**"WHAT I PROP
SURGICAL NUCLEAR STRIKE AGAINST
THE IMPERIAL POWERS. NOW THAT
THEY ARE COMPLETELY BLIND TO
OUR EFFORTS HERE AT TYURATAM,
WE WILL BE ABLE TO TAKE OUT ANY
TARGET IN NORTH AMERICA."**

Vadim Sobolev carefully scrutinized his guest. Seeing just a hint of weakness in the bureaucrat's tired face, the general refilled their glasses and toasted.

"To the lucky star that brought us together! Because of our meeting, the dreams of our forefathers will at long last be realized!"

Tossing the fiery liquor down his throat, Sobolev eyed the map of the world that graced his wall. Substituting massive, mushroom-shaped clouds for its red flags, his inner vision sharpened. He couldn't help but pity the poor Americans, for they would never know what hit them.

FLIGHT OF THE CONDOR

ACTION ADVENTURE

SILENT WARRIORS (1675, $3.95)
by Richard P. Henrick
The Red Star, Russia's newest, most technologically advanced submarine, outclasses anything in the U.S. fleet. But when the captain opens his sealed orders 24 hours early, he's staggered to read that he's to spearhead a massive nuclear first strike against the Americans!

THE PHOENIX ODYSSEY (1789, $3.95)
by Richard P. Henrick
All communications to the USS *Phoenix* suddenly and mysteriously vanish. Even the urgent message from the president cancelling the War Alert is not received. In six short hours the *Phoenix* will unleash its nuclear arsenal against the Russian mainland.

COUNTERFORCE (2013, $3.95)
Richard P. Henrick
In the silent deep, the chase is on to save a world from destruction. A single Russian Sub moves on a silent and sinister course for American shores. The men aboard the U.S.S. *Triton* must search for and destroy the Soviet killer Sub as an unsuspecting world races for the apocalypse.

EAGLE DOWN (1644, $3.75)
by William Mason
To western eyes, the Russian Bear appears to be in hibernation — but half a world away, a plot is unfolding that will unleash its awesome, deadly power. When the Russian Bear rises up, God help the Eagle.

DAGGER (1399, $3.50)
by William Mason
The President needs his help, but the CIA wants him dead. And for Dagger — war hero, survival expert, ladies man and mercenary extraordinaire — it will be a game played for keeps.

FLIGHT OF THE
CONDOR

RICHARD P. HENRICK

ZEBRA BOOKS
KENSINGTON PUBLISHING CORP.

ZEBRA BOOKS

are published by

Kensington Publishing Corp.
475 Park Avenue South
New York, NY 10016

First printing: August 1987

Printed in the United States of America

This story is dedicated to the U.S.S. Blueback (SS-581), the last and best diesel attack submarine in the U.S. Navy. Diesel boats forever!

"Once you have tasted inner space, you will walk the earth thinking of the ocean's depths. For there you have been, and there you long to return."

—Lou Eyerly

Chapter One

For the third consecutive morning, Andrew Weston's dreams woke him from a sound sleep. Each time, the vision was the same. He found himself in a lush, pine-covered valley. A single, thin trail cut through the rolling hills. With not another human in sight, he walked down the path with a brisk pace, drawn by an unknown goal. It was just as he passed over a tumbling mountain brook that a booming peal of deep thunder resonated from above. Directing his attention skyward, he searched the crystal-blue heavens for any sign of an advancing storm. When he saw no known source for the thunder, a heavy, ponderous feeling possessed his limbs and, for a second, he swayed back dizzily. It was then that his eyes sharpened their focus, picking out a single, massive creature circling high overhead. It was larger than any bird he had ever viewed before, and he knew in an instant that it was a condor.

Soaring effortlessly on the thermals, the powerfully built bird sported a lean body and a glossy, black-feathered wingspan well over eleven feet in length. As in each of the preceding dreams, Andrew continued looking upward, completely mesmerized by the creature's huge size, as the condor swooped down and passed only a few hundred feet overhead. A loud swish of air accompanied this movement, and Andrew got an excellent view of the bird's long, hooked beak, which grew almost straight out from its flat forehead. Curiously, its head was completely bald, yet the top of the scalp was a bright yellow. The rest of the condor's body was covered by black feathers, except for a strip of white ones situated under the front of each wing.

With a smooth, graceful motion, the bird rolled upward and initiated another low pass. Once more, Andrew looked on with awe. Unbelievable as it may have seemed, he could have sworn that the condor met his inquisitive glance directly. Then, for the briefest of seconds, the two creatures traded a rare moment of silent inter-species contact. Appearing wise beyond its years, the shaggy-feathered bird, which represented the last of its species in the wild, transferred a mental picture telling of its lonely struggle to survive at all costs.

As in the two previous mornings' dreams, it was at this point that Andrew awoke. Still curiously affected by the bird's sad plight, he reluctantly merged back into waking consciousness. With the vision still fresh in his mind, he vainly attempted to identify the lush valley he had been crossing before spotting the condor. Unable to place it, he stirred uneasily, his concentration broken by a rustle in the sheets beside him. A familiar, sweet scent met his nostrils, and Andrew quickly reorientated himself. Reaching out affectionately, he grasped the warm, soft body of the woman he had been living with these past two weeks. In a matter of seconds, thoughts of his dream were soon far from his mind, to be replaced by physical longings of a most primal nature.

Wendy had been sound asleep and Andrew's gentle hands nudged her abruptly awake. Without a second's hesitance, she allowed her lover's sensual touch to rouse her completely. A minimum of foreplay sent their hearts pounding, and all too soon the two were merged as one. An intense, passionate coupling followed.

Though they had known each other for just a few short weeks, Andrew and Wendy were most compatible. Each knew precisely what the other needed to insure complete satisfaction. This morning proved to be no exception.

Mounted side by side, Andrew started slowly and soon had his lover sighing in utter ecstasy. As his own need rose, his pace likewise increased, until both parties were shuddering in shared pleasure. Temporarily spent and exhausted, they parted. With hands still linked and shoulders touching, each savored the tingling warmth that coursed through their bodies. This delight was amplified, as both realized that they would not have to immediately part and run off to work, as had been the case too often in the past. For this morning signaled the beginning of a joint three-day leave. Andrew would never forget how difficult it had been for them to manage this mini-vacation together.

As a ten-year veteran, senior technician with NASA, he certainly had these days coming to him. He couldn't begin to count the hours of earned leave time due him. Yet his current assignment at the Kokee tracking station on Kauai, Hawaii's northernmost island, was a unique one to say the least. Perpetually overworked and understaffed, the Kokee facility managed its operations with a minimum of trained personnel. Because of this, Andrew had to practically beg a co-worker to assume his shift times. This would cost him dearly in the weeks to come, in the form of taking double shifts himself, yet Wendy had so anticipated this time together and he didn't dare disappoint her. As a Navy ensign stationed at Kauai's Barking Sands missile test-range facility, Wendy had to pull in a few favors herself to get her own pass.

Since meeting at a base cocktail party less than thirty days before, their relationship had progressed most rapidly. Attracted to each other from the very start, they were lovers in a matter of days. Two weeks before, their relationship had taken on an additional degree of permanence when he had agreed to move into Wendy's one-bedroom apartment in Waimea. As it turned out, this had been a decision Andrew had yet to regret.

Not only was his present habitation more comfortable than the cramped trailer he had been sharing with two other NASA technicians, his entire outlook on life had been broadened. An avowed bachelor, he had sworn to keep his life free from the complications a woman would necessitate. Yet, in Wendy's case, it was certainly worth the trouble.

For the first time in months, he began taking an interest in something other than his work. Although he had been stationed on Kauai for over six months, he had seen little of the magnificent sights the island was famous for. Since Wendy's duties at Barking Sands had kept her equally as busy, both had agreed that they would spend these three days together, exploring the island's natural beauty.

Only when Wendy rose to shower and then prepare breakfast did Andrew reach over to the end table to pick up a road map of Kauai. With anxious eyes, he began charting the course of their wanderings.

Spouting Horn would be their first stop. Located on the southern edge of the island, this beachside attraction derived its name from a lava tube that directed the Pacific waters into the air in a high, surging column. Then it would be on to nearby Koloa, a quaint shopping area that had once held the headquarters of Kauai's first sugar plantation. Continuing to the east, on the Kuhio highway, they would make their way to Wailua Beach. There they planned to cruise the Wailua River inland to view the magical Fern Grotto. Proceeding to the northern shore of the island, they would tour the Kilauea Lighthouse, picnic on the white sands of Anini Beach, then go on to explore Princeville and historical Hanalei. If time permitted, they even considered jumping on an interisland flight for a quick ride to Oahu, Maui, or the big island of Hawaii itself.

The smell of perking coffee and sizzling bacon redirected his attention from the map. For the first time in much too long, he found himself really anticipating the day's events. Jumping from the covers, he made his way to the bathroom. No sooner had he brushed his teeth and begun shaving than the shrill ring of the telephone sounded. His gut tightened when the ringing stopped to be replaced with Wendy's high-pitched voice.

"Andy, it's Dr. Lindsay!"

With his face still half-covered with shaving cream, Andrew put down his razor and silently cursed to himself. Fighting the impulse to ignore the call altogether, he sighed and hastily caught his reflection in the bathroom mirror. A disgusted, pained expression twisted his face as he turned to pick up the bedroom receiver. The mere tone of the caller's deep voice verified Andrew's worse fears.

"Andy, sorry to do this to you, lad, but we need you up here pronto. Keyhole Alpha is falling from orbit much quicker than we had anticipated. It's doubtful that she'll be able to give us another pass over the U.S.S.R. To replace her, Colorado Springs wants us to activate Baker. Since she's been your baby from the beginning, I thought you'd like to do the honors."

Although a major part of his being rebelled at the very thought of returning to the tracking station, Andrew's conscience got the best of him.

"I'm on my up, Doc," said Andrew sighing heavily.

"Very good, lad," returned the director of the Kokee station. "We'll hold the fort for your arrival. Drive carefully."

As he hung up the receiver, Andrew noticed a dejected-looking figure standing at his side. Her deep blue eyes expressed her frustration. Overtaken by an emotion he was just beginning to understand, he reached out and pulled his love close to him. Only then did he realize that half his face was still covered with shaving cream.

Five minutes later, he was fully dressed and on his way up Waimea Canyon Drive. Though the tracking station was less than twenty miles away, the curving road was steep, narrow, and, as he was soon to learn, at this hour, filled with tourists on their way to Kokee State Park. Settling his jeep behind a long line of slow-moving rental cars, Andrew cursed at his misfortune. Struggling to contain his rising anger, he pounded the wheel, hardly aware of the spectacular scenery passing on each side of him.

Fortunately, Wendy had taken his abrupt call to duty all in stride. Though she had been disappointed that their plans would have to be temporarily put on hold, she was most aware of the fickle nature of their governmental positions. Having entered the Navy over two years before, she had known that the call could have very well been for her. Not even bothering

14

to question the nature of the crisis that was ruining their plans, she had dutifully filled a thermos with coffee and packed Andrew a bacon-and-egg sandwich.

Parting with a kiss and a hug, Andrew had promised to call her as soon as he had a better idea of the length of his present assignment. If all went smoothly, he knew that the reunion could take place as soon as that afternoon. Since things in his field rarely went as planned, though, he couldn't say for sure. Resigned to this fact, he now directed his attention to the road before him. A total of seven cars lay between him and the slow-moving, diesel-belching tourist bus that was delaying their progress. Since there would not be a safe passing lane for another three miles, Andrew did his best to remain patient. After determining a prudent following distance, he allowed his thoughts to drift to the nature of his present work.

For over a decade, his duty with NASA had included a variety of assignments. These included work on the Explorer project, the space-shuttle program, and, most recently, a stint with the Air Force's satellite control facility at Sunnyvale, California. In fact, it was in Sunnyvale that he had absorbed the knowledge that he was presently being called in to apply—the exact positioning of satellites consigned to a polar orbit.

Of course, there could be no denying the extreme importance of the project he was currently involved with. That was why, when Dr. Lindsay's call had arrived earlier, Andrew hadn't dared to turn him down. The security of the very nation could well be at stake.

The Keyhole satellites were the most effective reconnaisance platforms that the United States ever had. Through the use of ultra-sophisticated optical techniques, such satellites obtained highly detailed pictures of portions of the earth from which America's security could be threatened. With the aid of high-resolution, multi-spectral cameras, objects as small as twelve inches across could be photographed from altitudes of several hundred miles. By using infra-red radar scanners, these cameras could even penetrate cloud cover. Needless to say, such platforms served as an invaluable instrument in determining a possible aggressor's intentions.

Because the nature of their assignments required a relatively low orbit, the Keyholes' lifetimes were limited. Earlier models had had an operational limit of less than four months, while the latest versions could remain aloft for over a year. Thus it was in the country's best interest to have several such platforms in orbit at all times, with replacements ready to launch whenever necessary.

Much to the Air Force's dismay, the U.S. would soon be in the precarious position of having only a single operational Keyhole platform in orbit. The reasons for this dangerous development were varied. With the loss of the space shuttle Challenger, and the subsequent delay of the entire shuttle program, the country had been temporarily deprived of its primary satellite-booster vehicle. The only available rocket powerful enough to carry such payloads as the Keyhole was the unmanned Titan 34-D. Less than three months after Challenger went down, a Titan carrying a Keyhole replacement had exploded over the coastline of central California, seconds after being launched from Vandenberg Air Force Base. This failure had left the U.S. with only a pair of Keyholes in orbit, and no foreseeable way in the near future of replacing them. Now, as the oldest of these two satellites fell from the heavens, at the limit of its operational lifetime, only a single platform remained aloft. This all-important surviving vehicle would have to remain on line until a reliable method of replacement could be achieved.

Andrew Weston's duty was to help the Air Force reposition, then activate this surviving platform, which was known simply as Baker. Nine months before, he had supervised its initial placement from the control room at Sunnyvale. Today, he would be responsible for bringing it back to life once again.

Most aware of the utter importance of his mission, Andrew sighed in relief when the long-anticipated passing lane became visible up ahead. Not waiting for the cars that preceded him to make their move, he pushed down on his horn, floored the accelerator, and veered the jeep to the left. Oblivious to the angry hand and facial gestures of those that he now passed, Andrew zipped by the bus and soon had the road all to himself.

As Waimea Canyon Road merged into Kokee Road, the landscape became noticeably different from that down below. Absent were the vast, flat fields of sugar cane and taro. In their places were steep, rounded hillsides, most of which were covered with thick stands of twisted oaks. From this new elevation, over two thousand feet above sea level, Andrew could view the broad canyon stretching out to his right. Developed after thousands of years of erosion, the colorful volcanic valley was known as the Grand Canyon of the Pacific, and rightly so. He would never forget the first time that he had viewed this landscape six months before.

Expecting to find Kauai completely filled with white beaches and coconut-laden palm trees, he had been shocked to find the Kokee tracking station situated on a pine-covered summit, twenty-five hundred feet above sea level, overlooking breathtaking Waimea Canyon. For the first couple of weeks, the fall weather had been gorgeous, with warm days and comfortable, crystal-clear nights. Andrew had quickly immersed himself in his work, as they all prepared to monitor a full schedule of seven space shuttle flights from Vandenberg the very next year. Yet all too soon both the rainy season and the Challenger disaster had quickly dampened their lofty plans. With the shuttle program on an indefinite hold, until the cause of the explosion was determined and subsequently corrected, the crew had done its best to fill in the empty hours. Andrew was soon to learn that the world's wettest spot, Mt. Waialeale, lay only a few dozen miles to the east. As might be expected with such a neighbor, the station had been deluged by weeks of constantly pouring rain. A boring routine had then followed, as the NASA tracking team strove to keep busy by assisting the military whenever possible.

It was immediately after the monitoring of a submarine-based launch that the crew had been invited to attend a reception at the Navy's Barking Sands facility, on Kauai's southwestern shore. Happy to escape the confines of his cramped trailer, Andrew had found Barking Sands a most congenial site. Not only had the sun been shining brightly on the afternoon that he arrived there, but it had also been the fateful day that he was to meet Wendy. Things would never be the same afterwards.

From her lips had come the stories of the island's natural history. This had included tales of the mysterious *menehune*, the so-called "little people," who had supposedly made Kauai their home, decades before the first Polynesians arrived. In fact, it was while on a subsequent visit to the Kokee tracking station that Wendy had told him of the tales of the *menehune* ghost-marchers, who wandered the hills of Kokee to this very day. Though he had taken such yarns lightly, his feelings towards Wendy had become more serious as each day passed. Now that he had moved in with her, he was even considering marriage. For a confirmed bachelor, this could prove to be a dangerous turn of events.

As he passed the twenty-five-hundred-foot marker, Andrew contemplated the events of the past few months and found his mood lightening. He would do his duty for his country, get Baker operational, and then return to his love to ask her to share the rest of her life with him. His lips curved in a satisfied smile, but suddenly the sky above darkened and soon he was in the midst of a blinding downpour. After switching on both his windshield wipers and lights, then decreasing his speed, Andrew did his best to stay on the winding roadway. Twice, his tires slid onto the muddy shoulder. Twice, he managed to return to the pavement. Just when he was considering pulling over to let the storm vent itself, the rains halted as quickly as they had begun. In their place was a ghostly, thick fog. Again, he struggled to stay on the road, yet seconds later the fog was gone, to be replaced by a sunny, brilliantly blue morning sky. A mile later, he guided his jeep to the right and began his way up the quarter of a mile of pavement that led to NASA's Kokee tracking station.

Inside the compact, concrete structure, Dr. Max Lindsay sat before a twelve-by-eight-foot perspex screen. Projected here was a full-scale map of the Union of Soviet Socialist Republics. With practiced eyes, the facilities director studied a single, flashing blue light, just visible over the Barents Sea, at the country's northernmost extremity. Shifting his unlit, well-battered briar pipe from one corner of his mouth to the other, Lindsay grunted anxiously.

So far, the morning had produced little news of a positive nature. Only an hour ago, the Ground-Based Electro-Opitcal Deep Space Surveillance (GEODSS) station located on Diego Garcia, in the midst of the Indian Ocean, had notified them that Keyhole Alpha was losings its orbit quicker than they had anticipated. Their original calculations had given the platform up to seventy-two hours of survival time. Whatever the exact time of the doomed satellite's final demise, it was Dr. Lindsay's responsibility to make certain that its replacement was on line the second that Keyhole Alpha failed.

Shifting his line of sight to the right, he watched a single, seated, white-smocked technician feed Alpha's exact coordinates into the computer. Beside him was a vacant terminal. It would be from this position that Baker would be reactivated. Checking his watch, Max Lindsay wondered what could be keeping the man responsible for this all-important task, senior technician Andrew Weston. If Weston didn't arrive soon, Lindsay would have to transfer this duty to Sunnyvale.

The staccato click of hard-soled shoes echoed off the tiled floor behind him. He didn't have to turn around to identify who those steps belonged to. Captain William Maddox had been stationed at Kokee for almost a month now. As NASA had become involved with more military projects, the Air Force had thought that it was fitting to have one of their own around to monitor the station's activities.

At first, Dr. Lindsay had been genuinely upset

20

with such a presence and had expressed himself vocally. He had argued that not only would the officer get in the way, but having such a figure around would be a complete waste of the taxpayers' money. The NASA crew was most capable of doing its routine work without a military flunkie continually snooping over its shoulders.

When his superiors had failed to get the officer recalled, Lindsay had reluctantly accepted the fact that they'd have to make the best of the situation. As it turned out, this was more difficult than he had anticipated, for Captain William Maddox was one of the coldest, most uncommunicative individuals that Lindsay had ever met.

Hardly ever breaking a smile, the dour-faced captain often seemed more like a robot than a human being. What really bothered Lindsay was the officer's complete lack of a sense of humor. In a place with such tight confines as the Kokee facility, trading a joke or two was often the only way the staff could relieve itself of tension. Why, Lindsay didn't even know if the man had a family or not. All that he knew was that Maddox was a graduate of the Air Force Academy, and had been assigned to the Consolidated Space Operations center in Colorado Springs, Colorado.

When the sound of clicking footsteps halted immediately behind him, Lindsay redirected his complete attention to the perspex screen. The blinking blue light had crossed the Arctic Sea and was well into Siberia by now. After smoothing down the two perpetually wild tufts of gray hair that lay beside each of his ears, Lindsay efficiently addressed his keyboard. As the lighted screen of his monitor blinked alive, a deep, no-nonsense voice spoke up from behind.

"What's Alpha's ETA over the Tyuratam ICBM

fields, Doctor?"

Expecting just such a query from Maddox, Lindsay answered without hesitation, "Approximately eleven and a half minutes, Captain."

"And what's the probability that Alpha will survive this pass?" continued the Air Force officer coolly.

Again Lindsay addressed the keyboard. "We still show the odds at better than fifty percent that Alpha will break up somewhere over the Indian Ocean. Diego Garcia is presently relaying to us the latest GEODSS data."

"I'm afraid that answer's not good enough, Doctor," retorted the captain. "Must I remind you again of the importance of this pass? If there's even a slight chance that Alpha won't make it, Keyhole Baker had better be ready for back-up."

With this, the captain stepped to Lindsay's side and directly caught his glance. Returning the officer's hard, probing stare, Lindsay answered firmly, "The present data indicates that Alpha will indeed be good for this one last look, Captain Maddox."

"Well, for our country's sake, it damn well better be," returned the officer. "There's no denying that the Russkies are up to something at Tyuratam. The last half-dozen passes show an unusual amount of activity there. The two most recent flyovers indicate that this activity is centered around the loading of a new type of warhead. Intelligence is damn nervous, and I don't blame them. Without these photos, the Soviets could be preparing a first-strike and we'd never know it until the missiles were already on their way. By that time, Doctor, it would be too late for all of us."

Taking in these harsh words, Lindsay struggled to contain himself. No one knew better than he the utter importance of the Keyhole system. Yet, if the Soviets were indeed readying themselves for a surprise attack, was there anything the U.S. could do to stop them? Almost four decades had passed and the world was still in the shadow of nuclear doom. If the politicians had only backed up their cries for disarmament with concrete actions, the threat of total apocalypse could have been substantially alleviated. As it stood now, the planet was living on borrowed time. There was no telling how much longer their luck would hold.

Sobered by this thought, Lindsay leaned forward expectantly as a high-pitched tone sounded from his monitor. As the screen began filling with data, his eyes narrowed.

"We're receiving the latest GEODSS telemetry from Diego Garcia, Captain. I'm afraid the odds are down to forty-eight percent that Alpha will make Tyuratam."

"That's just great," replied Maddox succinctly. "My gut told me that she'd never make it. Bring down Baker and let's get done with it."

Turning to his right, Lindsay could see that Andrew Weston had still not returned to his console. Though the station's director was very well capable of reactivating the satellite himself, the importance of this particular mission demanded the attentions of a specialist. If Weston did not return soon, he'd be forced to pass the responsibility onto Sunnyvale. As it turned out, the sudden, piercing wail of an alarm siren served to make up his mind for him.

"Christ, it's Alpha! She's breaking up!"

"Then damn it, Doctor, bring down Baker!" cried Maddox.

No sooner had Lindsay's hand reached the yellow handset that contained the direct line to Sunnyvale than he noticed that a newcomer had arrived at the previously vacant console to his right. Immediately he stood and made his way to this individual's side.

"Thank God that you got here, Andrew," said Lindsay breathlessly. "We just lost Alpha. If you had arrived a few seconds later, I would have already transferred Baker's reawakening to Sunnyvale."

"Sorry about the delay, Doc," commented Weston, as he efficiently began feeding data into his keyboard. "I can give us booster phase on Baker in forty-seven seconds."

While the senior technician continued his adept accessing, the blue-uniformed figure of Captain Maddox positioned himself behind Andrew's right shoulder. "Exactly where's Baker at the moment?" quizzed the officer.

Lindsay, who stood to his left, pointed towards the perspex map. "We should see her coming over the Arctic Circle any second now. She's traveling the same orbit as Alpha, at an altitude of twenty-five hundred miles. We've got to get her down to three hundred miles before she becomes operational."

Both men had their eyes glued to the screen when a single blue dot began flashing to the north of the island of Novaya Zemlya.

"We've got her!" cried Lindsay excitedly. "How much longer to booster ignition, Andy?"

Not bothering to take his eyes from the monitor screen, the senior technician replied, "Twelve seconds and counting."

The atmosphere was tense, and all heads were turned to the digital clock that crowned Weston's console. With excruciating slowness, the seconds ticked away. Only when the counter hit zero did the senior technician access a series of rapid commands.

Another thirty seconds passed. This time it was Lindsay who broke the tenseness by pointing toward the perspex screen and commenting.

"She's over the coast of Siberia now. The booster phase should be shutting down just about now. Do we have a confirmation as yet, Andy?"

The senior technician was quick to answer. "I show a negative on booster ignition. We've as yet to receive data from Diego Garcia."

"What the hell is taking so much time?" cried Maddox impatiently. "We should have brought down this Keyhole hours ago, instead of waiting until the last minute to do so. She's already over central Siberia. If we miss Tyuratam, we could have all hell to pay."

Not bothering to respond to the officer, Dr. Lindsay kept his eyes glued to Weston's monitor. He found himself holding back a smile when the screen began filling with a series of coded telemetry data. He allowed Weston to interpret it.

"Diego Garcia reports booster ignition. Keyhole Baker is approaching operational altitude. Presently awaiting verification of an attainment of the three-hundred-mile threshold before continuing with function activation."

A serene grin flashed across Lindsay's face as he turned to address Maddox. "If all continues as planned, Captain, we'll have Baker on line in plenty of time to photograph those ICBM fields. Don't you worry so."

The director's words did little to ease the captain's doubts. Not knowing what had gotten into the Defense Department to even consider asking for NASA's assistance in the first place, Maddox silently cursed the ineptitude of the system he served. Military matters were best handled by military personnel. Civilian involvement, however well intended, just never worked out. When NASA's programs had been put on hold several months before, the Government should have immediately replaced these technicians with an Air Force staff. At least *their* competency couldn't be questioned. At the moment, he didn't know whom to trust.

"Verification of Baker's operational orbit has just been received," commented the seated NASA technician dryly. "Proceeding to activate all optical and digital transferral systems."

Captain Maddox took in this positive report, yet the tenseness in his gut remained. His glance went to the perspex screen and he saw that the flashing blue dot was still well north of the Aral Sea. If all continued smoothly, perhaps there still was a chance that they'd have those photos of Tyuratam after all. Yet inwardly he doubted it. Forcing himself to keep an open mind, he hoped that his instincts were wrong.

Beside him, Dr. Lindsay also studied the map of the Soviet Union. The director's thoughts were of a much more optimistic nature. Surely, any second now, the first pixels would be transmitted. This would give them plenty of time to fine-tune the camera's focus to insure that the ensuing photographs were of a first-class quality. Knowing very well that the next few minutes would be critical, he found himself instinctively crossing his fingers as Weston's monitor again activated.

"We're receiving an incoming signal," announced the senior technician. "Transmission frequency appears strong. Awaiting primary pixel receipt."

As Weston prepared the specialized printer that would duplicate the film currently being processed aboard Keyhole Baker, the two observers, who stood behind him, stirred uneasily. When a full minute passed and the printer had yet to trigger, this uneasiness became amplified. Captain Maddox was the first one to voice his frustrations.

"Baker's rapidly approaching those missile fields, Doctor. Are we going to be able to get those photographs that we need?"

Not really certain what was causing the delay in transmission, Lindsay bent over to query his senior technician. "What's going on up there, Andy? Baker should have had plenty of time to transmit those initial pixels."

Still concentrating on his keyboard, Weston took several seconds before responding. "I don't understand it, Doc. The platform shows a one-hundred-percent operational capability, yet we're unable to receive a photographic transmission."

"Perhaps the problem lies in our end," offered Maddox.

"I doubt that, sir," returned Weston. "Our receivers are copying all other satellite transmissions."

"Then maybe Baker is in an improper orbit," suggested Lindsay. "That could account for us being unable to pick up her telemetry signals."

Weston shook his head solemnly. "GEODSS has a tight lock on her, Doc. I'll bet that Baker's altitude is precise to the foot."

Maddox's glance returned to the perspex screen, where the flashing blue dot was passing to the east of the Aral Sea. "Sweet Jesus, can't you guys do something? She's passing over Tyuratam now!"

Desperately attacking his keyboard, Weston appeared genuinely confused. "I still don't understand it. All systems continue to check out fine. There just doesn't seem to be any logical reason for us not to receive those pictures."

Lindsay nervously pulled his pipe from his mouth. "Run a complete failure analysis through the computer, Andy. I'll see if Sunnyvale can give us a hand."

Captain Maddox watched as the director reached

out and grabbed the yellow handset. When his glance returned to the perspex screen, it was most obvious that the flashing blue dot was well south of Tyuratam by now. Not knowing whom to pin the blame on, he could only be certain that, for the moment, the United States of America could no longer monitor the Soviet Union's largest ICBM field. A painful spasm coursed through his abdomen as the seated technician commented dryly, "Initial computer failure check indicates three possible areas of fault. It shows a sixty-three-percent probability that the transmission difficulties are due to some sort of inherent mechanical failure. The various sub-systems are in the process of being cross-checked. We show a twenty-two-percent probability that the difficulties are due to a cosmic anomaly such as a sunspot. The National Observatory data banks at White Sands are being queried to investigate such a possibility."

"And the third area of fault?" prompted the Air Force captain.

Clearing his voice, Weston continued. "The computer indicates a fifteen-percent probability that Baker's failure to transmit was due to intentional interference by a third party."

"Jesus Christ, that would mean that the Russkies have figured out a way to jam our signals!" exclaimed Maddox.

"Easy now, Captain," cautioned Lindsay, who had just hung up the telephone. "This is all still supposition. I just got off the horn with Sunnyvale and they're presently giving Baker a try themselves. Their consensus is that most likely we're facing some sort of mechanical glitch in the digital-reprocessing system. The Agency is recommending that if Baker fails to respond within the next twenty-four hours, one of the two remaining Keyholes in our land-based inventory be immediately put into orbit."

This time it was Weston who dared to question. "And just how are we going to do that, Doc? With both the shuttle and Titan programs on hold, what are we going to use as a primary booster?"

Unable to answer his colleague, Lindsay could only offer him a solemn glance. Meanwhile, Captain Maddox reached over to activate a red telephone that would give him a direct line to the Consolidated Space Operations center in Colorado Springs. As the officer initiated his scrambled conversation, a massive boom of thunder sounded overhead.

Looking past the director, Weston focused his complete attention on this strange rumble. With the speed of a heartbeat, he found his thoughts returning to the strange dream he had experienced for the past three mornings. Oblivious to his current surroundings, his mind's eye returned to the pine-laden valley. With remarkable detail, he recreated the single, thin trail that cut through the rolling hills and passed over a tumbling brook. It was at this point that another booming peal of deep thunder resonated from above, and once again Andrew's sight was drawn upward to the clear blue sky. Waiting for him there was the massive, soaring condor, whose wisdom seemed so total. The struggle to survive at all costs was the secret this endangered creature had tried to communicate. Andrew knew then that this message was to be applied to his own species, as the shadow of nuclear doom lay over the earth like an ever-present shroud of death.

Chapter Two

Fifty-seven miles to the northwest of Santa Barbara, California, a massive peninsula extends out into the Pacific. Isolated, except for a handful of small towns, this rugged piece of landscape is dominated by rolling, scrub-filled hills, deep, fertile valleys, and forests of oak, cypress, and pine. It was because of the absence of any significant human population that the Army had decided to base an artillery range here. Camp Cooke, as it was called, had served its country well until 1956, when the Defense Department had decided that it would be an ideal spot to initiate the Air Force's fledgling missile program. It wasn't until 1958 that the base had been renamed Vandenberg, in honor of Hoyt S. Vandenberg, the second Air Force Chief of Staff. Occupying over 98,000 acres, it had become America's third largest Air Force installation.

By 1985, over 1,550 missile launches had taken place here. About a third of these had been to send unmanned satellites into orbit. The majority of the other launches had been to test elements of the nation's intercontinental ballistic missile force.

Although the area's significant modern history goes back less than four decades, the peninsula's ancient heritage is a rich one. For hundreds of centuries, the rugged peninsula had been home to the Chumash, a highly advanced Indian people who had flourished there.

Vandenberg's 154 square miles held a wealth of Chumash relics. Many of these sites had been initially discovered by Robert R. Baray, a Blackfoot Sioux who had been the great-grandson of the illustrious warrior Sitting Bull. As the first American Indian to attend West Point, Baray had served as the general staff engineer for planning and development at the base. It was under his auspices that the first Chumash remains had been catalogued.

Fortunately, the Government had continued making every effort to preserve those ancient sites that recorded the everyday lives of a people first documented by Juan Rodriguez Cabrillo in 1542. This effort had included opening the highly classified area to trained archaeologists. It was in such a manner that Miriam Rodgers had received permission to dig there.

For the past month, Miriam and her team of university students had been perched on top of Tranquillon Ridge, located in Vandenberg's southern sector. There, they were in the process of excavating a particularly rich Chumash site. So far, the artifacts unearthed included several excellently preserved tule-willow baskets, dozens of slender, stone spear-points, arrowheads and bone-scrappers, and a magnificent Olivilla shell necklace. Because these objects had been all found within the confines of a single twenty-by-thirty-foot rectangular square of rocky soil, it was supposed that the ridge had once held either a small village or a burial plot. To determine its exact purpose, a full-scale excavation was now in progress.

From a position on the hillside's summit, Miriam watched her crew at work. Though the majority of the half-dozen men and women working below her were barely in their twenties, they worked more like dedicated professionals. Proud of their effort, she knew that she was very fortunate to have their services. In an era of ever-decreasing research budgets, actual field work was becoming one of the most difficult areas to finance. Enormous liability insurance premiums and the high logistical costs of the digs themselves had put many a researcher's dreams on permanent hold.

For three years now, Miriam had fought to put together this particular expedition. Even though there could be no question that the sites chosen were full of exciting promise, each of her quarterly budget requests had been curtly turned down. Ninety days before, when the dean had called her into his office and given her the go-ahead, she had hardly believed what she was hearing. Genuinely astounded by the news, Miriam had actually hugged the elderly, silver-haired administrator and then kissed him firmly on the cheek. Blushing at this unexpected show of exuberance, the dean had regathered his decorum and, after explaining that her monetary request had been significantly paired down, had wished the thirty-six-year-old senior researcher the best of luck.

Well aware that she could live within the confines of the resulting budget constraints, Miriam had done all that she could to immediately get the ball rolling. The area on the central California coastline that she wished to concentrate on was well known for its fickle environment. A summer dig would guarantee not only a semblance of decent weather, but also the availability of an experienced, relatively inexpensive crew comprised of her own students.

In what was later to be called a bureaucratic miracle, Miriam had not only assembled the myriad of equipment and supplies needed for a three-month field effort, but had also gained permission from the Department of the Defense to work on Vandenberg. All this had been accomplished with plenty of time to choose a qualified work force from a long list of anxious students. As the school year had ended, the young professor had closed up her office and readied herself to tackle the type of work that had prompted her to enter the field of archaeology in the first place.

Watching the crew at work, Miriam remembered well her first official dig. It was almost two decades before when she had joined a team of freshmen classmates on a Malibu hillside. There, utilizing the same tedious procedures that they used today, Miriam had gotten her first taste of actual field excavation. Never would she forget the fateful moment when her rake had made solid contact with an object buried in the dry soil below. How her heart had pounded in her chest as she carefully extracted an exquisite object buried in the earth for almost five hundred years.

The ceremonial knife had been over twelve inches long. It had a handle of dark gray whalebone, and its whitish, sharpened stone tip was bound to the shaft with the sinew of a deer and completely coated with a tar asphaltum. Standing there in the hills of Malibu with this Chumash relic firm in her trembling hand, the impressionable teenager had had no doubt as to the course of her future studies.

Years of intense research had followed. Both an undergraduate and a master's degree had been soon attained. And now Miriam was well qualified to instruct her own groups of impressionable students in the intricacies of her chosen profession.

Though the knowledge gained during her hours of study was great, her appetite for field work was as insatiable as ever before. Semesters of rote class instruction had done little to satisfy this undying urge.

As befitting her initial discovery, Miriam had devoted the bulk of her research to a study of the Chumash Indians. Completely fascinated by this highly advanced people who for thousands of years had flourished in what was now Ventura, Santa Barbara, and San Luis Obispo counties, she had neglected the distracting calls of her friends and family. By no means unattractive, Miriam had yet to marry or, for that matter, even to have been seriously engaged. Such a relationship would only divert her from her life's work.

She certainly hadn't lacked for interested suitors. These individuals had been drawn to her natural good looks, which were enhanced by a shining mane of long red hair, gleeming green eyes, high, etched cheekbones, perfect teeth, and a five-foot, nine-inch body kept lean and fit with daily five-mile hikes. The University atmosphere had provided a succession of interested men, yet Miriam had never been ready to share herself with them. Whereas the bulk of her ex-girlfriends now had a houseful of children to keep them occupied, Miriam had nothing but her work, and for her it was enough. For the moment, marriage would just have to wait.

A cool breeze blew in from the west, and the thirty-six-year-old researcher looked out toward the Pacific from the rock outcropping that she had been standing on. It was turning out to be another ideal day. Already the customary morning fog was dissipating. Beyond the scrub-filled hills, another two miles distant, was the shoreline. From where she stood she could just make out the white, frothing surge of surf as it broke over the jagged rocks of Point Arguello. Appearing as violent and unpredictable as ever, the ocean provided little haven for boaters or divers. Possessed as it was by strong undertows and deadly riptides, not even the most expert swimmers dared its currents.

Further out to sea, just visible in the dissolving fog bank, was the outline of a single drilling platform. This structure was perched like a lonely sentinel, with the sole purpose of tapping the reservoirs of oil locked deep within the continental shelf.

A familiar hollow-metallic tone howled in the distance, and Miriam diverted her glance to her right, where she could just make out a rapidly advancing locomotive. Seconds later, the rest of the freight train was visible as it snaked its way down the coastline southward. Soothed by the sound of the clatter of its wheels on the tracks, Miriam surveyed the valley that lay between the rails and the ridge on top of which she currently stood. Known as Space Launch Complex 6, or Slik 6 for short, it had a series of huge, man-made structures that dwarfed the landscape. It would be from this site that the first West Coast launch of America's space shuttle would take place.

Miriam had been given a hasty tour of this complex by an Air Force public-affairs officer upon her initial arrival. Though she had been working beside the series of buildings for a month now, she still couldn't help but be impressed with their sheer size. Dominating the complex was the immense white shell of the shuttle-assembly building. Painted on its side was a colossal American flag. Beside this were a number of brightly painted red, white, and gray buildings belonging to various control centers, preparations rooms, access towers, and storage tanks. All this was situated on a gleaming white concrete pad, which the public affairs officer had told her was comprised of the equivalent of a twenty-five-mile-long stretch of four-lane interstate highway.

Of course, all this was quite a contrast to the relatively crude operation that she was currently in charge of. Angling her line of sight back to her left, Miriam studied her crew at work. They were presently concentrating their efforts on a single plot of land, located on top of Tranquillon Ridge, approximately nine hundred feet above and a half mile to the southeast of Slik 6.

The site they had picked was one of those originally discovered by Robert Baray. Though his primary excavation had indicated that a possible wealth of buried relics lay there, little professional excavation had been attempted until their arrival. As in the case of any potential dig site, their first priority had been to carefully survey that portion of land into which they planned to dig. After staking out their initial twenty-by-thirty-foot rectangular plot, they had begun the tedious task of removing the first few inches of covering topsoil.

The dry ground was hard and rock-filled. To complicate matters, a thick ground cover of spiky cactus had had to first be eliminated. Not accustomed to such strenuous work, her students had done their best to ignore their newly calloused hands, strained muscles, and sunburnt skin.

Of irreplaceable assistance had been the strong arms and shoulders of her senior teaching assistant, Joseph Solares. A full-blooded Pomo Indian by birth, the twenty-five-year-old graduate student had instinctively taken charge of the primary excavation. With his long, dark hair tied down by a red bandana, and his muscular, bare chest perpetually sweat-stained, Joseph had taken on as much of the heavy work as possible. His tenacious effort alone had allowed them to proceed as scheduled.

As was the case on most mornings, Joseph was occupying the focal point of their present efforts. Miriam couldn't help but notice how the other members of the dig flocked around him as he squatted before a roped-off, twelve-inch sector of dirt. With his tanned back glistening in the early morning sun, he gently probed the earth with a hand-sized shovel. Whatever he had chanced upon must have been of some significance, for a ripple of excited chatter coursed through the crowd of onlookers gathered at his sides. Curious as to what he had found, Miriam left her perch on the ridge's summit and climbed down into the excavation area.

By the time she reached her fellow crew members, Joseph had exhumed a large, circular object from its earthen grave. Completely covered by a thick hemp net, it was recognized by Miriam as being one of the lap-sized sandstone bowls which the Chumash were famous for. As Joseph began carefully shaking the dirt from its inner cavity, it became obvious that this artifact was far from normal. Two novel designs made this most apparent.

Miriam was first attracted to the bowl's lip. There the outer edge was completely encircled with a series of intricately formed five-pointed stars. These tiny pentagrams were apparently made from shell and abalone bits, which were stuck into the rock lip with asphaltum. Such a tedious process had to have taken hundreds of hours to complete, and could have only been reserved for the most sacred of purposes.

Though the outer surface of the bowl was bare of design, its inner skin was not. Though it was still covered by caked layers of dirt, a unique series of concentric circles was visible, painted into the relic's bottom. Miriam recognized the bright yellow central disc as being representative of the sun. She failed to understand the significance of the thick black and red rings that encircled this disc several times.

As the bowl was placed on the ground for all to see, it was most apparent that Joseph was genuinely thrilled by his discovery. Cognizant of this fact, Miriam broke her silence.

"That's a beauty, Joseph. I don't believe I've ever seen a Chumash bowl decorated in such a manner before."

Breathlessly, Joseph responded, "Neither have I, Boss, although I must admit that I've heard of such a motif's supposed existence before."

"How's that?" asked Miriam, who now had the attention of the rest of her crew.

Aware of his audience, Joseph picked his words carefully. "It was my grandfather who first told me the tales of the spirit bowl in whose bottom was captured the sun and in whose lip was encased the stars of the heavens. Designed by the greatest of shamans, it was supposedly stolen by the crafty coyote, who snagged it in a net and took it from our land for all time."

At that point one of the students hastily asked a question. "Joseph, since your tribe lived in northern California, couldn't this Chumash design be totally unrelated to your grandfather's tale?"

Catching the alert eyes of the young man who waited for an answer, Joseph replied, "As I've told you before, even though the Pomo lived in the north, our mythology and that of the Chumash were amazingly similar. Many say the Pomo were but an offshoot of the Chumash, who subsequently migrated northwards. Whatever the case, both peoples tell of a spirit bowl designed in a fashion much like the one here. Both tribes tell of this bowl's similar purpose, which is to indicate the site where the souls of the newly dead pass into the afterlife."

"Then we've found the portal to Similaqsa!" exclaimed Miriam triumphantly.

Before Joseph could respond, an unexpected noise diverted the crew's attention. Each member looked to the south, where a single blue jeep was visible, making its way to the summit of Tranquillon Ridge. Less than a minute later, the four-wheel-drive vehicle pulled up beside the excavation site, leaving a thick cloud of brown dust in its wake. The jeep's three occupants were quick to exit. Miriam could only identify one of these individuals, for she had had run-ins with Master Sergeant Crowley on several occasions before.

The thick-necked, stocky sergeant led the way, followed by his two smartly uniformed escorts. It was most obvious that both of these no-nonsense-looking young men wore side arms. As they approached the crew, Miriam stepped out to greet them.

"Good morning, Sergeant Crowley. Can I help you?"

The sergeant hastily surveyed the ragtag group gathered before him and answered, "Good morning to you, Miss Rodgers. Is your entire group assembled here?"

Not sure what he was getting at, Miriam retorted, "This is all of us, Sergeant. Why do you ask?"

Crowley cleared his throat. "I'm here to relay orders from Lieutenant Colonel Lansford's office, ma'am. According to these instructions, you and your crew are to leave Tranquillon Ridge at once. We have been assigned to escort you back to your campsite at Ocean Beach Park."

Not believing what she was hearing, Miriam was not in the least bit intimidated. "We're in the midst of an important excavation here, Sergeant. We just can't go leaving it at the drop of a hat. Besides, we have the lieutenant's colonel's personal permission to dig here uninterrupted through the summer."

"I'm afraid that permission has been temporarily lifted, ma'am," returned the master sergeant, who went on to check his wristwatch. "Now, if you'll just stow your equipment, we'd better get under way."

Still not about to give in so easily, Miriam was set to continue to argue their case when Joseph stepped to her side. Whispering into her ear, he attempted to calm her down.

"Say, Boss, do you really think we've got a chance against these guys? Those are forty-five-caliber pistols on their hips. Let's lick our wounds back at camp. At least there we can call the lead honcho and find out what all this is about."

Well aware of the wisdom in these words, Miriam caught her assistant's playful wink. Stifling a smile of her own, she reluctantly surrendered to their new order. Though it would mean the loss of a perfectly good day's field work, there was plenty to keep them busy back at their trailers. Mentally calculating what this new course of action would entail, she knew that her own first priority would be a single phonecall.

Ocean Beach Park was located approximately five and a half miles due north of Tranquillon Ridge. Situated at the spot where the Santa Ynez River flowed into the Pacific, the park was one of the few areas on Vandenberg open to the public. It was comprised of a large asphalt parking lot and over one hundred acres of direct beach access. To get from the lot to the sand, it was necessary to travel a narrow dirt trail that led beneath a Southern Pacific railroad trestle. From there it was but a short hike to the pounding surf itself.

It had taken the direct authority of the base commander for Miriam and her group to be allowed to park their trailers there. After a bit of bargaining, they had been given a compact sector of ground located immediately east of the trestle. Though they had no direct ocean view, this positioning allowed them to be sheltered from the persistent, often blustery offshore winds that swept in from the Pacific.

The crew's four travel trailers had been parked in a semicircle. At the center of this semicircle, several picnic tables had been set up. It was there, when weather permitted, that meals were eaten and artifacts catalogued. This evening, the group had gathered around a large campfire, which had been built beside the table area. Sipping their teas, coffees, and hot chocolates, they watched the crackling flames and contemplated the day's strange turn of events.

Seated at the head of the fire was Miriam Rodgers. At her right was her assistant, Joseph Solares. Both sat cross-legged on the cool ground, their stares focused deep into the burning embers. Taking her last sip of deep, rich coffee, Miriam shook her head angrily.

"You know, I still can't believe that the colonel didn't have the courtesy to speak to me on the phone. Why, his aide wouldn't even bother contacting him."

Joseph shrugged his shoulders. "I still think that you're silly to let this bother you, Boss. The colonel's a busy man. He must have a damn good reason to want us off the ridge."

"At least he could share it with me," returned Miriam. "If we're going to be secluded here much longer, perhaps we should be looking for another dig site."

The crackling flames emphasized Joseph's sharp cheekbones as his eyes narrowed. "You're not thinking of abandoning the ridge now, Boss? Why, it's just starting to get interesting."

Miriam sighed. "I'm afraid that decision has already been made for us."

Not liking her tone, Joseph caught her glance directly. "That doesn't sound like the lady who practically moved a mountain to get us here in the first place. At least give the Air Force a couple of days before even thinking of pulling us off of Tranquillon. That site is just too promising."

As if to emphasize this observation, a young girl's voice came from behind them. "Excuse me, Professor Rodgers, but we've completed the initial cleaning of this morning's find. Would you like to have a look?"

"Why, of course, Margaret," replied Miriam. "Bring it by the fire."

With the help of a muscular co-worker, the skinny brunette guided the precious artifact to the fire's side. There the bowl took on a drastically new character. Gone was both the net and the layer of dried mud that had covered its surface before. In their place was a shiny, dark gray stone surface, polished smooth by hundreds of hours of patient craftsmanship. Unable to take her eyes off the series of sparkling pentagrams that lay embedded in the bowl's upper lip, Miriam felt her spirits lighten.

"Why, you did an excellent job, Margaret. It's positively breathtaking!"

"Oh, it wasn't just me," responded the blushing sophomore. "Each one of us had a hand in the cleaning."

"I'll say," said the muscular lad who had helped carry out the artifact. "Why, I almost scraped the skin off of my hands cleaning off the dirt from the bottom. It was as hard as a rock."

"What do you expect after five hundred years?"

asked Joseph lightly.

"Does this bowl really have something to do with the dead?" queried the inquisitive male undergraduate.

Before answering, Joseph looked to Miriam. Only after receiving a positive nod did he continue.

"From what we know of the design etched into its surface, this piece certainly looks like an authentic spirit bowl. Yet if it is, it's the first one to be uncovered."

"Why is it called a spirit bowl?" questioned Margaret.

Again, Joseph looked toward Miriam before responding. "Most of you know the Chumash legend of the soul's journey to Similaqsa. It tells us of their belief that, three days after a person has died and been buried, the soul comes up out of the grave to wander the world, visiting the places it used to frequent in life. On the fifth day after death, the soul is drawn to an isolated coastal spot, rumored to be somewhere near Point Arguello. There it prepares for the final trip to Similaqsa, the Chumash version of heaven and hell.

"Though it was all thought to be mere story-telling, the elders told of a magical spirit bowl inbued with the power to draw the soul to this final earthly portal. Buried on the coastline, this relic would divert the soul to a hand-cut royal road. Following this route westward, the deceased would come to a temple, formed from a circle of enchanted charmstones. Only after positioning itself in the exact axis of this circle would the soul be free to soar westward. I believe our esteemed leader beside me is better qualified to tell us just what awaits the soul in this other land."

Taking this cue, Miriam sat forward and, well aware of the total attention of her rapt audience, continued. "Before reaching the gates to Similaqsa, the soul had to pass a variety of tests, to make certain that it was still not alive. This included crossing through a valley of pounding rocks, and surviving an attack by a number of grotesque monsters. Just beyond the land of these beasts was the body of water that separated this world from the next. Spanning this liquid void was a single narrow bridge. Pity the poor souls of those that had done evil in their mortal lives, for they would be diverted into the waters to be transformed for all eternity into mutant, snake-like creatures. Yet those who did good in their lives could fear no punishment, for they would be led safely over the bridge and past the gates of Similaqsa. There they would live for all eternity, to wander in a blissful paradise free from mortal want."

With the conclusion of these words, a moment of pure silence followed. All of those present kept their thoughts to themselves, as all eyes remained glued to the blazing fire. As the flames crackled and hissed, the howl of the night wind rose in the distance. Beyond this sounded the crash of breaking surf. The spell was only broken when a far-off metallic tone permeated the night air.

"It's the southbound freight train right on schedule," offered Bobby Whitten, the group's comedian. "I wonder what that engineer would have to say if he knew that he was guiding his train smack through a doorway to the afterlife."

Though the majority of those present laughed at this comment, two of them took it quite seriously. Catching Miriam's look of concern, Joseph expressed himself in a whisper, so that only she could hear him.

"You know, Bobby could be very well onto something. If we have indeed stumbled upon the portal to Similaqsa here in Vandenberg, the elders would be far

44

from pleased. To defile this most sacred of spots with weapons of war would be a sin of the greatest degree possible. I seriously doubt that the judgment of the gods would be very favorable in our behalf."

Taking in these ominous words, Miriam shifted her gaze from the fire to the heavens above. A rare, crystal-clear evening sky was visible overhead. After easily picking out the Big Dipper, she looked on as a series of shooting stars streamed through the Dipper's interior. Most aware of how little they knew of the mysterious workings of the vast universe that surrounded them, Miriam anxiously shivered. Feeling small and alone, she stifled a yawn, and knew without looking at her watch that it was well past time to douse the campfire and send her crew off to their sleeping bags. For the dawn would all too soon be upon them, and once again they would have an ample opportunity to work on a solution to this greatest of all mysteries.

Six and half hours later, the first member of the team awoke to the distant cry of a hungry gull. It was as the twenty-year-old sophomore went to put on his morning coffee that his sleep-laden eyes wandered to the tiny trailer's only window. Outside, Coast Road was barely visible in the morning mist. Occupying its usually vacant length was a long line of vehicles, most of which had flashing red beacons on their roofs. All of this traffic seemed to be moving slowly to the south. Well aware that something unusual was occurring, he hurriedly pulled on his jeans and sprinted off to awaken Joseph Solares.

As he expected, the teaching assistant didn't mind this early wake-up call in the least. Scurrying from his bed, the broad-shouldered Indian took in the line of traffic still visible on the road and whistled appreciatively. Joseph didn't have to awaken Miriam, for two minutes later she was knocking at his trailer's door.

In the early light of dawn, the team assembled on the parking lot. Piping-hot coffee was served to temporarily alleviate the morning chill. While the crew members milled about the campgrounds, curious as to what the line of traffic visible a half-mile away meant, a single van cut off towards Ocean Beach Park. A cloud of dust trailed behind it as the vehicle snaked down the narrow access road and ground to a halt in the lot's far corner.

Four men immediately emerged from the van's interior. Two of these individuals proceeded to the rear of the vehicle, where they began unloading a large television camera and other video equipment. Another of the men began setting up a tripod, on top of which he mounted a sophisticated 35-mm. camera. The fourth individual merely stood beside the van, catching his reflection in its side windows. Tall, handsome, and immaculately dressed in a suit and tie, he studied his appearance as Miriam and Joseph approached.

"Good morning," greeted Miriam rather sheepishly.

Not in the least bit surprised by this intrusion, the man made a final adjustment to his collar, then turned and flashed the two newcomers a broad, toothy smile.

"And a top of the morning to you two," said the tanned gentleman, his dark eyes quickly sizing up his visitors. "And I thought we had this story all to ourselves."

"You're Roger Winslow, the TV news reporter, aren't you?" queried Joseph, his dark eyes beaming.

"This is me in the flesh," answered the anchorman boldly. "KXBC's finest will scoop the networks yet once again."

"What do you mean by that?" quizzed Miriam, who was an infrequent television viewer.

"You've got to be kidding me," replied the reporter. "You mean to say you honestly don't know what we've been called out of our warm beds to witness this morning?"

Catching the pair of puzzled expressions on the faces of his two ragtag visitors, Roger Winslow stifled a laugh. "And here I thought that you guys were from *Rolling Stone*, or some other ecological journal, here to record your own story. I guess we'll have an exclusive after all. May I ask what brings you guys to this god-forsaken portion of the California coastline? It sure can't be for the surfing."

It was Miriam who answered. "We're here on an archaeological dig for the State University."

"Ah, a bunch of genuine bone-pickers," jested Winslow.

Rather impatiently, Miriam continued, "Would it be too presumptuous of us to ask exactly what you're doing here this morning?"

Checking his watch, Winslow then angled his line of sight to catch the progress of his cameramen. "I guess a single leak won't hurt in this instance. You're going to damn well know what this is all about soon enough anyway. Might as well be ready for it."

Shifting his glance to the south, the direction the assembled cameras were now facing, the reporter pointed to the fog-shrouded hills that lay in the distance. "In a couple of minutes, if all goes as scheduled, we'll be witnessing the launch of a Titan rocket."

With this revelation, a look of genuine surprise

showed on Miriam's face. "So that's why they made us leave Tranquillon Ridge! At least Colonel Lansford could have told us about it."

"I'm afraid not, lady," retorted the newsman. "This whole launch is strictly a hush-hush affair, on a need-to-know basis only. We only heard about it late last night, through one of our ever-loving moles stationed inside Vandenberg. From what he gathered, it seems even the Air Force was caught off guard by the speed with which this whole thing came down."

"Well, this should really be something!" exclaimed Joseph. "I've always wanted to watch a real launch. Why don't I go over and tell the kids what this is all about. They're going to be thrilled."

As Joseph hurriedly crossed the lot to share the news with the rest of the dig team, Miriam found her gaze locked on the southern horizon. There, the surrounding hillsides were barely visible, covered in a cloak of thick, gray fog.

"Do you think this fog will delay the launch any?" she asked softly.

"I doubt it," answered Winslow. "If the Air Force was worried about fog, they sure wouldn't have chosen Vandenberg as their Pacific missile-launch site. As I'm certain you're well aware, if you've spent more than a couple of days here, clear mornings are an exception, and definitely not the rule. I seriously doubt if this fog is going to stop them."

The reporter's attention was diverted by a hand signal from one of the nearby technicians. Checking his watch again, he squared his shoulders and took a last look at his reflection in the van's window.

"It looks like it's show time. I'd better get over to my crew and check out those last-minute details. If you're still around afterwards, maybe we could get together. I'd like to know more about what you folks are digging for up here."

Not giving Miriam time to respond, the reporter took off to join his crew. Miriam watched as he stationed himself before the tripods. A tiny microphone was clipped to his tie and a dab of make-up applied to his cheeks and forehead. Standing there with his back to mist-shrouded Tranquillon Ridge and the hills beyond, the handsome anchorman looked out of place in his suit and tie. It was while Miriam was contemplating this fact that a familiar voice came from behind her.

"Hey, Boss!" cried Joseph. "Why don't you join us? We're going to climb up the railroad trestle to see if we can get a better view of the launch site."

Deciding that this didn't sound like a bad idea, Miriam crossed the parking lot and rejoined her group. Seconds later, they were off to the path that led towards the beach.

Once the group had made it to the top of the hill that held the railroad tracks, they settled down on its sandy shoulder. The view indeed proved to be an excellent one. From this vantage point, the Pacific could be seen crashing to their right, while both the parking lot and the valley leading to the city of Lompoc were visible to their left. But all eyes remained focused straight ahead, to the hills lying to the immediate south.

One of the students had thought to bring a thermos of coffee and a supply of cups, and they were soon available to all those who desired them. Contentedly sipping her coffee, Miriam savored its warmth and taste. As she brought the mug to her lips, she noticed a bright blue patch of sky visible above them. Well aware that the morning fog was already beginning to burn off, she stirred when a strange deep-throated rumble sounded in the distance. Steadily rising in intensity, the resulting noise was almost ear-shattering. Accompanying this deafening blast was a burst of brilliant white light. This was soon followed by a plume of billowing smoke as the first portion of the rocket became visible.

Larger than she had expected, the missile rose skyward from the valley directly adjoining Tranquillon Ridge. It was comprised of a long central fuselage, painted white and silver, and two shorter white boosters that straddled it. Ascending steadily into the air, the rocket roared with great power from its engines. It was unlike any sound that she had ever heard before, and Miriam found herself invigorated and thrilled. Only when the Titan momentarily disappeared into a low bank of clouds did she turn to share this unique experience with her team.

With eyes glued skywards, her crew seemed mesmerized. Only Joseph Solares met her gaze. A wide, wondrous smile etched her assistant's lips, and Miriam returned a simple nod of acknowledgment. When her own glance returned to the heavens, she found herself searching the skies in vain for any sign of the huge rocket. It was veiled by a bank of dark clouds, and she could only wonder what it was carrying and where it was ultimately bound.

The deep-throated, bass rumble noticeably abated, to be replaced by a single, explosive crack. This foreign sound was followed by a brief flash of intense light, visible even through the fog bank. Several seconds passed, and all was unnaturally quiet, when the area filled with the banshee-like wail of a warning siren.

Confused as to what this meant, Miriam looked to Joseph, who pointed straight into the air. Following the direction of his finger, she caught sight of a strangely shaped cloud of bright orange smoke drift-

50

ing high overhead. Still not sure what this indicated, she turned to her left as a loud claxon began sounding. She soon realized that this racket was coming from a single jeep that was rapidly approaching the parking lot. Miriam's senses prickled alive when a man's voice was heard emanating from this vehicle's powerful public-address system.

"Attention all civilians, there has been a failure of the Titan launch. You must evacuate the area at once because of the danger of toxic gases. I repeat, you must evacuate the park confines at once. Seal yourselves in your vehicles and head immediately for the Coast Road access to Lompoc."

Immediately Miriam snapped into action. Efficiently, she herded the team down the railroad trestle. With a minimum of panic, they made it to their van in less than a minute. Thirty seconds later, they were well on their way down the gravel road leading from the park, with the vehicle holding the journalists close on their tail.

Chapter Three

One-hundred and eighty-eight nautical miles to the southeast of Vandenberg, the attack submarine U.S.S. Razorback cut beneath the cool waters of the Pacific. The last vessel of its class, the twenty-seven-year-old sub obtained its power, not from a nuclear reactor, but from a trio of diesel-electric engines. Though this propulsion method was the same as that which had run the subs of World Wars I and II, a reliance on fossil fuels was about the only thing that the Razorback had in common with those vessels of old.

One of the primary design innovations that made the Razorback unique was its "tear-drop" hull. Unlike past classes of submarines, which had sharp, knife-like bows, the Razorback's hull was cylindrically rounded. This feature, combined with a more efficient power plant, allowed the sub to be more maneuverable than its predecessors, and to cruise faster and dive to greater depths. When a sophisticated electronics and weapons package had been added, the Razorback had embarked on her first deployment as a first-line man-of-war. Almost three decades later, in an age of digital electronics and reliable nuclear-propulsion systems, the Razorback still held its own. This was something its current skipper was most proud of.

Commander Philip Exeter had been assigned to the Razorback for over nine months. Though the forty-one-year-old officer had originally desired service aboard a 688-Class submarine, the Navy's latest nuclear-powered attack vessel, he had been thrilled with the chance to have a command of his own. As it turned out, he hadn't been the least bit disappointed.

Their present mission was certainly not disappointing. Only recently returned from a month-long deployment in the northern Pacific, the Razorback was now over six hours out of Point Loma. It had been ordered from its tender berth at the tip of San Diego Harbor, in the dead of night. Though dawn had already arisen above the sub, the crew would never know it, for the sub had submerged soon after clearing the final buoy. Exeter knew it was very possible that they would remain beneath the seas for a good portion of the next three days, until the exercise they were currently involved in was due to be terminated. He was preparing to explain this fact to the boat's Executive Officer, Lieutenant Patrick Benton, and its Navigator, Lieutenant Edward McClure.

Seated at his customary position at the head of the wardroom table, Exeter studied the charts that had been laid out before him. To his left sat the Navigator. An eight-year Naval veteran, Lieutenant McClure had quickly pointed out the Razorback's current position. Adjusting his wire-rim glasses, the softspoken junior officer had related their coordinates in a most scholarly fashion.

The XO had watched this briefing in a rather detached fashion. Seated directly across from the Captain, Patrick Benton thoughtfully sipped his mug of strong, black coffee and munched on a hot cinna-

53

mon roll. Sporting close-cropped red hair, with a pair of inquisitive, clear blue eyes, Benton was well known for both his dry wit and his trusty corncob pipe, which he always kept close by.

It proved to be the XO who broke the contained silence that had possessed the wardroom during the past few minutes. "We're well on our way into the Outer Santa Barbara Passage by now, Captain. If we're not heading into the open sea, then exactly where are we bound for?"

Exeter subconsciously twisted the end of his moustache. "Actually, we won't be traveling much further than this. Operation Mauler restricts the Razorback to a relatively tight triangular sector of water, roughly bounded by San Nicolas Island to the west, San Clemente to the south, and Catalina to the north. Our goal is to remain undetected for seventy-two hours, while three as yet unknown surface platforms attempt to track us down."

"This could be an interesting one," reflected the XO, who sat back and returned his attention to his cinnamon roll.

"Every time we leave Point Loma it's a new challenge," said the Captain, as he circled the area on the chart that they were restricted to. "This could very well be the Razorback's most important test. The waters here are relatively shallow and the current's extremely tricky. A trio of modern destroyers, complete with their combined helicopter forces, could easily tag us. It's imperative that this not be our destiny!"

The emotional force of this last sentence caused the XO to immediately sit forward and take notice. It was most evident that the Captain was taking this exercise most seriously. Wiping the remaining cinnamon crumbs from his fingers, he fumbled for his pipe,

54

which he had stored in his pocket. Only when its familiar scarred tip was between his teeth did he speak.

"We certainly showed them up in the Gulf of Alaska that the Razorback can outperform the best of them. Not even the Canadian airdales could tag us. We can surely hide once again, especially here in our home waters."

With this, the Captain's dark gaze directly linked with that of his XO. "That had indeed better be the case, Mr. Benton. I don't want any screw-ups with this one. Command has got to be assured that the Razorback can still take the best that they can throw at us, and then some.

"Now, I want the word spread throughout the boat that for the next seventy hours each and every crew member is to be alert to his every sound. Make certain that all unnecessary movement is curtailed. When the men are not on duty, they're to stay in their bunks. Silence is our most reliable ally. If it is properly maintained, it will never let us down."

Still surprised with Exeter's somberness, Benton nodded. "I'll pass the word, Captain. Do you want me to relieve the present OOD?"

Hastily checking his watch, Exeter responded. "We've still got some time left until we penetrate the southern boundary of the exercise perimeter. Let's allow Lieutenant Willingham to continue driving the boat until then. From what I've seen so far, that kid seems to be cut out of the right stuff for command, and I'm impressed."

It was from the lips of the Navigator that the next question emanated. "Excuse me, sir, but what strategy will we put into play once we cross the perimeter?"

The Captain managed a bare smile. "I guess that's

the million-dollar question, isn't it, Lieutenant? I'd say that the best way to start things out is for you to find us a nice, deep hole somewhere between San Clemente and Catalina. If nature cooperates, perhaps we'll also come up with a clearly defined thermal to further mask us. Then all we have to do is shut down all systems and wait for our pursuers to show themselves. Once we know precisely who's after us and where they're coming from, determining a tactic to further evade them will be a hell of a lot easier."

Pushing his chair back from the table, the Captain continued, "If there are no other questions, gentlemen, I'd say that it's time for both of you to get down to some serious work."

Taking this cue, the XO stood and allowed the Navigator room to slide out from the booth and stand beside him. Benton watched as Lieutenant McClure, noticeably taller and thinner than his own five-foot, nine-inch frame, efficiently gathered the charts that had been spread out before the Captain. Once this task was accomplished, both officers exited through the forward hatchway that led to the boat's control room.

Alone now in the wardroom, Exeter gazed at the framed picture hung above the booth to his left. Here was drawn a full-colored representation of the fierce animal they were so aptly named for. With eyes bulging and showing no fear, the lean, long-bodied wild hog prepared to charge a full-grown bear. Oblivious to the fact that it was clearly outsized, the razorback was about to initiate its attack with stubborn determination and pointed tusks as its only apparent strong points.

How fitting it was that this beast should be their namesake, thought Exeter. Like the charging hog in the picture, his submarine faced a most formidable challenge. Designed in a technological era that had yet to put a man in space, their twenty-seven-year-old vessel had been forced to prove its current worth time after time. Manned by sailors who weren't even born when its hull was laid, the Razorback found itself in a totally new world of micro-chips and mini-computers. Were they a mere anachronism as many in the Navy currently believed, or did they still have a valuable purpose to serve? In Philip Exeter's mind, there was no doubt about the answer to this question. As long as he was the commanding officer, the sub would give its all and prove her critics wrong.

Distracted by the presence of another individual to his right, Exeter pivoted and set his glance on the doleful-eyed seaman presently responsible for upkeep of the officer's galley.

"Excuse me, Captain, but can I fix you a platter of fresh scrambled eggs and sausage? Cooky's just pulled a mess of hot biscuits out of the oven, and there's still some cinnamon rolls left to boot."

Though he had yet to eat a thing since the previous day's late lunch with Carla, thoughts of food didn't entice Exeter in the least. "I'm afraid I'm going to pass on that, Simpson. I'd like you to fill my thermos with some fresh coffee, though. Please set it up in my quarters."

"Aye, aye, Captain," replied the soft-spoken seaman, who immediately began carrying out the request.

Most aware of the work that still faced him, Exeter stood and stretched his cramped frame. Crossing the hallway, he took less than a half-dozen steps to reach the space reserved for his private domain. Seaman Simpson was just leaving as he shut the folding door behind him and took a seat before his compact, wall-mounted desk.

Because the Razorback had been in San Diego a mere three days after returning from their month's assignment up north, he found himself faced with a variety of memos and reports and a stack of unopened mail. Each of these documents would have to be carefully scrutinized. Before tackling this time-consuming project, he decided that his attentions should be first turned to the sealed manila envelope his own wife had given him the previous afternoon. Slitting open the flap with a letter opener, he pulled out the envelope's contents, a single eight-by-eleven-inch photograph.

The picture was of Carla and his two daughters, Connie and Carmen. It had to have been taken recently, for his wife was wearing that new kimono he had brought her from Seattle only four days before. Carla loved it when he bought her new clothes and, as always, she had been quick to make a fuss over this newest outfit. In fact, she had been modeling it for him the previous afternoon when the messenger had arrived with the surprise order calling him back to the base. Just as shocked as she was, Philip had accepted her offer to drive him over to Point Loma to see what the order was all about.

One look at his CO's face and he knew that they'd be going off to sea once again. Even though they had just returned from thirty days of joint U.S.-Canadian ASW exercises in the Gulf of Alaska, Command needed the Razorback for yet another mission. Ever mindful of his sworn duty, he had sent Carla homeward with her heart full of disappointment and her eyes full of tears. It was as she prepared to leave the base that she had handed him the sealed envelope and had made him promise he'd open it once they were out of port.

As he studied the glossy photograph, he became

58

aware of his own rising emotions. His girls appeared before him, glowing with life and full of inner beauty. His Carla looked as gorgeous as the day he had first met her, over twenty-one years before. The pink kimono he had bought her fit her tiny figure perfectly. He knew her size well, for her waistline hadn't changed for over two decades. Considering her cooking skills, this was quite an accomplishment.

Standing on Carla's right was their oldest, Connie. Appearing like a carbon copy of her mother, from her slim, compact figure to her pixie-like haircut, Connie seemed full of intense energy. Considering her busy schedule of late, Philip was surprised that Carla had been able to get her to take some time out for this photo. Why, even after being gone an entire month, he had only gotten to see Connie a single time, on the first evening he had returned home.

Far from taking it as a personal affront, Philip knew that she was at the age at which there just didn't seem to be enough hours in the day. Lord knows she had never been the type of girl he had ever had to worry about. A straight-A student for as long as he could remember, Connie was the kind of kid a parent dreamed of. Level-headed and most aware of her responsibilities, she complimented her excellent schoolwork with both a weekend and full-time summer job.

For the last four years she had been working at Sea World. There she had become particularly fascinated with the dolphins. So intense was her interest that she even planned to make oceanography her major when she entered the University of California at San Diego as a freshman that fall.

Philip shook his head with wonder upon realizing that he'd soon have a girl in college. The years' swift passage were even more apparent in the face and figure of the young woman standing at Carla's left. Even though she was three years her sister's junior, Carmen was already the taller of the two, and still growing. Even her full figure seemed to be more developed. Philip knew this could be trouble in the months to come, because Carmen was having enough problems with the boys as it was. Drawn to her long, dark hair, baby-blue eyes, and warm, devilish smile, the boys at Loma High were already falling under her spell, just as he had.

Though Carmen was in many ways Connie's opposite, Philip always had a soft spot in his heart for her. Perpetually in disciplinary trouble, and struggling just to keep a C average, Carmen found it hard to keep her attention focused on a subject for any significant length of time. Particularly weak in science and mathematics, she was right at home in physical education. Tennis, swimming, and jogging were her favorites. A natural athlete, Carmen had a closet full of trophies and ribbons. Most of these awards had been won at the Navy country club.

Only two months before, she had turned sixteen. The day of her birthday, Carla had taken her downtown for her driver's-license test, which she had barely passed. Her latest crusade was to convince her parents to lend her the money to buy a car.

Philip's first answer had been a definite no. Carla had enough trouble disciplining Carmen as it was. A car could make things considerably worse.

When she had offered to take a summer job at the country club as a junior tennis instructor, Philip had found himself wavering. His daughter had never shown an interest in working before. Perhaps a car would make her more responsible.

In the end it had been Carla who had definitely put her foot down. Not influenced at all by Carmen's baby-blue eyes or heart-warming smile, Carla had put off even considering getting another car, at least until the first report card of the fall was received. Then, if Carmen's grades showed a substantial improvement, she could once again bring the subject up for consideration.

Though his youngest had pouted for an entire evening after he had agreed to this, she was soon her old self over breakfast. After polishing off half a cantelope, a bowl of cereal, three pieces of french toast, six slices of bacon, and two glasses of milk, she had been off to the tennis courts with her racket in tow and her new beau to charm. Though this had only occurred the previous morning, for some reason it felt like a lifetime ago.

Shaking his head and smiling, Philip felt closer to his wife than he had ever felt before. Twenty years was a long time to spend with one person, and he knew that he was very fortunate to have her as his wife. They had met during college. Both had attended the University of Kansas. He had known from the first date that she was the one for him. The way Carla told it, he had never had a chance of escaping even if he had wanted to.

They had been married soon after graduation, and she had been with him on that proud day he was commissioned an ensign in the United States Navy. Because his area of special study had been nuclear physics, he had been invited to attend submarine school in New London, Connecticut. He had immediately accepted and had not been sorry since.

Raising a pair of rambunctious girls out of a suitcase wasn't the easiest of jobs, but like all military parents, they had managed. Now, all too soon, both girls would be on their own, and he and Carla would have the house all to themselves. Perhaps now Carla could at long last complete her Master's and get that college-level teaching position she had always dreamed of. And of course there was his own desire to some day get his Doctorate.

Thus lost in thought at the picture of his beloved family, Philip Exeter found his concentration abruptly broken by the harsh ring of the comm line. With practiced ease his hand shot out to pick up the black handset mounted on the wall before him.

"Captain here."

The voice on the other end was smooth and sure of itself. "Captain, it's the XO. I thought you'd like to know that we're just about to cross Mauler's southern perimeter."

"Very good, Lieutenant Benton," returned Exeter, who was still a bit shaken by this sudden call to duty. "I'm on my way up to the control room."

Hanging up the receiver, he stood and, well aware of the pile of unread correspondence that still awaited his examination, left the confines of his cabin. As he entered the hallway, he noticed a single figure seated at the wardroom table. Completely captivated by the plateful of sausage and eggs that he was hungrily wolfing down, the Razorback's Engineering Officer, Lieutenant Theodore "Smitty" Smith, was startled by Exeter's sudden appearance.

"Well, good morning, Captain. I thought I was all alone back here."

"You soon will be, Smitty. How's our ventilation system looking?"

Putting down his knife and fork, the lieutenant was quick to answer. "We've just about got it one hundred percent, Captain. Of course, that main condenser still has to be replaced, but with a little luck she should get us through this cruise without too much sweat."

"Good job, Lieutenant. Keep me informed if she

gives you the slightest hint of trouble."

"Will do, Captain," snapped the junior officer, who waited for Exeter to completely disappear through the hatch before returning to his breakfast.

Not giving this encounter a second thought, Exeter continued on toward the Razorback's control room. The passageway he was presently crossing was narrow and cramped. On his left was the sealed door to the radio room. The massive vault-type combination lock on its door was an after-effect of the Walker spy case. Whereas the room used to be open to the entire crew, entry was now strictly limited.

The staccato noise of a typewriter broke from the right side of the corridor. Hastily Exeter poked his head into the sub's general office. Inside this elongated cubicle was a copier machine, various file and storage drawers, and just enough space for the boat's Supply Officer to do his thing in. Currently pecking on the typewriter was the most junior officer on the staff, Ensign Oliver Tollbridge. Without drawing his attention, the Captain peered over the ensign's skinny shoulders, and saw that he was typing up a revised list of the Razorback's current video library. Not desiring to interrupt this all-important task, Exeter silently backed out of the office and continued on towards the boat's bow.

Swiftly now he passed through a corridor lined with a myriad of pipes, cable, and copper fittings. This area of the sub also held the gyroscope, various ECM gear, and their unmanned Mark 101A fire-control system. The stairwell on his left led downward, to the boat's second level. There was stationed the sonar and torpedo rooms, the crew's quarters and galley, and, toward the stern, the Razorback's engine compartment. Continuing on past this stairway, Exeter emerged into the control room.

As always, this section of the boat buzzed with activity. Bisecting the room was the periscope station. It was here the captain and the current Officer of the Deck usually positioned themselves.

An alert seaman noticed Exeter's arrival and spoke out clearly for all present to hear. "Captain's in the control room."

With familiar ease, Philip Exeter scanned the compartment to determine the boat's exact status. Before him, he identified the lean figure of the current OOD, Lieutenant Scott Willingham. In the process of scanning the horizon with their forward periscope, the blond-haired khaki-clad officer quickly circled the metal-mesh platform, his shoulders bent, his eyes snuggled firmly into the periscope's sights.

To this station's left was the boat's nerve center. Here Chief of the Boat Lester Brawnley parked his hefty figure before the diving station. Ever alert to any change in their depth status, the chief sat before the board responsible for adjusting their trim and determining their buoyancy. By merely triggering the opening or closing of a variety of valves, he could vent air into their ballast tanks or add heavier sea water. The actual up, down, or sideways movement of the boat was regulated by the two planesmen, seated in the forward portion of the room, to the chief's right. Two seamen first class presently sat in the upholstered "drivers' " chairs, their hands carefully gripping the aircraft-type steering wheels that guided the Razorback's wanderings. Before them was mounted the ever-important depth gauge, which read a steady sixty-five feet.

Exeter took in the calm chatter of the control room's personnel and, satisfied with what he heard, crossed over to the compartment's rear. Here was placed the navigation station. Perched before its compact metal table, both the XO and Lieutenant Mc-Clure scrutinized a detailed bathymetric chart of the Gulf of Santa Catalina. The Captain was just taking in their current position, in the waters between San Clemente and Catalina islands, when the firm voice of the OOD spoke out excitedly.

"I have a surface contact, bearing three-two-zero, relative rough range five thousand eight hundred yards!"

Instantly, Exeter's attention snapped back to the periscope station. His ensuing orders were delivered crisp and clear for all to hear.

"Down scope! Take us down to two hundred and fifty feet, at one-third speed. Has sonar got anything on this contact?"

The seaman responsible for manning the direct comm line to sonar responded a few seconds later. "Sonar's got them on passive, sir. They apologize for not picking it up earlier, but the ship was apparently just lying there, dead in the water. She's a major combatant, all right, Captain, and she's coming towards us with a bone in her teeth."

"Change our course to two-six-zero," ordered Exeter firmly. He was aware of the sudden tilt of the deck as the Razorback's sail-mounted planes bit into the Pacific and the 2,800-ton vessel plunged downwards.

The Captain's eyes were locked on the depth gauge as they dropped beneath the one-hundred-fifty-foot level when the comm line from sonar again activated.

"Sir, sonar has another pair of surface contacts, bearings two-eight-five and two-two-zero respectively. Relative rough range for both contacts is five thousand yards and rapidly closing."

Genuinely shocked by this revelation, Philip Exeter silently cursed. Here he was less than an hour into the exercise and already they were boxed in and about to be tagged. To escape this rapidly tightening net the Razorback would have to play its alternatives most carefully.

"All stop!" he ordered. "Level us out at two-five-zero feet."

While these directives were being relayed, the boat's senior officers gathered around the navigation table. Fresh from his own recently concluded conversation on the comm line, the XO briefed them of his find.

"Sonar had time to do a preliminary signature ID on those contacts, Captain. The first one that we picked up was a dual-shaft gas turbine. Lefty bets his pension that she's a Spruance. The other two are single-shaft geared turbines, most probably belonging to a pair of Knox-class frigates."

"If that's the case, I'll bet they're the Roark and the Joseph L. Hawes," added the OOD. "I personally saw those two frigates trying to sneak out of Loma two nights ago. And here they've been just waiting for us all this time."

Aware that the angled tilt of the deck was decreasing, Exeter sighed. "Whoever they are, you can be certain that all three ships have got choppers and variable depth sonar. That means that we've got to make our move quickly or forever hold our peace."

With his glance locked on the bathymetric charts of the waters they were presently plying beneath, the Captain's eyes momentarily brightened. "Lieutenant McClure, do you think you could find us a nice, sandy portion of sea floor nearby for the Razorback to settle into?"

Already taking into account their new course, the sub's Navigator bent over the chart and responded. "I believe I can find us a good spot approximately seven nautical miles from our current position, Captain. The only trouble is that we're going to have to go down to six hundred and twenty-five feet to reach it."

"We can handle that," retorted Exeter, who briefly met his XO's concerned glance. "Chart us the quickest course and let's get going. Mr. Willingham, rig us for a deep dive. Then I want the boat to be buttoned up as quiet as a church. Spread the word that a state of ultra-quiet will prevail until further ordered. The only way we're going to evade these guys is by convincing them that we're no longer here, so let's get moving! The U.S.S. Razorback isn't about to get licked so easily."

One floor beneath the control room, Seaman First Class Todd "Lefty" Jackman sat in the narrow compartment reserved for the sonar monitors. The light here was veiled in red, the atmosphere hushed, as Lefty concentrated on the myriad of sounds being channeled into his headphones. He had been exclusively monitoring the Razorback's passive-detection system for over two hours. During this time, the noises created by their own vessel had been at a minimum, for they had been lying on the ocean's bottom, hushed in a state of ultra-quiet. This condition was fine with the senior sonar technician, for it gave his hull-mounted microphones a clearer sweep of the surrounding waters.

The sounds that he had continued to pick up these last one hundred and twenty minutes were far from reassuring. Above them, it was most obvious that the trio of destroyers had yet to be convinced that their target had moved on. He clearly heard the characteristic chugging of their turbines as they circled and probed. Thirty minutes before, the largest of these vessels had even sailed right over them. Lefty had been able to pick out the oscillating hum of its towed VDS unit, being pulled in the destroyer's wake, seeking any sign of the sub. In this case, fortune had been with the Razorback, for the Spruance-class ship had merely kept moving on. Currently, their pursuers were still in the area, though none were closer than 20,000 yards.

Lefty sat back in his chair and tried to stretch his cramped, muscular limbs. His hands were cold, and his feet practically numb. What he needed was a good thirty-minute workout in the gym. That would get the blood pumping through his body once again. He had heard that the larger subs, such as the 688's and Tridents, had such facilities right on board. This was not the case with the Razorback. In fact, he was fortunate just to have a bunk of his own. When he had been first assigned to the sub seven months before, Lefty had been forced to hot-bunk with a torpedo man, and he hadn't had many kind thoughts as to his draw of assignments. It wasn't until a month before, when he had finally passed his sonar qualification, that the XO had assigned him a space of his own. Though he couldn't even turn over without getting out of the bunk first, he wasn't about to complain. The torpedo man had stunk of cordite and machine oil, two scents that Lefty could certainly live without.

The exercise that they had just completed in the North Pacific was his first as a seaman first class. Comfortable with his specialty, Lefty was beginning to enjoy the Razorback and its crew. Being the last of her kind meant that the boat deserved extra-special attention. He was proud of this fact, and never wanted to be the one who let the tradition down.

Temporarily lifting the headphones from his sore ears, Lefty turned to see what his co-worker was up to. Seaman Second Class Seth Burke, who sat to his left, was also taking a breather, and the two conversed in a whisper.

"Well, what do you think, Lefty, will our playin' possum fool them?"

Lefty shrugged. "We'd better hope so. Otherwise the Captain is going to have our heads for sure. We should have heard that destroyer long before they saw it on the periscope."

"It sure is getting nippy down here," added the seaman second class as he zipped his gray sweatshirt up to his neck. "What happens if they wait us out and we have to surface to snorkel?"

"Then we lose," returned Lefty, who was beginning to feel a bit chilly himself.

"It's times like these that I wish we were in a nuke," observed Burke. "Then we could stay down here almost indefinitely."

"I don't know about that, Seth. If we had been in a 688, I'll bet that Spruance would have tagged us for sure when they passed over us. Those nukes can't shut down like we can. They've always got to have some sort of coolant pump going, and that means additional noise. For good-old quiet, I'll take the Razorback's battery power any day of the week. Say, have you ever heard the sound of your flashlight going?"

This question seemed to stump the seaman second class, who pondered an answer. Meanwhile, Lefty Jackman's attention was drawn back to his headphones as a far-off, crackling noise sounded from their stern hydrophone. Of a different pitch than that of a turbine engine, the faint noise was somehow familiar. Positioning himself squarely before his console, Lefty began to investigate it more fully.

On the floor immediately above Lefty, Commander Philip Exeter and three of his senior officers stood before the chart of the Gulf of Santa Catalina. The atmosphere that surrounded them was tense. The rest of the control room's complement of men was hunched in front of inactive instruments, waiting for the word that would get them going once again.

Around the navigation station, a whispered discussion was taking place. Lieutenant Smith, the Engineering Officer, had just figured out that they had a little less than sixty minutes of battery time left. Then they'd be forced to ascend and recharge their batteries. Since Operation Mauler extended another ten hours, if the destroyer and her escorts stayed close by, the Razorback would come up on the short end. Smitty also informed them that the boat's heating unit was close to failing. It was impossible to repair in a condition of ultra-quiet, and the temperature inside the vessel had already dropped a full ten degrees.

Philip Exeter and his fellow officers had long since put on their short khaki jackets. The additional chill was the least of their problems, and Exeter opened their predicament up for discussion.

Lieutenant Willingham was the first to offer his opinion. "I think we should attempt to creep away under battery power while we still can. Directly to the east of us there's all sorts of shallow trenches we can take advantage of along San Clemente's eastern shore. There we can safely ascend to snorkel depth, and if necessary, take on additional air in quick sips. When night falls, it should be a relatively easy run around the island's southern edge, and then we're home free in open ocean."

Contemplating this plan, Exeter turned to query his XO, who was standing to his right. "You've been unusually quiet this morning, Mr. Benton. What do you think is our best course of action?"

Pulling his pipe out of the corner of his mouth, the XO studied the chart a few seconds before answering. "Lieutenant Willingham's idea is interesting, but I'm afraid, in this instance, it's just too dangerous. The currents around San Clemente are extremely treacherous. This drastically increases the risks of us going aground. Not only could we fail the operation, we could lose the boat as well.

"I'd say we'd have a much better chance following the bottom of the trench we currently occupy northward. That will put us smack in the middle of the Outer Santa Barbara Passage. Once our batteries get us there, we can find ourselves a thermal and use it to veil us until it's safe to ascend. Right now, I've got a feeling that those surface ships topside aren't really certain where we are. Pushing on to the north could lose them for good."

Taking in this suggestion, the Captain was just about to offer a comment of his own when the comm line activated. The excited seaman relayed the message breathlessly.

"Sonar reports an underwater contact, sir. The bearing is one-eight-seven, with a range of fifty thousand yards."

Hastily rechecking the chart, Exeter realized that this would place the contact well within the southern perimeter of Operation Mauler. Since no U.S. submarine but the Razorback was authorized to be in this triangular sector for the next seventy hours, the Captain's pulse quickened. Tapping the comm line to the sonar room himself, he issued a single query.

"Can you get me a signature I.D. on it, Lefty?"

Recognizing this voice's source, Seaman Jackman's voice nervously faltered. "I believe I can, Captain.

Though it's at the limit of our range, it's making speed and really kicking up a ruckus. Don't hold me to this, sir, but I could swear this is the same sub that we picked up off Washington. Though I can't definitely prove it as yet, my gut tells me it's that outlaw Soviet Victor!"

Shocked by this revelation, Exeter stirred. "Good work, Lefty. Keep me posted on any developments."

Disconnecting the line, he pivoted to address his officers. "Well, this certainly throws a new log on the fire. Seaman Jackman feels this newest contact is none other than that Victor we chased out of Juan de Fuca. Do you believe the gall of those guys? It looks like it's time for us to teach our comrades another lesson about trespassing in American waters. Prepare the boat to get under way. I'm going to want flank speed."

"But what about the exercise?" offered the XO.

"Damn the exercise!" countered the Captain. "I'm not about to just sit here twiddling our thumbs while one of the Soviet Union's most advanced attack subs scoots right through our own backyard. Even if we can't pull thirty-two knots like they can, at least our pursuit will lead our ASW force to them. I say that it's time to put the fear of God in them!"

It was while he was initiating the flurry of orders that was putting new life into the Razorback's control room that one of the vessel's radiomen proceeded to the Captain's side. He handed Exeter a single, folded sheet of white paper. Opening it with a flourish, the Razorback's senior officer paled upon reading its contents.

Conscious of this message's effect, the XO approached him. "Is there anything the matter, Captain?"

Philip Exeter managed a small grin. "Just when it

seems most confusing, the U.S. Navy has a way of stepping in and making your decisions for you. Cancel that intercept, Mr. Benton. We've just received a top-priority transmission from COMSUB. In effect, the Razorback has been ordered to abandon all operations and proceed with all due haste to the seas off Vandenberg. There we're to assist the Air Force in the salvage of a Titan 34-D rocket that has just gone down in the Pacific."

"Jesus, you've got to be kidding!" returned the XO. "What about the Victor?"

Exeter shrugged his shoulders. "I guess we'd better radio those destroyers and let them know where the real enemy lies. Right now, I'd better get going on that course to Point Arguello.

"Prepare to ascend, Mr. Brawnley. Lieutenant Willingham, our new depth will be sixty-five feet. All ahead full on course three-zero-zero."

To a roar of venting ballast, the Razorback shuddered and slowly began rising. Invigorated with new purpose, the black-hulled vessel appeared imbibed with life itself as its planes rotated upwards and its single screw whipped into action with a frantic hiss.

Chapter Four

The morning was hot and steamy as Lieutenant Lance Blackmore walked out onto the exposed bridge of the tender U.S.S. Pelican. This was only his seventh day in Hawaii, and already he had found little to be excited with. Although the scenery was beautiful, unfortunately his first Naval assignment was turning out to be a real disappointment. And to think that his classmates had been actually envious of him when he'd opened the orders directing him to Pearl Harbor!

He had arrived here fresh out of sub school and full of expectations. What little he had read about DSRV duty had seemed interesting and most challenging. Designed especially to rescue the occupants of a submarine accidentally immobilized on the sea floor, the Deep Submergence Rescue Vehicle was a relatively new phenomenon. Able to be transferred by a tender, such as the Pelican, or on the back of a full-sized submarine, such a vessel had enormous value. The DSRV's practicality was significantly augmented by the fact that it could fit into the cargo hold of a C-5A transport plane, allowing speedy access to the far corners of the globe.

When he had first set eyes on the Marlin, the fifty-foot-long, black-hulled, cigar-shaped vessel had been sitting rather inelegantly on the back of a flatbed truck. Fresh from a touchdown at Hickam Air Force Base, the Marlin had just arrived at Pearl when Blackmore had been guided onto the sub base for his very first visit. It wasn't long afterwards that he had been introduced to the vehicle's present Officer-in-Charge, Commander Will Pierce.

Dressed in a pair of grease-stained khakis, Pierce had appeared nothing like the dapper, nattily uniformed officers Blackmore had been exclusively exposed to in ROTC and later at New London. This disparity had been even more obvious when a crude selection of four-letter words had flowed from the commander's mouth, after one of the hoist operators had prematurely begun lifting the Marlin. A heavy feeling had filled the newly arrived junior lieutenant's stomach when introductions and handshakes were later exchanged.

Completely gray-haired, yet tanned and in amazingly excellent physical shape, the forty-seven-year-old commander had checked Blackmore out with a probing, blue-eyed stare. A veteran of Viet Nam, and over a dozen different surface vessels and submarines, Pierce had silently appraised his new lieutenant, and Blackmore had somehow felt that he had already failed. Inexperienced and naive to the workings of the real Navy, the all-too-recent college graduate only knew the world through books and research. Little had his hundreds of hours of classroom work prepared him to meet the commander's stare of inspection straight on, instead of cowering like a frightened child. From that moment on, their relationship had seemed to steadily deteriorate.

Merely contemplating this initial confrontation caused Blackmore's already low spirits to additionally sour. Not even the magnificent scenery so readily visible around him helped alleviate this feeling of depression. This had been their second day anchored there in Maui's Lahaina Harbor. It was one of the most visually stunning areas on the entire planet, and one couldn't ask for a better setting. Lying to their left was Auau Channel. This glistening blue expanse of water stretched to the western horizon, where the island of Lanai was visible, its distant shoreline rising like an encroaching sentinel.

To their right, less than a half mile distant, was Lahaina, one of Maui's most quaint, picturesque villages. Set on the island's northeastern sector, Lahaina was a mecca to locals and tourists alike, who were drawn to its unique boutiques and excellent restaurants. Once a bustling whaling center, the town had been restored to capture its past splendor. Walking down Lahaina's narrow, cobble-stoned streets, which were given added character by the brightly painted, wooden buildings with open verandahs that lined each side, one indeed got the impression that he had been magically conveyed back a century or two.

Lance Blackmore knew, from the way the crew had acted the previous night during shore leave, that the Marlin's complement could be easily mistaken for an unruly gang of decadent whalers. This lack of discipline was visible even today, with a trio of beer-sipping skin divers lying on the Pelican's bow. Watching them with disgust as they soaked up the morning rays, Blackmore silently cursed his bad duty draw.

This was not the gentleman's Navy he had dreamed of serving in since childhood. Why couldn't he have been sent to a Trident or a 688? Such duty would certainly be more to his expectation. But no, he had to be sent to an outlaw ship, where discipline meant merely getting the job done. And who knew if they'd ever even get a real chance to show what they could do?

Distracted by the excited cries of their pot-bellied chief petty officer, who had just hooked into a large fish from the Pelican's fantail, Blackmore failed to notice that he was no longer alone on the bridge.

"Oh, sweet Lord," pleaded the newcomer painfully. "Will someone please turn off these lights!"

Shading his bloodshot eyes from the morning sun, Ensign Louis Marvin leaned up against the bridge's railing. Blackmore couldn't help but find his mood lightening upon examining the pitiful sailor who stood beside him, naked except for his skivvies.

To a detached observer, the two officers appeared as a study in contrasts. Though both were twenty-four years old, they had nothing else physically in common. The most obvious difference was their height. Blackmore stood a solid six feet tall, while his skinny co-worker barely reached Lance's broad shoulders. Whereas Blackmore sported a thick head of close-cropped blond hair, Ensign Marvin was almost completely bald, except for two unruly strands of frizzy black wool that lay behind each of his rather large, pointed ears. In need of a shave, the Ensign massaged his creased forehead.

"Never again will these lips sample another sip of rum. Oh my poor aching head!"

Lance found it hard not to have compassion for his hungover shipmate. "Those pineapple coconut drinks start out innocent, but look out."

"Now he tells me," replied the Ensign mockingly.

"Of course, you could have stopped after six drinks," continued the taller of the two men.

Marvin gently rubbed the back of his neck. "Who in the hell was counting? Boy, was that some party! Did everyone make it back to the ship all right?"

Nodding that they had, Blackmore found his mood darkening as the Ensign began a blow-by-blow description of the previous night's shore leave. It had all started out well, when a group of them had had dinner at an excellent outdoor seafood restaurant. By dessert, it had gotten completely out of hand.

To begin with, one of the barmaids had taken an immediate interest in their senior diver. The big Californian was far from the shy type and had been quick to take advantage of the situation. After consuming his share of chi-chis, the diver had playfully pulled the long-haired Hawaiian onto his lap. Unknown to everyone present, however, the girl's insanely jealous boyfriend had been watching from across the street. With a trio of good-sized locals at his side, the boyfriend had crashed into the restaurant and immediately started swinging. Seconds later, a full-sized brawl had begun taking shape. Only the arrival of a single individual had kept the situation from getting completely out of hand.

Commander Pierce had been in the process of taking an innocent stroll along the streets of Lahaina, when he had passed the seafood restaurant just as the first punches were being thrown. Quickly realizing that it was his own crew that was involved, Pierce had jumped over the verandah and headed straight into the action. Oblivious to the greater sizes and younger ages of the combatants, he had picked out the troublemakers and cold-cocked two of the locals with a flurry of expertly thrown punches. With the battle now diffused, Pierce had herded the lot of them hastily outdoors. With a promise to behave themselves, the group had sworn to continue its drinking in more friendly environs. Not doubting their word, the commander turned to continue his stroll, whistling a tune from *South Pacific* and appearing as innocent as a newborn lamb in his starched Navy whites.

Needless to say, Pierce's heroics had been the talk of the rest of the evening. Since he was already a larger-than-life figure to the majority of the crew, the commander's past service record had been rehashed in intricate detail. This had been the first time that Blackmore had been privileged to hear these stories. But though Pierce had certainly had his share of colorful close calls, the Lieutenant still held fast to his belief that this wasn't the type of man they should be emulating. A brute, coarse individual, prone to over-indulgence in both drink and women, Will Pierce was an anachronism. He had no place in today's modern, high-tech Navy.

Still thinking about the previous evening, Blackmore failed to notice when Ensign Marvin halted his rambling. Certain that he knew just what was on Blackmore's mind, the ensign spoke out directly.

"Jesus, Lieutenant, will you please lighten up! That prudish look on your face reminds me of my headmaster at military school. I know we can't ask you to condone all of the unorthodox behavior you've seen aboard the Pelican this past week, but please keep an open mind. Duty aboard the Marlin is special. Though your first impressions might tell you otherwise, one thing that you can be certain of is that, when the Marlin is called into action, you can count on us to get the job done.

"As to what came down last night, you should just forget it. Command's been pushing us awfully hard these past few months. Believe it or not, this has been our first real R and R in over sixty days. Guys will be guys, and they deserve to be able to let their hair down on occasion. We're just lucky to have the commander around to save our scalps for us when things get out of hand."

Failing to see the humor in this, Blackmore stood there impassively, his serious gaze locked on the mist-shrouded island of Maui visible on his right. Conscious that he had failed to change the newcomer's mind, Ensign Marvin was in the process of pivoting to return to his cabin to pick up some more aspirin when a strange surging noise came from the surrounding waters. Turning back to the bridge, he hastily scanned the nearby seas for the source of this commotion, and his eyes caught sight of a bubbling expanse of white water visible two hundred yards west of the Pelican. Before he could even call out to inform Lieutenant Blackmore of his find, the characteristic black tower of a submarine's sail broke from the ocean's depths. By this time, the lieutenant had also sighted it. The two men stood there speechless, as the vessel surfaced completely. From its massive size, almost twice that of the Pelican, and its rounded hull, both officers identified it as a nuclear attack boat.

The silence that they shared was suddenly broken by the harsh, ringing tone of the tender's underwater telephone. It was Ensign Marvin who picked up the receiver. Blackmore was close by his side as the captain of the submarine briefed them of an accident that had just taken place beneath the waters surrounding Kauai, Hawaii's northernmost island. There, a 688-class attack sub had been in the process of utilizing an experimental vertical-launch missile system when something had gone wrong. An explosion had followed, and the huge 360-foot vessel had become immobilized on the sea floor, some 800 feet below the pounding Pacific. The Marlin was being called on to immediately initiate a rescue operation of its trapped crew.

Quickly sobered by a rush of adrenalin, Ensign

Marvin went to awaken Commander Pierce. This left Blackmore alone on the bridge once again. With his eyes glued to the submarine, Blackmore knew the time had come when he'd see for himself just what kind of stuff the crew of the Marlin was really made of.

The Barking Sands Pacific Missile Range facility occupied an eight-mile-long strip of prime beach property on Kauai's western shore. Run by the U.S. Navy, the site included some 700 square miles of surrounding ocean. There over 900 missile launches a year were monitored.

To assist in the research and development of new weapons systems, and to insure the reliability of old ones, the Barking Sands Tactical Underwater Range (BARSTUR) was littered with bottom-mounted hydrophones and three-dimensional tracking sensors. These systems allowed the technicians to know just what was going on below the ocean as well as above it. This ability was especially important in the testing of submarine weaponry.

It was to the facility's central engineering station that this data was channeled. Displayed visually in the form of a massive, opaque, 3-D bathymetric chart, the sea floor appeared visible without its covering of water.

On this particular morning, the technicians huddled around this lucite chart were monitoring no mere test. Instead, their attentions were rivoted on a life-and-death struggle taking place right before their startled eyes. Each of them knew that somewhere beneath the Kaulakahi Channel, between Kauai and Niihau, the crew of the 688-class submarine Providence was fighting to survive.

None of these technicians were more aware of their predicament than Dr. Richard Fuller. As project manager of the launch that the Providence had been in the midst of when the accident had occurred, Fuller was responsible for determining the vessel's exact location. This was of vital importance if a successful rescue attempt was to be initiated. By utilizing the range's unique underwater sensor grid, the Naval Oceans System Command (NOSC) scientist had been able to determine that the sub had settled on the sea floor 845 feet beneath the water's surface. Fortunately, this was well within the incapacitated vessel's depth threshold. Otherwise, the loss of life would have been significantly greater. Most cognizant of this fact, Fuller knew that they had been lucky so far. Now, if the Navy could only complete the rescue of the remaining crew members, they could all breath a sigh of relief.

Only minutes before he had personally relayed the sub's precise coordinates to the vessel the Navy had assigned to effect this rescue. It was presently on its way from Maui. The lives of over 100 men were now in the hands of the DSRV Marlin.

Fuller had worked with such craft on several occasions, though this would be the first time that he would get to see it perform the function for which it had been originally designed. Thankful that the Marlin had only been a couple of hundred miles away when the Providence went down, Fuller anxiously awaited its arrival.

With his arms cocked behind his back, the six-foot, three-inch researcher nervously paced the engineering station's floor. Except for his white lab jacket, Fuller didn't appear to be the type of individual one would expect to find indoors very often. With his skin tanned a deep bronze and his curly brown hair bleached with streaks of blond, it was evident that the middle-aged scientist spent his fair share of time in the sun. More at home on the exposed bridge of a destroyer, or the sail of a submarine, he surrendered to inside duty only when absolutely necessary. This morning was one of those occasions.

They had been in the midst of a test of a new submarine-borne launch system when disaster had struck. The Providence had been one of the first 688-class attack subs to be fitted with a dozen vertical-launch tubes built into the bow section of its outside pressure hull. Specifically designed to hold a Tomahawk cruise missile, the 688's with this capability would have an entirely new offensive weapon at their disposal, allowing them to hit surface targets well inland.

Three previous launches had taken place without a hint of trouble. Then this morning, only seconds after the captain of the Providence had been given permission to fire the fourth prototype weapon, a searing explosive blast had decimated the cruise missile while it was in the process of exiting its launch tube. Fuller could only assume that this explosion had originated in the Tomahawk's mid-body fuel tank. Regardless of the cause, the resulting blast concussion had been focused downward, directly at the sub's hull. As a result, three seamen had been instantly killed, with six others severely burnt. Quick action on the part of the surviving crew members had allowed the ruptured compartment to be subsequently sealed, yet not before the vessel's hydraulic system had been severely damaged. Unable to control its trim, the sub had spiraled downward to its present location on the sea floor deep below the Kaulakahi Channel.

Though he was a civilian who never wore a Navy uniform, Richard Fuller had a deep respect for the brave men who lay trapped inside the hull of the Providence. Living constantly in a dangerous, alien environment, such individuals went about their daily work far from the notice of the general public. No strangers to either personal sacrifice or risk, these young men were the country's true heroes. Knowing this, he had to do everything within his capability to insure their survival. Certain that the coordinates that he had relayed to the Marlin were precise ones, Fuller could only count the minutes left until the DSRV would arrive.

The trip up from Maui took the Pelican the better part of the day. With the Sturgeon-class submarine Sea Devil at its side, the tender immediately pulled up anchor only minutes after receiving its new call to duty. Monitoring each advancing nautical mile of their progress northward was the weathered, gray-haired figure of Commander Will Pierce. The Marlin's Officer-in-Charge had positioned himself on the tender's bridge soon after being awakened by Ensign Marvin. Only after being satisfied that their navigator had chosen the quickest route to the Kaulakahi Channel did Pierce allow himself a cup of coffee and a hasty bite of breakfast. Beard-stubbled and dressed in a wrinkled pair of khakis, Pierce then proceeded to the Pelican's stern, where the Marlin was nestled, secure in its elevated carrying blocks. With his men around him, he briefed them of their situation, and then made absolutely certain that the Marlin would be ready to go once they reached the waters west of Kauai.

It was shortly after Pierce completed his inspection of the DSRV that he called together his officers in the Pelican's corrugated-steel storage compartment, located amidships. With probing blue eyes, he studied all those present and emphasized the utter importance of their mission. Then, almost nonchalantly, he made the following assignments. Pierce would pilot the Marlin himself. Seated to his right would be Lieutenant Lance Blackmore. This newest member of their complement would serve as co-pilot and be responsible for all of the vessel's various navigation, communication, and mating systems. This would leave Ensign Louis Marvin as the DSRV's third and final crew member. As the sphere operator, Marvin would operate all the life-support systems and manipulator controls and assist those rescued as they transferred themselves into the Marlin itself. After conveying this information, the commander excused himself, to return to the Pelican's bridge.

Needless to say, Lance Blackmore found himself shocked to have been picked as the co-pilot. Though he was somewhat familiar with the systems he'd be in charge of, he had only acted as co-pilot on a single previous descent. Surely Pierce had more experienced individuals available, who were better qualified to carry out this all-important mission. Somewhat dumbfounded, he positioned himself beside the ship's starboard railing and watched the island of Molokai's western shoreline disappear in a veil of haze.

Their crossing of the Kaiwi Channel was a rough one, for the Pelican's throttles were kept wide open. During this time, Blackmore's nervousness was given an additional measure of misery as he succumbed to a full-fledged case of sea-sickness. Nauseous and dizzy, he pointed his "muzzle to the wind," and all too soon had his stomach empty.

By the time he viewed the island of Oahu passing before him, Blackmore's plight had eased considerably. Not only had they reached calmer waters, but

Louis Marvin had arrived at his side to console him. As before, the skinny ensign displayed the remarkable ability to be able to determine precisely what was on Blackmore's mind. A veteran of dozens of DSRV submergences, Marvin shrugged off the lieutenant's relative inexperience. The commander would have not ordered the newcomer along as co-pilot unless he was absolutely certain that he could do the job. If anything else, Blackmore should be taking this invitation as a compliment. The lives of over 100 men were at stake and Will Pierce would never think of needlessly jeopardizing them. As long as Blackmore remembered the locations of the systems he was responsible for, and followed his instructions precisely, he would do just fine.

After reminding the Lieutenant that he would always be close by should he need assistance, Marvin recommended that they both go below deck. A shower, meal, and a nap would have Blackmore feeling like himself again. Because the day would prove to be a long one, he would be thankful for this rest later on. And there was even plenty of time for him to study the Marlin's operational manual, should the desire arise. The Pelican's flat bow was already biting into the waters of the Kauai Channel when the two junior officers disappeared into the tender's interior.

Four and a half hours later, the mad grind of the Pelican's diesel engines decreased markedly. Most aware of the new waters that they were entering, Commander Pierce studied the horizon. To their bow's starboard side lay the cloud-enshrouded southern coastline of Kauai. Less than a half-dozen nautical miles to the north were the coordinates relayed to them from Barking Sands. The sun was already sinking to the west when he ordered his men topside.

A stiff easterly wind had stirred the waters of the Kaulakahi Channel with a moderate swell as the Pelican dropped its anchor. With an ease tempered by hundreds of hours of endless practice, the crew prepared the Marlin to descend.

The operation would be a relatively basic one. If the location of the downed sub indeed proved accurate, the Marlin merely needed to take on additional ballast and dive to the sea floor. There they would mate with the Providence and begin removing its crewmen, twenty-four at a time. The Marlin would then locate and mate with the Stugeon-class vessel that had followed them up from Maui. The submarines would be discharged and the operation would again be repeated. A total of five trips would be needed to transfer the entire crew.

Even if this complicated process went smoothly, they would be forced to work well into the late hours of the night. Thus Pierce desired to get things under way with all possible haste. After making his final contact with the captain of the Sea Devil from the Pelican's bridge, the gray-haired commander pulled on his overalls and made his way to the tender's stern. Last-minute instructions were passed to the support staff, and Pierce followed his two junior officers into the Marlin's topside hatch.

Lance Blackmore was the first one inside. There it was cool, damp, and dark. Following the steel stairway down into the central pressure capsule, he entered a cramped world far removed from that topside. The equipment-cluttered sphere in which he presently stood would be where the Providence's crew was to be placed. Behind this sphere, in the Marlin's stern, were the vessel's main propulsion and hydraulic units. It was in the opposite direction that he was drawn. Contorting his solid six-foot figure so that he could fit through the narrow hatchway, Blackmore entered the command module feet first. Careful not to hit any of the dozens of valves and switches that surrounded him, he slid into the chair placed to the right. Barely twenty seconds later, Pierce slid into the chair next to him. With a minimum of conversation, the two began the task of bringing the Marlin to life.

Once the mercury-filled ballast tanks were trimmed and the hydraulics system checked, Pierce triggered the battery-driven motor. A slight whirl sounded behind them as the Marlin's single screw began biting into the surrounding water. Blackmore was busy readying the communications gear when he noticed the angle of the DSRV's bow begin to dip downward. Even though it was pleasantly chilly inside the module, a thick band of sweat formed on his forehead. His heartbeat quickened when the angle of descent steepened further.

The familiar voice of Louis Marvin temporarily broke the tense atmosphere. "Well, we're off to the races. Pressure looks good in the main capsule, Skipper. All other systems continue to be right on."

"Good show, Ensign," replied Pierce matter-of-factly. "Are we all set for guests back there?"

"That we are, Skipper," returned Marvin with a thumbs-up sign.

"Then let's see about telephoning our guests to see if they can make the party," continued Pierce, whose hands were gripped tightly around the steering column. "Lieutenant Blackmore, you may do the honors."

Spurred by this request, the lieutenant nervously picked up the underwater telephone unit. After turning up the volume gain, he spoke into the transmitter of what appeared to be a normal, everyday telephone handset.

"U.S.S. Providence, this is the Marlin. Do you copy us, over?"

Blackmore repeated this message before flipping the receiver switch. When a response failed to materialize, he again repeated the message. This time, the quick hand of Ensign Marvin reached in beside him and triggered the transmit button. Because Blackmore had failed to depress this switch, his initial message had gone no further than the command module. This time, with his co-worker's help, a garbled response soon flowed through the telephone's speaker.

"DSRV Marlin, this is the Providence. We read you loud and clear. What took you so long?"

Grinning at this response, Pierce took the transmitter and answered, "Better late than never, Providence. Are you guys ready to get the party started?"

This time the signal from the disabled sub was substantially clearer. "That's affirmative, Marlin. The line is already forming at the stern escape hatch, and we're ready to start the dance whenever you are."

"Well, hang in there just a little bit longer, Providence. The band is coming on down."

With this, Pierce handed the receiver back to the lieutenant, who secured it in its cradle. A check of the depth counter found them already passing the 100-foot level. As the gauge continued spinning, Blackmore looked out of the column-mounted viewing port and took in a black wall of sea water, barely penetrated by their hull-mounted spotlights. How they ever hoped to spot another vessel in this muck was beyond his wildest imagination.

As if again reading his mind, Ensign Marvin offered his own observation. "I sure hope Barking Sands gave us an accurate set of coordinates. Otherwise, this could be like finding the proverbial needle in a haystack."

Before this comment could be returned, the Marlin was suddenly tossed on its side by a powerful current of water. Thrown backward by this concussion, Marvin tumbled from his precarious perch into the rear pressure capsule. Fortunately, both Pierce and Blackmore were held fast to their command chairs by their safety harnesses. A sickening heaviness formed in the lieutenant's gut upon realizing that their angle of descent had drastically increased. His heartbeat quickened, the sweat rolling off his forehead, as he watched the commander struggle to regain control of the Marlin. All of this took on an entirely different perspective when the lights unexpectedly flickered and then failed altogether.

"Lieutenant, hit that circuit breaker!" ordered the stern voice of Pierce.

Struggling to control his panic, Blackmore knew this directive was aimed at him, yet his ponderously heavy right hand failed to move. He knew right where the breaker was located. Why couldn't he trigger it?

The Marlin rolled hard to the right and their diving angle became even steeper. The pitch blackness that prevailed gave Lance the distinct impression that he was in a nightmare. His heart was practically pounding out of his chest when Pierce's voice again sounded.

"For God's sake, Lieutenant, hit that breaker!"

Summoning his every last ounce of self-control, Blackmore managed to release the iron-like grip his right hand had on his thigh. Trembling and icy cold, he fought to raise it overhead and reverse the overloaded circuit. An eternity seemed to pass, until his index finger finally found the breaker and pushed it forward. Instantaneously, the lights flickered on in response.

It took several seconds for Blackmore's eyes to adjust to the alien brightness. When they did focus, he caught sight of Pierce, coolly sitting at the pilot's station in complete control. Even without the benefit of light, the commander had managed to safely guide the Marlin out of the swift current. He had even been able to regain control of their angle of descent. Blackmore had just noticed that they were 500 feet below the water's surface now when Pierce spoke again.

"Ensign Marvin, are you still with us?"

Several anxious seconds passed before a shaken voice sounded out from behind them. "You didn't lose me that easily, Skipper. What in the hell hit us?"

"Just a little underwater current," returned Pierce. "They can run something fierce in these channels. Let's just hope that's the last we've seen of it. Shall we get on with active and see what we've got down there? Lieutenant Blackmore, begin that sonar search."

Though his hand still trembled, Blackmore managed to get it to do the commander's bidding. The sonar was activated and, as a result, a wavering pulse of intense sound energy surged from their bow. With bated breath, he awaited the characteristic metallic ping of a return that would indicate another solid object was close by.

By this time, the lieutenant's heartbeat had calmed itself considerably. No longer did sweat pour from his forehead. Certain that Pierce had seen his panic, Blackmore wondered if this dive would be his last. Even with this somber thought in mind, a greater priority took center stage. Somewhere down below them in the icy blackness over 100 of his fellow seamen depended upon him to save their lives. No matter what it took, he would not let them down.

And from the seat to Lieutenant Blackmore's immediate left, the Marlin's pilot deftly operated the DSRV's controls. Still shaken by the sudden underwater current that had almost taken them to their graves, he too contemplated the goal that was guiding them downward. A quick glance to his right showed that the young lieutenant seemed in much better emotional control. Just before the lights had failed, he could have sworn that Blackmore was close to a full-fledged panic attack. Though to lose control in such a situation could have disastrous implications for all of them, Pierce had to give the kid another chance. He would never forget his first dive in a DSRV, when the vessel had inexplicably lost total hydraulic pressure. Spiraling into the ocean's depths, Pierce had not only frozen up in fear, he had wet his pants as well. Saved by the masterly expertise of the pilot, who had passed to him his present command, Will had lived to dive once again. Of course, he had sworn to himself that he never would panic again. This had been a promise that he had somehow managed to keep through the years.

As to the emotional strength of the young officer who sat beside him, only time would tell. The lad certainly seemed bright enough. His grades in school were excellent, yet he was a bit too overly sensitive. Perhaps if he'd learn to relax more and have a good time, this sensitivity would dissipate. Only then could he develop the right attitude for command.

Pierce's ponderings were broken by the metallic ping of a solid sonar return. It was soon evident that this return belonged to none other than the U.S.S. Providence. As the Marlin passed a depth of 820 feet, the position of the 688's stern was determined. With the delicacy of a surgeon, Will Pierce then began the delicate task of linking the DSRV's transfer skirt with the downed sub's rescue hatch.

* * *

It was the sensitive transducer of a hydrophone that first relayed to the technicians at Barking Sands proof that the DSRV had mated with the Providence. A scratchy, scraping noise emanated from the deep as the Marlin's transfer skirt attached itself onto the sub's emergency trunk. Seconds later, the characteristic sucking whoosh of equalizing pressure was followed by the distant sounds of the submariners themselves as they began their short climb to safety.

The receipt of this signal caused a shout of relieved joy to spread throughout the engineering station. Patting each other on the backs like new fathers, the white-smocked scientists celebrated for a full minute before returning to their consoles.

A bare sigh of relief passed Dr. Richard Fuller's lips. If all continued well, the Marlin could have the Providence completely evacuated by midnight. Only then could he totally relax.

Of course, their real work would come in the days that followed. Hopefully, a repair team could be sent down to somehow patch up the hydraulic damage and get the Providence topside. Then they could better initiate the comprehensive examination that would be needed to find out just what had caused the explosion in the first place.

Though Richard had his own ideas as to what caused the cruise missile to blow up as it had, the way things looked he would not be an immediate part of the NOSC investigation. Less than a quarter of an hour ago, a sealed envelope had arrived that was to drastically change the direction of his thoughts.

The orders were from the Chief of Naval Operations in Washington, D.C. Fuller had met Admiral Carrington during a Submarine League symposium only the previous year, yet he had never dreamed of hearing from the white-haired senior officer officially again.

The directive was tersely written. Addressed to his eyes only, the orders instructed Fuller to join the crew of the Marlin immediately after the transfer of the Providence's complement had been completed. At that time they were to proceed to the airfield at Barking Sands, where a C-5A transport plane would be waiting to fly them to Vanderberg Air Force Base in California. There they were to assist the base commander in coordinating the salvage of a Titan 34-D rocket that had failed over the Pacific earlier that same morning.

Confused by these instructions, Fuller had to read them several more times before they finally sank in. He had been exclusively involved with the submarine-borne vertical-launch missile system for over a year now. Why they would want to abruptly change the direction of his study now was beyond him. The only thing that he could think of was that something awfully important must have been on top of that Titan when it went down. And now the military was desperately depending upon them to get it back.

He had worked with the Air Force on a single past occasion. As it turned out, this had also been the last time he had worked with a DSRV. The incident had involved the crash of one of the Air Force's most sophisticated jet fighters. The F-15 Eagle had gone down in the ocean off the coast of southern California, near the beach town of Carlsbad. It must have been packed with top-secret hardware, for no sooner had the aircraft settled into the sand of the continental shelf than the orders asking for his assistance had arrived at NOSC headquarters in San Diego. An hour later, he had been on his way to the crash site by helicopter.

It had apparently been his expertise in the field of ocean currents and sea-floor topography that had attracted the Air Force to him in the first place. The F-15 had been subsequently recovered, and Fuller had soon been back in San Diego resuming his work in advanced naval weaponry.

Since then, this study had been his exclusive domain. But now the orders from the CNO would once again abruptly divert him. Somewhat disappointed that he wouldn't be present to examine the initial evidence regarding the failure of the Tomahawk launch, Fuller knew that he was powerless to express his displeasure. His country needed his expertise elsewhere. As in the past, he would not let it down.

Even as his eyes strayed to the lucite chart of the channel of water between the islands of Kauai and Niihau, his mind was already searching for any information that he might have picked up regarding the ocean off Vandenberg. Most aware that those waters sported dangerous reefs and treacherous currents, he knew that he would need the special bathymetric chart book that sat in his library back in San Diego. He was already visualizing the main currents influencing central California's coastline when word arrived that the first load of the Providence's crew had safely made it back to the Sea Devil.

Chapter Five

General Vadim Sobolev's day had started off splendidly. Not only was the Central Asian weather perfect, but the news from Moscow was equally as agreeable. In fact, at this very moment, the Premier's personal aide, Valentin Radchenko, was already flying down from the capital to meet with him privately. This was quite an accomplishment for Vadim, considering he had only asked for this audience late the previous afternoon. To properly prepare for this all-important meeting of minds, he decided to awaken himself thoroughly with a long, brisk walk.

Though he had been brought up in the thick pine forests of northern Russia, the sixty-eight-year-old general was finally getting used to the rather bare plains of Turkestan. He supposed that, after two decades of service there, this had better be the case. Of all the hikes he presently had to chose from, his favorite was an earthen footpath that brought him to the banks of the Syrdar River. He particularly enjoyed this route because it crossed through a rather dense stand of gnarled oaks, before ending at the Syrdar's banks.

So far this morning, his travels had taken him from his quarters located outside of Tyuratam's Baikonur Cosmodrome. The dawn broke clear, mild and full of promise, as the white-haired officer drank down his tea, threw on his clothes, and, with walking stick in hand, began his way across the base itself. The new recruits were already well into their exercise routine when he passed by the airfield's barracks area and reached Tyuratam's western gate. A look of genuine surprise flashed across the guard's previously bored face upon identifying the broad-shouldered figure of his commanding officer. Even with his rank, Vadim was forced to sign the registry that indicated his precise destination.

The path he was soon trodding upon began only a quarter of a kilometer from the guard shack. For a good hour, this trail led over a sparse, rolling plain, bare of any noticeable vegetation but a dull variety of low-growing shrubbery. The air was fresh and invigorating, though, and he soon spotted his beloved woods another kilometer distant.

To pass the time more quickly, he lengthened his stride and focused his thoughts on the long career that had precipitated this fated day. It had all begun almost five decades before, when he was but an innocent, long-legged teenager. How anxious he had been at that time to enlist in the Army. After all, the Motherland's borders had needed to be protected from the demonic Nazi hordes gathering to the west. After participating in his share of bloodshed, the young private had come under the scrutiny of General Pavl Yagoda, a man who was destined to change his life.

It was Yagoda who had noticed the glimmering spark of intellect that simmered in Vadim's mind. Invited to join the illustrious general's personal staff, Vadim had blossomed into manhood. A quick learner who knew how to command the respect of those beneath him in rank, he was to spend hours under the general's direct tutelage. Eventually, as the fates would have it, their division had captured an entire warehouse of German V-2 rockets. Equally as important had been the Nazi scientists that they had come upon, hiding in the structure's basement.

With Vadim at his side, General Yagoda had soon gone off to Moscow to personally brief Stalin of their great find. Faced with the imminent conclusion of the Great War, the Motherland had been attempting to determine its future ranking in the new world order to follow. Pavl Yagoda had been one of the visionaries who realized that strategic nuclear forces would be the keys to power in the new age. He had argued that only by developing a new generation of nuclear weapons could the Soviet Union challenge the might of American Imperialism.

Hesitant to accept his advice, Stalin had gone to his grave leaving the country with no strategic master plan. A confused era had followed, when such leaders as Georgi Malenkov had voiced their desire to abolish all nuclear weapons before mankind itself was totally destroyed.

Fortunately, Malenkov and others like him had been ousted from office, to be replaced by Nikita Khrushchev. In his speech of January 14, 1960 before the Supreme Soviet, the fiesty Premier had put his weight totally behind the concept of developing a massive nuclear strike force as the ultimate expression of national policy. Five months later, Vadim had been at Pavl Yagoda's side as the old-timer was named Commander-in-Chief of the Strategic Rocket Forces. Spurred by such embarrassments as the Cuban missile crisis, the Soviet ICBM program had shifted into high gear.

The ascent of Brezhnev had signaled the switch from Soviet strategic inferiority to parity and more.

By early 1970, the U.S.S.R. had even passed America in the number of operational ICBM's.

Vadim Sobolev had begun seriously developing his own reputation during the SALT-I negotiations. At that time he had argued vigorously that the Soviet Union had to be allowed to continue its research in the field of multiple warheads, MIRV's for short. America had granted this concession, and the Motherland had been quick to exploit the full limits of this rather one-sided treaty. Unlike the U.S., the U.S.S.R. had continued to improve its forces. This had culminated in the development of the giant SS-18 missile, whose massive boosters were able to carry ten 600-kiloton MIRV'd warheads. For the first time ever, the Motherland now had the capability to destroy even the most hardened targets anywhere in the Northern Hemisphere.

Merely knowing that two dozen of these immense giants lay buried beneath the ground of the base he had just come from warmed Vadim's heart considerably. Though Pavl Yagoda was long in his grave, his protégé had survived to make certain that his dream was fulfilled. Inspired by this responsibility, Vadim briefly halted and surveyed the meandering path that was visible, stretching beyond to the western horizon.

The trail had already dropped into the tree line. He had passed the first bent oak several minutes before. Yet he knew that he still had a hike of approximately a quarter of a kilometer to reach the densest part of those woods. A songbird cried to his left, while a fat squirrel scurried over the ground before him. Merely being in this setting caused a great joy to overcome him. Breathing in a deep lungful of fresh air, Vadim continued on.

This brisk stride was not that of a sixty-eight-year-old man, thought Sobolev, who felt like a young buck again. Though betrayed by a mane of flowing white hair, he was proud of the fact that he had worked hard to remain in such excellent physical shape. Eating the right foods and taking walks such as this one were the secrets to his success.

A raven cried harshly above him, and Vadim's gaze turned upwards. Beyond the twisted branches of the ancient oaks was a cloudless blue sky. A single black bird soared effortlessly there. Viewing this scene caused a new vision to raise in his consciousness. It represented a chapter in his life that he was most proud of.

On April 26, 1962, he had helped initiate the Motherland's fledgling space program by organizing the launch of Cosmos 4. This rather primitive spacecraft had only stayed in orbit three days, yet its payload of camera equipment was to revolutionize military science for all time. As the first Soviet reconnaissance satellite, Cosmos 4 had led to a succession of sophisticated platforms, the latest of which could photograph an earthbound object of less than twelve inches in diameter from an altitude of over 200 miles.

Vadim was especially proud of the military version of the Salyut space station that was presently the country's equivalent to the American recon satellite known as Keyhole. Not only could this platform's cameras scan the American military fields and command bunkers, it also utilized a variety of sensors to provide surveillance over the seas themselves. A powerful radar array could locate even the smallest of surface ships in any weather condition, day or night. Infra-red sensors could sniff out the warm wakes of U.S. nuclear subs, putting an end to the conjecture that this portion of their "triad" was invulnerable.

Vadim had seen the results of such a scan only

hours before. After a single pass, the current Salyut was able to relay certain proof that one of the Americans' latest 688-class attack subs had sunk off the Hawaiian island of Kauai. Earlier, it had conveyed a disaster of equal proportions, when the recon platform had recorded the actual failure of the launch of a U.S. Titan rocket over the coast of California.

Knowledge of this last incident was particularly satisfying to Vadim, for he knew just what the Titan had been carrying as its payload. Now, perhaps, the Premier would be more receptive to his daring plan, which had taken a lifetime to formulate.

Who knew if such an opportunity would ever present itself again? They had only a few days left to take advantage of it. That was why his meeting later that morning with Valentin Radchenko had to go smoothly.

Hastily checking his watch, Sobolev calculated that he would have just enough time to reach his goal before being forced to return to Tyuratam. He would empty his soul by the banks of the Syrdar River, then return for the fateful meeting that could very well change the balance of power of the entire planet. Stimulated by this thought, he pushed himself forward.

From an altitude of 4,000 meters, the landscape of Soviet Turkestan appeared flat and uninteresting. Except for the blue expanse of the Aral Sea glistening on the southern horizon, Valentin Radchenko could pick out few spots of scenic interest. Instead, endless plains of parched scrub stretched in all directions. Few highways were visible traversing these expanses. In fact, if it weren't for the railroad tracks that they had been following for the last hour, one could have sworn that this was a spot that civilized man had completely passed by.

Catching his reflection in the helicopter's fuselage window, Valentin studied what he saw. Predominant was a pair of heavy, black plastic glasses that gave his small, featureless face a scholarly appearance. Even with the dim light, the gray that lined his once-coal-black hair was most visible. This coloring made him look considerably older than his forty-three years.

To the monotonous chopping clatter of the Mi-24's rotor blades, the bureaucrat pondered the causes of his premature aging. As a junior aide to Premier Viktor Alipov, he was kept on the move twenty-four hours a day, seven days a week. With no time for a family life or children, he was exclusively married to the State.

Today's activities were typical of a schedule that allowed precious little time for leisure. Strange as it might seem, only eighteen hours before a trip into the wilds of Turkestan had not even been on his agenda. Busy in Moscow preparing for the following week's visit of the American Secretary of State, Valentin had learned of his mission early the previous evening.

The call to Premier Alipov's office had caught him completely off guard. Thinking that this summons had to do with the Western diplomat's visit, he had entered the Premier's paneled office ready to take on a long list of last-minute responsibilities. Instead, he had found the usually sour-faced Alipov in a most cordial mood. Inviting Valentin to have a seat and share a vodka with him, the Premier had asked him in the most undemanding of tones if he would mind flying off to Tyuratam the first thing in the morning. One did not easily turn down the Premier of the Soviet Union, and Valentin had offered his services without question. A quick briefing had followed, at which time Alipov had conveyed the purpose of this hastily scheduled trip.

General Vadim Sobolev was a larger-than-life figure whom Valentin had enormous respect for. As Commander-in-Chief of the Motherland's Strategic Rocket Forces, Sobolev held one of the most important military positions in the country. This responsibility included the direct leadership of a force of over 1 million men.

Only an hour earlier, Sobolev had called the Premier and asked him to send a representative of his office to Tyuratam. Once at the Cosmodrome, this emissary would be briefed on a matter of the utmost sensitivity. This individual would then be free to return to Moscow, to share this new knowledge with the Premier.

Curious as to the nature of the information that would soon be passed on to him, Valentin had left Alipov's office and begun making arrangements for the flight southward. It was the Defense Ministry that had chosen his means of transportation. A massive Ilyushin IL-76 jet had picked him up before dawn outside Moscow and whirled him off eastward to the Air Force base at Sverdlovsk, at the foot of the Ural Mountains. Valentin had been somewhat surprised to learn that this was as far as the jet was going. Not knowing what to expect next, he had been led to a fully armed, Mi-24 helicopter gunship. Having only seen such a craft in photographs before, he had found the camouflaged chopper most impressive. It was only when its pilot had walked over to him and greeted Valentin by name that he had learned that this unusual vehicle would take him on the final leg of his journey.

The gunship's main cabin was more comfortable than he had ever imagined. Though it was designed to carry eight fully armed troops, he was the only apparent passenger. An hour after they had lifted off from Sverdlovsk, the co-pilot had come back to visit with him. Sharing a hot thermos of sweetened tea and some tasty poppyseed cakes, the young officer had divulged that, after stopping at Tyuratam, they would be off to the front in Afghanistan. Valentin had learned that this would be the second tour of action there for each member of the helicopter's current four-man flight crew. A battle-scarred veteran of a war the young bureaucrat had heard of only in reports and in the newspapers, the co-pilot had brought the conflict to a very real level.

The war stories that he had subsequently related to Valentin were genuinely shocking. It seemed that battlefield atrocities of the most distasteful kind were almost an everyday occurrence. And it wasn't always the rebels who were the perpetrators.

One couldn't help but notice the bitterness that had flavored the young officer's words. It had reminded Valentin of the dissension expressed by many American troops during the Viet Nam conflict. He supposed this similarity was due to the very nature of the two wars. Like Viet Nam, Afghanistan was racked by a guerilla war. Unable to apply the full brunt of its superior firepower, the Soviet military was tied down in a frustrating, time-consuming battle against an ill-trained, poorly equipped rebel force. If the tide of victory didn't shift soon, the Soviet Union's armed forces could have a major morale problem on their hands. Valentin had made a mental note to share this observation with the Premier as soon as he returned to Moscow.

The co-pilot had eventually returned to the cockpit, and Valentin had been left alone to his current thoughts. What in the world awaited him in Tyuratam? A slight decrease in the sound of the gunship's rotors was followed by a noticeable drop in altitude, and he knew he'd all too soon know the answer to this question. Expectantly, Valentin's gaze returned to the window. There a river was visible, snaking its way beneath them. A relatively dense stand of woods lay on each side of its banks. Minutes later, a two-lane highway could be seen. This strip of asphalt pavement led directly to an extensive, fenced-in compound. Even from this height, Valentin could make out the chain-link barrier's barbed-wire top and the groups of armed sentries that patrolled its length.

Valentin had visited the base once before to witness the launching of an SS-18. At that time he had been greatly impressed with the sophisticated facilities that had been developed here. This visit proved no different. The Mi-24 continued losing altitude, and he was afforded an excellent view of Tyuratam's ultra-modern research and development test facility, massive fuel-storage area, and breathtaking main space-launch complex. An airfield was also visible up ahead, and he soon picked out the huge, domed roof of the Baikonur Cosmodrome. It was before this structure that the gunship landed.

The quiet was most noticeable as the helicopter's rotors spun to a halt. As he left his seat to retrieve his briefcase, the fuselage door popped open. With his case now in hand, he made his way outside.

A gust of hot, dry wind hit him full in the face as he stepped onto the tarmac. Waiting for him there were a pair of smartly uniformed sentries, and a single smiling, white-haired individual whom Valentin had no trouble identifying. General Vadim Sobolev was quick to greet him with a warm hug and a kiss to each cheek. Appearing as vibrant as ever, and in remarkably good shape for his age, the Commander-in-Chief of the Motherland's Strategic Rocket Forces welcomed Valentin like a long-lost son.

"Welcome to Tyuratam, Comrade Radchenko. I hope your journey here was a smooth one."

Valentin grinned, already infected by his host's enthusiasm. "That it was, General. I must admit, though, that I was a bit surprised by the manner in which the Defense Ministry routed me down here from Sverdlovsk. That was my first ride in an Mi-24."

"That's quite a machine," observed Sobolev, who turned to get a better look at the vehicle.

Valentin followed the general's gaze and took in the chopper's box-like cockpit, dual turboshaft engines, and characteristic stub wings, onto which were attached a pair of gun pods and a missile launcher.

"She's a lethal one, all right," continued Sobolev admiringly. "I imagine this one is bound for Afghanistan. How I wish we could accompany its brave crew into action. A man doesn't know how to live fully until he has enemy bullets flying at him. Only then can he really appreciate the great gift of life. Did you have the honor of serving in the armed forces, Comrade Radchenko?"

Vadim replied proudly, "That I did, General. For five years I was a deputy member of Admiral of the Fleet Gorshkov's personal staff."

"So you served with old man Gorshkov," reflected Sobolev. "You were a most fortunate lad, comrade. The Motherland should only have more great men like that one."

Turning from the helicopter, Sobolev pointed toward the domed hangar that lay behind him. "I want you to take a look at something inside the Cosmodrome, Comrade Radchenko. Then we will go on to my office for tea and get down to the matter which has brought you these hundreds of kilometers."

Nodding in compliance, Valentin followed his host toward the hangar. Doing all that he could do to match the general's stride, the bureaucrat silently cursed his poor physical conditioning. Here was a man over twenty-five years older and he could hardly keep pace with him. He just had to make time for a serious exercise program. And then he'd even consider giving up smoking.

Suddenly conscious that he hadn't had a cigarette since leaving Sverdlovsk, Valentin's hand went to his jacket pocket, and he brought out a thin, silver case. From it he removed a single filterless American cigarette. He placed it between his lips, and was just about to light it when the general abruptly stopped him.

"Please, Comrade Radchenko. If you must insist on consuming those cancer sticks, please wait until we are well clear of the Cosmodrome. Jet fuel is extremely volatile."

Valentin needed no more urging to pocket his lighter and return the cigarette to its case. His face blushed with embarrassment as they entered the hangar and were greeted by a huge Soviet flag hanging from its rafters. It was cool and dark inside, the stagnant air tainted with the scents of warm oil and alcohol-based coolant. As they continued to walk inside, he noticed a line of sleek jet fighters parked toward the back of the structure. Evidently, it was toward these vehicles that they were headed. Their conversation was kept to a minimum until both individuals stood directly before the line of six shiny, silver jet fighters.

"As an ex-military man, I thought you'd enjoy taking a look at these beauties," offered the proud general. "They're MiG-27's, just off the assembly line. My test pilots are currently breaking them in before they're placed into action over the skies of Afghanistan."

Valentin studied the sleek lines of this combat fighter, while Sobolev continued, "Especially designed for low-level attack missions, these aircraft should put the fear of Allah into the rebel riffraff who continue their feeble resistance. From rockets to cluster-bombs these beauties can deliver an awesome punch at speeds well over Mach One. Nothing will be able to knock them from the air."

Nervously clearing his throat, Valentin dared to express himself. "The crew of the Mi-24 gunship that brought me down here was comprised of Afghan veterans. I couldn't help but notice the undertone of resentment behind their words as they briefly described their experiences there."

"Why, of course!" exclaimed the general. "Those poor lads are totally frustrated! How would you feel if you were asked to fend off an adversary with one hand tied behind your back? That is precisely what has happened to our brave soldiers. If only our esteemed leaders would give the military a free hand to deal with the rebels as we see fit, the entire problem could be alleviated in a matter of days. What more would you expect from the greatest military machine ever assembled on the earth's surface?"

Taking in this passionate response, Valentin found himself agreeing with the general. As the Americans had learned in Viet Nam, a modern war could not be won with a half-hearted effort. Yet, ever concerned with world opinion, the Kremlin had attempted to keep the conflict in Afghanistan as low-key as possible. If such a meagre effort continued for long, they would be faced with nothing less than tragedy.

As the general pivoted and led the way out of the hangar, Valentin found himself startled by the nature of his thoughts. Far from enjoying his years of military service, the bureaucrat had until now understood the importance of attempting to reach a peaceful accord before needless hostilities were precipitated. His host's hardline military policies, on the other hand, were common knowledge in Moscow. By dedicating his entire life to the building of a strategic force second to none, Sobolev had given the U.S.S.R. the ability to cower to no one. Perhaps it was time to pay a little more attention to the old man's thoughts.

There was no question that the rebellion in Afghanistan was just taking too long to resolve. And how could they neglect the grumblings of their own people, who found their drab, hard-working lives often without the bare necessities of food, clothing, and shelter? With the strain of a budget that was too rapidly being devoured by military expenditures, their leaders faced some major decisions. Could they neglect the everyday dissatisfaction of their very own citizens? And what of the dissatisfaction that was evident among the members of the Warsaw Pact? For the Soviet Union to lose its allies would be a tragedy in itself.

As Valentin followed his host out into the midday sun, he remembered that the hardline posture Sobolev called for was deceptive. No problem could be solved by might alone. Still struggling to keep up with the general's pace, the bureaucrat knew he'd have to remain strong and keep an open mind. As the Premier's eyes and ears, he couldn't afford not to.

Sobolev's office was located in the launch center's main support building. Occupying an entire corner of the structure's top floor, the suite was decorated in such a manner as to give one a comfortable, down-home feeling. This included a full-sized fireplace, a set of well-stocked bookshelves, and an ample supply of overstuffed sofas and chairs. It was to the pair of high-backed, upholstered chairs set before the fireplace that Valentin was led. Choosing the seat to the left of the marble mantle, he anxiously settled himself in.

The general remained standing in front of Valentin as his uniformed orderly appeared. The young soldier pushed in a silver tea cart, which he left beside the fireplace, then silently excused himself. Checking the cart's contents, Sobolev smiled.

"I can personally vouch for the caviar sandwiches, Comrade Radchenko. The black bread is fresh, the cream cheese rich, and the caviar most delicious. If you'd prefer it in place of tea, we could substitute a drink of a bit more substance. I have some excellent potato vodka, which I'm certain you'll find most tasty."

Finding his throat unusually parched as a result of the dry winds of Tyuratam, Valentin agreed to this suggestion. His host beamed in response.

"Excellent choice, comrade, one which I'll enjoy with you."

From the cart's bottom shelf, Sobolev removed a clear crystal decanter and two matching glasses. After pouring a pair of healthy drinks, he handed one of them to his guest.

"To your health Comrade Radchenko, and to the future well-being of the Motherland."

Accepting this toast, Valentin downed his drink in a single gulp. The fiery spirits were indeed of excellent quality and went down most smoothly. His host noticed his satisfied grin and handed him a lap-sized silver platter.

"Now try some of the caviar, Comrade Radchenko.

You won't be disappointed."

Unable to resist the bite-sized finger sandwiches that lay invitingly before him, Valentin popped one into his mouth. Smacking his lips in delight, he responded.

"This is indeed excellent caviar, General. We haven't had anything like this in Moscow for quite some time now."

"It's one of the benefits of being stationed so close to the Caspian Sea, Comrade. Now, take some more to snack on while I refill our glasses. Then it will be time to get down to business."

After filling a small plate with several more appetizers, Valentin sat back to enjoy them. With his vodka conveniently perched beside him, he found himself content to munch away while Sobolev ambled over to his desk and picked up a large manila envelope. Returning to the fireplace, the general pulled out what appeared to be two medium-sized photographs, one of which he handed to Valentin.

It took several seconds for Valentin to make sense out of the glossy black photo. Taken out at sea, it showed a strangely shaped, square-hulled surface vessel bobbing in the rolling surf. Immediately beside this ship, which from the cranes that projected from its stern appeared to be some sort of tender, was the top portion of a mini-sub.

"What in Lenin's name am I looking at?" queried the confused civil servant.

Relishing the moment, Sobolev took a full sip of vodka before answering. "That, Comrade Radchenko, is the U.S. Navy tender Pelican, with her precious cargo, the Deep Submergence Rescue Vehicle Marlin, floating at her side. It was taken yesterday morning from an altitude of two hundred and forty kilometers, and shows them operating in the waters off Hawaii."

"Ah, then it was photographed from our Salyut recon platform," observed Valentin.

"Precisely," retorted the General, who beamed with pride.

Shaking his head with wonder, Valentin continued, "The quality is most excellent considering the height at which it was taken. Yet what does it all mean?"

Sobolev stifled a chuckle. "What this shows, Comrade Radchenko, is a desperate attempt by the Americans to save the lives of over 100 of their brave seamen trapped beneath those same seas. For, if my intelligence source is correct, this photo is proof positive that the Imperialists have lost one of their latest 688-class attack subs here. The Premier will be thrilled to see that their overly rated submarine force isn't so invulnerable after all!"

Absorbing this observation, Valentin grasped the second photograph. Pictured there was some sort of strangely shaped, exploding cloud of airborne vapor. Not having the faintest idea what this could be, he scratched his forehead and looked up into the eagle-like gaze of his host.

"Don't fret, Comrade Radchenko. I didn't expect you to identify this remarkable photo either. Taken yesterday morning from the same Salyut platform, it shows the actual failure of an American Titan missile launch over the coast of central California. The fates were indeed smiling on our cosmonauts when their cameras chanced upon this tragic incident, just as they initiated their first dawn pass over the North American continent."

Aware now of the circumstances, Valentin was indeed impressed. "I must be the first to congratulate you, General Sobolev, on these unbelievable photographs. Once again, our military intelligence services have outdone themselves. Yet I still don't understand what was so important to warrant yesterday's call to the Premier."

Sobolev's eyes gleamed as he positioned himself before his guest and spoke out succinctly. "The information I am about to pass on to you is of the most confidential nature. I would have flown to Moscow myself to personally share it with Viktor Alipov, but my responsibilities here made such a trip impossible. Unable to trust the reliability of scrambled telephone lines or encrypted telegrams, I was forced to ask the Premier to send me a trusted member of his staff. We are indeed fortunate that he choose you, Comrade Radchenko. Your probing intellect and rare ability to get things done in the capital are known even on the plains of Turkestan."

Blushing at this compliment, Valentin nodded in acknowledgment of the unexpected praise, while his host took a deep breath and continued. "Earlier in the week, America's primary Keyhole reconnaisance satellite burnt up in the atmosphere high over this very installation. This event in itself did not surprise us, for we were well aware that the platform had reached the end of its operational lifetime and was due to fall from its orbit eventually. It was as this satellite's back-up was called down to replace it that our telemetry technicians in Kapustin Yar notified me of a totally unexpected development. Without any outside interference on our part, this second Keyhole platform also failed. I don't have to remind you what this means, Comrade Radchenko, for it leaves the Imperialists with no effective eye in the sky over the Central Soviet Union!"

Calmly taking in this revelation, Valentin offered his own observation. "This is all rather fascinating, General, but surely this condition is only temporary.

Don't the Americans merely have to launch a new Keyhole satellite to replace the failed unit?"

Though he was anxious to answer his guest, Sobolev waited a full thirty seconds before responding. "And just what do you think was the payload of the Titan, whose remains are so graphically displayed before you?"

Shocked by this disclosure, Valentin suddenly realized this was the news the general wanted passed on to Premier Alipov. Surely it would cause a ripple of interest within the Kremlin, yet he couldn't help but feel that there was still more behind this hastily called meeting.

As if he were reading his guest's mind, Sobolev turned and walked over to the fireplace's far corner. There a piece of blank wooden paneling lay between the marble mantle and the bookshelves. The general triggered a recessed button and the oaken panel slid upward to reveal a large map of the world. A bright crimson star lay over Tyuratam, with dozens of smaller red flags interspersed over the rest of the planet, the majority being situated in North America. A satisfied grin was on the general's face as he pivoted to again address Radchenko.

"What you see before you, comrade, is the culmination of this old soldier's hard-working life. For over five decades I have ceaselessly toiled to allow this vision to be possible. Now, without any help of my own, the fates have presented us with a situation that we can't possibly ignore. For who knows if such an opportunity will ever be handed to us again?

"The glorious plan that I am about to share with you is not my humble work alone. It is a synthesis of unselfish efforts. Though most of these individuals are long cold in their graves, they come from the ranks of our country's greatest heroes. Foremost in

114

helping plant this vision in my mind was my beloved predecessor, Pavl Yagoda. As the first Commander-in-Chief of the Motherland's Strategic Rocket Forces, Pavl had a unique genius that allowed this dream to become a reality. I will not bore you with further accolades. Rather, I will get right down to an explanation of the operation which will at long last allow the entire world to share in the bounties of our Socialist State.

"What I propose is a surprise surgical nuclear strike against the Imperialist powers. This attack can be accomplished with a minimum of casualties, for it will be focused on the West's vulnerable communications and command centers. By destroying these installations, we will render the enemy unable to order a counterstrike. Total victory will thus be ours in a matter of mere minutes!

"What presently makes such a strike most attractive is the current status of America's satellite-borne, intelligence-gathering platforms. Now that they are completely blind to our efforts here at Tyuratam, we can go about the business of refitting our SS-18's with the new Tartar weapons packages. I'm sure you've read the latest material on the Tartar system. It allows each of our longest-range ICBM's to be fitted with ten independently targeted nuclear warheads, each with a yield of eight hundred kilotons and a CEP of less than one hundred meters. For the first time ever, we will be able to take out any target in North America, no matter how hardened it may be.

"The red flags you see pinned to the map before you correspond to ninety carefully chosen, vital counterforce sites that the West depends on to issue an attack of its own. By knocking them out, we will render the West completely defenseless. As you can see, the eighteen SS-18's that we currently have ready to go here at Tyuratam will be more than adequate to take out these targets. Since each rocket holds the equivalent of ten separate warheads, we can have the luxury of striking these sites with a pair of bombs each. Not even their Cheyenne Mountain facility will escape this attack unscathed!"

A moment of hushed silence filled the room, and Valentin found his thoughts spinning. Though he had been briefed on the possibility of such a strike in the past, hearing it so convincingly described by the general caused him to look at it in a new light. Merely contemplating such an attack used to be unthinkable. The dangers of it developing into a full-scale nuclear exchange were just too great. Yet now, he was beginning to have second thoughts.

Sobolev carefully scrutinized his guest, as Valentin's brow tightened in the midst of his difficult mental deliberations. Seeing just a hint of weakness in the bureaucrat's tired face, the general continued his offensive.

"Well, Comrade Radchenko, now you know why it was necessary for me to ask the Premier for a personal representative. Can you imagine me conveying such an operation over the telephone? Now that you know my innermost dreams, and the extenuating circumstances that prompted my original call, how do you think such a plan would be received in the Kremlin? No one has his hand on the pulse of the Premier as you do, comrade. Tell me, would Viktor Alipov be presently open to my operation, or would I be merely spewing more hot air onto the summer winds?"

Valentin sat forward and responded thoughtfully. "That is hard to say, General. The mood in Moscow is a strange one these days. Impatience and frustration run rampant everywhere. It is even prevalent in the Premier's office. One day the talk is of the vital necessity of reaching an arms-limitation agreement with the West, and the next day we are all smiles over the development of yet another new nuclear warhead that will hold the Imperialist hordes at bay for the next decade. This swing in policy is impossible to gauge, although I feel it will be forced to attain some stability when the American Secretary of State arrives in Moscow next week. Rumor has it that the Secretary will be carrying with him a major arms concession by the U.S. President. If that's the case, it could make that disarmament treaty a reality."

Solemnly, Sobolev interjected, "I wouldn't be surprised, comrade. Don't forget those photos you still hold in your hand. The Imperialists know when they've been licked. Their latest missiles explode in the air, while their most advanced submarines sink to the ocean's depths. The Motherland has sacrificed much to attain our present position of strategic superiority. And now the Americans will come begging for peace. What a waste it will be to negate our people's efforts for the signing of a stupid, meaningless treaty."

At that moment, the general appeared tired and ready to concede defeat. Valentin couldn't help but feel compassion for the old-timer. After all, the man before him was a hero in all senses of the word. His vision shouldn't be so easily ignored. Though part of him urged his inner self to hold his tongue, Valentin spoke out anyway.

"I shouldn't be sharing this with you, General, but I think it could affect your plan's acceptance in Moscow. Several days ago, I came across a top-secret intelligence briefing while organizing the Premier's desk. Though it wasn't intended for my eyes, I skimmed it anyway. The report concerned the American reconnaissance satellite program. It indicated that there were only a pair of Keyholes available in the U.S. ground inventory. But now this photograph that our cosmonauts have relayed to us shows that one of these replacement units is no more. Perhaps if you were to devise a plan to eliminate the remaining Keyhole, the Premier would look at your plan with new eyes. As I told you before, his mood is most fickle of late. But in no way could he simply ignore the situation that the fates have so kindly handed us. With the U.S. completely blind to our preparation, maybe a limited surprise attack would indeed have a chance of success. At the very least it warrants more study."

"That's just what I wanted to hear!" exclaimed Sobolev emotionally. "I knew that I had been most fortunate when I was told that you would be the one coming down from Moscow. Radchenko, my friend, you have lived up to your reputation as one of the brightest minds in the Kremlin. No wonder the Premier depends on you so. I can never thank you enough for sharing the secrets of your soul with me. The least I can do is offer you another sip of our Motherland's blood."

Nodding that this was fine with him, Valentin looked on as the general refilled their glasses and toasted. "To that lucky star that brought us together! Because of our meeting, the dreams of our forefathers will at long last be realized. Tarry just a little bit longer, you slaves of Capitalism. Your yokes shall soon be cut and all men will finally be equal!"

Tossing the fiery liquor down his throat, Vadim Sobolev anxiously stirred. The time for his dream's fruition had arrived after all. He only had to think up a simple scheme to destroy the final Keyhole. With the invaluable assistance of the young bureaucrat who sat beside him, the Premier would then be approached, and final approval would soon be his. Most aware of what this would mean, he looked again at the map of the world that graced his wall. Substituting massive, mushroom-shaped clouds for its red flags, his inner vision sharpened. He couldn't help but pity the poor Americans, for they would never know what hit them.

On the other side of the world, the dawn was just breaking over the northeastern coast of South America. The morning was already proving to be another hot and muggy one as the thirty-eight-foot sailboat belonging to Colonel Jean Moreau cut through the crystal-clear blue waters of the Atlantic. Perched on the vessel's stern, with its tiller in hand, the boat's six-foot, four-inch owner stood ever alert to the changing wind patterns. An expert sailor, Moreau scanned the seas and the skies in an effort to read Mother Nature's fickle mind.

Even after fifty-three years of life, Moreau remained an excellent physical specimen. Broad-shouldered and muscular, he stood his watch in only a worn pair of khaki shorts. His present environment's perpetually hot, steamy climate made such minimal attire both comfortable and practical.

The only feature that hinted at his advanced age was a full head of close-cropped, salt-and-pepper-colored hair. It seemed that, to the women, this sprinkling of gray only served to make him appear more distinguished. Contrasted with his deeply bronzed skin, it enhanced his already ruggedly handsome face and superbly toned body. Of course, there could be no ignoring the fine lines that gathered around his eyes and neck. Yet Moreau never let their development bother him. To the colonel, age was but a relative number. Living life to its fullest extent was the secret to delaying the reaper's inevitable call.

A frothing line of surf slapped against the boat's hull, and Moreau rode out the resulting swell with an expertise honed by many hours at sea. As always, the fresh ocean air had an invigorating effect on him. He was feeling relaxed and mentally at peace since his two-day fishing excursion had been a great success. Not only was the boat's refrigerated locker filled with a half-dozen tasty yellowtail, four fat bonita, and a small hammerhead. In addition, his mind had been far away from the pressures of his everyday job. As it turned out, it wasn't only his success with a rod and reel that had helped achieve this rare state of relaxation. For below deck, in the main cabin, lay a catch of a completely different kind.

Theresa was a precocious seventeen year old whom Moreau had been employing for less than three weeks. She had signed on as a maid, but it hadn't taken much time for the pert Brazilian to find her way to her master's bed. Small-boned and with petite, dark features, Theresa didn't even come up to Moreau's shoulders. Yet what she lacked in stature she more than adequately made up for in passion.

It had been years since the colonel had come across a young woman with such a voracious sexual appetite. Though the length and width of his manhood had never generated a complaint before, Theresa couldn't seem to get enough of him. The previous night's lovemaking had proven no different.

They had been anchored off the infamous Devil's Island. There, palm trees and thick scrub had long since covered any evidence of the man-made hell-hole that used to scar this innocent-looking archipelago. After a delicious dinner of fresh sauteed yellowtail, brown rice, and steamed zucchini squash, they had proceeded to finish off the good portion of a full liter of rum from the boat's fantail. Theresa spoke a credible French, and it was in this language that he had gotten to know a little bit more about her upbringing.

Born in the coastal town of Fortaleza, Theresa had been raised in a middle-class family. Her father had been an engineer with the state's petroleum development board, and as such spent at least three-quarters of the year in the Brazilian jungle far from home. This had left her in the hands of her mother and grandmother, who protected her as though she were the crown jewels of England. Struggling to attain an average grade in school, Theresa had been more interested in boys, rock music, and partying. This conflict of interest had all come to a head the afternoon her mother caught her necking in the back alley with a neighbor boy. A furious argument had followed, as her mother called her a tramp and savagely beat her with a leather belt. That evening, still bruised and inwardly hurting, Theresa had made the decision to leave home.

The employment opportunities in the French Guiana town of Kourou were well known to her. Developed from a sleepy jungle town by a European consortium, Kourou was becoming a center of space age technology. It was common knowledge that all who came to this coastal city would have no problem starting a new life. So, with a minimum of personal belongings at her side, and the contents of her piggy bank in her purse, Theresa had sneaked out of her house and begun the long, arduous voyage to Kourou.

Once she had entered French Guiana she hadn't been the least bit disappointed. Especially on the fateful morning the employment agency had sent her to the home of Colonel Jean Moreau. From the first time her eyes had linked with those of the handsome foreigner, she had known she'd get the job. She had also been aware of the strange tingle of desire that coursed through her body, for her employer was just as handsome as the legendary Paul Newman, her favorite actor.

Her one big worry had been that the Frenchman wouldn't find her attractive enough. She had done her best to catch his eye whenever possible, making certain that she always wore her tightest shorts and skimpiest halter-tops whenever he was around the house. This display had soon had its desired effect. She would never forget that memorable evening the two had become lovers. When her boss had then invited her on this fishing trip, she had been certain that she had him completely hooked.

Just thinking about the young girl who shared the boat with him brought a grin to Moreau's handsome face. There could be no denying that she was an exotic little thing. Her long black hair capped a pretty face, which was dominated by a pair of dark, doleful eyes. Her body was just flowering into womanhood. How sensitive was her compact bosom, the pointed, erect nipples beckoning with the sweetness of the finest of brandies. And how could he deny her soft, velvety skin, firm thighs, and luscious, tight love channel?

The previous night he had ridden her like a young stallion in heat. Inflamed by the brandy, he had entered her right there on the open deck. Somehow, they had later made it below deck to the bedroom. For hours on end, he had filled her with his all. Respondent to his every demand, Theresa had proven as supple as a gymnast. Never had a woman felt so good beneath him.

Only when he was certain that her desire had been adequately quenched had he let himself go. Fulfilled beyond his wildest expectations, he had begun drifting off into blessed sleep, when he felt her tiny, warm hands massage his crotch, vainly attempting to coax new stiffness back into him. Moreau knew that there was a time not long ago when he would have responded to this occasion without question. Yet the call of his fifty-three-year old body had soon led him to a deep, dreamless slumber.

He had awakened less than an hour before feeling rested and refreshed. Taking care not to awaken his young lover, who slept soundly beside him, Moreau had slipped from the narrow cot and hastily washed himself. After donning his shorts, he had made a pot of strong, black coffee, poured himself a mug, and made his way topside.

Above, the night stars still glowed in a crystal-clear sky, yet his practiced gaze observed the first glimmer of dawn painting the eastern horizon. As he prepared the boat to get underway, he was conscious that the new day had long ago risen over the capitals of Europe. How distant the bustling streets of Paris and the lush woods of his native Normandy seemed to him at that moment!

The hot, gusting tradewinds soon filled the newly unfurled sails and Moreau pondered the fact that, with the conclusion of the summer, he would have dedicated seven years of his life to this god-forsaken wilderness. Of course, there were the yearly trips home to spend the holidays, but even though his body was transported over the seas, part of his mind always remained here. He imagined this had to do with the great responsibilities of his present job. This had been especially true in the earlier years, when his total effort had been needed to accomplish a task of unbelievable proportions.

The Consortium had chosen one of the most remote corners of the entire planet for the Ariadne facility. From the very beginning, the challenge of developing the project had been placed squarely on his shoulders. From the moment the first Consortium jet had landed at Kourou's primitive airport, Moreau had known he'd have his work cut out for him.

First there had been the task of clearing the actual site itself. Faced with a logistical nightmare, Moreau had somehow managed the impossible. Happy to have finally gained employment, the native population had pitched in to hack away at the thick jungle of coconut palms and mangrove. The swamps had been drained, and the malaria problem somewhat alleviated. Supplies and equipment had begun flowing more freely when the airport's runway had been lengthened and repaved and the port facility completed.

Ever mindful of the huge expenses that they were incurring, the Consortium had greeted his superhuman efforts with one new demand after the other. Never known as a quiter, Moreau had persevered. This effort had all come to fruition two and a half years before, when the first Ariadne missile had left its launch-pad. Only two months over schedule, the launch had successfully placed a Consortium-owned communications satellite into a perfect earth orbit. Over the next year they had managed to put at least one additional satellite into orbit each and every month.

Moreau knew that if all were still well at the facility, they'd be launching yet another missile that very morning. Their rocket would be carrying the first in a series of Japanese communications satellites into orbit. The completion of such a project could very well signal the attainment of their financial break-even point. Though their past projects had been exclusively European in nature, the addition of the Asian market would open their coffers to a totally new source of badly needed revenue. All too soon, Ariadne would be not only self-sufficient, but a major profit center as well. This was the day that Jean Moreau was praying to see, for the moment Ariadne became a commercial success, his life's greatest goal would be achieved.

His sailboat shuddered beneath him as the hull bit into yet another swell. Angling the tiller to take advantage of the rising offshore breeze, Moreau approximated his position. Devil's Island had long since disappeared in his wake. In the heavens, the morning star was the only planet visible, as the sun prepared to break the whitening horizon. In the illumination of this first light of dawn, he could just make out a distant formation of dense storm clouds to the southwest, in the direction that he was headed. Not alarmed by them in the least, Moreau was most aware that these clouds perpetually hugged the coastline during this, the rainy season. They would dump their steamy torrents sometime around noon, hopefully long after the Ariadne was high in the heavens.

He guessed that if the winds remained favorable, they'd be sailing into Kourou in another two hours' time. That should give him plenty of time to drop Theresa off at home and then get over to the base.

Of course, this entire fishing excursion wouldn't have been possible without the invaluable aid of Jacques LeMond. His thirty-three-year-old administrative assistant was turning into quite a leader in his own right. Personally trained by Moreau for two years, Jacques was definitely coming of age. Now he was even capable of handling a launch of his own.

Anxious to know if the youngster were having any unexpected difficulties, Moreau silently cursed his boat's broken radio. Though he should have returned to Kourou immediately after it had failed the previous afternoon, he hadn't. Several years before, this wouldn't have been the case. At that time, a mere two-hour fishing trip would have been a luxury.

Wondering if his days at Kourou were already numbered, Moreau found his concentration broken by a sudden movement amidships. There, Theresa was visible, her shapely, naked body invitingly lit by the first rays of direct sunlight. Teasingly, she beckoned him to join her down below. Though his thoughts had been far away from any such sensual delights, a sudden stiffening coursed through his loins. Ravaged by a hunger he had assumed to be more than satisfied, Moreau locked in the boat's auto-pilot. Without a second's hesitation, he then rose to once again sample the sweet nectar that was all too soon flowing from the Brazilian's young, ripe body.

Two hours later, the boat carrying Colonel Jean Moreau and his teenage lover sailed into Kourou's harbor. As the vessel was expertly tacked into its proper slip, it seemed dwarfed by the massive pair of sleek, ocean-going cargo ships that were tied up nearby.

Jean Moreau wasted no time locking up the boat and escorting his companion to the parking lot. There they jumped into a battered jeep and took off down the port's only roadway. Minutes later, they were out of the congested harbor area and into the relative seclusion of the surrounding jungle. The road there was narrow yet easy to follow. A minimum of traffic allowed for excellent progress.

While Theresa nodded off back to sleep beside him, Moreau savored the passionate coupling that they had just completed. For the first time in their brief relationship, he had had the fiesty brunette whimpering in ecstasy after leading her to a long series of drawn-out orgasms. Careful to hold back his own pleasure, he had only released himself after she had positively begged him to do so. Totally spent and satiated, she had nestled back to sleep, while he had returned topside to guide the boat back into the harbor.

Such was the pleasant course of his contemplation while he guided the jeep off the main road and pointed it up a familiar driveway. A quarter of a kilometer later, he pulled up to a white-stucco ranch house with a red-tiled roof. The hum of the jungle creatures rose from among the thick stands of surrounding vegetation as he put the jeep into neutral and turned to awaken his passenger. Several shakes of her shoulder were needed to accomplish this.

"Come on, sleeping beauty, the vacation's over. It's time to get back to work."

Her eyes were heavy with sleep as she slowly opened them to reorientate herself. "Oh goodness, *mi amore*, are we back at the house already? In my dreams, you had taken me far out to sea."

Enraptured by Theresa's innocent tone, Moreau bent over to kiss her on her moist lips. "Sorry, but not this time, my little beauty. Now, get going before I have to paddle your behind. I want the house completely cleaned and full of groceries by the time I arrive for dinner."

Theresa seemed puzzled by his haste. "But, *mi amore*, aren't you coming in to shower and change your clothes first? You can't go to work looking like that. Why, you haven't even shaved."

Conscious of the late hour, Moreau reached over and hit the passenger-door latch himself. "*Au revoir, ma petite*. Now get along, before I call your mother and have you shipped off back to Fortaleza!"

This last remark was all that was needed to get Theresa motivated. A sad pout could still be seen on her face as she reluctantly left the jeep and watched him drive off.

As Moreau guided the four-wheeled vehicle back onto the main roadway, the rumble of distant thunder boomed from overhead. In response, the colonel floored the accelerator. Oblivious to the abrupt increase in speed, he expertly maneuvered the jeep through the jungle.

He didn't have long to go until his progress was halted by a closed, sturdy steel barricade. Stopping before it, Moreau was greeted by a serious-faced, uniformed sentry. No words were exchanged as the fully armed guard caught sight of the jeep's sole occupant. With a crisp salute, he triggered a switch and the barricade slid open.

Moreau put the vehicle into gear and continued with his forward progress. The rumble of thunder again echoed overhead, and he passed a compact, military-like sign that read, "Welcome to Ariadne."

The paved roadway significantly widened at this spot. Absent along its shoulders was the heavy vegetation that hugged the previous section of pavement. In fact, a full kilometer of bare ground lay between this section of road and the encroaching jungle. Moreau had been here when this portion of the complex had been originally cleared. Never would he forget how difficult this task had been. Even today, it took the full-time efforts of a team of muscular laborers to keep the jungle back.

Up ahead, he caught sight of a pair of massive,

round liquid-oxygen tanks. Located on each side of the clearing he was soon crossing, these snow-white containers were positioned beside various fuel-storage tanks and a central oxygen-holding area. Next he passed the complex's largest structure, the payload-preparation facility. It was inside this huge edifice that the satellites were prepared for orbit and eventually attached to the Ariadne rocket itself. Moved in and out of the preparation complex on a set of railroad tracks, the assembled booster was then conveyed to the actual launch mount with the support of a moveable service tower.

Though he had witnessed many a launch there, he never failed to get an emotional charge out of seeing the assembled rocket as it awaited the signal to lift off. This morning proved no different. As he passed by the preparation facility, he looked to his right, and set his gaze on the silver-skinned Ariadne perched securely on its launch pad. Over fifty meters in length, the missile appeared sleek and powerful, its four bulging boosters secured to each of its fins. A cloud of whitish vapor streamed from its fuselage, and several support vehicles were busy seeing to the last-minute refueling and pre-flight check-out.

Once again, the colonel was diverted by the rumble of distant thunder. A line of black clouds could be seen gathering to the south. It wouldn't be long now until they would make their presence known here at the facility.

With the hope that they'd be able to get the Ariadne skyward before this storm struck, Moreau guided his jeep towards a nearby, low-level concrete bunker. Taking a last look at the advancing clouds, he parked his vehicle and walked quickly to the bunker's central access door. Before he was allowed entry there, he needed to enter an identification code into a frame-mounted key-pad. Once this was accomplished, he inserted his personalized ID card into a slot positioned beneath the computerized lock. Several seconds passed, and then the door slid open with a loud hiss.

Inside it was dark and noticeably cooler. Hastily, he followed the single tile-lined hallway to the preparation room. There he chose a spotlessly white jumpsuit from several outfits that had been hanging on the far wall. Only then did he press for the elevator that would efficiently whisk him three floors underground.

The environment that he soon entered was drastically different from that he had encountered upstairs. Flashing digital consoles, blinking video screens, and the hushed tones of the dozens of white-suited technicians now visible met his eyes and ears. Without hesitation, Moreau proceeded to the console marked Meteorology. There he encountered a white-haired individual nervously hunched over his display screen.

"*Bonjour*, Marcel. Tell me, old friend, are we going to have time to get Ariadne skyward before the rains begin?"

A warm smile spread across the grizzled meteorologist's face upon catching sight of the source of this query. "Good morning to you, Jean Moreau. If LeMond can keep us on schedule, we will just make it. Otherwise, it doesn't appear promising."

Absorbing this observation, Moreau looked up into the screen of one of the several wall-mounted video monitors that were conveniently placed inside the control room. He took in a close-up view of the same rocket that he had inspected outside. Most aware that a launch delay would be costly, he scurried over to the room's central console, to check the progress firsthand. Just as he reached this station, which was dominated by several manned, interconnected computer terminals, the room filled with the cold, feminine voice of the launch monitor.

"T minus five minutes and counting."

Relieved that the lift-off appeared to be right on time, Moreau approached a rather lanky, long-haired figure seated at the station's center. Before the colonel could greet this technician, the young man caught sight of him out of the corner of his eye. Smiling, he rose to exchange handshakes.

"So you made it back, Colonel," greeted Jacques LeMond with a wink. "How was the fishing?"

Brushing aside this question, Moreau offered one of his own. "Meteorology indicates that we won't have time for a single delay. How do the systems look?"

The young technician seemed surprised with his haste. "Have you no confidence in your own protege, Colonel? Everything appears just perfect. I see no reason that we won't have a lift-off right on schedule."

With this, Moreau's mood lightened. "Of course I have confidence in you, Jacques LeMond. Otherwise, I would have never left in the first place."

Meeting his assistant's broad grin, Moreau looked to the nearest video screen as the room's monitor speakers again activated.

"T minus three minutes and counting. All ground personnel should be clear of the launch pad."

With his gaze still glued to the picture of the Ariadne visible before him, Moreau didn't even notice Jacques LeMond return to his console. The colonel's mind was cluttered with thoughts, and he was hardly aware of the continued passage of time, until the familiar female voice again sounded.

"T minus sixty seconds and counting . . . five, four, three, two, one, ignition!"

With a wall of flame and a rumbling roar, the

Ariadne's four solid-rocket engines burst forth above a fiery tongue of spent propellant. As this mixture of powdered aluminum, ammonium perchlorate, synthetic rubber, and other exotic additives interacted, a thrust of over one million pounds was generated. In response, the Ariadne soared off skyward.

The atmosphere inside the control room was thick with tension as the video screen filled with the sight of the rising behemoth. This tenseness was relieved only after the monitor speakers once more activated.

"Trajectory appears good. All conditions go for full throttle."

This revelation was met by an excited chorus of cheers and applause, for with full throttle the most critical phase of the launch had passed.

Jean Moreau's attention remained glued to the video screen until he was certain that the solid-rocket motors had jettisoned from the booster cleanly, and that the Ariadne's first stage had fired properly. Only when this was confirmed did he allow himself a sigh of relief.

The Ariadne's main engine was but a speck on the television screen when Jacques LeMond gathered at his side. "That looks like another one for the Consortium, Colonel. I hope our Japanese customers will be satisfied. Oh, by the way, in all the excitement, I forgot to give you this envelope. It arrived by special courier late last evening.

Moreau's assistant handed him a sealed manila envelope, which he quickly opened. His eyes lit up upon reading its contents, yet all too soon a distracted, serious glow colored his expression.

"Well, Colonel, what's it all about, or can't you tell me?"

Moreau seemed called back to life with this comment. "I'm sorry, Jacques, but it's a dispatch from the Commandant's office. The old man wanted to share with us some rather unfortunate news regarding the Americans. It seems they lost another one of their Titan 34-D's. It went down over Vandenberg early yesterday morning."

"Those poor Yanks," returned LeMond with a shake of his head. "First it was the shuttle, now it's the Titan. Even with all their billions of dollars, they can't even get a satellite into orbit. Who knows? Until they get their difficulties ironed out, maybe they'll come to us for help."

Moreau grinned wisely. "You just might have hit upon something, my friend. It would sure beat asking the Soviets for assistance, and just think what the Consortium could do with all those extra funds."

LeMond's response was influenced by the voice of their monitor, who announced that the Ariadne's second-stage motor had fired right on time. With youthful exuberance, he flashed his superior a hearty thumbs-up.

Jean Moreau was barely conscious of this gesture, his thoughts a million miles away. While his mind's eye focused on the Ariadne's payload as it prepared to deploy itself in outer space, he carefully folded the dispatch he had just received and placed it inside the flap of his jumpsuit's breast pocket. Deep within his subconscious, he was already beginning to calculate the novel opportunities this news could portend.

Chapter Six

It was late afternoon by the time Lieutenant Colonel Todd Lansford finally made his way to the bluff overlooking Vandenberg's Point Arguello. He had spent most of the day indoors, studying the bathymetric charts of the waters he presently stood before. Seeing firsthand the raw immensity of the area of ocean his search was to be centered in gave him a new respect for his present assignment. Added to the difficulty of this herculean task itself were the political pressures that he was already beginning to feel. From the contents of the various phone calls he fielded throughout the day, it was most obvious that Washington was in a hurry for results. Of course, he had been the lucky one chosen to fulfill their impossible bidding.

As a senior officer with SAMTO, the Air Force's Space and Missile Test Organization, Lansford had been given the tough assignment of coordinating the search for any debris that might have survived the recent Titan 34-D failure. Such evidence was of major importance in determining the exact reason the missile had gone down. Since a design fault would mean that the entire Titan program could be threatened, no Titan would be launched until a reason for this most recent failure was determined. This fact made his present mission that much more significant.

Carefully scanning the surrounding terrain, the fifty-four-year-old officer was well aware that most of the search operation would be taking place under the Pacific. The reason for this was simple, for the Titan had just began arcing over Pacific waters when it had exploded in a fiery mass of debris and flame.

Compounding the difficulty of this underwater search was the fact that the topography of the sea bed there was extremely inhospitable. The jagged nature of the very bluff he presently stood on was a prime example of the type of physical environment that they'd be facing.

Cut from primordial volcanic rock, Point Arguello was a wild, desolate spot. It was formed by a semicircle of serrated rock with needle-like pinnacles and razor-sharp reefs that had been a nightmare for navigators throughout the decades. Originally labeled La Guijado del Diablo, or the Devil's Jaw, by the Spaniards, the reefs had been responsible for the sinking of dozens of tall-masted, treasure-laden galleons.

On this particular afternoon, the ocean appeared deceptively calm. Noticeably absent were the surging riptides, pounding surf, and pea-soup fogs that not only cut visibility down to zero, but distorted and muffled sound as well. Each of these factors helped give the Point its tragic notoriety.

Direct proof of the area's dangers lay immediately to Lansford's left. There, placed on a bed of concrete, was a rusted anchor, raised from the surf in 1973. It belonged to the U.S.S. Chauncery, one of seven Navy destroyers that had plowed into the Devil's Jaw on the night of September 8, 1923. Lansford had read an account of this tragedy upon his initial deployment at Vandenberg. At that time he had been shocked by this incident that had somehow been kept out of his collegiate history books.

It had been a simple navigational error that had led this squadron of high-speed warships onto the reefs off Point Arguello. Though all seven ships had been sunk, miraculously only 23 seamen out of a possible 800 had been killed. The tragedy had occurred when the navigator of the lead destroyer, the U.S.S. Delphy, had miscalculated a directional radio beacon signal. Veiled by a thick nighttime fog, the ship's officers had thought they were well south of Point Conception, on their journey from San Francisco to San Diego. Because of this error in their calculations, they had ordered the ships to turn due eastward into what they had presumed was sheltered Santa Barbara Channel. Yet, in reality, they had yet to pass Point Arguello, three miles north of Point Conception. The destroyers had been running in a tight battle formation, and ship after ship had plowed into the awaiting rocks, their horrified captains unable to halt their forward progress until too late. And once again the Devil's Jaw had added yet another pile of debris to its already bone-littered sea floor.

Pondering this unbelievable tale, Lansford noticed the weird, brooding silence that seemed to haunt the spot. No seabird or gull cried overhead, the only sound audible being that of the wind and the incessant, surging surf.

Angling his line of sight back out to sea, he studied the breakers that formed in long frothing sets over a quarter of a mile beyond. It was beneath these crashing waves that his search would begin.

Preliminary reports from the submarine U.S.S. Razorback showed the initial debris field to lay approximately three and a half miles offshore. There, in 150 feet of water, the first major pieces of wreckage had been spotted. A subsequent sonar scan of the ocean's bottom had picked up over 500 additional pieces of debris, lying in a sector 5 miles long and 400 feet wide. Because this path led out to sea, much of the wreckage could lie in depths of over 800 feet.

Their first objective was to completely search, localize, and visually classify. Then, utilizing such unique platforms as the Deep Submergence Rescue Vehicle Marlin, they would initiate the difficult task of exhuming as many of the pieces of wreckage as possible. Without benefit of the DSRV's articulated manipulator arms, such a task would have been impossible.

Aware of the time limitations all too recently placed upon him, Lansford prayed that relatively stable weather would continue to prevail. A series of storms now could delay their efforts for weeks. At last report, the base meteorologist had seen no significant low-pressure systems in the immediate area. If this remained constant, the first actual piece of debris could be extracted as early as the next day. Of course, this still depended upon various logistical concerns that he had absolutely no control over, such as a mechanical breakdown in their equipment. Yet, as it stood now, his superiors would be accepting no excuses. What they demanded were results. This was the bottom line that he would have to be working for no matter the cost.

Stifling a yawn, Lansford ran his hand through his crew-cut. There would be little time for sleep until they learned just what had taken the mighty Titan down. Glad that Marjorie and their two boys were off in Florida visiting her parents, he was prepared to give this project his all. The vital importance of its ultimate ramifications couldn't be ignored.

The lieutenant colonel had known the identity of the Titan's top-secret payload from the very beginning. Thus he hadn't been surprised when the first calls had begun arriving from the Pentagon as news of the missile's failure reached Washington. What he was having problems understanding was the unusual speed with which his superiors were demanding results. An investigation of this type could take weeks to complete. Even then, it was somewhat doubtful if they'd ever know the exact cause of the explosion.

Lansford had only begun understanding just how vitally important it was for the Air Force to get the last remaining Keyhole in orbit late the previous night, when orders had arrived instructing them to ready Slik 6 for a possible launch. He had been shocked to learn that this directive also included instructions to get the Condor out of storage and ready to fly.

Both the launch complex and the shuttle vehicle had been mothballed, ever since the Challenger disaster had put the whole program in a state of indefinite suspension. Only recently had NASA agreed to a series of design corrections which were to be implemented on the surviving shuttle vehicles to make flight safer. Yet the Condor, a top-secret military version of the shuttle, had yet to be adapted. It was designed to be launched from Vandenberg, with as little public fanfare as possible, its ultimate mission veiled in secrecy. Lansford and his coworkers had not expected to see it fly for at least two years, when the design changes were scheduled to be completed. That was why these new directives had come as such a shock to him.

He could only assume that the nation's very security was currently being threatened. There could be no denying the effectiveness of the Keyhole reconnaissance satellite program. As the space-borne eyes and ears of the nation, such a platform would give the

U.S. its first hint of an enemy's hostile intentions. Though such an important satellite always had a back-up in orbit, something must have occurred to necessitate the tragic, rushed launch of the Titan. Since that previously reliable delivery system was now in question, and since a replacement Titan would take over a month to assemble, a decision had been made to ready the Condor.

As a member of the military, Lansford was no stranger to risk. His daily assignments often sent him to the far corners of the globe. Oblivious to the dangers involved, he did his duty without question. Yet, in this instance, he couldn't help but find himself doubting the rationality of those he served. Even if a Keyhole had to get airborne, did it necessitate risking a billion-dollar space craft known to be deficient, and its brave crew besides?

The shrill ring of his car phone interrupted his thoughts. Shifting his line of sight from the surging Pacific, he turned his attention to his current means of transportation. The dark-blue Air Force station wagon was parked less than a quarter of a mile away. The earthen roadway was cracked and dusty as he crossed the plateau and approached his vehicle. Without opening the automobile's door, he reached inside the open window and picked up the black plastic receiver.

"This is Lieutenant Colonel Lansford speaking."

The familiar voice on the other end replied instantly. "Sir, it's Master Sergeant Sprawlings. I thought you'd like to know that the C-5A you've been waiting for from Hawaii is on its final approach. E.T.A. is at half past the hour."

Hastily checking his watch, Lansford responded, "Very good, Sergeant. I'm down at the Point presently, and should have just enough time to get over to the airfield to greet them."

"Do you want me to meet you there, sir?"

"You'd better continue to hold down the fort. By the way, any more calls from D.C.?"

"Nothing since you left, sir. You did get one inquiry from Roger Winslow over at KXBC. He wanted to know if you had anything new about the cause of the Titan failure. I just told him he'd have to bide his time with the other reporters until an official news bulletin is released."

Lansford grinned. "Keep those dogs at bay, Sergeant Sprawlings. Now, I'd better get moving. See you in the office shortly."

Hanging up the receiver, Lansford entered the car and turned its ignition. The engine responded with a roar and the senior officer carefully guided it up the steep, rough earthen roadway that led to Coast Road. As he continued on to the main thoroughfare, he passed through a series of scrub-covered hills. Filled with razor-sharp cactus and thistle, the dry landscape was home to jackrabbits, mice, and plenty of rattlesnakes. Having had plenty of close encounters with this species of reptile, Lansford was happy to have the shelter of his automobile around him.

The car's shocks got a full test as the vehicle passed over a washed-out ravine, skirted a large pothole, and bounded over a rock-filled trench. On the other side of this trench were the railroad tracks, which Lansford quickly crossed. This placed him facing Coast Road. There his progress was momentarily halted, for he had to wait for a convoy of southward-bound trucks to pass before pulling onto the paved, two-lane roadway.

The huge semis were of a similar size and design. He had no doubt in his mind that they were all bound for the same location, for nestled in the parched hills to his right was Space Launch Complex 6. After months of inactivity, he could just imagine the frantic activity taking place there now as the site crew struggled to get Slik 6 back to life. Fighting the impulse to check their progress, he instead turned his car to the left after the last of the trucks had passed. This section of the Coast Road led directly northward and was fortunately free of traffic. Thus he was able to make excellent progress. With the blue Pacific passing on his left and the rolling foothills, where the Titan launch complexes were situated, to his right, Lansford focused his attention solely on his driving. All too soon, he was crossing the Coast sentry gate and rounding the broad curve that led to the entrance to Ocean Beach Park.

Continuing on down Ocean Avenue, away from the Pacific now, Lansford wondered how that crew of archaeologists were doing. Though he would have liked to take some time out to apologize to them for the rather abrupt manner in which they had been removed from their dig site on Tranquillon Ridge, he had been too busy to do so. Once he got the active search for the Titan debris under way, however, he would contact the young woman in charge of the archaeology project. Since the Air Force's renewed interest in Slik 6 would keep Tranquillon off limits for the time being, perhaps a new excavation site could be found for them. Otherwise, their summer fieldwork program would soon be over. With this in mind, he made a left hand turn on 13th Street, and after crossing the Santa Ynez River passed over what appeared to be a large, vacant field. Strategically placed within the clumps of raw woods visible there, were not only various telemetry installations, but also the security kennels where the base's police-dogs were trained and boarded. He continued up a steep hillside, and set his eyes on a number of structures set on both sides of the road. Only after passing the unassuming brick building containing Base Headquarters, where his own office was situated, did he turn to his left on Airfield Road.

Vandenberg was one of the few Air Force bases in America that didn't have a single fixed-wing aircraft under its auspices. In fact, the only airborne vehicles on its inventory consisted of a detachment of Bell UH-1N Iroquois helicopters that were used for aerial launch surveillance, security, and other rescue and recovery operations. This was in spite of the fact that Vandenberg had a 15,000-foot runway, one of the largest of its kind in the world. Specially designed to accommodate such unique craft as the space shuttle, the airfield was quite capable of handling the likes of the giant transport plane currently approaching from the southeast.

Lansford arrived at the terminal building in time to see the Lockheed C-5A Galaxy initiate its final descent. This lumbering silver-and-white-winged giant was the largest airplane in the Air Force's inventory. Sporting a fuselage length of over 247 feet, it had a 222-foot wing span that offered an available wing area of 6,200 square feet. This amazing feature, plus a quartet of 41,000-pound-thrust General Electric turbofan engines, allowed the C-5A to lift an unprecedented payload of one quarter of a million tons.

With its massive wings drooping and its engines squealing, the Galaxy lowered its twenty-eight-wheel landing gear and prepared to touch down. Leaving the confines of his automobile in time to see this event, Lansford could hardly believe it when the MAC transport ground to a halt after using barely half the available runway space. Whistling in appreciation of this remarkable feat, he looked on as the plane began taxiing towards him.

The loud, grinding report of a diesel engine's sudden activation sounded to his left, and Lansford turned and set his eyes on the cab of a large tractor trailer as it pulled off the runway's shoulder toward the approaching plane. Though it appeared to be a normal truck cab, he knew that it held a specially designed motor, and had just been driven up from San Diego. It was to be used to transport the C-5A's main piece of cargo to Vandenberg's Point Arguello docksite. Most satisfied that all appeared to be going smoothly, Lansford made his way over to the spot on the taxi-way where the Galaxy was in the process of braking to a final halt.

Just as the Lieutenant Colonel reached the plane's side, the C-5A's forward fuselage hatch popped open. From this opening, a self-contained stairway was lowered. First down its length was a blue, jumpsuited MAC airman. Greeting Lansford with a smart salute, the airman led the way for a group of khaki-clad Navy personnel. Appearing fit, tanned, and happy to be on the solid earth once more, this group assembled beside the plane's nose. There Todd Lansford greeted them.

"Gentlemen, you must be the crew of the Marlin. I'm Lieutenant Colonel Lansford, and I'll be your host during your visit here. On behalf of the United States Air Force, I'd like to welcome you to Vandenberg."

Making his way out of the group was a single officer. Easily the oldest individual of the bunch, he sported a head of gray hair, a beard-stubbled face, and probing blue eyes. Though his khakis were a bit wrinkled, his handshake was firm and voice strong.

"Thank you, Lieutenant Colonel Lansford. I'm Commander Will Pierce, Officer-in-Charge of the

DSRV Marlin, and this bunch of malcontents are the rest of her complement. I'd like you to meet Lieutenants Marvin and Blackmore, my junior officers."

Stepping out of the pack to trade handshakes with Lansford were a pair of officers who could never pass for twins. The smaller of these two individuals, Ensign Marvin, was skinny as a rail and almost completely bald, except for two strands of frizzy black hair that lay behind his rather pointed ears. Lieutenant Blackmore was in every way his opposite. Serious-faced and hesitant to meet Lansford's stare, Blackmore stood at least six feet tall, with a muscular build and a thick head of blond hair.

A quick round of introductions followed, as Lansford hastily met the group of petty officers and seamen who made up the rest of the DSRV's crew. In general, they seemed a young, congenial bunch. It was evident from their bronze complexions that they spent much of their time outdoors. Ever mindful of where they had flown in from, Lansford wondered what it would be like to have duty in a paradise such as Hawaii.

A loud, hydraulic hiss sounded from the fuselage, and each of the men looked up as the C-5A's lower nose section began to lift upward. Soon it covered the cockpit windows and was directed straight into the sky. This opened the interior of the aircraft for their examination. Barely visible under the plane's interior lights was the sleek, cylindrical, shiny black DSRV. Securely fastened to a full-length flat-bed trailer, the Marlin had been loaded nose first. This left its circular, tilting white shroud and single propeller directly facing them.

While the crew joined the MAC team as they prepared to extract the mini-sub completely, Lansford stepped aside to get a better view of the whole picture. It was as the tractor cab began backing its way up the C-5A's extended-lip cargo ramp to attach itself to the flat-bed trailer that Lansford noticed that another individual had just left the plane's forward hatch. Dressed in khaki pants and a denim work shirt and wearing a Dodger baseball cap, this tall, tanned figure seemed vaguely familiar. As this newcomer started walking down the stairs Lansford placed his face, yet still failed to remember his name. They had worked together several years before, when an Air Force F-15 Eagle had crashed off the coast of Southern California. As a scientist with NOSC, he had aided Lansford considerably, for he had been able to give a detailed description of just what the sea floor looked like in their search zone. Assuming that he was still with NOSC and was there once again to help him, Lansford walked over to greet the man.

"I believe we've worked together once before. I'm Lieutenant Colonel Todd Lansford, your host here at Vandenberg."

After scanning the officer's face, the newcomer smiled in recognition. "Of course. We pulled that Eagle out of the waters off Carlsbad. I'm Dr. Richard Fuller."

The two traded handshakes and Lansford continued, "I didn't realize that you were coming along with the Marlin. Your presence here is most appreciated."

"Why, thank you. To tell you the truth, I'm as surprised to be here as you are."

"Is this your first visit to Vandenberg?" asked the lieutenant colonel.

Fuller nodded. "That it is. I've certainly read a lot about this place, though. I understand you've got quite a facility here."

"We sure do," responded Lansford. "As soon as you

145

get settled in, I'd be happy to show you around the place. In fact, I just have to make a quick stop at my office before dinner. I'd love for you to join me. I've got some excellent charts of the area's waters there that I'm sure you'd be interested in taking a look at."

"Sounds good to me," replied Fuller, whose attention was drawn to the C-5A's nose. There the diesel truck cab had just linked with the flat-bed trailer on which the Marlin was strapped. As the DSRV began inching its way out of the cargo hold, the two men were joined by the vessel's gray-haired Officer-in-Charge.

"Is everything all right with you, Commander Pierce?" queried Lansford.

With his eyes still glued to the trailer, Pierce answered, "It looks good so far. Exactly what's on the agenda after we get Marlin out of there?"

Lansford found himself having to raise his voice to be heard over the straining grind of the diesel truck's engine. "The Marlin's to be pulled to Vandenberg's Point Arguello docksite. That's approximately twelve miles south of here. The submarine U.S.S. Razorback is currently awaiting your arrival there. The Marlin is then to be loaded onto the sub, with your first cruise scheduled to begin tomorrow morning."

"What are the facilities like at this docksite?" probed Pierce.

"I think you'll find them most satisfactory," returned Lansford. "It was formerly a 1930's-era Coast Guard lifeboat station, now specially modified to receive the space shuttle's two 154-foot-long 69,000-pound external tanks. Not only will you find a variety of transfer equipment there, but also a well-lit, spacious work area. And by the way, the route your trailer will be following out of the airport is the same one the shuttle follows. The roadway south of here has been designed to carry its seventy-six wheel transporter. Rocky hillsides have been excavated, and you'll find all turns have a minimum radius of 162 feet."

A contained chorus of cheers broke from behind them as the Marlin was pulled completely out of the C-5A's cargo hold. Conscious of what this meant, Lansford added, "Looks like you're in business, Commander. Would you like to join Dr. Fuller and myself for some dinner now?"

Pierce patted his abdomen. "Though my stomach says yes, I'm afraid I'm going to have to decline the offer, sir. It's best that I stay with the Marlin while she's being moved down to the water."

"I understand, Commander. I'll be down at the docksite myself right after chow. If it's all right with you, I'd like to quickly brief you at that time as to what we're looking for out in the Pacific. And please, if you encounter the least bit of difficulty, don't hesitate to call my office. Making your stay here as smooth as possible is what I'm here for."

Tipping his hat in response to this, Will Pierce turned to rejoin his men. While the crew of the Marlin loaded into an awaiting Air Force van to begin the slow trip to Point Arguello, Lieutenant Colonel Lansford escorted his new guest into the confines of his station wagon. Before taking off themselves, they took a last look at the Marlin as it began its journey off the taxi-way. Looking like a huge, beached whale, the black DSRV sat squarely on its transport. Following attentively behind was the van holding its weary crew. Confident that they would encounter few difficulties in their journey, Lansford initiated the short drive to his office.

As they sped down Airfield Road, Lansford addressed his guest. "Well, Commander Pierce certainly

147

seems like a grizzled old veteran. What do you make of the rest of the crew, Doctor?"

With his gaze focused on the passing landscape, Fuller answered, "They're young, but extremely competent. You should have seen them in action off the coast of Kauai. Without a second's hesitation, they took the Marlin into depths plagued by tricky currents and vicious riptides. Because of this effort, over one hundred brave submariners survived an incident that could have had a very tragic outcome."

"Sounds like just the sort of crew that we need around here," commented Lansford. "By the way, are you still with NOSC?"

"That I am," replied Fuller. "Since we've worked together last, I've been involved with the Naval Weapons lab. My present work concerns the sub-launched Tomahawk cruise-missile program. How about yourself, Colonel? How long have you been here at Vandenberg?"

Lansford was quick to answer. "Actually, I left the Tactical Air Command shortly after the F-15 incident. At that time I was transferred from George Air Force Base to the Space Command Center in Los Angeles. After a full year of training, I was assigned to the Space and Missile Test Organization here at Vandenberg."

As they began passing through the main administrative area, Richard Fuller viewed a series of simple, multi-storied brick structures. One of these buildings had a full-scale model of a Minuteman missile perched at its entrance. While studying this object's sleek lines, Fuller spoke out directly.

"You know, Colonel, I'm aware of the fact that something awfully damn important must have been loaded aboard the Titan to warrant calling the Marlin out of Kauai. It's not every day that the Navy leaves one of its 688-class submarines laying on the sea floor completely disabled. Tell me, does its payload have something to do with the Strategic Defense Initiative?"

Lansford grunted a response. "No, it doesn't, Doctor."

Not put off by the officer's recalcitrance, Fuller tried again. "Then I bet it carried a reconnaissance platform of some type."

Though his host didn't answer, the mere look on Lansford's face indicated that Fuller's second guess was a correct one. Taking in the contained silence that now filled the car, he sat back as Lansford turned the vehicle into an asphalt parking lot. After parking it in a reserved space, the officer led the way out of the vehicle and toward an elongated, four-story brick office building. Quick on his heels, Richard Fuller followed Lansford into this structure's entrance. Once past security, they began their way up three flights of stairs. This brought them to a wide, linoleum-tiled hallway. The lieutenant colonel's office was the second one to the left.

No sooner had they walked into the doorway than they were excitedly greeted by the stocky, red-haired figure of Master Sergeant Vince Sprawlings. "I was just trying to get you on the car phone, sir. You just got a call from Secretary Fitzpatrick's office. I told them that you were probably in transit, and that you would return the call at once."

Taking this all rather calmly, Lansford beckoned towards his guest. "Master Sergeant Sprawlings, I'd like you to meet Dr. Richard Fuller of the Naval Oceans System Command. The good doctor arrived along with the crew of the Marlin and will be assisting us with the Titan salvage operation. Please see what you can do to speed along his every request.

Now, how about getting me Mr. Fitzpatrick on the line? It's not every day that we're graced with a personal call from the honorable Secretary of the Air Force himself."

Guiding Fuller inside the door to his inner office, Lansford seated himself behind a rather large walnut desk. The Doctor took his own seat in one of the two high-backed leather chairs that faced this desk. His gaze remained on his host, whose hand was about to pick up the telephone when its intercom button chimed a single time.

While Lansford proceeded with a rather formal, polite conversation, with few words actually spoken by him, Fuller scanned the office's interior. Except for the desk, chairs, a single table, and a compact bookshelf, the floor furnishings were at a minimum. This wasn't the case with its walls, which were covered with all sorts of commendations, pictures, and maps. Studying these more closely, he spotted a series of framed eight-by-ten-inch photos that showed a variety of aircraft. Fuller identified a Fairchild A-10 Thunderbolt, a General Dynamics F-16 Fighting Falcon, a Lockheed C-130 Hercules, and a McDonnell-Douglas F-4 Phantom. Set on an opposite wall was a large poster of a Rockwell B-1B bomber in flight. Pinned to the wall beside this awesome-looking aircraft was a detailed map of the base itself. It included a good portion of ocean, which formed Vandenberg's western boundary. It was while he was visualizing the currents that undercut this portion of the Pacific that Lansford hung up the phone and addressed him.

"Sometimes I seriously wonder just what makes those guys in Washington tick."

"I know what you mean," replied Fuller. "You look like you just heard an earful, Colonel. Can you share it with me?"

150

For a good thirty seconds Lansford merely sat there, silently appraising his guest, before replying. "I really shouldn't, but you're going to be figuring it out sooner or later anyway. Of course, I'd appreciate your discretion. In the hands of the wrong people, the information I'm about to pass on to you could cause us all sorts of problems."

Accepting Fuller's solemn nod, Lansford continued, "The failed Titan missile that you will be helping us piece back together indeed carried a top-secret reconnaissance platform as its payload. This particular model of Keyhole was the most sophisticated version that we had yet attempted to get into orbit. Beyond its normal capabilities, it had cloud-piercing radar, night-vision sensors, and a new type of digital-transfer ability to insure photos of an unprecedented quality.

"It is the practice of the United States to have at least two Keyholes in orbit above the Soviet Union at all times. Unfortunately, our primary platform has fallen from orbit and its back-up has mysteriously failed. With the loss of the Titan, only a single land-based Keyhole remains in our inventory. To boost it into space, a suitable Titan rocket will take over a month to assemble. This leaves us with only a single vehicle readily available to get it into orbit, the military space shuttle, the Condor.

"It was only late last night when orders were received here directing us to prepare both the moth-balled orbiter and its launch site for possible action. That call from the Secretary confirms those directives, and raises our intended level of preparedness only one notch away from an actual launch. Though Vandenberg has yet to put a shuttle in space, that may all change in the days to come."

Solemnly absorbing this information Fuller sat

151

forward and asked, "Has the Condor been adapted to meet the Challenger board's recommendations for design changes?"

Lansford shook his head. "I'm afraid those changes have yet to be implemented either here or anywhere else as yet."

Clearly disturbed by this revelation, Fuller protested, "Then how in the hell can they even think of using the Condor just to get a damn satellite in orbit? Not only could they very well lose the last remaining Keyhole, but the shuttle and its crew as well!"

Lansford nodded in agreement. "You're right, the risk is great. Yet what else can we do? Though I still don't know for certain, rumor has it that the Soviets are up to something that seriously upsets the current balance of strategic power. Because of this, it's imperative that we get that Keyhole skyward no matter what risks are involved."

"I still can't see it," replied Fuller. "There's just too much at stake."

"That's just it," said his host. "Washington wouldn't even be thinking of putting the Condor into the air unless there were no other alternative. I can only pray that they know what they're doing. Right now, all that I can do is perform the job at hand to the best of my abilities. Which reminds me, I imagine you'd like to take a look at a chart of the Titan's preliminary debris field as determined by the U.S.S. Razorback's sonar."

Without waiting for a response, Lansford reached into his drawer and removed a folded chart. Smoothing it out before him, he handed it to his guest. With practiced ease, Richard Fuller examined this bathymetric chart of the Pacific Ocean off Point Arguello. Its unique feature was dozens of tiny red dots that began approximately three and a half miles from shore and stretched in a thin, elongated pattern westward.

"That debris field is comprised of over five hundred separate contacts," commented Lansford . "It's over five miles long and four hundred feet wide. Your mission, and that of the Marlin, is to determine its exact extent. Then you're to begin the job of classifying each separate piece of wreckage. Your priorities are twofold. Not only are we desperate for any evidence that might point to the reason the Titan failed, but we also must know if any portion of its payload has survived. If the Soviets were to pick up that Keyhole, our entire space intelligence program would be completely compromised."

With his eyes still glued to the chart, Fuller responded, "I'll need a complete set of maps showing the sector's topography, current, and magnetics. Bathymetric charts of the sectors both to the immediate west and south would also be appreciated."

"Just ask Master Sergeant Sprawlings and it's yours," returned Lansford, who pushed back his chair and stretched his legs. "I want to thank you again for giving us a hand with this, Doc. The Air Force is indeed fortunate to have the benefit of your expertise. Now, how about hitting that chow line? I don't know about you, but all this thinking has got me famished."

Chapter Seven

Vadim Sobolev could think of no better way to end this momentous day than by capping it off with a hike to the Syrdar River. That morning, when he had taken this same walk, he had never dreamed that the results of his recently concluded meeting with the young bureaucrat, Valentin Radchenko, would bear fruit so quickly. Yet only two hours before the call from Viktor Alipov had arrived. Without a hint of hesitation, the Premier had given his blessings to the plan Vadim had sketched out to Radchenko earlier that same day.

Sobolev could only guess that the aide had caught the Premier in one of those fickle moods that he'd been prone to lately. Once again, the Commander-in-Chief of the Strategic Rocket Forces thanked the fates for sending Valentin Radchenko to him. This entire operation couldn't have blossomed without his invaluable assistance. Of course, those two extraordinary photographs Radchenko had delivered to Alipov must have had their effect also.

The distinctive cry of a quail broke from the oak wood, and Vadim searched the tree line for any visible sign of this elusive creature. It was as his eyes skimmed a fallen, moss-covered trunk that he spotted an entire covey of the fat, feathered game birds. Sorry that he had neglected to bring his shotgun along, Sobolev watched them scurry into the cover of the thick underbrush.

A gust of cool, fresh air blew in from the west, and Sobolev gratefully filled his lungs with this sweet essence. As the tree limbs swayed in response above him, he could think of no other place on this planet where he'd rather be. With his life's work on the verge of total fulfillment, complete satisfaction would soon be his. Excited with this realization, Sobolev continued on down the pathway.

Because the sun had already fallen behind the tree line to the west, he knew he'd have just enough time to reach his goal before the gathering darkness sent him homeward. With renewed effort, he lengthened his stride, and five minutes later found himself standing on the Syrdar's bank.

Positioning himself on a clover-filled clearing, Sobolev took in the glistening expanse of water that flowed before him. Soothed by the sound of the current, as it crashed upon the rapids in frothing white torrents, he found his being completely at peace.

It was as he scanned the woods that lay on the opposite bank that a strange movement caught his attention. Moving himself carefully downstream to get a better view of this disturbance, the old general began to grin as he identified its source. Lying on the other side of the Syrdar were a pair of lovers in the midst of a passionate coupling. Oblivious to the world around them, they went about their lovemaking with total abandon.

Though voyeurism was not a habit of his, Sobolev couldn't help but find himself stimulated by watching the two go at it. A massive, gnarled oak trunk

155

provided adequate cover for him to take in the frolicking, naked bodies without the threat of discovery. From their appearances, the two couldn't be but mere teenagers. The lad, who was mounted firmly on top, was lean and wiry. With a frantic swiftness, he plunged his hips continually downward between the chubby thighs of his trembling lover. Most probably from a neighboring village, these two youngsters obviously enjoyed the seclusion and peace of this spot just as much as the old general did.

Curiously, Sobolev found his thoughts soaring far away from sex. Widowed for over a decade now, he had for a long time been afforded the love of a wonderful woman. Though they had never had children, his Tanya had often been the source of his strength and inspiration. Without her backing, he could have never aspired to attain his current rank.

How genuinely excited she would have been to know how splendidly his dream was actually progressing. For even as he stood here, the operation was already in progress.

Intelligence showed the only remaining American ground-based Keyhole platform to be located in central California, at Vanderberg Air Force Base. Because this base's western boundary was bordered by the Pacific, he didn't foresee any difficulties in landing a Spetsnaz Special Forces squadron there. Vanderberg would be penetrated and the Keyhole destroyed. This would leave the Americans totally blind to Soviet efforts. Already his crews were readying the final Tartar warhead packages. These would be loaded onto Tyuratam's force of SS-18's. Then they merely had to wait for the final okay from Alipov to send the warheads skyward.

A surge of adrenalin coursed through Sobolev's

body as he watched the young male lover's torso freeze in the midst of orgasm. Far from ponderings of a sexual nature, his inner eye visualized the utter destruction their warheads would wreak. Like a sperm in the act of fertilization, the nuclear blasts would spawn a new society. Finally freed from the blind material greed of Capitalism, the West would anxiously join hands with its Soviet brothers, and the world would know an unprecedented era of peace and prosperity.

Stirred by such a vision, Sobolev sighed. The harsh cry of a raven sounded behind him, and he looked up and found dusk rapidly descending. Taking a last look at the lovers, who still lay intertwined, he reluctantly began his way back to the footpath with a single thought in mind. As it now stood, the outcome of the operation he had already set into action lay in the capable hands of a single individual. If his protege, Pavl Yagoda, could only know that his grandson now held the very fate of the Motherland in his hands! It was as Vadim rejoined the narrow path that would take him back to Tyuratam that he wondered if Grigori's orders had yet reached him.

Five hundred and forty kilometers to the southeast of Tyuratam, Lieutenant Grigori Yagoda sat in the co-pilot's seat of an Mi-24 helicopter gunship. Below him, his blue-eyed gaze was rivoted on a desolate, rock-filled valley. Presently thirty-seven kilometers due east of the village of Bamian, in central Afghanistan, the blond Spetsnaz operative searched in vain for any sign of the armored column they were expecting to meet up with there. Shifting the weight of his muscular body, Grigori was most conscious of the ever-advancing dusk. If the column were not intercepted within the next forty-five minutes, they would be forced to return to Kabul, their mission a failure. Such a possibility was not in the least bit attractive, and the big-shouldered Naval Infantry commando diverted his attention to the pilot, who sat to his left.

Grigori's powerful bass voice easily penetrated the loud clatter of the chopper's rotors. "Are you certain that we are over the right valley, Captain? Ten armored vehicles can't just disappear in this wasteland."

Not bothering to take his eyes off the cockpit instruments, the pilot responded, "Of course we're over the right valley, Lieutenant. That is, unless General Valerian has decided to penetrate Bamian using another route."

"Not Valerian," returned Grigori. "He'd follow the plan of the day if it meant walking right into the gates of Hell. Perhaps he was able to make better progress than we anticipated. Though, from the rugged look of the terrain down there, I don't know how this would be possible."

Sitting back in his seat, Grigori adjusted the black beret that signified his position in the Soviet Union's most exclusive fighting unit. Except for the blue-striped sailor's shirt, the neck of which was just visible beneath his camouflaged fatigues, there were no other markings on his uniform to divulge his status as one of the Motherland's most elite warriors.

The profile of the heavily armed gunship reflected off the surrounding hillside as Grigori surveyed that portion of the valley that they were about to enter. It was as they rounded a broad bend that he first spotted the smoke. The thick, black plume rose from a portion of the valley still several kilometers distant.

His gut instinctively tensed as the pilot also saw the smoke and opened up the gunship's throttles. In instant response, the dual Isotov turboshafts roared alive, and the helicopter surged forward with a speed of over 275 kilometers per hour.

Less than two miles later, their worst fears were realized as the gunship reached the burning remains of the column that they had been sent to intercept. As they hovered above the wreckage, Grigori identified the burnt-out shells of three BMP infantry combat vehicles. Lying on their sides, in front of the BMP's, were a pair of eight-wheeled BTR-6 armored personnel carriers. Next to these were the remains of four troop carriers. Even from their present height, Grigori could pick out the dozens of bodies that lay beside these trucks. A wave of anger possessed him as the gunship circled the smoking hulk of the convoy's lead vehicle, a T-62 main battle tank.

"Take us down!" ordered Grigori Yagoda sternly.

"But the ones who were responsible for this massacre," countered the pilot, "surely they're close by."

Not believing that he was being challenged, Grigori swept his icy stare to his left and directly caught that of the pilot. No more words were needed, and the captain pushed forward on the gunship's stick. Its nose dipped in response.

The Mi-24 landed on a rock-strewn clearing immediately beside the troop carriers. First out of its fuselage was a pair of Spetsnaz commandos. As experienced members of Grigori Yagoda's squadron, both Konstantin Lomakin and Dmitri Andreyev knew their responsibilities. Angling their Kalashnikov rifles upwards, the dark, moustached soldiers, who could have passed for twins, took up defensive positions at the clearing's perimeter. With the gunship's rotors

159

still madly cutting through the air above them, their leader jumped onto the clearing from the Mi-24's interior.

Armed with an AKS-74 assault rifle, Grigori signaled the chopper pilot to return the vehicle to the sky. Each of the soldiers covered his eyes as the gunship's engines increased their whine. To a whipping cloud of dust, the Mi-24 broke contact with the ground and began a wide sweep of the surrounding hillside.

The relief was instantaneous. The dust soon settled and the engine's roar faded. Grigori Yagoda took in the sickening scene that he had viewed from above.

The mountain air was cool with dusk, yet the ripe, putrid scent of death was everywhere. Fighting back the nauseous urge to empty his gut, Grigori crossed through a line of stiff, blood-soaked bodies. Each of these lifeless corpses was dressed in the khaki fatigues of the Motherland's infantry. When he noticed that his unfortunate countrymen were stripped of their weapons and some of their clothing, Grigori's pulse quickened. When his forward progress interrupted a trio of vultures feeding on the body of a sergeant, his rage exploded. Whipping his rifle upward, he let loose with a deafening blast, and seconds later the birds of prey were nothing but a pile of bloody flesh and feathers.

His limbs were still trembling as he made it to the lead truck's side. Surprised that the rebels were able to take out such a heavily armored vehicle, he inspected its shell to determine the cause of its demise. It was as his eyes spotted the jagged black hole created by an exploding land mine that he stumbled over the legs of one of his fallen comrades. He peered down to identify this corpse and recognized it instantly. Though the body was decapitated, with the head nowhere to be seen, there could be no denying the officer's bars that decorated this soldier's corpulent torso.

General Pavl Valerian had been the senior Soviet officer stationed in Afghanistan. Though his rank afforded him the relatively safe luxury of remaining at their base of operations in Kabul, the old-timer wouldn't think of missing real action. A veteran of the Great War itself, Valerian had personally served with Grigori's grandfather. Together they had accounted for hundreds of Nazi barbarians in that greatest of all modern military conflicts.

For Valerian to have met death in such an inglorious manner, in this god-forsaken, desolate wilderness, was a travesty of justice. Surely a hero of the Soviet Union deserved better. With this thought in mind, Grigori stood upright and issued a resounding curse at the top of his lungs. The urge for revenge guided his steps as he breathlessly rejoined the other two members of his squad and called the gunship back to pick them up.

"What kind of force could have been responsible for this massacre?" queried Konstantin Lomakin as they waited for the helicopter to return from its sweep of the hills. "Never before have the Mujahiddin demonstrated such firepower."

"I'll bet they were using our own weapons," observed Dmitri Andreyev bitterly. "May our soldiers who trade their guns for hashish die a thousand horrible deaths!"

Grigori Yagoda watched their gunship sweep in from the northwest. "Well, the one thing that we can be certain of is that the rebels who caused this slaughter are even better armed now. They've gained over one hundred of our last rifles in this attack, and untold amounts of grenades and ammunition."

"My gut aches for revenge!" spat Dmitri Andreyev, who looked up as the Mi-24 began its descent.

Screaming over the roar of its engines, Grigori Yagoda added, "Join the crowd, comrade. I'd say it's time we begin to start evening the score. How about it?"

There could be no ignoring the expressions of pure hatred on the commandos' faces as they piled into the gunship. When it again took to the sky, Grigori watched the fading line of smoldering wreckage from the co-pilot's position.

"Shall we return to Kabul and bring back the entire company?" quizzed the pilot.

Grigori's response was delivered without hesitation. "There's no time for that, Captain. By the time we got back here, the ones responsible for this massacre will be long gone. I want you to take us to Bamian."

"What can we possibly do there alone?" queried the pilot. "We need back-up on this."

"Like hell we do!" screamed Grigori, his face flushed with contained anger. "Turn this gunship westward, comrade, or I'll be forced to fly it there myself."

Most aware that the man sitting next to him was quite capable of this feat, the pilot turned the nose of the Mi-24 back towards the sunset. Outside, the horizon was tainted with gold as the sun inched behind the encircling mountains. As they continued on down the valley's spine, a hushed silence settled inside the cockpit's interior. The pilot's attention returned to his instruments, and Grigori's inner vision returned to the smoking column.

Though he was certainly no stranger to death, the

162

thirty-two-year-old commando would take to his grave the tragic sights he had just experienced. To see so many stiff corpses in one spot truly sickened him. With their putrid scent still flavoring each breath that passed his nostrils, Grigori craved only a single course of action. Revenge would be the medicine that would purge this poison from his system.

The monotonous chop of the gunship's rotors rattled on, and Grigori stirred with impatience. Below him, by the light of the gathering dusk, he noticed that the terrain was gradually changing. Thick stands of low-lying scrub and an occasional gnarled tree gripped the ground that had supported only rocks and sand before. When their progress took them over a tumbling stream, he spotted acre after acre of ripening wheat in the distance. As they crossed over these fields, the first shabby human habitations became visible. Crudely constructed out of bleached rock and dried timber, these simple structures made for an inviting target. Grigori fought the impulse to spray them with bullets. Nevertheless, his hands gripped the fire-control panel as the gunship roared over a series of needle-like hillsides and broke into a wide, fertile clearing.

Dominating this clearing were two huge Buddhas, carved into the surrounding mountains. Well aware that they had finally reached their goal, Grigori stirred in anticipation. His eyes narrowed as they swept over the collection of sand-colored stone huts that comprised the village of Bamian. It had been a mecca for the decadent, hashish-smoking American hippies in the 1970s. Now the Mujahiddin considered their rule there undisputed. He'd soon show this rabble how wrong these so-called Warriors of God were in this assumption.

His mouth was dry, his glance expectant, yet he couldn't pick out a single human being visible beneath them. Swearing under the cover of his breath, he looked on impotently. Had their elusive quarry escaped them once again? And would the lives of his fallen comrades go unrevenged?

He was just about to admit defeat when a massive rectangle of flaming torches became visible, lighting up a distant field. Catching this sight at the same instant, the pilot exclaimed, "It's the entire town! They're down there on the Buzkashi field. We must have caught them in the midst of some sort of festival!"

Most conscious of what this meant, Grigori smiled and his fingers tightened their grip on the gunship's weapons controls. Without further comment, they soared in to attack.

For the next few minutes, all Grigori Yagoda was aware of was the steady staccato blasting of the gunship's four wing-mounted gattling guns. Instinctively, his index finger depressed the firing trigger and the 12.7-mm. bullets flew forth in a hydraulic flurry of 2,000 rounds a minute. Designed to pierce the surface of a light armored vehicle, the bullets played havoc with human flesh. This fact was most evident as the casualties below steadily mounted.

The Afghans had been in the midst of their national game when the Mi-24 swept in from above. Hundreds of villagers were watching the Buzkashi tournament and they were apparently caught totally off guard. During their first pass, Grigori was afforded an excellent view of the match itself, which his bullets all too soon disrupted. Dozens of horsemen had been visible in the center of the torchlit field, busy trying to gain possession of a stuffed burlap sack. The object of the game was to secure this sack and ride it around the two poles placed at either end of the rectangular field. In days of old, a sheep's head was this sack's contents. As he remembered the decapitated body of Commander Valerin, Grigori's fury intensified.

They had completed over a half-dozen passes, and the area was now littered with hundreds of prone, bloody bodies, yet still Yagoda craved more. It was only when an anti-aircraft tracer shot out from a surrounding hillside that Grigori cried out angrily.

"There's the bastards responsible for the deaths of our comrades, they're in the hills! Let's show those spineless cowards what it is to fight like real men. For the glory of the Motherland!"

Possessed by the intensity of battle and the strength of Yagoda's words, the pilot didn't hesitate to turn his attention to this new target. With throttles wide open, the gunship streaked through the dusk-colored sky, its nose pointed straight for the rugged hills that lay to the north of the village. Again a tracer shot out toward them. To answer this blast, Grigori released a pair of 5.7-mm. rockets, which streaked out from their storage racks and smacked into the hillside with a fiery vengeance. As the Mi-24 turned to make another pass, Grigori noticed a good-sized contingent of armed rebels scurrying for cover among the rocks beneath them. Signaling the pilot of their presence, Grigori spoke out.

"We'll never get them all from this vantage point, comrade. I want you to drop me and my squad off on the crest of that hill. Then we'll show that rabble what it means to provoke the ire of the Motherland's finest!"

A quick scan showed them clearly outnumbered,

yet the pilot didn't dare challenge Yagoda's request. Even though standard military practice would have them call in reinforcements, he guided the chopper over to the rocky crest the commando had pointed out. Yagoda stood and flashed him a victory sign.

"Don't go far, Captain. This won't take long. Take us down to twenty meters. We'll use ropes to go the rest of the way."

Signaling that he understood, the pilot saw the tall, blond-haired Spetsnaz operative turn and disappear back into the Mi-24's main cabin. With practiced ease, he then began the difficult task of settling the lumbering gunship over the proper landing site.

As the chopper hovered and slowly began descending, three sets of ropes flew from its opened main hatchway. Lit by the light of dusk, three figures, with rifles strapped over their backs, expertly slid down the ropes. Hardly had their boots touched the ground when they sprinted for cover behind some nearby boulders. The down draft of the now-ascending gunship veiled the crest in waves of dust, and all too soon the helicopter's racket was gone, to be replaced with a hushed, primordial silence.

Utilizing a system of birdcalls to communicate with each other, the three men silently leapfrogged down the mountainside. It was Dmitri Andreyev who first chanced upon the enemy. As he crawled from the cover of a particularly jagged boulder, he found himself face-to-face with a trio of startled rebels. Taking in their characteristic baggy pantaloons, long, loose shirts, and beard-stubbled faces, Andreyev put a bullet neatly into each man's forehead long before they could even raise their Kalashnikovs.

The report of these shots caused a half-dozen Mujahiddin to suddenly show themselves from the rocks immediately to Andreyev's left. Just as he turned to put his own weapon into play, six shots sounded out from behind him. Before any of these Afghans could even hit their triggers, each of them received a single, fatal wound from the hidden barrels of his two comrades. Still not certain exactly where they were located, Dmitri allowed himself a sigh of relief. He had been caught off guard and that breath could very well have been his last.

The shrill cry of a quail sounded to his right, and Andreyev knew it was time to be on the move once again. Answering with a call of his own, he continued on down the hillside. This time it was the booming blast of an automatic weapon that caught his attention. Unlike any rifle that the members of his squadron used, he picked out the distinctive whine of a 7.62-mm. PK machine gun. A series of bullets ricocheted off the rocks immediately before him, and he desperately scanned the surrounding hills to pick out their source. Only when a raven's harsh cry emanated from his left did he know that the machine gun was set up behind him. With his back pressed up against a solid ledge of rock, he cautiously moved in the direction the raven had called from. Again the machine gun whined, and this time its bullets bit off several chips of nearby rock. One of these fragments grazed his cheek, and for the first time in weeks Dmitri Andreyev tasted his own blood.

Not certain how he would extracate himself from this situation, the commando froze. His extensive training taught him to think out a problem fully before committing himself too hastily. As it eventually turned out, his savior was crouched only a few meters away from him. Waiting patiently beside the large rock ledge to his left was the grinning figure of

Grigori Yagoda.

Only when Yagoda was certain of Dmitri's position did he stand up and lob a single RGD-5 hand grenade into the rocks behind them. The machine gun instantly coughed alive, and Yagoda was forced to dive for cover. Three seconds later, the grenade's 110 grams of TNT burst with an ear-splitting crack. The sound of this explosion echoed off the rock cliffs and the distinctive whine of the machine gun became noticeably absent.

Dusting the debris off his fatigues, Grigori Yagoda stood and signaled that the obstacle behind them had been cleared. Only then did Dmitri join him.

"It looks like the Afghan marksmen have finally drawn the blood of Russia's finest," whispered Grigori, as he pointed to the wound that lined his comrade's cheek.

Wiping the blood off with a handkerchief, Dmitri retorted, "This is no war wound, comrade, it's only a mere scratch. I wonder where Konstantin has run off to."

As if to answer this query, the gentle cry of a quail sounded to their right. An all-knowing grin spread across Grigori Yagoda's face.

"I believe that's our esteemed comrade calling to us now. I'll give you odds that he's cornered our quarry down below, and that he's only waiting for our presence to do them away."

"I learned long ago never to bet against you, Grigori Yagoda, and this time proves no exception. Let's go see what he's found."

Dmitri's cheek wound had already stopped flowing by the time they spotted their co-worker. Perched on a rocky ledge, several meters below them, Konstantin Lomakin pressed his index finger to his lips and beckoned them to join him. A minute later, they were at his side.

"We've got the whole lot of them, comrades. While you were busy with that machine gun nest, I spied over a dozen Mujahiddin crawl into a cave whose entrance is right below us. Not only were they heavily armed with two rifles apiece, but they were carrying several ammo crates that could have only come from our convoy."

With this revelation, Grigori Yagoda couldn't help but smile. Not taking the time out to verbally respond, he began examining the composition of the rock shelf on which they currently stood. Only then did he speak.

"This limestone should be easy to fracture. I'd say that, if we lay a line of plastic explosive along the lip of this ledge, we should be able to take down a good chunk of the hillside above us. If the concussion doesn't return them to Allah, I'll guarantee you that they'll be trapped inside that tomb of rock for all eternity. That should give these Warriors of God plenty of time to contemplate the type of adversary they've chosen to challenge."

Most happy with this plan, the three Spetsnaz commandos began the task of lining the ledge with white, clay-like chunks of plastic explosive. It was Grigori who expertly connected the remote-controlled detonators. Then he led his men off to shelter. Once they were settled at a safe distance, Grigori held up the battery-powered detonator trigger and, before pressing it, whispered vindictively, "This is for the lives of General Pavl Valerian and the rest of his brave troops. May their deaths be not in vain!"

With the completion of this brief valediction, he hit the button and a deafening series of blasts sounded.

This was followed by the terrifying sound of an avalanche, as the wall of rock lying above the exploding ledge tumbled downward in a single, swift motion. The crashing wave of solid rock caused a huge veil of debris to form over the blast site. It took almost five full minutes for this cloud to settle and for the commandos to check the results firsthand.

Careful not to slip on the tons of loose rock that their detonation had created, the three soldiers picked their way down the mountainside. They were surprised to find that the ledge on which they had set the explosives no longer existed. In its place was a tumbled mass of huge boulders. Since this ledge had also served as the cave's roof, there was no doubting that the Afghans who had been hiding inside it were nothing but crushed heaps of bloody flesh and smashed bone. With this in mind, the soldiers knew their revenge was finally completed.

A hushed silence possessed their ranks as Grigori Yagoda led them back up to the hillside's crest. Once they had reached the summit, Dmitri Andreyev activated a flare. Minutes later, they were aware of a chopping clatter echoing down the valley's sheer walls. It was Konstantin Lomakin who first spotted the Mi-24 gunship as it swept in from the northeast. A single rope ladder was visible, swaying from the vehicle's fuselage hatchway. Soon it was hovering above them, and one by one the squadron made its way upward into the helicopter's main cabin.

Taking only the time to straighten his beret, Grigori Yagoda proceeded immediately to the cockpit. There he was greeted by the anxious pilot.

"Welcome back, comrade. I hope your mission was a successful one because top priority orders are calling you back to Kabul. I've been instructed to return you there with all due haste."

Without further comment, the pilot turned his attention back to the vehicle's controls and initiated a long sweeping turn. Soon they were headed back down the valley, toward the southeast.

The dusk had turned to night, and Grigori sat back emotionally drained. This empty feeling always accompanied him when he returned from combat. The thrill of standing on the precarious border between life and death was an exhausting one. Fighting the heaviness that weighed down his eyelids, Grigori thought about the nature of the orders that were calling them back to Kabul. He could only hope that this directive would further allow him to take the war deeper into the enemy's homeland. This anticipation dominated his thoughts as he surrendered himself to a sound, dreamless sleep.

As darkness enveloped the dry, desolate hills of Afghanistan, the noon rains were drenching the plains of French Guiana. No one was more aware of this downpour than Colonel Jean Moreau. For the past five minutes he had been guiding his jeep down the mud-splattered roadway, towards Ariadne's southern security perimeter. At his side sat his assistant, Jacques LeMond.

Both men did their best to see out of the vehicle's windshield, yet the rains fell in such a volume that the jeep's wipers fought a vain battle. Inside the non-air-conditioned vehicle, it was hot and sticky. In order to keep the inside of the windows free from steam, Moreau was forced to keep his window cracked open several inches. Oblivious to the rain that completely soaked his left shoulder, he hunched forward in an attempt to get a better view of the road before them.

Not a word was exchanged between them, as Moreau focused his total concentration on his driving. Even then, the kilometers seemed to pass by with a maddening slowness. Hesitant to increase their speed, the colonel fought the instinct to hit the brakes when the jeep plowed into a rain-swollen depression. Only when they passed through a familiar, overgrown portion of the jungle did a breath of relief pass his lips.

On the other side of this thick copse of fern and coconut palms was a wide clearing. There the road skirted its southern flank. A seven-foot tall, barbed-wire-topped, chain-link fence separated this portion of the clearing from the jungle beyond. They followed the fence, visible on their right, for almost a half kilometer before Moreau spotted the parked security jeep blocking the road before them. Pulling in behind this vehicle, he hit the brakes and turned off the ignition.

"Well, here it goes, Jacques," observed Moreau solemnly. "I have a feeling it's not going to be pretty."

Responding to this comment with a shrug, Le-Mond pulled down the visor of his Montreal Expos baseball cap and shoved the door open. Moreau was quick to join him outside.

The rain fell in blindingly thick sheets, yet they spotted the three armed sentries almost at once. Standing beside the fence, the sentries had their attention locked on the ground beside them. By the time the newcomers joined them, both Moreau and his assistant were thoroughly soaked.

To a crackling boom of thunder, Moreau caught sight of the sickening scene that held the guards' attention. Lying on their backs in a straight line were five black laborers. They were stripped to their waists, and each of the corpses had its throat cut and a bullet hole squarely in its forehead. Because the rains had long ago washed the stiff bodies of blood, they seemed like artificial mannequins, yet Jean Moreau knew otherwise.

"Bon jour, mon Colonel," greeted the senior sentry. "We found these poor fellows less than a quarter of an hour ago. It looks as if they've been dead for several hours. All five were assigned to field maintanence. There's something over here that I think you'll be interested in seeing."

Nodding to lead on, Moreau and his assistant followed the sentry toward the fence. There, a long length of chain-link wire had been neatly cut. It allowed plenty of room for a full-grown man to pass through. Protruding from the soaked ground beneath this break was a single rusty machete. Tied to its handle was a red bandana.

"It's the calling card of the Third Brigade," said the sentry disgustedly. "After months of absence, those filthy leftist bastards have finally returned."

Taking in this observation, Moreau shook his head. "It certainly appears to be the work of the Third Brigade, *mon ami.*"

"What in God's name is the Third Brigade?" asked a bewildered LeMond.

"It's hard to believe that they've been inactive in these parts for over two years," continued Moreau. "We had our share of this kind of foolishness when we first started work here." He turned to LeMond. "Apparently the Brigade is a Maoist guerilla organization that wants Ariadne out of Guiana. For the first couple of years we put up with their threats, until they started making this kind of sick gesture. A full year before you arrived here, we were forced to move into the back country with a large contingent of

Legionnaires. Our boys found their headquarters on the banks of the Sinnamary River, and blew away over four dozen of them. Until today, that was the last we'd heard of them."

"There've been rumblings in Kourou that they've returned for sometime now, *mon Colonel*," offered the senior sentry. "Yet this bandana and machete are the first actual proofs of this fact."

"We still must be cautious," returned Moreau. "Someone could be merely copying their calling-card to cover up a simple, brutal murder. That's why I want a complete investigation. Photograph the area thoroughly before taking the bodies off to Kourou for an autopsy. Then an emergency security meeting is in order for later this afternoon."

A rumbling boom of thunder emphasized these words. This was followed by the piercing electronic tone of Moreau's carphone. It was Jacques LeMond who slogged over the muddy field to answer it.

A quick conversation followed. LeMond hung up the receiver and called out to his superior.

"Colonel, it was Winston. He says it's most urgent that you return to your office at once."

Knowing that his administrative assistant wouldn't bother him needlessly, Moreau excused himself and returned to the jeep.

"Would you like a ride back, Jacques?" questioned Moreau as he climbed into the driver's seat.

LeMond stood on the field before him. "That's okay, Colonel. I'll hitch a ride back with security. If you don't mind, I'd like to give them a hand with the initial investigation."

"Be my guest," returned Moreau, who added, "Just keep an eye on that tree line, *mon ami*. If it is indeed the Third Brigade, I'll bet they're watching us at this very moment. Good hunting."

The last he saw of his assistant was as he pivoted to return to the fence. The soaked, tall, lanky figure was soon out of his line of sight, and Moreau turned the jeep around and headed back on the same drenched road that he had just passed over.

The rains had yet to diminish and the colonel was most aware that the freshly starched shirt and pants that Theresa had prepared for him that morning were now completely saturated. Wiping the moisture from his forehead, he did his best to drive as fast as possible.

A single vision remained in his mind's eye. The five dead laborers had been laid out in such a dramatic fashion that the heinous nature of the needless crime that had taken their lives could almost be overlooked. It was as if the deaths themselves meant nothing. Rather, it was a mere political point that the perpetrators were trying to convey. Sickened by the type of low-life that could stoop to such an act, Moreau cursed his misfortune. Whenever things appeared to be going smoothly, the jungled hell that surrounded them would place yet another obstacle in their way. First it had been the logistical difficulties of establishing an adequate supply line. Then there were the mosquitos and the snakes to contend with. The appearance of the leftists only made a miserable environment that much worse.

Moreau guided the jeep through a dense copse of palms and realized that in a way they'd been lucky these past few years. Only a fool would have thought that the Legionnaires had been able to do away with all the trouble-makers. As with a malignant cancer, only a single remaining cell needed to be left behind in order for the disease to propagate once more. If the

175

Third Brigade had indeed returned, the only course of action would be to strike them quick and sure. Since several members of Ariadne's current security force had previously worked on Devil's Island, he was confident that they would be able to do the job themselves. This could all be discussed during the afternoon's meeting.

A crack of lightning lit the nearby sky and the colonel nervously jumped. Beyond, a rain-swollen creek had overflowed and the stream was in the process of flooding the road. Shifting his vehicle into four-wheel drive, he plowed into this current. The wipers continued their futile battle to clear the windshield and Moreau was forced to open his window wider to allow in more air. The jeep skidded, yet he quickly regained control.

A half kilometer passed before the grade of the road improved. Though the rain still fell in blinding sheets, he was able to make out the outline of the payload-preparation facility and, beyond, the Ariadne's launch tower. No rocket currently sat on this pad.

He cursed when a mosquito bit him on the neck. Slapping it dead with the palm of his hand, Moreau wondered what could be so damn important to warrant this unusual call back to the office. He knew he'd soon find out for himself, for the two-story, concrete-block structure holding command headquarters was visible off the road, directly to his left. Turning into its lot, he parked the jeep and sprinted to the building's entrance.

He needed to utilize both his security code and identification pass to gain entry there. Ignoring the trail of mud and water he left behind him, Moreau climbed up two flights of steps. At the head of the stairway was a frosted-glass door on the surface of which was printed, "Colonel Jean Moreau—Director, Ariadne Project." Quick to enter this door, he was greeted by his black male secretary, who sat before his typewriter pounding out a memo.

"Oh, *mon Colonel,* thank the Lord that you got back here so quickly. The Commandant himself called you less than a quarter of an hour ago. You're to call him at once, on the private line at his summer place in Cannes."

"Why thank you, Winston," said the breathless Moreau, who only then was aware of the puddle of water that had gathered beneath him. "Sorry about the wet mess, *mon ami,* but the rain just won't stop falling out there. I'll place the call myself in my office."

Without waiting for a response, Moreau rushed through the double doors that led to his inner sanctum. It wasn't every day that he received a personal call from the Commandant. In fact, it had been over a week since he had last heard from the director and founder of the Consortium. With this in mind, he positioned himself behind his desk and, punching in the series of numbers that only he was priviledged to know, activated the computerized telephone.

A succession of electronic tones emanated from the phone's speaker. Moreau visualized the signal as it was received by the Ariadne communications satellite that soared in a geosynchronous orbit high over the Atlantic. Seconds later, this same signal found itself beamed eastward, to a receiving dish located in far-away southern France. Just as quickly as he could complete a call to neighboring Kourou, a deep voice sounded with utmost clarity from the receiver.

"Commandant here."

"*Mon Commondant*, this is Colonel Moreau."

The voice on the other end lightened. "Ah, Jean, it's good to hear your voice. As always, it sounds like you are calling from just down the street. I hope things are well at Ariadne."

Moreau answered guardedly. "I'm afraid we had a bit of a tragedy here this morning. Five of our maintenance workers were found murdered in the southern security sector. Preliminary evidence points to the Third Brigade as the ones responsible."

Seconds passed before the Commandant responded. "That is indeed sad news, Jean. Please convey my respects to the poor victims' families. Will you be needing assistance from the Legion once again?"

"I believe this time we will be able to handle the situation ourselves. If we are unable to correct the problem, I will inform you at once."

"Very good, *mon ami*," retorted the Commandant, whose tone then turned flat. "For a while there, I thought that we might have ridden the earth of that scum for good, but *que sera, sera*. I hate to add more darkness to your already gloomy day, but I thought that you'd like to be one of the first to know that the United States Government has turned down our bid to assist NASA in their time of difficulty."

Surprised with this revelation, Moreau sat forward. "But how will they put their satellites into orbit without the services of their space shuttle or Titan?"

Aware of the tension that flavored the colonel's voice, the Commandant replied coolly, "Believe it or not, our man inside NASA informs us that the military shuttle Condor is currently being brought out of mothballs to place America's top-priority payloads into orbit, until a safer, more reliable platform is available. The first launch of this vehicle could take place as soon as forty-eight hours from now."

Hardly believing what he was hearing, Moreau exclaimed, "Are those Americans crazy? Have they forgotten the results of Challenger already? I can't believe they'd risk the lives of a brave crew when we hold the alternative right here at Ariadne. They are as stubborn and cheap as they are foolish."

The Commandant allowed Moreau to catch his breath before continuing. "Only hours ago, I was summoned to a hastily called meeting of the Board of Directors. At that time, our esteemed finance director informed us that, even with the additional Asian business, the Consortium faces serious cash-flow problems in the near future. The nature of this ever-increasing deficit could put Ariadne completely out of business as soon as the end of this year. Only one source of revenue remains untapped that can reverse this position before it's too late. I'm afraid I have no other alternative but to instruct you to immediately initiate Operation Diablo one more time."

The instruction cut into Moreau's soul like a knife into butter. Most aware of just what the Commandant was asking of him, the colonel struggled to summon a proper response. Abandoning his emotions, he allowed his duty to take over.

"Yes, *mon Commandant*, I will get to work on implementing Diablo at once. Am I to assume that this is not a practice alert, sir?"

"Your assumption is correct, Jean Moreau," answered the icily cool, deep voice of his superior. "A full packet of instructions is currently on its way to you via a Mirage jet fighter. You will be receiving them within the hour. Please don't hesitate to call me if you have the slightest of questions. I don't have to

179

remind you that the very survival of Ariadne is at stake here. Though our actions might seem a bit harsh, we have no other choice. I do hope you understand this. *Au revoir, mon ami.* May the Lord be with you."

Barely offering a goodbye of his own, Moreau managed to hang up the receiver. His mind was still awash with tangled thought as he swiveled around to view that portion of the facility visible from his office's central picture window. He hardly flinched when a jagged spear of lightning flashed from the heavens and struck the top of a nearby coconut palm. A wave of solid water splattered onto the window's exterior surface, and Moreau found himself focusing in on the sight of his own reflection visible in the glistening glass pane.

Appearing pale and completely drained of energy, the white-haired figure sat there listlessly, his thoughts struggling for rational order. Though he had been well aware that this day might come, he had never considered it seriously. Now that the unthinkable had happened, he could do but one thing. Otherwise, an entire life's effort would be totally wasted.

Chapter Eight

The morning fog came in from the Pacific with swirling, thick gray fingers. Blanketing the central California coastline in a shroud of cottony vapor, it played havoc with both seafarers and landlubbers alike. With visibility down to near zero, only the most daring of travelers risked penetrating such an environment.

Miriam Rodgers was well aware that this was an excellent morning to keep their vehicles parked at camp. Since their promising excavation on Tranquillon Ridge had been put off limits by the Air Force, she had allowed her senior teacher's assistant to find them an alternative dig site. Fortunately, Joseph Solares had been able to find one within walking distance of their circle of trailers. Thus their method of transportation was by foot, and not even the fog could hold them back.

The majority of the crew had left for this new site at the first crack of dawn. This left only Miriam and one of her students back at camp. There they were kept busy cataloguing a precise list of every single artifact so far uncovered in their work at Vandenberg. This included the remnants of an excellent collection of Chumash basketry. So far, they had identified a wide assortment of superbly crafted designs, weaved from such materials as juncas, sumac, tule willow, and the roots of sedge and fern. Several of them were even decorated with flicker quills. Their shovels had also uncovered hundreds of obsidean arrowheads and a variety of scrapers, spear points, knives, and awls. Miriam took exceptional pride in the magnificent Olivilla shell necklace that she had personally uncovered only a week after they had initially arrived there. It was unlike any piece of Chumash jewelry that she had ever viewed before, and she imagined that it had to have been the property of a village matriarch.

Of course, the most spectacular of their discoveries had been their latest. The shiny gray stone spirit bowl had been exhumed from Tranquillon Ridge only minutes before the Air Force sentries had arrived to drive them away. Each time that she studied it, she couldn't help but be impressed with the hundreds of hours of intricate workmanship that must have been needed to create its lip of tiny five-pointed-star shell bits. And then there was the unique symbol painted on its bottom. If Joseph was correct, the ball of bright yellow and the concentric circles of black and red that surrounded it could be symbolic of the journey of the very soul after death. Quick to stir the imaginations of Miriam and her impressionable co-workers, the lap-sized bowl hinted at even greater discoveries yet to come.

Robert R. Baray, the Sioux Indian staff engineer for Vandenberg, had been correct in his assumption that Tranquillon offered the trained archaeologist a wealth of possibilities. Yet Miriam couldn't help but wonder if Baray had been aware that this spot could be the location of the legendary Chumash portal of the dead. How her juices had flowed when Joseph had related to them the story of the paved royal road and the circular charmstone temple that would prove this very fact. Aware that such a discovery could have been as close as the next shovelful of dirt, Miriam couldn't have been more disappointed when the Air Force sentries had arrived to abruptly put her dreams on hold. Powerless to fight their authority there, she could but lead her crew back to camp, where they regrouped and eventually diverted their efforts elsewhere.

Once again it was from Robert Baray's journal that they had found this new site. Located only a mile from camp, on the other side of the foothills that separated the parking lot from the beach itself, this spot was supposedly a Chumash fishing village. A preliminary excavation had showed it to be promising, and all too soon the students had been ready to abandon Tranquillon and see what treasures awaited them at the new site.

Though a month's worth of work couldn't be so easily walked away from, Miriam had somewhat reluctantly given this new project her blessings. Anxious to be working in such a close proximity to the beach, the kids had gone to the site this morning in better spirits than she had seen them in weeks. Since they had to be kept busy doing something of value, she looked upon this whole excavation as a mere diversionary project. The Air Force couldn't keep Tranquillon off limits forever. Hopefully, the ban would be lifted soon, and she could proceed with the effort her instincts told her would produce the most treasures.

Conscious of the varied collection of relics that cluttered the picnic tables before her, Miriam sat back and put down the arrowheads that she had been sorting through. Aware again of the unusual density of the morning's fog, she rubbed her raw hands together. Her relative physical inactivity had allowed a moist chill to settle in her limbs. Not even the hot mug of coffee that she had been sipping was able to alleviate it.

Her co-worker, Margaret, didn't seem in the least bit effected by the cold. Dressed in a thick, woolen turtleneck, the sophomore honors student was carefully measuring each of the arrowheads, then labeling and registering them in a ledger. She was seemingly lost in her work and Miriam hated to bother her, yet she did so anyway.

"Hey, Margaret, do you mind holding down the fort on your own for a while? It's time for me to get the old blood circulating."

Jerking her head upward, as if emerging from a trance, the student archeologist smiled. "Go for it, Miss Rodgers. I've got plenty here to keep me out of trouble."

Certain of the legitimacy of these words, Miriam stood. "Thanks, Margaret. I think I'll mosey on down the beach and see what the rest of the crew has come up with. See you at lunch."

"Don't get lost in the fog," said the straight-faced student, who was already turning her attention back to her work.

Not desiring to disturb Margaret any further, Miriam did her best to leave the campsite as quietly as possible. Hastily she left the semicircle of trailers and crossed the parking lot. As she began her way down the sandy trail that followed the southern bank of the Santa Ynez River downstream, she found herself disappearing in a solid wall of swirling fog. Already, the trailers were no longer visible behind her. To ward off the moist chill, she pulled up the zipper of her quilted vest and significantly lengthened her stride. This action barely neutralized the icy current of offshore air that struck her as she rounded the bend leading toward the trestle of the elevated railroad tracks. Constructed there to convey the train safely over the river bed, the wooden trestle had a walkway cut beneath it. Miriam followed the narrow path that led under the bridge and passed a series of sand dunes.

The wind died down, to be replaced by a strange, hushed stillness. In the distance rose the constant muted tones of crashing surf. Above her, still veiled by the fog, a lonely gull cried out. Since her travels would now turn southward, she decided to follow the Santa Ynez down to the sea itself. There the firmer sand would be easier to tread upon and allow her quicker progress.

The smell of the estuary was ripe with life as she followed a mussel-lined path down to the ocean. Only able to see a few inches before her, Miriam halted when she arrived at the surf line. A clear morning would have afforded her an excellent view of Vandenberg's northern coastline at this spot. Situated there were the base's Minutemen launch silos, where the Air Force trained its ICBM crews.

With the sound of the crashing surf all-prevalent, she turned in the opposite direction and began her way southward. The path she now followed was determined by the tide. Careful to keep out of the water whenever possible, she walked briskly down a beach littered with all sorts of flotsam and jetsam. Because the portion of beach immediately in front of her step was the only thing that she could see, she spotted an assortment of shells, rocks, and bits of coral. Interspersed between them were thick, green, bulbous strands of freshly deposited kelp. As was the case on most beaches, evidence of man was present also. Soft-drink bottles and beer cans lay beside pieces of smashed Styrofoam and cut wooden planks of all sizes. Sharp, jagged slivers of rusted metal pointed upward out of the sand like awaiting snares. Keeping as far from them as possible, she settled into a steady, brisk pace.

The chill that had bothered her earlier was no longer noticeable. With the fresh supply of blood that pumped through her veins, Miriam was even beginning to feel a bit warm. To compensate for this, she unzipped her vest.

To properly monitor her progress so that she would be able to determine the right spot to turn inland, Miriam checked her watch. She decided that a hike of ten minutes should put her where she desired. Otherwise, unable to spot a familiar landmark, she could find herself walking all the way down to Point Arguello.

The muted cry of a foghorn was audible far in the distance, and the archaeologist found her thoughts returning to the excavation they had been recently asked to relinquish. How very frustrating it was to again ponder their predicament, yet Miriam couldn't help but be aware of the great potential the site at Tranquillon Ridge promised. After only a month's work, it had already produced a variety of priceless treasures. Surely, they had yet to even sample the artifacts that lay beneath the sandy soil there. Perhaps if the next afternoon's meeting with Lieutenant Colonel Lansford went well, they could return to the Ridge without further delay.

She had to admit that she was somewhat surprised when the note inviting her to the base headquarters had arrived the previous evening. Prior to that, Lansford had been completely unresponsive to her queries. Of course, she understood now the reason they had been ordered out of the foothills overlooking Space-Launch Complexes 5 and 6. They had come close enough to breathing the toxic fumes falling in the failed Titan's wake as it was. There was no telling what type of debris had descended upon Tranquillon, which was less than a mile from the missile's launch site.

What disturbed Miriam the most was the abrupt manner in which they had been originally ordered to leave the Ridge. At the very least, Lansford could have shared with her the reason for this hasty resettlement. As it turned out, they had to learn of the Titan launch from the lips of a newscaster only minutes before the missile actually sped skyward.

Then there was the manner in which the lieutenant colonel had ignored her subsequent phone calls. She had responsibilities just as he did. At the very least he could have given her a mere minute of his precious time.

The previous day's decision to begin work at the alternative dig site had done much to release some of the tensions that were beginning to build up at camp. For a while there, she had even been seriously considering cancelling the rest of the summer's work. After fighting for three long years to get funding for this project, it was not an easy decision to come by, yet what else could she do?

Joseph Solares had proven to be their unlikely savior. The good-natured Indian, who was a joy to work with, had come across the alternative location while thumbing through Baray's journal. With the lieutenant colonel finally responding to her inquiries, perhaps Joseph's last-minute discovery had saved her from a hasty decision that she could now be extremely sorry for. She was conscious that the permission to return to Tranquillon could be in her hands as soon as the next afternoon, and her mood lightened. Patience was a virtue she had largely ignored during her quick rise up the scholastic hierarchy. Perhaps she should be a little more aware of its merits. With this in mind, she put her back into her stride and, after checking her watch, proceeded south down the beach for another three minutes.

The first evidence that the fog was beginning to lift came when she looked to her left and viewed a clear section of beach that had previously been veiled. By the time she reached the end of her planned ten-minute hike, the sun was even visible overhead. Though it was still substantially masked, enough direct rays were penetrating to burn off a good amount of the mist that had formed inland. Because of this new clarity, she was able to view a wide patch of human tracks leading from the water line to the distant dunes. Since this line crossed the beach approximately an eighth of a mile beyond her present location, she had yet to overshoot her mark. Proud of her directional skills, Miriam chartered her own course to the dunes.

As she left the firm wet sand of the tide line, her progress was significantly slowed. The soft sand she was now crossing shifted beneath her every step and she soon felt its effects on her ankles and calves. Regardless of this new obstacle, she pushed herself eastward with a renewed determination. A wide band of sweat had gathered on her forehead as she reached the first of the dunes and began climbing over it.

From the top of the rolling, twelve-foot-high ridge of sand, Miriam was afforded an excellent view of the surrounding terrain. The fog had completely lifted, to reveal a clear blue sky. Checking the progression of the tracks that she had been following, she saw that they crossed over a succession of lower dunes. There the sandy ground was covered with a variety of desert-like shrubs. The predominant plant was a prickly type of miniature cactus. Careful to remain clear of its razor-sharp thorns, Miriam picked her way eastward, towards the railroad tracks that lay another half mile inland.

The ground was hilly, the sand giving way to a coarse, rocky soil. After passing over a series of ever-steepening ravines, Miriam spotted a familiar-looking canyon. Cut from the dry ground, this narrow valley was shaped by two precipitous walls over thirty feet high. She couldn't help but grin upon spotting her ragtag crew, busily working at the canyon's base. So busy were their efforts that they didn't even realize her presence. Their backs were to her, their attentions focused on a low ledge of sandstone, as she approached them.

Joseph Solares was the bare-chested figure that they were gathered around. His muscular torso was sweat-stained, his long dark hair tied back with his customary red bandana. In the process of lecturing to his spellbound audience, Joseph proved to be the one who first set eyes on the newcomer.

"Hey, Boss, welcome to Sun City. You won't believe what we've been excavating all morning."

Nodding toward the quick succession of smiling faces that soon greeted her, Miriam made her way to the ledge and focused her line of sight downward. There, embedded in the arid soil, was the outline of a narrow, elongated, nine-foot-long vessel. Having only seen such a primitive canoe in a museum before, she gasped.

"Is that a *tomolo*?"

"The very same," replied Joseph proudly. "Mr. Whitten chanced upon it five minutes after we arrived here."

"Does this mean that I get to skip finals?" jested the class clown, who arrogantly puffed out his chest.

"Not while I'm teaching this class," countered Miriam, as she bent down to examine their find more closely.

Kneeling beside her, Joseph chipped away a section of blackish rock that lay between the bleached remnants of the canoe and the surrounding soil. "My preliminary guess is that the vessel was somehow preserved by a pocket of asphaltum. It just has to be over five hundred years old. Brother, did Robert Baray hit this site right on the spot!"

"I'll say," observed Miriam, who ran her fingers cautiously over the canoe's outline. "What are the chances of exhuming it intact?"

Joseph grinned. "It could take a little effort, Boss, but did you expect any less from the finest crew of bone-pickers this side of the Colorado. We'll get this sucker out in one piece okay, although I doubt that she'll be very seaworthy afterwards."

Meeting this comment with a facetious scowl, Miriam shook her head. "Then get on with it, Mr. Solares. You never know how much longer we'll have to work here."

Issuing a mock salute, Joseph began explaining just how he thought the excavation should go, just as an excited voice came from up above.

"Hey, you guys, take a look at this!"

Angling his line of sight upward, Joseph spotted a tall bean-pole of a figure standing on the upper wall of the canyon. "What in the hell has Thompson spotted now? I only sent him up there to scout for arrowheads."

"I'll go check it out, Joseph," volunteered Miriam. "You're doing such an excellent job with this *tomolo* that I'll only get in the way here."

Joseph shrugged his shoulders. "Be my guest, Boss. Only be careful on the way up. It's rather steep.

And by the way, if Thompson's pulling our legs again, send him down here so that I can personally fill that creep's mouth with sand."

Not bothering to respond to this, Miriam stood and, after slipping off her vest, rolled up the sleeves of her cotton T-shirt and ambled over to the path that led upward. Five minutes later, she arrived at the canyon's summit, her forehead soaked and her lungs wheezing for breath. Not giving herself any time to recover, she immediately approached the lanky figure of sophomore Mick Thompson, who stood on the ledge, his gaze focused westward.

"What have you got, Mr. Thompson?" asked Miriam between gasps of air.

Pointing toward the Pacific, clearly visible beyond, the student stuttered, "You can still see it about a half mile out there. I've never seen anything like it before!"

Following the direction of his forefinger, Miriam looked out to the surging ocean. The first thing that she was aware of was the fact that the fog had completely dissipated. Miraculously, not even a hint of the thick mist remained. As she looked out past the pounding breakers, it took her almost thirty seconds to finally spot the object that had caught the youngster's attention.

Over two hundred feet long from its rounded bow to its tapered stern, the sleek black submarine cut a frothing line through the relatively calm blue seas. Fluttering proudly from its protruding sail was an American flag. Immediately behind the conning tower, an odd-shaped object sat strapped to the vessel's backside. Appearing as though it could be either a large bomb or even a mini-sub, it was like nothing she had ever seen before. No stranger to submarines, since her own father had been a twenty-eight-year underwater veteran, Miriam watched the vessel continue up the coastline.

It was only when it passed directly before them that she sighted the trio of tiny figures that stood on the sub's conning tower. Wondering where in the world they were bound for, she looked out with her curiosity piqued as the submarine turned to the west and, ever so slowly, began descending into the ocean's black depths.

"We're at sixty-five feet, Mr. Willingham."

Taking in this information from Chief Brawnly, the Diving Officer, the Razorback's current Officer of the Deck, Lieutenant Scott Willingham, efficiently approached the vessel's periscope station. "Secure from the dive. All ahead one-third on course two-six-zero. Up scope. Seaman Powers, how's she handling?"

From his seated position to Willingham's left, the Razorback's bow planesman responded. "She's a bit sluggish with that load on our back, but nothing that we can't handle, sir."

Expecting just as much, the OOD hunched over and pressed his forehead into the periscope's rubber viewing coupling. The sun was bright, the sky blue, as he grasped the scope's two handles and slowly circled. Other than an occasional slap of water, the viewing lens was clear of any surface traffic. While he continued his careful scan of the horizon, he was barely aware of the gathering taking place behind him at the control room's navigation station. Huddled around a bathymetric chart of the waters off of Point Arguello were the Captain, the XO, and the Navigator. Comprised of a variety of squiggly lines detailed in various shades of blue, this chart showed a fairly accurate description of the ocean's depth.

Their present course was drawn in pencil. Beginning at the dock facility on the Point's southern tip, they were heading in a straight line toward the west. Currently they were six and a half nautical miles off the coastline, with over 300 feet of water between their hull and the seafloor. From this point westward, the Pacific's depth increased rather rapidly, to a sounding of over 10,000 feet in nearby Arguello Canyon.

"Exactly where will we be dropping off the Marlin?" queried the XO, who shifted his ever present corncob pipe into the corner of his mouth.

Exeter made a small X mark at the extreme eastern tip of submerged Arguello Canyon. "This position should serve us perfectly. The ocean floor is some two thousand feet deep here. Since it's rather doubtful that the debris field extends further westward, the crew of the Marlin plans to begin their initial sonar scan at these coordinates. If the bottom looks clear, they'll gradually work their way eastward. This will allow them to double-check our initial scan."

"When will they begin the job of actually conveying the debris topside?" asked Lieutenant McClure.

Exeter was quick to answer. "That depends on Will Pierce. Though his primary task is to determine the field's exact perimeters, he's got the green light to begin the recovery of any debris fragments which catch his eye."

"Scuttlebutt has it that commander Pierce is a strange one," observed the XO nonchalantly. "The Marlin's senior chief was telling me just last night that the commander even insists on personally doing minor maintenance on the DSRV. He treats it like it was a part of him."

"We can all sleep easier tonight with that in mind," added Exeter, who caught the glances of his two senior officers. "I'll be the first to admit that Will Pierce is a unique officer all right. We worked together during a joint exercise several years ago, and even then his manner of command was solely his own. Half the time his khakis had more grease on them than those of our own engineers. Though there's certainly nothing wrong with an officer rolling his sleeves up and getting down to nuts and bolts, perhaps Pierce does take such things to an extreme. Some even whisper that this particular eccentricity comes to haunt him at promotion time, yet who's to say? The one thing that the Navy can be sure of is that, when duty calls, Will Pierce and the Marlin will be there to do the job. Perhaps he might not do it with all the finesse of an Academy graduate, but the results will be there, and that's the bottom line."

Returning his eyes to the chart, Exeter continued, "I'm going to slip back to my cabin and try to make a dent in some of that paperwork that's waiting for me there. Give me a ring when we're about to let the Marlin go. Until then, put sonar on active bottom search. Perhaps some of that debris down below us has shifted. If there's nothing else, gentlemen, I'll be expecting to hear from you in another half hour or so."

Exeter's efficient movements were all business as he pivoted from the navigation table and crossed the control room's width. Upon passing the periscope well, he noticed that the Razorback's current OOD was anxiously hunched over the scope, in the process of scanning the surrounding waters. Well aware of Lieutenant Willingham's continued diligence, he knew it wouldn't be long until the young officer had a command of his own. Ever mindful of his own spirited efforts during his first years of duty, Exeter silently admired the youngster's gusto while turning down the corridor that lay to his right. As he passed the stairway that led down to the sub's second level, his thoughts were already returning to the pile of correspondence that waited for him beyond the next hatchway.

Meanwhile, downstairs in the Razorback's galley, Seaman First Class Lefty Jackman was busy wolfing down his second stack of buttermilk pancakes and his third helping of sausage of the morning. Seated in the booth opposite him was Seaman Second Class Seth Burke, who was still working on his first stack. Both sonar technicians were in the process of filling their stomachs for the long duty shift that would soon be theirs.

Oblivious to the hushed chatter of the sailors who were seated in the booths around him, Lefty was arguing his point while waving a piece of link sausage in the air. "I tell you, Tex, that Russian sub is following us."

Seaman Burke answered skeptically, his words flavored by a West Texas drawl. "Ah, c'mon, pawdner, there's no way the Russkies would waste one of their nukes following this ole rust-bucket. It's got to be a coincidence."

Stuffing the sausage into his mouth, Lefty was quick to reply. "Coincidence? You've got to be kidding me. I'll accept a chance meeting off the Straits of Juan de Fuca, but for us to tag 'em again down by San Clemente, less than two weeks later, is a bit much. No, I tell you that they've been trailing us all along."

Still not buying his co-worker's argument, the freckled Texan shook his head. "The important thing is that we were able to pick 'em up on both occasions.

195

Billy Powers tells me that the Skipper sure was pissed when Command called us off the last pursuit. The way Billy told it, the Old Man almost bust a gut when he was forced to divert us up northward to look for this missile wreckage."

"I don't blame the Captain," retorted Lefty. "It's hard to believe that the Brass still don't have their priorities straight. The Razorback's a first-line man-of-war. Sure, we might be a bit slower and have to surface for air a few times more than a nuke, but we can still hold our own. To place us on a salvage mission is a complete waste of the tax-payers' money. We're an attack boat and ought to be treated as such. To let those Russians off the hook like we did gives me a belly-ache."

Looking on as Lefty stuffed another mouthful of hotcakes into his mouth, Seth grinned. "I doubt that's the cause of your tummy problems, pawdner. I still don't know where in the blazes you put all that chow, but you certainly can pack those vittles away. Have you always had this kind of appetite?"

Lefty answered after gulping down a mouthful of milk, "This ain't anything, Tex. You should see me at mealtime when I'm in training. Why, during football practice I can never get enough inside of me."

"Your poor family must have some food bill," reflected the fair-skinned Texan.

Lefty nodded. "My father always said from the day I first joined the Navy that I'd eat Uncle Sam broke. I must say that Cooky sure turns out some awfully tasty chow, although it can't begin to compare with my mom's cooking."

After carefully soaking up the remaining maple syrup with his last sausage, Lefty gobbled it down. Only then did he push his plate away and issue a satisfied burp of approval.

"That should hold me until lunch," said the senior seaman, whose glance went to the wall-mounted clock. Suddenly aware of the time, he bolted upright.

"Jesus, Seth, we'd better get moving! We've got exactly one minute to relieve the chief before we get our butts kicked."

Following close on his co-worker's heels, the gangly Texan stood and proceeded to make his way hastily out of the galley. Fortunately, they didn't have to go far. Less than a dozen steps separated the mess hall from the sonar room. The narrow, dimly lit compartment was located off the central corridor, immediately across from the crew's bunk area.

Senior Seaman Jackman was the first one to make his way inside. Waiting for his arrival there, from the seat of an elevated stool, was Chief Petty Officer Lawrence Desiante. The moustached New Yorker greeted him anxiously.

"Christ, Jackman, I thought you were gonna stand us up."

Calmly checking his watch, Lefty responded, "What do you mean, Chief? We're a whole fifteen seconds early."

Not about to dignify this remark with a response, the khaki-clad chief removed the headphones that he had hanging from his neck and stood. "The Captain's got us on active at the moment. He's interested in knowing if that debris field has shifted any."

With this revelation, Lefty's gut instinctively tightened. An active sonar search meant unnecessary noise, something that an attack sub wanted no part of. Powerless to voice his objections, he stood aside as the chief and his assistant prepared to vacate the room.

"Our passive hydrophone arrays are a bit screwed up with the racket that DSRV is creating strapped to our hull like it is," added the chief with a yawn. "So concentrate your attention on that missile wreckage. And for Christ's sake, don't screw up! I've been going for eighteen hours now, and I hear my bunk calling. I'm counting on you guys for me to get some decent shut-eye. So please, don't let me down, *capisce*?"

Signaling that he understood, Lefty watched as the chief and his assistant exited into the hallway. Relieved to be on his own, he turned toward his co-worker.

"What was I just telling you about Command?" emphasized the senior seaman disgustedly. "We've got no business shooting off our active sonar like this. Why they can hear us all the way back to Vladivostok! If you don't mind, I'll monitor passive for the time being. I don't think that I could take hearing all those pings wasted."

"That's fine with me," returned Seth Burke calmly.

Still not certain what had gotten into his high-strung co-worker, the Texan seated himself on the same stool that the chief had been utilizing. As he adjusted the headphones over his ears, he noticed that Jackman was settling in before the passive console. With high hopes that Lefty would soon calm down, the seaman second class focused his own attention on the loud, wavering blast of sound energy that was continually pulsating from their bow.

Beside him, Lefty Jackman was in the process of adjusting his own headphones. Unlike his co-worker's set, his were attached to a series of sensitive microphones placed strategically throughout the Razorback's hull. Designed to pick up the sounds of an enemy vessel before they were tagged themselves, the passive arrays were of enormous value.

With a familiar ease, honed by hundreds of hours

of practice, Lefty swept the surrounding seas. It didn't take him long to pick up the strange racket that the chief had warned about.

The streamlined nature of the Razorback's hull was designed to create a minimum of noisy, free-flowing holes for water to be forced through. This was one of the unique features that allowed them almost silent operations. But because they were currently carrying a DSRV piggyback on their stern, this feature was completely negated.

For the Marlin to be carried, a special cradle had to be bolted onto the Razorback's deck. The temporary nature of this bulky structure created a great deal of drag. Not only was their top speed reduced, but the sub's sound signature was drastically altered. Far from being silent, their forward progress was all too audible.

Lefty took in the resonant surge of this noise and silently cursed. Until the DSRV was released, the stern hydrophones would be practically useless. A quick check of the bow array found these sensors in much better condition. Though he had to turn up their volume a bit more than usual, he was soon able to begin an accurate scan of the sea before them.

Ten minutes later, he was in the process of penetrating the waters off their port bow when a barely audible hiss sounded beyond the normal clicks and moans of the sea creatures themselves. Quickly he reversed the scan and, after isolating the noise's precise location, amplified the signature fivefold. Since it emanated from a portion of the ocean located at the extreme limit of their sensors, Lefty closed his eyes to concentrate more fully. Gradually this noise took on a fuller definition.

Unlike the modern nuclear subs that had a variety of computerized equipment to interpret such signals, the Razorback's passive sensors relied solely on the ears and the memory of their human operator. Lefty Jackman prided himself on his hearing ability. Three years before, he had even heard the sound of a miniature screw as it broke loose from his mother's glasses and dropped to the kitchen floor. This feat was even more unforgettable considering the fact that the radio was blasting a Cardinal baseball game at the very same time. Able to pick out the merest bit of distortion on a record or tape, Lefty had trouble appreciating most modern music because of its generally poor musicianship and engineering. Rather, his tastes ran more to the classical. Violins were his very favorite. In the hands of a master, there could be no more pleasing sound for him.

What he was hearing presently grated his nerves like the loudest, crudest heavy-metal rock and roll. Twice in the previous couple of weeks a similar distant chugging surge had been picked up by their hydrophones. Only when he was certain that he had not dropped off into a dream did he turn to inform his co-worker.

"Sweet Mother Mary, Tex, I hope I'm not going bonkers, but take a listen to this signature that I'm picking up off our port bow. It sounds too damn familiar!"

After removing his headphones and replacing them with an auxillary set connected directly into the passive console, Seaman Second Class Seth Burke attempted to determine just what his partner was getting so excited about. At first, he could hear nothing unusual. It took a full thirty seconds for him to pick out the barely audible, distant surging sound. It took him another half minute to identify it.

"You've got to be kidding?" observed the shocked Texan. "It can't be!"

Nodding his head that it was, Lefty rechecked the signature's bearing. "She's coming in on a course of two-two-zero. Now do you believe what I've been trying to get into that thick skull of yours? I don't know why, but one of the Soviet Union's most sophisticated attack subs seems to pop up wherever the Razorback is sent. Not even the Secretary of the Navy is going to be able to keep the old man from giving them a chase this time. Captain Exeter just won't believe it!"

Seth Burke was having trouble believing it himself as Lefty's hand shot out to activate the comm line. Seconds later, the boat's XO was receiving a detailed description of just what they had chanced upon.

"I don't give a damn about our current mission!" exclaimed a very determined Philip Exeter. "This time the Razorback is going to give those Soviets a run for their money. Our first task has to be to dump the Marlin."

A tense silence possessed the control room, until the XO's voice broke from the circle of officers gathered around the navigation table. "That should be easy enough, Captain. We're only a few miles from our pre-planned drop-off point anyway. I'll ring the Marlin on the underwater telephone and tell them to prepare to deploy."

Accepting the Captain's nod of approval, Patrick Benton proceeded over to the communications station. Meanwhile, Exeter turned to address the sub's current OOD.

"Lieutenant Willingham, bring us down to one hundred and fifty feet and issue an all-stop. As soon as the Marlin is safely clear, we'll be diverting to a new course of two-two-zero. Ring engineering and let

Lieutenant Smith know that we're going to need flank speed. Battle stations are to be sounded, and then we'd better get to work on determining a decent attack angle."

Spurred into action by these directives, Scott Willingham barked out the orders that soon had the control room buzzing with activity. While the Diving Officer carefully readjusted their trim, and the planesmen began the task of guiding the sub to its new depth, the young Weapons Officer picked up the comm line and calmly called engineering.

With his eyes still glued to the bathymetric chart of the waters off Point Arguello, Exeter's hushed voice was directed solely toward his Navigator. "I'd say those Soviets have been prowling around our territorial waters long enough, Lieutenant. Let's see what we can do about making their stay here a bit less hospitable. Since we can't outrun them, what's the best course to intercept?"

While the Razorback's command team prepared their pursuit, three fellow Naval officers found themselves anxiously perched on the sub's stern, in a fifty-foot-long cylinder of high-tensile steel. From the Marlin's pilot chair, Commander Will Pierce efficiently activated the various switches that were bringing the DSRV's power plant back to life. Beside him, Lieutenant Lance Blackmore remained glued to the underwater telephone, in the process of receiving a message from the Razorback's XO. Watching them from the shelter of the vessel's central pressure capsule was Ensign Louis Marvin.

No sooner did Blackmore disconnect the phone than he turned to address the gray-haired officer seated on his left. "That was the Razorback's XO, sir. We've been ordered to immediately disengage."

Having suspected as much, Pierce called out to the Marlin's sphere operator. "Release those capture bolts, Ensign! Prepare the boat for separation."

While Marvin pivoted to hit the trigger switch that would free the DSRV, Pierce double-checked their hydraulics system. Satisfied that all looked good, he activated the aft thrusters just as the security bolts disengaged with a loud, metallic click. The main propulsion unit was set into gear, and the Marlin was now on its own.

It wasn't until the vessel had completed a ninety-degree turn at full throttle that Pierce again spoke. "Contact the Razorback and let them know that we're all clear, Lieutenant Blackmore."

Without hesitation, the junior officer activated the radio telephone unit and hit the transmit switch. Only seconds after he conveyed Pierce's directive, each of the three members of the Marlin's crew could hear the distinctive whirl of the Razorback's single screw. Steadily increasing in intensity, this roaring sound was accompanied by a pronounced shudder as the sub's gathering wake deflected off the hull of the Marlin. The disturbance quickly passed, and soon even the sound of the sub's engines faded in the distance.

"What in the world was that all about?" queried Marvin. "I thought we still had a couple of miles to go until we reached our pre-planned drop-off point."

"It appears that the Razorback had a little uninvited company to check out," offered Blackmore. "They seem to suspect that there could be a Soviet Victor-class attack sub cruising in the waters south of here. Do you think that we should scrub today's mission, Commander?"

In the process of checking out a bathymetric chart

that he had unfolded on his lap, Pierce shook his head. "I don't see any reason to go to that extreme, Lieutenant. The Soviets are always poking their noses where they don't belong, and I can't see how their presence here could effect us. Even if we were in a state of war and they meant us harm, the Razorback is quite capable of keeping them off our backs. So for the time being, it's business as usual."

With his glance still locked on the chart, Pierce continued, "Though we're a bit east of our ordered position, this looks like a good spot to take the Marlin down. We've got a good sixteen hundred feet of water to play with here. We'll continue heading westward until we reach the eastern tip of Arguello Canyon. The ocean depth increases rapidly there, and we should only be able to explore the first couple of miles of the canyon's bottom before reaching our depth threshold.

"If our sonar has no luck, this could signal the western extreme of the Titan's debris field. If that's the case, we'll turn eastward here, and retrace the preliminary scan completed by the Razorback. If this plan is all right with you, gentlemen, I think it's time to earn our day's keep. Ensign Marvin, prepare the Marlin for a deep dive. Lieutenant Blackmore, activate the bathymeter and begin an active sonar search. I want to know every bit of man-made debris that lies beneath us, no matter how small it may be."

While his junior officer turned to do his bidding, Pierce grasped the DSRV's control stick and angled their tilting propeller shroud upwards. Next, he flooded the ballast tanks. The additional weight of tons of sea water soon had the Marlin plunging downward. Minutes later, their depth gauge passed 850 feet, the point where most submarines would be forced to level out. Oblivious to the clearly audible moaning strain of the hull around them, Pierce continued their dive.

Also watching the depth gauge increase was Blackmore. As they passed 900 feet, he realized that this was the deepest that he had ever been. Though his feet and limbs were already icy cold, a narrow band of sweat formed on his forehead. Far from the panic that gripped him off of Kauai, he experienced a mild feeling of tense apprehension that he supposed was only normal.

At least he hadn't screwed up this time, when they were in the midst of those vital communications with the Razorback. Now, if only he could keep from freezing up in an emergency. This remained his greatest fear.

He would never forget those nightmarish moments when the Marlin had been swept out of control by the Kauai Channel's underwater currents. When their interior lights had failed, Blackmore had found himself so scared that, for a few seconds, he had been unable to hit the emergency breaker switch that he was responsible for. With his heart beating wildly, and his arms heavy as lead, he had been totally useless. Yet somehow he had managed to snap back and, with the lights' reactivation, had gradually regained his cool.

For the rest of that mission, any sense of panic had been totally absent. He guessed that he had been so busy with the five round trips it took to remove the Providence's crew that he had had no time for fear. After the rescue had been completed, he remembered being possessed by a feeling of complete exhaustion, unlike any he had ever felt before. Fortunately, the flight on the C-5A had allowed him six hours of uninterrupted sleep. He had awakened to find himself at Vandenberg. While being briefed on their new mission, Lance had been again surprised when the commander had again chosen him to be the Marlin's co-pilot. He was certain that Pierce had seen him freeze up before, yet the senior officer hadn't said anything about it. And here he was, hardly twenty-four hours later, once again putting his life in Lance's inexperienced hands.

Marvin had said that this was an excellent sign. The commander wouldn't give Blackmore a second chance unless he was certain that Lance could handle the job. Once again the spirited ensign had advised the Marlin's newest officer to lighten up. Everyone who dove deep beneath the seas felt such apprehensions at first, it was only natural. Thus, Blackmore had to quit being so tough on himself. He had to learn to relax and let things take care of themselves.

Never one to take life lightly, Lance took in this advice, yet knew it would be difficult to follow. He had always been tough on himself, even in school. Raised by a pair of college-educated parents, he had been expected to live up to their high ideals. This included the attaining of a 4.0 grade-point average.

As it turned out, Lance had made the grade. Yet in return, he had had to sacrifice much. His one great passion had been swimming, and his high school coach had even promised him a spot on the varsity team if he'd only take the time out for practice. Because his full schedule of studies had made such free time rare, he had reluctantly turned the coach down. This had been fine with his parents, who had promoted grades as his number-one priority.

His position on the Dean's List had allowed him his choice of colleges. Like his father, in college he had immediately enrolled in Naval ROTC. Though this had originally been intended only to provide him with financial assistance, Lance had found himself genuinely enjoying his military studies. Since oceanography had been his minor, he had been particularly fascinated with submarines. Though his parents would have preferred that he seek a desk job, he had graduated with the full expectation of receiving his commission as a submariner.

A year later, he was plunging into the icy waters of the Pacific. Conscious of the long road that had led him there, he sighed in sudden awareness. His greatest challenge wouldn't be in scholarship after all, but in conquering his own inner fears. Only in this way would he be able to stand on his own two feet and be a true man.

The clatter of the bathymeter began on his right, and Blackmore shifted his attention to study the pattern the instrument's stylus was recording. The laser printer showed the outline of a jagged underwater canyon passing four hundred feet beneath them. This subterranean valley was formed from walls approximately fifty feet high and three hundred yards apart. It would be into this void that their sonar would soon be penetrating.

A quick check of the depth gauge showed them to be under 1200 feet. It was evident that Commander Pierce was set on guiding the Marlin as close to the canyon's floor as possible. Considering the inhospitable composition of this geological formation, Blackmore shuddered to think what would happen if they encountered any unusual turbulance. With a minimum amount of space in which to maneuver, the Marlin would be hard-pressed to survive any unexpected change of lateral course. Knowing that any sudden collision at this great depth would be instantly fatal, Blackmore attempted to wipe any such thoughts from his consciousness. Worrying about such a thing would certainly give him nothing but an ulcer.

To divert his attention, he sat forward and peered into the viewing scope. Even with the help of a pair of powerful, hull-mounted searchlights, he could pick out nothing but the black liquid void of inner space. Yet merely being aware of the alien medium around him served to ease his nervousness, for here was the fascinating world that had always called to him.

Covering three-quarters of the planet, the oceans were man's last frontier. Unbelievable as it may seem, man knew more about the landscape of the moon than that of the ocean's floor. Plunging to depths over three times Mt. Everest's height, portions of the sea were completely unexplored. Only recently had man been able to actively operate at the Marlin's current depth. Even with this advance, this still left almost ninety-nine percent of the ocean's floor virtually unexplored.

Lance stirred when a small jellyfish suddenly became visible in the viewing lens. This opaque marine coelenterate sported a flat, saucer-shaped body and a myriad of free-flapping tentacles. Though it was only visible for a matter of seconds, the young officer already felt more at one with the surrounding environment. When a long, tapered squid shot beneath them, he felt almost at home. Any thoughts about the rather innocent nature of his past college studies came to an abrupt halt when the wavering sound of a returning sonar ping emanated from the speaker mounted above him. He looked up to determine just what their sound waves had detected.

With the commander's expert assistance, Blackmore was able to determine the exact spot where the suspected object apparently lay. Beneath them, the canyon floor stretched in a ribbon of sandy silt. Yet somewhere in this flat muddy bed, at a depth of over

1800 feet below the surface, was what appeared to be a rectangular-sized, sharply edged object.

"Well, that certainly looks interesting," observed Pierce coolly. "What do you say about going down and taking a look close up?"

Not waiting for a response, the Marlin's pilot began guiding the vessel downward, ever conscious that they were rapidly approaching their own depth threshold. With practiced ease, he initiated the tricky task of angling the DSRV in between the valley's jagged walls. The job of then getting the thirty-six-ton vessel to hover only a few precious feet above the canyon's floor was not easy in itself, yet the veteran officer accomplished it with a minimum of delay. Only then did he issue a sigh of relief.

Blackmore needed no invitation to join Pierce for a look through the viewing scope. The first thing that met his eyes was the silty composition of the sea floor. Clearly visible beneath them, the patch of muddy ocean bottom appeared as if it belonged to a huge fishless aquarium. It only began to come to life when their continued forward progress took them over a pair of bright-yellow starfish. Next, their lights illuminated a colony of sea urchins. Scattered among those spiny creatures were a number of elongated worms and dozens of tiny, darkly colored fish.

When their video camera set its lens on an advancing shelf of sharp rock, Pierce hit the Marlin's thrusters and the vehicle jumped upward. Most aware that they had missed colliding with his object by a matter of inches, Blackmore found his pulse fluttering and his mouth dry. He had even begun to believe that this rock was the source of the suspected sonar return when he realized that the commander was once again maneuvering the Marlin downward.

He couldn't help but feel that they would all be

better off if the Marlin were headed instead in the opposite direction. The great depth and geological instability of the canyon made working there much too risky. Surely no piece of wreckage was worth losing the Marlin for. A crewless, remotely powered vehicle would be much better suited to operate in these dangerous waters. Not certain if he'd have the nerve to share his opinion with Pierce, Blackmore felt the familiar tension return. Once this took command of his nerves, he knew that he would be powerless to express himself. Deciding to fight it at all costs, Lance bent over to re-examine the viewing scope. The object his eyes locked onto there quickly brought him back to normalcy.

Beside him, Pierce had also set his startled gaze on the same object. There could be no question of its source, for protruding from the sea floor there was a torn, rectangular segment of thick silver metal, with a bright blue circle and a white, five-pointed star painted clearly on its side. Upon viewing this, he found himself smiling.

"Well, I'll be. It looks like we've stumbled onto a piece of that Titan that the Razorback's initial scan missed. We're at least a mile from the presumed western limit of that debris field. If this guy's for real, it could drastically change our search area. What do you say about latching onto it and bringing it topside with us?"

"It might not look like much, but that segment probably weighs quite a bit," offered Blackmore. "Can we handle it at this depth and all?"

"We'll have to call in a specialist on that one," returned Pierce. "What do you think, Ensign Marvin, can we manage it?"

Scooting in between the two officers, Louis stretched over to peer out Pierce's viewing scope.

"Bingo, Commander! She could prove a challenge, yet how can we resist the try?"

"That's the type of prognosis I like to hear," answered Pierce. "Get back there and ready the articulated manipulator arms, Ensign. We'll soon all know just how much muscle this little lady can throw around."

A familiar knot had returned to settle in Blackmore's stomach as he watched Marvin pull himself back into the pressure capsule. A vacant, distracted stare was on his face when a calm, deep voice sounded from his left.

"Hang in there, Lieutenant. We'll pull this off yet."

Meeting the probing stare of the man these words came from, Blackmore could hardly believe what he was seeing. Had a split-second of compassion actually emanated from behind that all-seeing gaze, or were his nerves merely playing tricks with him?

He'd never know for certain, for the commander soon returned his attention to the controls. Cold and efficient, he went about the job of positioning the Marlin over the piece of debris with a surgeon's deftness. Inspired by his professionalism, the young lieutenant bent forward to assist the grizzled veteran in whatever way possible.

Chapter Nine

It was a call from Lieutenant Colonel Lansford's office that sent Richard Fuller packing for Vandenberg's Point Arguello docksite. As he left Lompoc, the late afternoon sky was a clear blue, and it continued that way until he passed Ocean Beach Park. There the sun was in the process of being blocked out by a thick bank of advancing fog. The mist increased in density as he continued on towards the coastline. By the time he reached the Arguello docksite, there were barely two feet of forward visibility.

With some difficulty, he managed to find the parking lot. Outside it was cool, moist, and strangely quiet. Beyond the hushed chop of the surf sounded the distant, mournful cry of a fog horn. Imagining what it would be like to be on the sea on an afternoon such as this one, he found it took his total effort just to find the walkway. The narrow, asphalt footpath he soon found himself on passed through a rolling section of desert-like scrub, sand, and volcanic rock. Barely able to see immediately before him, he knew he was approaching the surf only because its characteristic sound gradually increased with each step forward. The ripe scent of its presence was thick in his nostrils and he soon spied the ghostly outline of his goal, the site's masssive corrugated-steel warehouse. Originally designed to hold up to five of the space shuttle's 154-foot-long, 69,000-pound external solid-rocket booster tanks, the facility currently housed an object of a much different nature.

Totally chilled by the moist fog, Fuller gratefully ducked into the warehouse's entrance. The structure's cavernous interior was dominated by a cathedral-like ceiling and, beneath it, an immense central work space. Brightly lit, it was presently empty except for a pair of figures standing at the room's center. It was towards these individuals that the NOSC scientist was drawn.

From his rumpled khaki uniform and full head of gray hair, Fuller was able to identify one of these men as being the commander of the DSRV Marlin. The young fellow that he was animately conversing with was dressed in black slacks, a white shirt, and a red tie. He carried a clipboard, and appeared to be some sort of engineer rather than a military man. Their attention was riveted on a jagged eight-and-a-half-foot-long, six-foot-wide piece of shiny metal which lay on the concrete floor before them. It wasn't until Richard Fuller arrived at their sides that he viewed the flame-scarred blue circle and white five-pointed star that was painted on this object's side.

"Good afternoon, gentlemen," said Fuller somberly. "Lieutenant Colonel Lansford mentioned that I could most probably find you down here. I see you've brought us up a little souvenir from the deep, Commander."

As the NOSC scientist kneeled down to examine the piece of wreckage more clearly, Will Pierce responded, "That we have, Doc. We brought it up from a depth of 1,640 feet, from the eastern tip of Arguello

Canyon."

"Ah, then you were coming in when you spotted it," returned Fuller, who carefully ran his hand over the object's cool metal skin.

Pierce knelt down beside him. "Actually, we were just going out. The Razorback had to drop us off early, to play tag with a suspected Soviet Bogy."

"You don't say," observed Richard thoughtfully. "I guess that was fortunate for us. Otherwise you might have passed this piece by. I must admit that its location certainly changes our projections as to the extent of that debris field. Apparently, it extends over twice as far as the Razorback's preliminary scan indicated."

"And who knows how much further west it lies," added Pierce.

"I doubt that you'll be encountering much more of the Titan's remains past this point," remarked the young man who still stood above them with his clipboard in hand. Having attracted the newcomer's attention, he added, "Hello, I'm David Downing with McDonnell-Douglas."

Fuller stood to exchange handshakes. "And I'm Dr. Richard Fuller with the Naval Oceans Systems Command. May I ask what makes you feel that we've hit upon the debris field's limit?"

"Why, of course," responded the engineer, whose eyes gleamed with intellect. "You see, this particular piece of cowling comes from the upper section of the Titan. It's placed where the missile's two solid-rocket boosters attach onto the second stage. My company manufactures the Titan's payload fairing that sits directly above this portion. Since the rocket failed while arcing up over the Pacific, this piece of debris should indicate that the nose cone lies nearby. This means that the remainder of the wreckage would most

214

probably be found in a rough line extending toward the shore."

"That makes sense to me," added Pierce, who stood stiffly to join them. "Let's just hope that the payload is indeed close by. Arguello Canyon drops off sharply west of the spot where we picked this guy up. And I don't have to remind you how unforgiving that valley's walls can be."

"Then I guess that's where you'll be returning to continue your search," said Fuller.

Suddenly conscious of the time, Pierce checked his watch. "Right on, Doc. The Department of Defense isn't going to rest easy until we snag that precious payload. So, to make certain that the Marlin is ready to go at first light, I'd better get back to the dock."

"Take care in this fog and all," said Richard.

The grizzled commander was already pivoting to exit as he answered, "When you're diving down over 1,600 feet, into a volcanic canyon whose floor isn't even as wide as three football fields, this fog is the least of our problems."

Both men looked on as the veteran Naval officer crisply exited. As the door echoed shut behind him, Richard Fuller returned his attention to the piece of debris that lay before him.

"Any guesses as to why this baby failed, Mr. Downing?"

The engineer shifted his weight uneasily. "Our first suspicion was that it was caused by an explosion in one of the two solid-rocket motors. Yet now, I'm not so sure. You see, if that were the case, this piece of cowling would have been totally disintegrated."

Taking in this observation, Richard once again knelt down to closely examine the scarred metallic skin of rocket cowling. As he did so, the young engineer added, "I'm afraid that I'm going to have to

215

be off myself, Doctor. I've got to get down to the Santa Barbara airport to meet a planeload of McDonnell bigwigs flying in from St. Louis. And with this fog, who knows how long that drive could take."

Absentmindedly nodding goodbye, the NOSC scientist kept his attention locked on the piece of jagged debris. Hardly aware that the engineer had left, Fuller used his hand to trace a somewhat familiar pattern of indentations imbedded above the star's upper point. About the size of a series of shotgun pellets, the circular pattern was formed by over a dozen separate dents. Not having struck with enough force to actually pierce the thick steel skin, they were nevertheless the after-effect of a fairly strong concussion.

After racking his brain unsuccessfully to remember where he had seen such a pattern last, Fuller knew it would come to him eventually. At the moment, he had another priority. For, if he didn't get going shortly himself, he'd surely be late for that afternoon's appointment with Lieutenant Colonel Lansford. Anxious to share with him Commander Pierce's revelation as to the position of the cowling when it was exhumed, the scientist stood and made his own way out of the massive storage facility.

Doing his best to ignore the dense fog that awaited him outside, Fuller arrived at his car and began the short, yet demanding drive to base headquarters. The extreme atmospheric conditions forced him to focus his attention solely on his driving, and the trip down Coast Road was cautious and slow. His nerves were frayed by the time he eventually pulled up to the brick building that housed the Space and Missile Test Organization. After passing security, he made his way up three flights of steps and turned to the second office on his left.

216

The stocky, red-headed figure of Master Sergeant Vince Sprawlings greeted him inside. "Good afternoon, Dr. Fuller. Did you have any problems finding us in this pea-soup fog?"

"At least I have an excuse for being late," said Richard.

The master sergeant's mouth turned in a boyish grin. "There's no worry about that, Doctor. We've been playing catch-up since early this morning. In fact, the Chief is currently on the horn with Washington right now. He said to show you in as soon as you arrived."

Motioning that he could handle this task himself, Richard entered the doors to Lansford's inner office. The atmosphere inside was noticeably tense. The Lieutenant Colonel sat solemnly behind his desk, the phone cradled beside his earlobe. It was evident that he was not the one who had initiated this call, for his responses were brief and monosyllabic. His usually neat desk was littered with scattered documents, and he distractedly beckoned his guest to have a seat.

Fuller silently passed up this offer, and instead walked over to the map of Vandenberg and its environs that was hung on the far wall. His eyes went to the elongated pattern of red flags that were set in the ocean, approximately seven miles from the shoreline. Taking hold of the flag placed on the westernmost extremity of this pattern, he moved the pin to the map's extreme border, over twice the distance to the west. Satisfied that he had accurately marked the site where the Marlin had made its discovery, he stepped back and pivoted as a voice came from behind.

"These guys in Washington are going to have my sanity yet," observed the senior officer, who had hung up the phone and stood to approach his new guest. "Not only do they expect us to get the Condor out of mothballs overnight, but now I've got to deal with the surprise arrival of Secretary Fitzpatrick tomorrow afternoon. Don't they know that there aren't enough hours in the day to accomplish all of this?"

Richard could only shrug his shoulders and offer a compassionate smile. This simple gesture served to lighten Lansford's mood considerably. Rubbing his forehead, he approached the scientist.

"I'm sorry, Doctor. I'm sure you don't care to hear my belly-aching. You probably have enough problems yourself. Did you make it down to Point Arguello?"

Stepping aside, Richard pointed toward the map. It took Lansford several seconds to spot the new flag. When he eventually did, his face lit up in amazement.

"Do you mean to say that the Marlin picked up that piece of debris way out there? Why, that almost doubles our search area! Is it possible that the currents swept it out there?"

The NOSC researcher shook his head. "That's extremely unlikely. The currents there run mostly in a north-south flow. Though there's always the possibility of a shift, it's doubtful that we'll ever witness one with enough force to move this debris such great distances. I'd say that it was lying right where it originally fell."

"Great," sighed the disgusted officer. "Now I've got twice the area to search. With only two salvage vessels, it could take us months to find that nose cone and then figure out just why the Titan went down in the first place."

Richard instinctively softened his tone. "It's not all that bad, Colonel. In a way, this new discovery could be a blessing in disguise."

"Why's that?" asked the officer.

Fuller responded slowly. "When I arrived at the

Arguello storage facility, I got a chance to meet with both Will Pierce of the Marlin and a Mr. David Downing with McDonnell-Douglas. Downing seems to think that the piece of debris that the Marlin chanced upon comes from the Titan's upper portion, directly below the payload fairing. If that's indeed the case, there's a very good chance that the Keyhole itself is lying close by."

This revelation brought a grin to Lansford's face. Before he got too excited, Richard Fuller added, "Of course, the subterranean canyon in which it may lie can offer us some unique difficulties in itself. Not only are its walls extremely rugged, but its floor is narrow and lies over sixteen hundred feet below sea level. Even if the Marlin can locate it, conveying it topside could be extremely hazardous."

"At least we seem to be getting closer to that nose cone," said Lansford, his eyes still on the map. "Did Downing offer any opinions as to what may have brought the Titan down?"

Richard answered a bit hesitantly. "One thing that he seemed to rule out was an explosion in the missile's solid-rocket boosters. If that had been the case, that portion of debris we recovered would have been blown to pieces. I think we should keep our minds open to the possibility that it wasn't necessarily a mechanical problem that brought the rocket down."

Lansford's curious gaze shifted to the face of his guest as the NOSC researcher continued, "Commander Pierce mentioned something about the Razorback chasing off a suspected Soviet submarine prowling close by. Is it possible that the Titan could have been sabotaged?"

Lansford's face reddened. "Oh, come now, Doctor, aren't you pushing things a bit far? By even mentioning such a ridiculous thing, you question the very ability of the Air Force to properly police this installation. Few areas on this planet are as tightly secured as Vandenberg. Just try penetrating the base's boundary without a proper pass. I guarantee you that you wouldn't get more than a hundred yards without us knowing that you were there. As to the possibility of Soviet sabotage, I won't give such a remark the dignity of further comment. I'd appreciate it if you would refrain from even mentioning such a thing, unless you have one hell of a case to back it up."

Surprised by the strong reaction this innocent suggestion generated, Richard felt like a chastised schoolboy. He was relieved when Lansford's eyes went to his watch.

"I'm afraid that's all the time I can spend with you today, Doctor. The Secretary's abrupt decision to visit us has thrown my schedule into a shambles. I'd appreciate it if you could put together a detailed chart of just where the Marlin will be exploring tomorrow. I'm certain Mr. Fitzpatrick will find it most informative."

"I'll work on it tonight, and bring it by in the morning," said Richard flatly.

Nodding that this was fine with him, Lansford escorted his guest to the door. "Now, I've got to attend an emergency staff meeting. We might have to work through the night, but this base is going to be positively shining by dawn."

"If this fog sticks around, the Secretary will never know the difference," said the NOSC researcher in an attempt to lighten the mood.

The lieutenant colonel couldn't help but smile. "You just might have something, Doctor. Yet, with all my luck, tomorrow the sun will be out in all its glory. No, the men need this shake-up anyway. Hell, if they're doing their duty right in the first place, they won't have anything to worry about, will they now?"

With this comment, Lansford opened the door and led the way into the outer office. Richard followed close behind.

Outside, waiting anxiously beside the master sergeant's desk, was Miriam Rodgers. Upon viewing this newcomer, the lieutenant colonel greeted her somewhat nervously.

"Ah, Miss Rodgers, you just caught me on the way out. I hope the master sergeant was able to conveniently reschedule this afternoon's meeting. I had been anticipating hearing how your progress is going, but unfortunately duty calls me elsewhere."

Not only had Miriam been looking forward to this appointment for a full day, she left the camp late and had been forced to drive down the fog-enshrouded roads faster than she would have liked to. Disappointed that their meeting had been abruptly cancelled, she was about to vent her frustrations when she set her eyes on the tall, blond-haired figure who followed Lansford out of his inner office. A lump formed in her throat, and she found herself speechless.

From the other side of the room, Richard Fuller couldn't help but spot the attractive redhead who stood there gaping at him. His own heart fluttered in his chest as he identified her as Miriam Rodgers, his first college sweetheart. He hadn't seen her in over a decade, and she was just as pretty as she had been fifteen years before. Still unable to find the words to greet her, he merely stood there while Lansford made his apologies.

As the officer prepared to hurriedly leave his office, with Master Sergeant Sprawlings at his side, he remembered his guests. "I'm sorry. Miriam Rodgers, I'd like you to meet Dr. Richard Fuller. I hate to run off like this, but my staff is waiting. I'll try to talk with you both tomorrow."

Without further comment, Lansford slipped out the door. Preparing the exit himself, the master sergeant quickly turned and addressed the two civilians who still stood inside.

"Sorry again, folks, but these things happen. Please be so good as to close the door behind you when you leave. Now, I'd better get trucking. Talk to you both soon."

With Sprawlings gone, Miriam and Richard had the outer office all to themselves. Only then did they slowly approach each other.

"This has to be a dream," mumbled the NOSC researcher as he took in the trim figure and shining face of the girl he had once loved.

"I feel likewise," responded the archaeologist shyly. "Is that really you, Richard?"

Unable to hold her emotions back any longer, she flung herself into Fuller's awaiting arms. When their lips finally met, her cheeks were already wet with tears.

"Good Lord, I missed you, Redhead," whispered Richard. "It's like I've been suddenly taken back into the past, yet this time you're even more gorgeous. What in the world are you doing here at Vandenberg of all places?"

"I hope you don't mind if I ask that same question. Are you in the Air Force, Richard Fuller?"

"Not I, Princess. Actually, I work for the Department of the Navy, with the Naval Oceans Systems Command."

"You've come a long way since those Viet Nam protests, my dear. Is your doctorate in biology?"

"Oceanography," replied Fuller, who stepped back to take in Miriam's full figure. "I've no doubt that, if you haven't signed up with the Air Force yourself, you're here digging up some old Indian bones."

"They are Chumash remains to be exact, and yes, that's what has called me down to Vandenberg. I'm presently here with a student crew, on a State University grant which covers the entire summer."

"Well, one of us was able to fulfill their lifetime goal," returned Richard. "I'm damn proud of you, Princess."

Following this remark with another kiss, he looked to her left hand. Seeing no wedding ring there, he cautiously probed.

"Have you accumulated any husbands or little ones through the years?"

Miriam's glance narrowed. "I guess I've been too busy with my career and all for that kind of thing, Richard. Although, maybe after you, I was just spoiled. How about yourself?"

"Same with me, Princess. There was someone a few years back who I thought I might be able to get serious with, but she ran off with a professional surfer to Hawaii. Since then, I've kind of written that chapter of my life off, and dedicated this new one to giving one hundred percent to my job."

A wave of emotion suddenly overcame Miriam, and she hugged her old love tightly. Responding to this, Richard stroked the soft, long hair that cascaded down her supple back.

"It's been much too long, Redhead. You don't know what seeing your smiling face has done for this tired old researcher. For some reason, I'm still waiting to open my eyes and find out that this is all a wonderful dream. Whatever broke us up anyway?"

Fighting back the tears, Miriam answered, "The years that we were together weren't the easiest to promote a personal relationship. The war and all forced us to look inward. When we finally rediscovered our social consciousness, we somehow lost the magic that brought us together. You know, too often I think about what our lives would have been like if we'd stuck it out."

"A lot less lonely," said Richard, who squeezed Miriam tightly, as if to make certain that she weren't an apparition. "Say, since your meeting's been cancelled, would you like to have dinner with me? That is, if you don't have any other plans."

Miriam looked up into his eyes. "I can't think of anything that I'd enjoy more. Have you made any of your famous fettucini lately?"

Richard's gaze sparkled. "As the fates would have it, I just bought the fixings earlier today, while stocking the condo that the Air Force has so graciously lent me. If you'd like, we could pick up some of that chianti you used to love, and I could whip you up a Fuller Special."

Kissing him on the cheek, Miriam responded, "That sure sounds more interesting than the grub we've been throwing together back at camp. Speaking of the devil, I'd better be giving them a call and letting them know I'll be missing dinner. With this fog, they'll be worried sick if I don't show."

Walking over to use the master sergeant's telephone, Miriam hastily dialed the number of the pay phone that was set up between the trailers. Watching her every movement, Richard Fuller, for the first time in months, found his mind stirring with an anticipation not focused on mere work.

The condominium that the Air Force had provided for Richard was located in Lompoc, only a couple of miles from the base's eastern boundary. Tastefully decorated with oaken furniture and a complete supply of household utensils, the one-bedroom unit provided a somewhat cramped, yet cozy temporary living space. The tiny kitchen proved more than adequate for the NOSC researcher to demonstrate his cullinary abilities. The results of this preparation had been served in the condo's dining room. Though two candles still burned from the glass table, the diners had already emptied their plates. They were presently relaxing in the adjoining living room.

Richard and Miriam sat on a white-shag throw rug. Before them blazed a compact gas fireplace that Richard had conveniently ignited with the push of a button. With wine glasses in hand, they leaned back onto the large pillows that lay at the couch's base.

"I hope you don't mind the champagne," reflected Richard, after taking an appreciative sip. "But I guess they just don't import those straw-wrapped bottles of Italian chianti like they used to."

"It's fine," answered Miriam dreamily. "To tell you the truth, I'm not much of a drinker these days. One thing that sure hasn't changed, though, is your cooking. That fettucini was as good as ever."

Richard grinned. "You know, that's still about the only decent dish that I can prepare. Other than a mean tuna-fish salad, that fettucini is the extent of my repertoire. I've got to admit that I've cut down on the butter and cream that I used to pour into it. That old thirty-inch waistline has gone the way of thirty-cents-a-gallon gasoline."

"I don't know, Dr. Fuller. You still look in pretty good shape to me. I doubt if you'll ever have to seriously worry about fighting the battle of the middle-aged bulge."

With his gaze set on the flickering flames, Richard fondly reflected, "Do you remember that Jimi Hendrix concert? Boy, was that a night!"

As her own thoughts went back in time, Miriam couldn't help but laugh. "What were you planning to do up on the stage with Jimi anyway?"

"I don't know, but when I saw his guitar go up in flames, something inside of my head called me up there to put that fire out."

"I think I know what that something was, my dear," admitted Miriam.

Well aware of the artificial stimuli that had most probably prompted his mad dash for the stage, Richard shook his head. "I don't know how, but somehow we managed to survive those crazy days. And now look at us. We've turned out to be just the type of responsible citizens that we swore never to become. It's ironic, isn't it?"

Not bothering to respond to this, Miriam snuggled up against Richard's side. Richard put his arm around her waist and hugged her tightly.

"I'm glad you called your people again and told them that you'd be staying in town tonight. There's no way that I'd let you out in that fog now."

"I'm glad that I called too," said Miriam. "Those kids are very capable of getting by without me. Sometimes I wonder who's taking care of whom. It's funny, but things seem different now. My students seem to have a much better idea of who they are and where they're headed."

"Don't ever forget who paved the way for them," said Richard. "It was because of our generation that the very consciousness of the country was altered. The kids today don't have to fight the same battles that we fought, because we've already made the sacrifice for them."

Absorbing this observation, Miriam sighed. "I guess I'm really not that excited to get back to camp anyway. Ever since the Air Force moved us off Tranquillon Ridge, it just hasn't been the same. Sure, we've got an auxilliary dig site now, a mile south of Ocean Beach Park, yet you wouldn't believe how promising our original excavation appeared."

Sensing Miriam's frustration, Richard pulled her closer. "Hey, no more talk of work, okay? I could easily get into my own current troubles, but it's better for both of us to just put them on hold for the time being. Believe me, they'll still be right there waiting for us in the morning however much we worry about them tonight."

Richard's words of wisdom hit home as Miriam took a sip of champagne and looked up into his eyes. "You're right, Dr. Fuller, this special evening's not for discussing problems. Take me back to those carefree days when we had no responsibilities but each other."

Richard responded by leaning over and kissing his guest's full, luscious lips. Miriam had earlier decided that she would let herself go completely this night, and she passionately returned his kiss. It had been much too long since either of them had felt real desire, and a tingling electric warmth passed between them.

With no other thoughts in their minds but each other, they put their glasses aside and returned to a much simpler, happy time. Since the fates had brought them together, both knew that they would never have such an opportunity again. Taking full advantage of this chance meeting, they surrendered to their hungers.

Richard took the lead, as his hand slipped beneath Miriam's sweater. Her skin was warm and soft, and his fingers all too soon found their way to her pert breasts. The intensity of her kiss indicated that this touch was most welcomed, and Richard delicately traced the stiffening aureoles of her nipples.

As their tongues continued their mad probings, Miriam's hands began their own wandering. Adroitly unbuttoning Richard's shirt, her fingers touched the tight skin of his chest. Only then did she push herself away.

With her gaze locked on that of her lover, she went about the task of removing her sweater and pulling off her pants. Richard followed by tearing off his own clothes, and soon both parties were completely naked. Taking in each other by the glimmering light of the fireplace, they each made a silent pledge, and both lovers knew that no further commitment was needed. As they had over a decade before, they would give themselves to each other without needless promises and future hopes. Only in this way could their trip backward in time be complete.

Unable to restrain himself any longer, Richard reached out and pulled his love tightly into his arms. No pleasure could be as great as that experienced when their bodies finally touched, and linked as one. Laying Miriam gently on her back, he slowly gave of himself until all was given. A whimper passed her lips as this gift was received deep in the tight, warm recesses of her womb.

For several minutes they lay there, barely moving. Visible in each other's eyes was a long trail of shared past experiences. The joys and heartbreaks, the innocent aspirations and torrid, passionate desires all came to the surface with this merging. New joys rose, as Richard slowly pulled his hips backward and then inched himself forward once again. This tempo gradually increased until a comfortable rhythm was achieved.

Long into the night this coupling continued, until

Miriam's womb burst in a hot, tingling current of pure ecstasy. As she begged her lover to join her, Richard let go of his own blissful current, and the ritual was at long last culminated. Lying there in each other's arms, their passions completely satiated, the two lovers tapped an innocent joy few mortals have ever discovered. For how many of us have been able to return to the past and not be disappointed?

While the flames flickered before them, new hopes and purposes came into focus. Yet all too soon the deep, deathlike sleep that only lovers share overcame them. With their bodies still intertwined, they surrendered to this call as the midnight moon rose over the coast of central California.

Sometime in the night Richard awoke, and without disturbing his love's slumber, picked her up and carried her into the bedroom. Though he would have loved to join her beneath the covers, the spell had been broken, and already thoughts of his present responsibilities rose in his consciousness. It wouldn't be long now until the dawn would break, and there was quite a bit of work that needed his attention in the meantime.

Carefully closing the bedroom door behind him, Richard yawned and stretched his lean body contentedly. Lit only by the still-flickering flames of the fireplace, the room was littered with the evidence of their lovemaking. Clothes lay scattered, glasses were overturned and pillows kicked aside. Though he had slept a mere five hours, his slumber had been deep and he felt more rested than he had in months. Still savoring the memories of their coupling, the NOSC researcher grinned with satisfaction. Aware of a renewed stiffening in his loins, he fought the impulse to turn back to the bedroom. Only when he saw his briefcase, which was set beside the dish-covered dining-room table, did he redirect his thoughts back to his duty. Reluctantly, he flicked on the lights and began clearing himself some work space.

His first priority was to work on the project Lansford had asked for. Since the recipient of this map would be none other than the Secretary of the Air Force, he proceeded carefully. After tracing his most accurate bathymetric chart of Point Arguello and the waters that lay west of it, he began the tedious job of drawing in the various curving depth lines. He extended these lines to a position eighteen nautical miles due west of the coastline. This portion of subterranean Arguello Canyon lay some 2,400 feet beneath the ocean's surface. Next, he began sketching in the Titan's supposed debris field. He had just finished indicating the position of the wreckage found during the Razorback's preliminary sonar scan when a pair of moist lips kissed him on the back of his neck. At first startled by this unexpected intrusion, Richard turned and set his eyes on the smiling face of Miriam.

"Well, good morning, Dr. Fuller. Aren't you the industrious one? Worked all through the night, have you?"

Realizing that he had been completely lost in his work, Richard caught sight of the clock that was hung over the fireplace. He could hardly believe that it read 6:45.

"Good morning to you, Princess," he said. "Actually, I've only been up a little less than two hours. How did you sleep?"

"Like a kid again," answered the archaeologist as she bent over to give him a peck on the lips. "How about you?"

"What I lacked in quantity, I more than made up for in quality. Would you like some breakfast? There's a fresh pot of coffee in the kitchen."

Pulling Richard's over-sized, white terry-cloth robe around her, Miriam nodded. "That coffee sounds great. I'm still not much of a breakfast eater."

As she began walking into the kitchen, she added, "What are you working on anyway?"

Richard's response was hesitant. "It's a project for Lieutenant Colonel Lansford. I'm sure you're aware that the Air Force lost a missile here the other day."

Miriam was in the process of pouring herself a mug of coffee when she answered him. "I'll say. Me and my crew had a ringside seat for the whole thing. We only got out of Ocean Beach Park in just enough time to escape a cloud of toxic chemicals that fell from the skies."

"Then I'm sure you know that the failed missile was an Air Force Titan. Because it exploded while arcing over the Pacific, I was called in to help determine the extent of the resulting debris field. That's what this chart is all about."

Positioning herself at the diningroom table's side, Miriam sipped her coffee and looked down at Richard's work. "Sounds like you could use an archaeologist's help."

Richard winked. "If we don't do our job correctly this first time, it will probably be someone from your field who stumbles onto a piece of the Titan in a couple of decades or so. Since these positions are only the result of a hasty sonar scan, and have yet to be verified, who knows if some of them don't turn out to be the wrecks of a fleet of Spanish treasure galleons."

"If that's the case, Richard Fuller, I expect to be one of the first ones to know of it. Now, I'd better jump in the shower and then get back to work myself. We came across a fully preserved Chumash *tomolo* canoe at our new beachside excavation site, and I promised to be there later this morning when the crew attempts to pull it out."

While Miriam continued on to the bedroom, Richard turned his attention back to the chart. He could hear the shower streaming in the background as he determined the exact spot where the Marlin had made the previous day's surprising discovery. Marking this site with an X, he then drew a line eastward, to connect it with the rest of the debris field some seven and a half miles away. Wondering what could account for the unusual distance between these two sites, the NOSC researcher could only hope that the Marlin's luck held. Perhaps, even as he sat there, the brave crew of the DSRV was already preparing to get under way. If fate were still with them, perhaps this day's findings would somehow help solve the puzzle that lay so visible before him.

Chapter Ten

Lieutenant Colonel Todd Lansford had been expecting this new day to be a full one, yet little could he have ever guessed how it was to start off. It all began with an emergency phone call that arrived at his home at 5:25 A.M. Awakened out of a sound sleep, Lansford groped for the telephone, and soon found himself on the line with the commander of Vandenberg's Second Weather Squadron. The warning this serious-toned officer had to relate was unlike any that Lansford had ever received before. It was from the National Oceanic and Atmospheric Administration's Honolulu office, and consisted of a tsunami alert.

Not yet fully awake, Lansford had to ask the commander to repeat himself. This time, the base's senior meteorologist related the following facts. At approximately 5:01 A.M., an earthquake registering 7.1 on the Richter scale had shaken the waters off Alaska's Kodiak Island. As the two subterranean crustal plates comprising the Aleutian fault line had snapped with a tremendous release of stored force, a fan-like quiver of energy had surged out into the Pacific basin. To the north, this energy took the form of a massive earthquake. As a result, dozens of buildings had collapsed in nearby Anchorage. Preliminary reports showed at least two dozen people dead and hundreds more injured there.

To the south, this unleased force was expressing itself in the form of a monstrous tidal wave. Traveling at a speed of over 500 miles per hour, this fifty-foot-high wall of water could hit the central California coastline as early as 10:00 A.M. that very morning.

By the time the commander had related these grim facts, Lansford was wide awake. A cold shiver of dread coursed through his body as he visualized the tidal wave crashing into Vandenberg's western boundary. Leaving the meteorologist with orders to give him updates on the half-hour, Lansford disconnected the line and then hastily dialed the apartment of Master Sergeant Vince Sprawlings. After explaining their situation, he directed Sprawlings to meet him at his office at once. Accepting the master sergeant's offer to pick him up on the way in, Lansford made one more call before sprinting to the shower. He found himself somewhat surprised to hear that the deputy commander of the 4392nd Security Police Group had already been informed of the alert. Though he had just been awoken from bed himself, the deputy commander was already sketching up a preliminary evacuation plan. Directing him to bring this blue-print over to base headquarters at once, Lansford ran straight from his bed into the bathroom. At it turned out, Vince Sprawlings was just pulling into his driveway when he emerged fully dressed from his front door.

The fog made driving hazardous, yet Sprawlings knew the route well. By 6:00 A.M. he had the lieutenant colonel in his office, in just enough time to greet Deputy Commander Bill Rose of Vandenberg's Security Police Group. With coffee cups in hand, the two senior officers huddled before a map of the base that the burly, crew-out security chief had pulled from his briefcase.

"This map is from the Master Contingency Disaster Plan," stated the no-nonsense deputy commander. "It shows the areas of our western boundary that lay within the tidal-wave inundation zone. As you can see, the only major structures directly threatened are those situated at the Point Arguello docksite. It's imperative that we order an immediate evacuation of all personnel, and get going with the transfer of all moveable equipment inland."

Lansford's face lit up. "We mustn't forget the Razorback and the Marlin. I wonder if the Navy has contacted them as yet."

Bill Rose replied icily, "Even if they haven't, the safest place for those two vessels to meet the wave is at least one mile offshore. When Point Arguello is contacted, we'll remind the Navy of this fact."

"What about the launch complexes?" queried Lansford.

The deputy commander traced a line from Point Arguello northward. "Most of the launch sites are situated high enough to be free from any threat of flooding. The only positions that could be marginal are the Minutemen silos located in the northern sector of the base, off Point Sal Road."

"Then seal them up," directed Lansford. "Also, once the evacuation is completed, both Point Sal and Coast Roads are to be closed to all traffic. Then I want the Civil Defense sirens activated, and the proper bulletins released over both radio and television."

"I think it's a good idea to scramble the Hueys," added Rose. "The choppers can comb the coastline and the immediate waters, to inform any strays who miss our warnings."

Lansford nodded. "Good idea, Bill. With your expert assistance, we'll ride this wave out with a minimum of damage. Secretary Fitzpatrick couldn't have picked a worse day for his surprise visit."

"It will all be over by the time his plane touches down at noon," said Rose. "He won't even know that anything out of the ordinary occurred here this morning."

"I hope to God you're right," retorted Lansford, whose weary eyes went to the wall-mounted clock. Taking in the time, he realized that in less than three and a half hours they'd all know the outcome for sure.

Two hours later, the exact manner in which they would meet their predicament was a bit clearer. Even from his office, Lansford could hear the warning sirens wailing in the distance. A similar sound could be heard in communities up and down the western coast of North America. Confident that Vandenberg was prepared for the worse, he still was concerned with the Point Arguello dockside facility.

Only minutes before, the base's security chief had called him from this site. There, the evacuation of men and material was going smoothly. Even the piece of Titan debris that the DSRV Marlin had recently exhumed from the ocean had been moved to higher ground. This left the massive, solid-rocket booster warehouse as the only installation of significant value that lay in the tidal wave's inundation zone. Most aware that there was absolutely nothing he could do to further protect the multi-million-dollar facility from the ever-approaching wall of water, Lansford could only pray that all base personnel were safely out of harm's way when the tsunami struck. He was about to call Bill Rose to reiterate this point when his intercom buzzed. This was followed by the deep voice of Master Sergeant Sprawlings.

"Sir, Dr. Fuller is here with that chart you asked him to draw up for the Secretary."

Having completely forgotten about this request, Lansford responded, "Send him in."

The NOSC researcher looked confused as he entered the inner office. "Sergeant Sprawlings was just explaining what these sirens are all about. Since I haven't heard a TV or radio yet this morning, I thought it was all some sort of practice drill. Actually, I would have guessed that the Russians were landing before associating the sirens with a tsunami alert. I haven't been in one of these things since the spring of '86, when I was working on the north shore of Kauai. At that time, it was another Aleutian quake that provoked the warning. Fortunately, the tidal wave failed to materialize."

"I only hope we're so lucky," said Lansford, whose tone was already heavy with fatigue. "We'll know in another hour and a half. Would you like to see a map of the inundation zone?"

"Of course," replied Richard, who was well aware that a tidal wave could be one of the most destructive forces Mother Nature could unlease against man.

As his eyes studied the chart that the lieutenant colonel handed to him, he noticed the black hatchmarks that completely covered the coastline. Those finely drawn lines were especially thick around the section of beach just south of Point Arguello. Drawn to show the extent of the overflowing waters as they crashed onto land, the hatch-marks continued up northward. He couldn't help but notice how they covered Ocean Beach Park.

"Has anyone thought of personally notifying that

crew of student archaeologists?" asked Richard.

Lansford answered matter-of-factly, "The park is well covered by sirens. I'm certain that they've heard the radio bulletins by now and that they're safe and sound in Lompoc."

"Maybe you can take such a thing for granted, but I certainly can't," said Richard. "I can't believe you didn't at least send someone down to check on them!"

"Easy now, Doctor. Those kids will be just fine. Our security force has the matter well in hand. We've even got helicopters combing the beach for any stragglers."

"That's still not good enough," retorted Richard, his face flushed with concern. "If you don't mind, I'd like to drive down there to make certain that they're out."

Unaware of what all the fuss was about, the lieutenant colonel reacted angrily. "As a matter of fact, I do mind, Doctor. As of 0800 hours, all roads leading down to the coastline have been placed off limits. The South Vandenberg Security Gate has been notified to admit emergency personnel only."

"Well, please notify them to let me through, Colonel. I won't be able to rest until I know those kids are safe."

Realizing that the researcher was not about to take no for an answer, Lansford reluctantly gave in. "I still think you're being silly, but go on down there if it's so damn important to you. Yet I'm warning you, if you're not out of there in another hour, I'm sending one of those choppers in to pull you out. Now, where's that chart that I asked you to draw up for the Secretary?"

Richard Fuller's mind was already concentrating on the route he'd utilize to drive down to the beach as he handed the map to Lansford and abruptly excused himself. Not even stopping to return Sergeant Sprawling's goodbye, Fuller sprinted from the office and headed immediately for his car. As he raced through the main administrative area, he took in the sound of the wailing sirens and the ever-present swirling fingers of thick, gray fog. Ignoring the base speed limit, he began his way down the long, sloping roadway that led directly into the only route to Ocean Beach Park. With the resulting elevation change, the fog closed in even tighter. So thick was it that he saw the locked sentry gate only at the last moment. To the squeal of grinding brakes, he skidded up beside the guardhouse.

It seemed to take an eternity for the smartly uniformed sentry to greet him. "Going a bit fast, weren't you, sir?"

Richard responded hurriedly. "I'm sorry, but it's imperative that I get down to Ocean Beach Park as soon as possible."

In no rush of his own, the guard shook his beret-clad head. "I'm afraid that could be a bit difficult, sir. You see, because of this tidal-wave alert, entry to all points west of here is no longer permitted."

Though he tried to hold back his temper, Richard exploded. "For God's sake man, I'm fully aware of that! My name is Dr. Fuller, and Lieutenant Colonel Lansford has given me permission to enter."

"That's news to me," returned the sentry, who didn't like his visitor's tone of voice. "If you'll excuse me for a second, I'll have to check this out with headquarters."

Richard's blood pressure was soaring as the guard turned to return to his kiosk with deliberate slowness. The NOSC researcher checked his watch and figured he would have just about an hour to reach Miriam before the tidal wave hit. Fighting the impulse to hurry the sentry with his horn, he contemplated the irony of it all. Here he had been without Miriam for over a decade now, and just as he had rediscovered how important she was to him, he ran the risk of losing her to a mere whim of nature's fury. He was in the process of remembering that fateful moment when he had first set his eyes on her in the confines of Lansford's office when the sentry stepped outside.

"Sorry about that, sir, but you have indeed received permission to pass. Please keep your speed down, and buckle that seatbelt. This fog's a lot worse down at the coastline, so be extra alert."

Taking in this motherly advice, Richard hit the accelerator the second that the gate popped open. Barely five minutes later he was somewhat cautiously pulling into the mist-shrouded parking lot that was his goal.

The semi-circle of parked trailers appeared like a ghostly apparition in the foreground. As he jumped from the car, he was aware of the faraway, banshee-like wail of a warning siren, and beyond this, the crash of distant surf. No other sounds were audible.

It took him only seconds to cross the lot and enter the camp. He found a single individual seated at a picnic table, her attention totally focused on the ornate shell necklace that she was delicately cleaning. In order not to frighten the brunette, who was dressed in a bright red ski jacket, Richard loudly cleared his voice while still several yards away from her.

"Hello," he added. "Is Miss Rodgers around?"

Even with the warning, the young woman seemed startled by his presence. Turning around quickly, she centered her gaze on the tall, khaki-clad figure who was emerging from the fog.

"I'm afraid not," she answered hesitantly. "Can I

help you?"

Striding up beside her, Richard could see that she was only in her late teens. "I'm Dr. Richard Fuller, a friend of Miss Rodgers. Have the rest of you been evacuated?"

"Evacuated?" quizzed the undergraduate. "What do you mean by that?"

No other words were needed for Richard Fuller to have his worst fears realized. "This coastline is under a tidal-wave alert. It's scheduled to hit here in another hour. Haven't you wondered what all the sirens were about?"

Shocked by this revelation, the young archaeologist's voice wavered. "The only time I've ever heard a siren like that was back home in Kansas during tornado season. Since I didn't think that we had twisters here, I assumed it was just some sort of military test."

"I wish it were," said Richard, whose own tone of voice softened. "Now, where's Miss Rodgers and the rest of your classmates?"

Having instinctively accepted this stranger's legitimacy, Margaret Samuels was quick to answer. "They're all down at the new excavation site. It's about a mile south of here, and accessible only by foot."

Again checking his watch, Richard asked nervously, "Do you think that you could lead me to them? It's vital that they reach high ground before that wave strikes."

Without hesitation, Margaret stood and pointed to the west. "The only way to get there is by crossing the beach. Come on, I'll show you."

Thankful for her trust, Richard followed her out of the camp, and down a sandy footpath that lay beside the Santa Ynez River. There, the fog progressively thickened. Barely able to see the wide channel of water that flowed on his right, he noted that the trail cut beneath a railroad trestle up ahead. An icy gust, full with the scent of the ocean, hit him as he crossed beneath this large, wooden structure and passed by the river's estuary. It wasn't until they actually hit the surf line that their progress turned southward.

Margaret kept a brisk pace, and Richard needed a total effort to keep up with her. Eventually, he settled in beside the young student, and with the waves crashing to their right, Margaret asked him, "How do you know Miss Rodgers? Are you with the Air Force?"

"Believe it or not, we went to college together. We met here, quite by accident, yesterday afternoon."

Still curious, Margaret continued, "What are you doing here in Vandenberg?"

Most aware of his companion's probing intellect, Richard cautiously answered, "I'm giving the Air Force a hand in the recovery of that missile that failed here the other day. I believe all of you saw it go down."

"We sure did," observed Margaret excitedly. "It was really an incredible sight. For a second there, when I set my eyes on that orange mushroom-shaped cloud that filled the skies, I was afraid that a nuclear bomb had gone off. From what I was able to view, I didn't think there was much left of that thing to recover."

"You'd be surprised," said Richard. "So far, we've catalogued over five hundred good-sized chunks of debris lying on the floor of the Pacific west of here. Now the tough part is to scoop up each piece and bring it to the surface."

Margaret didn't seem impressed. "I wonder how many millions that exploding rocket cost us taxpayers. If the leaders of the world would only grow up, they'd realize that all this needless military expenditure is not only a colossal waste of money and resources, it's life-threatening as well. Someday, some poor fool is going to push the wrong button, and goodbye Planet Earth."

"I agree with you on that, young lady. We've been lucky for four decades, but who knows how much longer our fortune will hold."

"By the way, my name's Margaret Samuels, and I'm in Miss Rodger's upper-level lab class."

Not breaking his stride, Richard smiled. "Pleased to know you, Margaret. I'm glad you were around. Otherwise I would have had a heck of a time finding this place. How much further do we have?"

Because the fog still veiled any familiar geographic features, Margaret could only check her watch. "The hike takes about twenty minutes, so we should be there in approximately ten minutes more."

Checking his own watch, Richard saw that this would get them there at 9:30. That should give him just enough time to get the crew to high ground.

The wet, firm sand provided excellent traction and Margaret didn't seem to tire in the least. Though Richard had been chilly at first, a thick line of sweat now soaked his forehead. His calves were sore, and he silently cursed his lousy physical condition. Daily swimming and cycling were what he needed to counter this. Of course, his advancing years didn't help much. And to think that, just the previous night, he had actually felt like a young, college-aged boy again. Reality set in only when he noticed that Margaret's stride was easily outdistancing his own. There had been a time not long ago when she would have been hard-pressed to catch him.

Margaret suddenly pointed anxiously ahead of her.

243

"There's the gang's footprints. We go due east here."

Sighting these tracks himself, Richard followed her as she swung to the left. The sand was softer there, the going a bit tougher. Yet just knowing that they were close put new spring into Fuller's step. The sound of the surf faded behind them, and as they approached a series of dunes, the fog began lifting. It had dissipated almost completely by the time they climbed around the dunes and crossed a hilly plain filled with low-lying scrub and cactus. As it turned out, it was 9:30 exactly when they spotted the first member of the crew, innocently working at the base of a steep, rocky canyon. Well aware that a good-sized tsunami could easily inundate this portion of coastline, Richard pressed himself to lengthen his stride.

They arrived just in time to witness the team in the process of lifting a long, narrow, canoe-like vessel from a crypt of dried mud and rock. Miriam had been supervising this effort, and was the first crew member to spot the newcomers. From the first moment that she set her astounded eyes on them, she had a feeling that this wasn't a mere social visit. Leaving the excavation, she walked over to issue a greeting.

"Good morning, you two. Well, Richard, this sure is a surprise."

Fuller didn't even allow himself a second to catch his breath. "All of you must leave this area at once to seek high ground. In less than thirty minutes, a wall of water higher than a ten-story building will crash into the coast here at a speed of over five hundred miles per hour."

Hardly believing what she was hearing, Miriam could only think of a single thing. "Do you mean a tsunami?"

Richard's eyes flashed. "Precisely. It was generated

244

as a result of a major earthquake in the Aleutian Islands. Since it's scheduled to strike the central California coastline at 10:00 A.M., we've got just about a half hour to get out of this inundation zone."

As the reality sunk in, Miriam paled. "First we witness a missile explode right before our eyes, and now this. The crew is never going to believe it. Come on, we'd better inform them."

Without further delay, she led them towards the floor of the rugged canyon. There, still concentrating totally on their work, the young archaeologists were in the process of admiring the object that they had just dug out of the rocky hillside. A tall, solidly built Indian in his early twenties stood at the group's head. It was towards this bare-chested figure that Miriam moved.

"Joseph, kids, we're going to have to wrap up our dig here right now. I know this sounds somewhat unbelievable, but in less than thirty minutes, this canyon could be awash with the after-effects of a tidal wave."

Joseph Solares shook his head in wonder. "Tidal wave? You've got to be kidding us, Boss."

Miriam's firm tone didn't falter. "I wish I was, but apparently this threat is very real. This gentleman beside me, who was good enough to hike out here with the warming, is Dr. Richard Fuller. Richard, would you like to add anything?"

Sizing up the looks of astonishment on the faces of his young audience, Richard responded, "Believe me when I tell you that I was just as shocked as you are when I first heard of the alert barely an hour ago. But unfortunately, it's a very real one. As an oceanographer, I've studied dozens of eyewitness accounts by tidal-wave survivors, and there's no denying the awesome destructive power that such phenomena can generate. Since we're presently standing in a major flood zone, our only defense is finding some high ground, and getting there on the double."

A tall beanpole of a lad pointed towards the summit of the adjoining canyon. "Is that high enough, Doctor?"

Shading his eyes from the sun's incessant glare, Richard peered upward and viewed the portion of hilltop that the young man indicated. "That will be more than sufficient."

This time it was Miriam who added, "Then it's settled. We'll pack up all that we can carry and start at once for the trail leading up there."

Only a single deep voice sounded out in complaint. "But the *tomolo*!" said Joseph Solares. "We can't just leave it here to get washed away. It's one of the best-preserved specimens that I've ever seen before."

Most aware that he was right, Miriam thought a minute before answering him. "Do you think that a couple of you could safely carry it up the hill?"

Without hesitation, Joseph retorted, "Of course we could."

"Then get going!" said Miriam, who added, "The University might not agree, but surely a couple of picks and shovels are expendable in this case. Now, move it, kids! We've all got some climbing to do."

While the youngsters scurried for whatever belongings they could carry, Richard's eyes went to his watch. Calculating that they'd just have enough time to reach the canyon's summit, he knew that he had been extremely lucky. A delay of a mere fifteen minutes could have had disastrous implications. It was while pondering this fact that he became aware of a distant chopping sound. As he scanned the horizon to determine its source, his gaze caught sight of a single green Huey helicopter, sweeping in from the south. The sound of its approach rapidly increased as the sleek vehicle initiated a sudden descent. Soon it was hovering only a few hundred feet above them.

A resounding, amplified voice emanated from the chopper's public-address system. "Attention all civilians, you must evacuate this area at once! Please proceed immediately to the nearest high ground. A tidal wave is expected to hit this coast in less than ten minutes, and you are presently occupying a predetermined flood zone."

The message was repeated, and Richard Fuller tried to signal the helicopter crew that they understood. Only when the first of the students began their way up the narrow canyon trail, did the chopper dip its nose and speed off northwards.

Better late than never, thought Richard, who realized that Lieutenant Colonel Lansford had come through after all. With this in mind, he looked on as three of the young archaeologists shouldered their treasured canoe with a grunt and began their own way to safety. Miriam filed in behind them and waved for Richard to join her. Certain that no one else was left behind, he gratefully did so.

Twenty-one miles to the west of the beachside canyon, the Pacific surged with a deceptive calm. The lapping blue waters gave little hint of the violent swell that continued its mad approach from the northwest.

This tranquility was especially apparent from a depth of 450 feet beneath the water's surface. There the U.S.S. Razorback had been positioned to meet the tsunami's fury. From his usual command position, at the rear of the torpedo well, Commander Philip Exeter surveyed the hushed control room. To his left was his XO, Patrick Benton. The calm-tempered redhead had his trusty corn-cob pipe between his lips, and was in the process of looking over the shoulder of Lieutenant Edward McClure. As usual, the scholarly Navigator was hunched over his charts.

Seated to their left was Lester Brawnley. The portly Chief of the Boat alertly waited at the diving station for any ordered change in their depth status. Beside him sat the young helmsman, whose steady hands ultimately controlled the boat's destiny.

The firm voice of the sub's OOD, Lieutenant Scott Willingham, addressed Exeter from the portion of the deck situated immediately before the Captain. "Sir, all hands are standing by at battle stations. The boat is secured to meet a concussion."

Studying the determined, clean-shaven face of the OOD, Exeter nodded. "Continue on course two-six-zero until further ordered, Lieutenant. I want you to remain at the helm until this wave passes, so hang in there.

Willingham's expression was all business as he pivoted to recheck their course and depth. The young man's no-nonsense approach was continuing to impress the Captain. Too many rookie officers tried to hide their insecurities with humor. Though there was a time and place for wisecracks, this surely wasn't one of them.

This would be the Captain's first experience meeting a legendary tsunami at sea. Though a certain amount of nervous anticipation possessed him, he didn't dare show it. His command position made it necessary that he set the example for the others to follow.

His eyes went to the clock and he saw that there were five more minutes until the wave was to arrive. At their present depth, the tsunami's after-effects should be minimal. Just in case it were otherwise, he made certain that there was plenty of water surrounding their hull. Twenty-one miles from the nearest land, and with the nearest subterranean geological feature an additional 3,000 feet beneath them, the Razorback was buttoned down and ready for the worst.

Six and a half miles due east of them, Commander Will Pierce hoped he had the Marlin in a similar condition. Even though the DSRV was considerably smaller than the Razorback, its deep-diving capability should keep them well out of danger.

Exeter found himself subconsciously wishing that the wave would go ahead and pass. Only then could he get on with the patrol that had made the previous twenty-four hours extremely hectic, frustrating ones. He still couldn't get over the fact that the Soviet Victor had successfully evaded them. Yesterday, they had chased the bogy all the way to San Miguel Island. It was in those tricky waters that they lost it.

He could only assume that the Soviet skipper had put his sub down on the bottom there, and then scrammed his reactor. Unless he was utilizing some sort of novel anechoic-coating masking device, this was the only way that they could have disappeared so thoroughly, in so little time.

In an attempt to relocate them, Exeter had resorted to a variety of proven tactics. This had included ordering the Razorback to sprint and drift. By shutting down the sub in a state of ultra-quiet, he had known that their hydrophones would be better able to listen in on the surrounding waters without their own noise interfering. When a scan proved fruitless, he had ordered the boat to move on to an adjoining sector, where the same listening procedure had been repeated.

This process had continued on for a good portion of the night, until the Razorback's prior commitment had ultimately forced them to return to Point Arguello. As it turned out, this usually simple, two-hour voyage had turned into one of the most demanding trips he had ever embarked upon. Veiled by the night itself, and one of the thickest fogs that he had ever witnessed, the sub had been able to get back to the Arguello docksite without a single scrape, by the grace of God and the cool skill of his crew. Special commendations had gone to their radar operator, whose expertise had allowed them to stay well clear of the jagged rocks that helped earn these waters the nickname "the graveyard of the Pacific."

No sooner had they arrived at port then preparations for reloading the Marlin had had to be initiated. Barely two hours had passed before the Razorback had been once again knifing its way through the fog-shrouded waters.

Dawn was just lighting the ghostly horizon, when they had been informed of the tsunami alert. Since standard operating procedure would send them to sea to meet the wave anyway, they had decided to continue on with their mission as planned. Fourteen and a half miles west of Arguello, the Marlin had been dropped off. An hour later, the Razorback had attained its current position.

A slight shift of the deck beneath him diverted Exeter's attention back to the bulkhead-mounted clock. He noted the time, 10:00 A.M., as the firm voice of the seaman assigned to monitor the comm line broke the relative silence that had prevailed.

"Sonar reports the receipt of an unusually loud tidal surge topside!"

Instantly knowing what this meant, Exeter called out calmly, "Brace yourselves, gentlemen. It's here."

250

No sooner were these words delivered than the Razorback violently lurched forward, as the tsunami sucked back the waters that lay before it. This was followed by a massive concussion that sent the submarine reeling on its starboard side.

Thrown to his right, the Captain strained to remain standing. Held upright only by the grip his hands had on the bulkhead security railing, Exeter felt the cold steel bite into his palms. The lights overhead momentarily blinked off, then on again, as the sub was tossed in the opposite direction. This time the Captain's grip failed, and he went slamming into the navigation table. The powerful grasp of his XO kept him from falling down completely. Unfortunately, this was not the case with Lieutenant Willingham, who was thrown to the deck immediately beside the harness-secured helmsman.

The deck canted again to the right, yet this time the angle was much less severe. Only then did the straining hull finally stabilize.

By the time the deck had settled beneath them, Willingham had already lifted himself up from his prone position. As he brushed aside his blond, wavy hair, it was evident that there was more injury to the young lieutenant's pride than to his body. Quick to station himself back at the periscope well, he lost no time in regaining his composure.

"Damage Control, I need an immediate report on the condition of the boat! Helmsman, how's she responding?"

As the control room drifted back into normalcy, Exeter was aware of a shooting pain in his right knee. Fighting to ignore it, he limped over to the OOD's side. Only when he was certain that the Razorback had ridden out the concussion with no serious injuries or mechanical failures did he turn back to the navigation station. There the XO swiftly intercepted him.

"Are you okay, Skipper? That was a pretty wicked knock you took on that table."

Rubbing his already swelling knee-joint, Exeter fought to control the pain. "I'll live, Mr. Benton, though if it wasn't for your strong arms, things could have been a lot worse."

The XO could see that the Captain was hurting, and found it impossible to hide his concern. "I think that it's best if you got off that leg for a while, Skipper. Some aspirin wouldn't hurt either."

Knowing that the XO was probably right, Exeter sighed. "I'll allow myself that luxury only when we know for certain whether or not the Marlin rode out that wave safely."

"She was a huge one, all right," offered Benton. "I never dreamed it would touch us down here."

"Neither did I," said Exeter grimly. "Now, let's just pray that Will Pierce put that DSRV in the deepest damn hole that he could find."

Only a few seconds after the tsunami passed over the Razorback, it bit into the waters where the Marlin was attempting to hide from its fury. Even though the DSRV was at a depth of 900 feet, the wave's powerful currents lifted the thirty-six-ton vessel as though it were a mere feather in the wind.

Commander Will Pierce had been expecting the worst, and he valiantly fought to guide the mini-sub from the tidal surge that soon had them in tow. Much as an experienced swimmer meets a riptide, Pierce attempted to steer the Marlin in a lateral course. This routine tactic was just showing some merit when an agitated torrent of sea water struck their hull and sent the vessel tumbling on its side.

Shocked by the unexpected strength of this surge, the crew was caught totally by surprise. As the lights flickered, and finally faded out altogether, Pierce and his co-pilot, Lieutenant Lance Blackmore, felt their safety harnesses bite into their shoulders. Behind them, Ensign Louis Marvin tumbled backwards, and only escaped serious injury by grapping hold of one of the bench-posts that lined the rear pressure capsule.

In the ensuing blackness, Pierce groped for the controls. Conscious that the vessel's bow was abruptly pointed downwards, he struggled to retrim the Marlin. When his hands finally grasped the ballast vents, he activated the proper switches even without the benefit of light. A feeling of sickening dread filled his gut when the familiar rush of venting sea water failed to meet his ears. Again he hit the switch, yet still the ballast mechanism would not trigger. He knew this could mean only one thing. The Marlin had lost the use of its hydraulic system. Without it, they would continue to be pulled downward, unable to counter the force of the current that now had them solidly in its grasp.

Seated on Pierce's right, the DSRV's co-pilot was also quite aware of their precarious trim. With limbs heavy and his pulse beating madly, Blackmore fought to contain the panic that was rising to possess him. Well aware that his first responsibility was to reset the circuit breaker to provide them with lighting, Blackmore struggled to raise his right arm upwards. As if caught in a recurring nightmare, the young lieutenant knew that this was no mere dream. His life, and that of two others, could very possibly rest on his current efforts. Oblivious to the terror that called him to escape in a tight, embryonic ball, Blackmore summoned his every last ounce of will, and somehow prevailed. His right index finger hit the plastic circuit breaker, and almost instantaneously the compartment filled with glowing, blessed light.

It took several seconds for his pupils to adjust to the illumination, and when they eventually did, he looked almost shamefully to his left. Expecting to meet the Commander's disappointed stare, Blackmore was surprised to find Pierce cowering in panic. Soaked in sweat and with limbs quivering, the gray-haired veteran officer sat rigidly forward, his eyes locked on the boat's depth gauge. Blackmore's own gut soured as he realized that they were in the midst of a spiraling, uncontrollable dive. Showing a depth well beyond twelve hundred feet at the moment, the gauge was spinning ever downward without apparent constraint.

His mouth was dry and throat tight, yet somehow Lance managed to speak. "Commander Pierce, what in God's name is happening?"

When this query didn't even produce a blink in response, Blackmore screamed out desperately, "Jesus, Commander, pull us out of here!"

Pierce still didn't budge, and his co-pilot could think of but a single course of action. Unbuckling his safely harness, he strained to his left and reached out for the steering yoke. Just as he was about to grasp this metallic handle, Pierce came alive and brushed his hand away.

"It's useless," observed the commander, his usually powerful voice subdued and cracking. "The moment that second concussion struck, we lost all hydraulics."

To demonstrate this point, Pierce pulled the yoke back into his lap with only a single finger. Completely ignoring this movement, the depth gauge continued its mad spin downwards.

"There's got to be something that we can do!" countered Blackmore. "How about jettisoning the emergency mercury-filled ballast tank?"

"Not without hydraulics," returned the commander weakly.

Still shocked with Pierce's state of mind, Blackmore forgot his own panic as his being struggled for survival. Reattaching his harness, he hastily scanned the console before him. With a desperate coolness that he was only now discovering, the co-pilot activated the vessel's sonar and triggered its bathymeter. It didn't take long for these systems to chatter alive, and he soon had an accurate picture of just what lay beneath them.

Three hundred and seventy-five feet below their hull was the jagged summit of this portion of Arguello Canyon. A thousand feet below this ridge was the floor of the valley itself. Even if they could make it to the bottom there without smashing into the surrounding volcanic walls, it would put them at the extreme threshold of their operational diving depth. Yet, without any effective means of steering the Marlin, there was little chance that they'd ever escape the razor-sharp precipices that were all too quickly approaching.

They were less than 100 feet from the first of these serrated ledges, when a voice groggily called out from the rear pressure capsule. "What in the hell is going on up there?"

Having completely forgotten about their ensign, Blackmore turned around to address him. "We've lost our hydraulics, Louis. Right now, we're in the midst of an uncontrollable dive, with the walls of Arguello Canyon directly beneath us."

"Wonderful," returned the ensign, without the least hint of panic. "Anyone think of checking the aft hydraulic power unit?"

"Go for it, Louis!" replied Blackmore. "But make

it snappy. Time is definitely not on our side."

Though Lance Blackmore had pretty well given up hope by now, there was always the slim chance that the ensign would stumble onto something. Consigning himself to meet death in the bravest manner possible, he took three deep breaths and turned to meet the glance of the man who sat beside him.

By this time, Pierce had regained control of his nerves. His stare was clear, his own breath steady, as he looked into the eyes of the young man who sat on his right. Appearing calm and collected, Lieutenant Blackmore glowed with an inner peace and maturity that had been absent beforehand. Invigorated by this show of strength, Pierce bravely smiled. Blackmore returned this grin, and the two officers found themselves closely linked by a common fate.

For men who daily risked their lives, panic was no stranger. Yet a thin line lay between those who controlled this natural anxiety and those who let it get the best of them. Both officers had seen each other in the midst of such an inner conflict. Both had also been around to watch their co-worker conquer this oldest of fears. The result was a bond that not even death could fracture.

Less than thirty feet from a series of needle-sharp volcanic pinnacles, the Marlin shuddered in a sudden spasm. A long-absent electronic whine accompanied this movement, and Pierce knew instinctively what this meant. With a familiar delicacy, he reached forward to regrasp the steering yoke. His pulse quickened as this time his touch met resistance. Hydraulic pressure had been miraculously restored!

Conscious of just what was occurring beside him, Blackmore snapped into action. "Turn hard aport to bearing two-seven-zero!"

With one eye on the bathymeter, the young lieutenant determined the course that would keep them from the jaws of death. Trusting his judgment implicitly, Pierce followed his directions without question.

The Marlin's hydraulics were still somewhat sluggish to respond, yet they provided just enough control to allow them to miss the first series of obstacles. As the ledge of rock passed only inches to their right, Blackmore couldn't help but express his relief.

"All right, Louis! What in hell did you do back there?"

The ensign replied boldly, "It just ain't my time to go yet, Lieutenant. Fortunately, after a good old-fashioned whack on the hydraulic pump, the good Lord concurred."

"Well, don't celebrate too prematurely," interrupted Pierce. "Though we've got our lateral control back, I still can't brake us from this dive. Lieutenant, what's it look like beneath us?"

Blackmore responded while rechecking the bathymeter. "We're angling in between the canyon's walls now. The bottom still lies some seven hundred feet away. If we do reach it, that will put us at least twenty-five feet below our depth threshold, sir."

"I figured as much," returned Pierce solemnly. "Yet until we get our venting systems back on line, the Marlin's just going to have to take it. Seal her up tight, gentlemen. We're about to see what this baby's really made of."

The depth gauge continued to register their descent, and the hull creaked and moaned in response. A tense silence prevailed, as Pierce did his best to slow the speed of the drop. Guiding the DSRV in a wide, spiraling circle, he was able to brake the rate of descent rather drastically.

"I hope you've picked out a nice, soft, sandy spot for us to touch down on," said Pierce to his co-pilot.

Blackmore still had his doubts as to whether the Marlin's hull would even get them to that point. Suddenly Marvin's voice sounded. "Try those vents again, Commander!"

Immediately reaching forward, Pierce hit the ballast trigger. The familiar gush of venting sea water met their ears, and the Marlin shuddered in response. With the assistance of the vessel's thrusters, the level of descent was gradually eased, until the DSRV lay hovering, level in the water.

"Glory be!" sighed Pierce, who only then took the time to wipe off the sweat that had gathered on his forehead. "And will you look at that! We've got a whole seventy feet of ocean left until we hit bottom. I knew we'd make this depth. What's down there anyway, Lieutenant?"

Blackmore's glance was rivoted on the sonar screen. "Good thing we didn't hit here, sir. Though it's certainly flat, the ocean bottom seems to be comprised of solid rock."

Pierce shrugged his shoulders. "Since the fates took us down this far, how about taking a closer look at it? Another fifty feet or so won't hurt us."

Offering no objections of his own, Blackmore hit the Marlin's bow spotlights, as Pierce gently directed the vessel downward. After tilting the video camera toward the sea floor, Lance bent over to peer into the lap-mounted viewing port.

At first he could see nothing but the swirling, turbid waters themselves. Even at this great depth, the thick, primordial ooze had been stirred up by the tsunami's passage. Only when Pierce lowered them another five feet did the sea floor become visible.

Formed from a series of flat, smoothly hewn rocks, the ocean bottom there looked more like some sort of cobblestone pathway. Lance Blackmore couldn't help but make this association as his eyes alertly scanned the depths.

"It almost looks like there's a man-made road down here," observed the lieutenant, who realized the absurdity of such a statement.

Quick to study his own viewing port, Pierce shook his head in wonder. "I'll be damned, it sure as hell does. I've never seen anything quite like this before. What's our current heading?"

Blackmore checked their course and answered, "We're cruising due west, sir."

"I'd like to see how far this phenomenon extends, Lieutenant. Zap the waters with our sonar, and see what it looks like ahead of us."

While Blackmore got to work on this, Ensign Marvin snuggled in between them. "What's so interesting, Commander?"

Without looking up from his viewing column, Pierce answered, "It almost looks like we found a section of the freeway grid that the auto club missed on their maps. What do you make of it, Ensign?"

Swinging the column over for Louis to have a look, Pierce waited for the ensign's response. "It certainly does, Commander. If this is a by-product of mother nature, it's awfully freaky. Those stones down there sure look like they were placed by hand."

"We're picking up something else straight ahead of us, sir," interrupted Lance. "It seems to be some sort of rock formation. Sonar shows that it's semicircular in shape and comprised of six separate, large stones, approximately seven feet tall and three feet wide. It's still a good mile distant."

"Anything else out there?" queried Pierce curiously.

"That seems to be it, Commander. Until you reach the canyon's walls, it's as flat as a pancake out there."

As he took this in, Pierce's brow tightened. "Then let's check this formation out firsthand."

Pierce opened the Marlin's throttle, and the vessel surged forward. Still hunched over the viewing column, Marvin scanned the stone thoroughfare that continued to stretch out beneath them. Though some of it was covered with sediment, most of it was unusually clear. He supposed that it could have been only recently swept clean by the deep currents which accompanied the tidal wave. Yet this certainly didn't explain how it had been formed in the first place. The one thing that he was certain of was that this was no freak of nature. The stones were too uniformly cut and laid out too perfectly for this to be true. This meant that it had to be the product of man.

With what little Louis knew of underwater geology, he supposed that this canyon could have once been part of the mainland. Most likely, an earthquake had caused its submergence many centuries before. Yet this still left in question who had originally designed it. Louis could only guess that it had been built by the ancient Spaniards, who had first visited there in the 1500's.

"We're two hundred yards in front of the formation, Commander."

Blackmore's words caused Louis to sit up, and Pierce slowed the craft to half speed. The steady hum of the Marlin's single propeller decreased proportionately. Since both officers were busy at the controls initiating their approach, Louis turned his attention back to the viewing column. Angling the tilt of the camera to scan that section of ocean directly before them, he focused in on a sight that would stay with him forever.

Projecting from the sea-floor were six massive monoliths of smooth stone. Appearing like those of Stonehenge, the monoliths were equally spaced in such a way to allow the stone roadway to neatly bisect them. Still following the center of this path, the Marlin continued its way westward.

Louis Marvin's eyes were wide with wonder as the DSRV passed into the semicircle itself. His pulse quickened as he viewed a huge black and red circle, etched into the very stone below them. He audibly gasped upon setting eyes on the object that lay at this circle's axis. For here was a white metallic nose cone, its skin fire-scarred, its base cleanly punctured. Only when he identified the five-pointed-star insignia of the Air Force that was imprinted on its base did a chill of awareness streak up his backbone.

"Jesue Christ, Commander, you're not going to believe this!"

Chapter Eleven

From an altitude of 78,000 feet above sea level, Lieutenant Grigori Yagoda sat in the cramped fuselage of the Tupolev Red Fox strategic reconnaissance aircraft. Perched before the compartment's single, heat-resistant glass porthole, the Spetsnaz commando peered down to the blue Pacific passing far below. He found it hard to fathom the fact that they were presently traveling at a speed of three times that of sound. This meant that they would be able to complete the 4,200-mile trip from Petropavlovsk in a little more than two hours' flying time.

Grigori had heard rumors that such an amazing aircraft was part of the Motherland's arsenal, and this flight proved them all true. Not only could it fly higher and faster than any plane on the planet, but, because of its design, it could do so while remaining completely undetected. Such engineering advances were beyond Grigori's comprehension. Yet, without such a platform, he doubted their present mission would have even been attempted.

Within the next half hour, they would be penetrating American airspace. He knew that the United States tactical air corps was extremely weak. Because the Soviet Union had never fielded a serious strategic bomber threat, the Yankees had put little effort into their coastal defense. With the advent of such amazing aircraft as the "Red Fox," this would soon change. Right now, they could but take advantage of their adversary's weaknesses as they best saw fit.

The roar of the Tupolev's dual continuous-bleed, after-burning turbojets filled the background with constant sound and Grigori stifled a yawn. He had slept little since leaving Afghanistan, seemingly a lifetime before. Fortunately, his two co-workers, Konstantin Lomakin and Dmitri Andreyev, had closed their eyes soon after they had taken off from Petropavlovsk. It was most important for them to be completely rested for the mission that faced them. As for himself, he'd get by with a minimum of sleep as he always did.

He looked over his shoulder and watched his companions snoring contentedly on the compartment's narrow floor. With barely enough room for the three of them and their equipment, the Red Fox was an efficient, yet uncomfortable means of transporting them into battle.

Returning his weary gaze back to the porthole, Grigori watched the sun settle towards the western horizon. Below them, a day was just about to end in America, while a new dawn was about to break over the eastern border of the Motherland. Well aware of the fickleness of time, he pondered the hectic series of events that had begun soon after they had arrived back in Kabul.

The sweet taste of revenge was still fresh on their lips as they had returned to their central base after the raid on Bamian. There, the officer in charge had seemed to have little interest in the loss of General Valerian and the entire armored column, and the team's subsequent exploits. Instead, he had accepted this news with a sigh, then handed Grigori a single set of orders. Coming directly from the Commander-in-Chief of the Strategic Rocket Forces, General Vadim Sobolev, these directives had ordered the team to be immediately flown to Petropavlovsk via an awaiting Backfire bomber.

Vadim Sobolev was an esteemed, legendary figure. A personal friend of Grigori's late father, the general was one of the highest-ranking officers in the Motherland's military. When he was a lad, his father would often take him to visit Sobolev, whom Grigori remembered as being a tall, heavy-set figure with a flowing mane of snow-white hair. Since his graduation from Leningrad's Frunze Naval War College, Grigori had seen little of the man who commanded over 1,000,000 soldiers.

Rather surprised to suddenly hear from him now, Grigori had followed his directive without question. Hardly having time to shower and change uniforms, they had loaded into the Backfire and begun the five-hour flight eastward to the Kamchatka Peninsula's southern tip.

It was cold and windy when they arrived in Petropavlovsk. Meeting them at the aircraft's hatch had been a stern-faced Spetsnaz colonel whom Grigori remembered from basic training. With a bare word of welcome, he had loaded them into a camouflaged Zil truck, and driven them to an isolated outpost.

There the team had been ordered to completely strip. Once this was accomplished, they had been each given a full set of United States Army Special Forces fatigues. From their underwear to the equipment they had been soon handed, each item was of American origin. Of special interest was the shoulder-fired, surface-to-air Stinger missile kit that he had been personally issued. Packed in a special, watertight, foam-padded carrying case, which altogether weighed less than thirty-five pounds, this weapon was a most effective one. With a range of over eight miles, and a speed several times that of sound, the Stinger's fragmentary warhead was guided to its target by an infra-red seeker that homed in on the objective's exhaust plume. He had shot one during basic training, and would never forget how deadly accurate it had been.

At this point, Grigori had been separated from his teammates. Alone in a cramped windowless room, he had waited for the arrival of the colonel, who had then begun a quick, cursory briefing. He had handed Grigori a pair of maps. One was of the island of San Miguel. This insignificant piece of desolate, volcanic rock was the northernmost outcropping in California's Channel Island chain.

The second chart was much more interesting. It provided an intricate cross-section view of the southern portion of California's Vandenberg Air Force Base. Grigori had looked up expectantly as the colonel had informed him that the first part of their mission would entail the transfer of the team to San Miguel Island. Descending by parachute, they would gather on the island's isolated western tip. There they'd place a specially designed homing device in the Pacific. This beacon would call in the Victor-class attack sub Volga, which was awaiting their arrival in the surrounding waters. It would be on the Volga that the rest of the mission would be revealed to him.

Somewhat disappointed at the extent of the briefing, Grigori hadn't even bothered questioning the colonel further. If Command had wanted him to know more, they would have told him. It was as simple as that.

Leaving Grigori with instructions to inform his men of their mission only when they had left Petropavlovsk, the colonel had wished him good fortune and abruptly exited. All too soon, they had been driven back to the airfield, where they had been loaded into their present means of transportation.

The monotonous roar of the Tupolev's engines accompanied his thoughts as Grigori remembered his first sight of the aircraft known as the Red Fox. Parked in a section of the field, far removed from the flight-line itself, the rather flat, needle-nosed plane had been covered by a protective hangar and surrounded by armed guards. Completely painted with a dull, crimson-red finish, the vehicle sported a large, delta-shaped wingspan set in the lower half of the thirty-seven-meter-long fuselage. It was in the center of each of these wings that a single, massive engine was placed. Set on top of these engines were a pair of rudder-like tails.

Developed primarily as a recon platform, this particular model had an extra humped, clamshell canopy set behind the cockpit. This special compartment was apparently designed especially for Spetsnaz squadrons such as their own.

Konstantin and Dmitri had been brimming with questions, yet Grigori had remained silent until they were well airborne. He found it somewhat peculiar that they never even saw the pilot. They did have access to an intercom system that lay on the sealed, forward bulkhead door.

The plane was buffeted by a stream of moderate turbulence, and Grigori had to reach out to steady himself. The flight had been quite smooth so far. If they remained lucky, the good weather would prevail when it came time to jump.

Though he had made hundreds of HALO (high-altitude, low-opening) free-falls before, this would be his first on American soil. Never had he dreamed that the Motherland would trust him with such a mission. Earlier, Dmitri and Konstantin had attempted to figure out just what this task would be. Both had agreed that because of the Stinger missile array that Grigori carried, it would involve the shooting down of some type of prototype Imperialist bomber. This made sense to Grigori, who was quite content to wait for their arrival on the Volga to find out the precise nature of their goal. Patience was a virtue he had learned quite early in his military career.

Grigori's thoughts were broken by the sudden activation of the intercom system. A penetrating electronic buzz sounded over the guttural whine of the turbojets. It was easily loud enough to awaken his two slumbering co-workers. While their heads popped up to see what the disturbance was all about, Grigori stood, and with his back hunched over so that he wouldn't hit the low roof, maneuvered himself over to the forward bulkhead. He picked up the red plastic receiver and spoke into its transmitter loudly.

"Yes, comrade, this is Lieutenat Yagoda speaking."

The voice that returned his greeting was deep and firm. "Good afternoon, Lieutenant, this is Captain Kalinin. I hope you've enjoyed the flight so far. Sorry that the accommodations aren't a bit more spacious, but such is the small price we pay for our great speed."

Grigori cleared his throat. "It doesn't matter, Captain. We are quite comfortable back here."

"Good," responded the Tupolev's pilot. "I figured three hardy Spetsnaz operatives like yourselves could survive this temporary discomfort. I've called to tell you that soon you'll have time to properly stretch your legs. You see, you're scheduled to jump in precisely fourteen and a half minutes."

Checking his watch, Grigori retorted, "Very good, Captain. We'll begin our preparations at once."

Hanging up the receiver, he turned to face his men. "Well, hello, my sleeping beauties. I hope your dreams were pleasant."

Looking like beard-stubbled, moustached twins, the two dark-haired soldiers yawned and stretched their limbs. Konstantin Lomakin crawled up to the porthole and peered outside.

"Some restful sleep," offered Konstantin. "Here we are at 78,000 feet, and all I dream of is blowing away a gang of Mujahiddin. Will that war ever leave my mind?"

"There will soon be plenty to take your thoughts away from that crude conflict, my friend," advised Grigori. "We'll be jumping in another fourteen minutes."

Continuing to gaze out of the porthole, Konstantin asked, "Then we're in United States airspace now?"

"I imagine so," offered Dmitri Andreyev with a grin. "Yet the Americans will never know it. I've heard tales of these so-called stealth aircraft, but the reality of it all is even more amazing."

"Let's just hope we indeed remain invisible to their radar," added Grigori. "Otherwise there will soon be a flock of angry F-15 Eagles on our tail. Now, let's get going with that gear. There's much to prepare, and the time is short."

Doing their best to stand in the tight quarters, the

two junior officers joined Grigori at the compartment's forward section. There they began slipping on the odd assortment of pressure suits, oxygen equipment, helmets, and goggles that would enable them to jump from a height of 40,000 feet. To insure a minimal target, nearly all of this would be a free-fall, with their altimeter-triggered chutes not opening until they reached a mere 1,200 feet above sea level.

After the various body gear was in place, each member of the team double-checked the others. Once this was accomplished, they proceeded to strap on their weapons. Special waist-carried, padded carriers were utilized to hold the assortment of American-made weaponry which they would take with them. Grigori had just buckled on the harness that held the Stinger package in place when the intercom again activated. This time it was Dmitri who answered it. Taking in the pilot's two-minute warning to jump time, he smiled at his co-workers with relief. Thirty seconds later, the Spetsnaz team stood at the hatchway.

All eyes were locked on the two lights mounted above the door there. At present, only the red one was lit. Any moment now, the hatch would automatically slide open, the green light would pop on, and they'd be free to go.

To prepare for the sucking blast of pressure that would meet them when the door opened, the men held onto a specially designed steel support rod. Dmitri would be first to go, followed by Konstantin and Grigori. Each did his best to calm himself, as the seconds ticked slowly by.

Grigori's pulse jumped when the hatchway finally slid open with a loud hiss. Pulled instantly forward by the resulting depressurization, he strained to keep himself in place. A wave of ice-cold air enveloped him and he was aware of the now-deafening roar of the plane's engines. He forced himself to yawn to equalize the pressure on his eardrums, and then the green light suddenly blinked on. Without further prompting, Dmitri soared outward, followed closely by his two comrades.

To catch up with his teammates, Grigori tucked in his hands and legs and rocketed downward like a lead weight. All too soon he was forced to slow himself. To do this, he merely fanned out his limbs, and the resulting drag did the rest. When Konstantin and Dmitri were finally level with him, he continued his free-fall, only a couple of arm lengths away from them.

The air was cold and thin, and it streaked by with a banshee-like wail. Far above him, the crimson wings of the Red Fox could be barely seen, as the jet initiated a sweeping turn that would take it home-ward. Diverting his line of sight downwards, Grigori took in the incredible view of the ocean below. Clearly visible were the Channel Islands, and further to the east, the actual mainland. A thick bank of fog was visible far offshore, yet for the moment their target, the smallest and most northerly of the islands, was clearly in sight.

Free-fall was a time of pure joy for Grigori. Nothing could exhilarate him in quite the same manner. Though the bulky HALO gear kept him from feeling the icy, stimulating air on his face, the mere act of falling through the skies invigorated and refreshed him. His fatigue was the furthest thing from his mind as he watched the planet's surface approach with an incredible speed.

His thoughts were free from fear and concern as

both his teammates' chutes opened almost simultaneously. Slowed dramatically, both were immediately pulled out of sight above. Guessing that his own pack would open any second, Grigori took in the ever-approaching earth and felt the first stirrings of panic. Quickly checking his wrist-mounted altimeter, he saw that he was past 1,100 feet. But why hadn't his own chute activated? He was well aware that he carried no spare, and his gut tightened as he imagined what it would be like to die in such a nightmarish manner. Had his equipment been packed improperly, or was a mechanical malfunction at fault? It was too late to place blame now, and he plunged ever downward.

It wasn't until he hit the 900-foot level that his pack finally popped open. Pulled to a near halt with a spring, he issued a breath of relief upon watching the silken-white chute billow outward. They had been issued the new rectangular, steerable parachutes, and Grigori gratefully took hold of the two steering cords that were beside each shoulder. His panic was long passed as he noticed that his comrades had good chutes also.

Remembering the map that had been given to him at Petropavlovsk, he aimed for the island's deserted western shoreline. There, a wide patch of sandy beach was visible, several meters from the rock-lined surf itself. The surface winds were at a minimum, and Grigori swept in from the ocean and hit his mark with the ease of stepping off the bottom rung of a stepladder.

The added encumbrance of the Stinger package made gathering his chute a bit awkward, yet by the time his teammates landed beside him he had his gear in complete control. Thankful to get his oxygen mask off, he took his first breath of Capitalist air. Beside him, Konstantin did the same.

"So this is what smog smells like," Konstantin said. "Tell me, comrades, where are all the surfers?"

Taking this in with a distasteful grin, Grigori beckoned them to keep their voices down. After all, this was enemy territory, and there was no telling who could be close by listening.

A ledge of sharp, volcanic rocks lay to their left, and Grigori signaled that this would be where they would seek shelter. It was behind this outcropping that their HALO gear was subsequently buried and their new equipment readied. In addition to their matching green camouflaged fatigues and corresponding berets, both Konstantin and Dmitri were armed with Colt .45-caliber pistols, several stun grenades, and M16 A2 rifles. Grigori carried the same side arm, yet in place of the eight-and-a-half-pound rifle he was armed with a lightweight Uzi 9-mm. submachine gun. This would allow him to more easily carry the still-packaged Stinger.

It was Dmitri who carefully unwrapped and activated the all-important homing device. Shaped much like a large, portable transistor radio, the instrument was subsequently carried out beyond the surf line and anchored to the ocean's floor. There it would send out a loud, pulse-like burst of high-pitched sound in a pre-designated, coded sequence. If all had gone as planned, the Volga should be close by to pick up this call. Only then would the next part of their mysterious mission be revealed to them.

To await the sub, they chose to remain hidden behind the rock ledge. From this covert vantage point, they were afforded an excellent view not only of the surrounding waters but of the beach and shoreline as well.

A pair of powerful binoculars was used to scan the ocean's surface for any sign of the Volga. As it turned out, a full hour passed before Konstantin made the initial sighting. He jumped forward and pointed excitedly as a thin column of red smoke issued forth from the ocean, approximately a kilometer offshore. Upon sighting this flare himself, Grigori stood up and beckoned his men to do likewise.

"That's them all right," he whispered. "I knew the Navy wouldn't let us down. Let's get that raft inflated and get off this desolate pile of sand and rock."

With a minimum of difficulty, the small raft was readied and the commandos began their way seaward. The surf was minimal and their progress swift. When they were half a kilometer from shore, the flare quit smoking. They didn't lose sight of their goal, though, for a slender black periscope now extended from the water and graphically showed the way. Seeing this structure put new spring into their strokes.

When they were a quarter of a kilometer away, the sleek, rounded black sail of the submarine slowly raised above the surface. Shaped like the back of a breaching whale, the conning tower's characteristic form could belong to only one class of underwater vessel. The rest of the boat's deck remained submerged as they continued their approach.

Grigori felt his chest swell with pride when a trio of figures appeared on top of the sail. One of these blue-suited sailors waved at them, while the others were busy lowering a rope ladder overboard. This operation proved without a doubt in his mind that the Motherland's finest could successfully operate right in the enemy's very backyard. Anxious to know exactly what this mission entailed, Grigori utilized his paddle like a rudder to swing the raft up against the steel conning tower.

"Welcome to the Volga, comrades," greeted one of the young sailors, who reached over to grab their bow line.

Nodding in response, Dmitri began handing one of the other sailors their weapons. This transfer proved to be a bit difficult, bobbing in the open ocean as they were, yet it was soon completed and the Spetsnaz operatives themselves began to board. Grigori was the last to do so. Satisfied that they had conveyed all their equipment, he grabbed the thick rope ladder with one hand, and hit the raft's air-release valve with the other. By the time he had climbed onto the sail's solid deck, the now-deflated raft was already sinking beneath the ocean's surface.

"The Volga's seen enough daylight for today, comrades," observed a burly sailor. "Please continue on down into the vessel itself so that we can submerge. Captain Antonov is anxiously awaiting your presence in the wardroom."

After carefully lowering their weapons inside the hatchway, they proceeded to climb down the steel ladder. It was dark and cool inside the sail's cramped superstructure. Doing his best not to bruise his limbs and torso, Grigori somewhat gratefully stepped off the last rung and found himself in the sub's central attack center.

The blond-haired commando looked out with astonishment as he studied the sophisticated electronic gear that now surrounded them. Appearing more like the computer room of a major university, the compartment glowed and chattered with dozens of digital consoles and high-tech keyboards. Manning these stations were over a dozen sailors. They were dressed immaculately in matching blue coveralls, and Grigori felt conspicuous in the camouflaged fatigues of their adversary.

"Ah, I see that you made it down the sail in one piece," jested one of the sailors, a warrant officer who dropped down to the deck beside them.

Before continuing, the warrant officer addressed a tall, distinguished-looking figure standing at the room's opposite end. "The sail is sealed and all deck crew and new passengers accounted for, Lieutenant Litinov."

Nodding in response to this, the officer wasted no time in calling out, "Dive! Dive!"

Three loud blasts of a claxon accompanied this directive, and a surging hiss of venting air and flooding sea water was immediately audible. Barely aware that they were descending, Grigori caught the exultant stares of his teammates, who humbly stood at his side.

"Now come, comrades, the captain is waiting," added the warrant officer as he beckoned them to follow him into the sub's interior.

Grigori was equally as impressed with the portion of the vessel they were soon led to. After passing down a narrow, cable-lined corridor, they climbed through an open hatchway and emerged into a somewhat spacious, wood-paneled compartment. Dominating this room was a large, rectangular table. A single uniformed figure sat at its head, his complete attention focused on a series of intricate nautical charts that lay spread out before him.

While his teammates climbed through the hatch behind him, Grigori took in the familiar strains of the second movement of Tchaikovsky's Symphony No. 4 in F minor emanating from a pair of elevated speakers. This particular piece had been one of his father's

275

favorites, and he had played it time after time on his record player. Hearing it blare out with such realistic clarity there beneath the waters of the Pacific did much to ease Grigori's tenseness.

When his eyes caught the framed photographs that lined the room, he felt even more at home. There were over a dozen superb pictures of the great river for which their present means of transport was named. Since he had grown up in the city of Gorky, which lay on the Volga's very banks, he was no stranger to the river's great beauty.

The photograph on the wall nearest to him showed a particularly breathtaking segment of the river. There the ever-flowing blue expanse of water cut through a thick oak wood on one side and an immense field of billowing wheat on the other. Grigori couldn't help but find his thoughts soaring back to his past.

"Makes you homesick, doesn't it, comrade?" boomed a deep, bass voice in a tone that reminded Grigori of his own father.

Brought back from his brief reverie, the blond-haired Spetsnaz commando realized this voice came from the figure seated at the table's head. Quickly, he looked over to confirm this fact. Staring up at him was a face he would not soon forget.

The first facial feature he was drawn to was the black patch that covered the right eye. This swatch of shiny cloth only enhanced the intensity of the dark green stare that projected from his left pupil. Seemingly hypnotized by this glance, Grigori took in the sharply etched cheekbones, aquiline nose, square, firm jaw, and tight, weather-worn skin. With dignity and grace, the black-haired officer politely nodded in response.

"Lieutenant Grigori Yagoda, I presume. Welcome aboard the Volga. I am the vessel's commanding officer, Captain Mikhail Antonov."

Standing to offer his handshake, the captain revealed a solid, trim, six-foot figure. Positioning himself beside the officer, Grigori found his grasp firm and warm.

"Captain Antonov, it is an honor to be here. May I present my fellow squad members, Lieutenants Konstantin Lomakin and Dmitri Andreyev."

Meeting their nods of greeting, Antonov slyly grinned. "The honor is ours, comrades. It's not often that the Volga has such esteemed guests. The brave exploits of the Spetsnaz are well known to us. As fellow Naval warriors, you do us most proud. Now sit, comrades, and enjoy the simple comforts of this humble vessel."

Snapping the fingers of his right hand, the captain beckoned his guests to be seated. As they did so, the warrant officer silently exited the compartment. Quick to enter in his place was a white-uniformed orderly. With practiced ease, this young sailor set the large silver tray he had been carrying down on the table. Displayed on its length was a china tea service and a platter of fresh oatmeal cookies. After serving them each a cup of tea and two cookies, the seaman smartly pivoted and left the room, shutting the hatch behind him. Only then did the captain continue.

"I hope this will hold you until dinner, at which time I'd like for you to join me for a real meal."

After consuming a sip of tea, he added, "By the way, Lieutenant Yagoda, I had the honor of meeting your illustrious father in Moscow several years ago. With his passing, the Motherland has indeed lost one of its greatest heroes. His vision alone was responsible for the likes of the amazing vessel that we currently sit inside."

"Why, thank you, Captain," returned Grigori, who noticed that the symphony that continued to surround them was about to begin its next movement. "My father rests in peace knowing that his thousands of hours of unselfish toil have not been wasted in vain. If only he could have lived to see this day come."

"I believe he's with us at this very moment," offered Antonov with a wink. "He lives through you, Comrade Yagoda. How very fortunate it is for the Motherland that you have lived up to his demanding standards and then some. The Spetsnaz is our country's finest fighting force. No other soldier on this planet is your equal. Since achieving the impossible is but an everyday occurrence for the Spetsnaz commando, I think you'll find your present task particularly challenging."

Taking in the rapt gazes of his curious audience, Antonov took another sip of tea before continuing. "I must admit that, so far, the timing of this mission has been most auspicious. Only a few hours ago, your transfer to the Volga would have been impossible to achieve. Though the ocean looks calm now, this morning these same seas were swept by a mammoth wave of water.

"We first learned of the approach of this tidal wave not long after sunrise, while monitoring the U.S. Coast Guard shortwave weather band. At first, we feared this alert could be a mere hoax, cleverly conceived to draw us out. Yet, when we checked our own weather satellite, we found it most legitimate.

"Fortunately, we were positioned near these same islands. Since the wave was coming in from the northwest, we stationed ourselves in a deep trough of water that lay to the southeast of San Miguel. Even though the island absorbed much of the tsunami's fury, we felt its after-effects a full eight hundred meters beneath the water's surface.

"Then, of course, in addition to this unusual phenomenon, an extremely thick fog has haunted these waters lately. This afternoon is the first in over a week in which the blue sky is even visible this far out to sea."

With this, Grigori sat forward. "I had a chance to personally view this fog bank during my free-fall from the Tupolev Red Fox that flew us here. I wouldn't be surprised if the waters above us were already veiled in its milky shroud."

"What would we have done if the fog had covered San Miguel Island?" questioned Konstantin, between bites of a cookie.

Grigori didn't flinch. "We would have jumped anyway and worried about where we landed later."

Expecting just such an answer from their fearless leader, Konstantin merely shrugged his shoulders. Taking the resulting silence as a cue, Captain Antonov spoke out once again.

"Just as worrisome as this unusual weather has been the actions of a certain American submarine. Yesterday will mark the third recent occasion on which we apparently crossed their path by mere accident. As was the case with our previous encounters, we easily escaped their crude attempt to pursue us."

Antonov shook his head. "To think that the United States would dare challenge the pride of the Motherland's Fleet with one of their twenty-five-year-old, obsolete, diesel-electric models. This only goes to show how very thin their supposedly unrivaled submarine force is actually spread. Why, the poor fools can't even effectively guard their own coastline!"

This last statement caused the captain's previously calm face to flush with excitement. Regathering his composure, he took another sip of tea and cleared his throat.

"Well, enough of this old sailor's rambling. I'm certain that you're most anxious to hear exactly what you've been sent these thousand of kilometers to do. So, here it goes.

"The orders I'm about to convey to you come directly from Premier Viktor Alipov's office. They were sent via a laser satellite transmission, and were received on the Volga barely two hours ago. Since they arrived scrambled, I'm the only one aboard who knows their contents."

Pausing to take a deep breath, Antonov scanned the faces of the three young men who sat before him. Certain that he still held their complete attention, he continued.

"At present, the Volga is on a course due northward. That will put us off the coast of the U.S. mainland in approximately another hour's time. As soon as I can guarantee you the protective cloak of dusk, I'm going to drop you off in the waters directly opposite the geological feature known as Point Arguello. I will do everything within my power to convey you as close to the shoreline as safety allows. I'll warn you now that these waters are extremely hazardous. They are haunted by wicked riptides and razor-sharp reefs. You must choose your course of entry carefully, for the pounding surf here can be most unforgiving."

"We are well qualified to overcome whatever obstacle Mother Nature might throw our way," interrupted

Grigori, whose curiosity was fully piqued.

"Of course you are," returned the captain. "I was only being overly fatherly, for caution in these waters can not be overly stressed."

Accepting Grigori's nod of awareness, Antonov returned to business. "Once you have penetrated the surf line, you will find yourselves in the southern sector of Vandenberg Air Force Base. From there you are to proceed to Space Launch Complex 6, which lies another kilometer inland. It is from this site that America's space shuttle will be launched into the heavens sometime tomorrow morning. Your mission is to simply terminate this flight using whatever means necessary. The Volga will then be standing by off the coast to pick you up, once this task has been accomplished. Needless to say, we'll waste no time in taking you home to a much-deserved heroes' welcome."

This last sentence barely registered in Grigori's mind as he contemplated the awesome scope of his mission. This was no mere airplane that they had been sent to take out, but America's most advanced space-delivery system!

Genuinely astounded by what he had just heard, Grigori looked to the faces of his co-workers. There was no hiding the shock and surprise that they too were experiencing. After silently offering them a compassionate gaze of understanding, Grigori slowly turned his stare back to Captain Antonov.

"Some morning's work the Motherland is asking from you, huh, comrades?" offered the one-eyed Naval officer.

Unable to respond, Grigori instead found his attention focusing on the picture mounted on the wall immediately behind Antonov. Once again this photo featured Europe's longest river. Innocently playing on the Volga's wide banks in this representation was a group of frolicking young children. Was it really only twenty years before that Grigori himself had been such a child?

Feeling old beyond his years, the blond-haired Spetsnaz lieutenant could only hope that the Premier knew what he was asking of them. It wasn't necessarily his own life that concerned him. Grigori had consigned himself long ago to the dismal fact that it would be a minor miracle if he ever made it past thirty. Rather it was on the generation pictured in the photograph that his concerns were centered. For if the overly proud Americans ever got wind of just why their precious Space Shuttle had gone down, they would respond with nothing short of World War III. Certain of this grim fact, Grigori knew it was now up to his team to insure that this impossible mission was completed without a hint of suspicion.

Chapter Twelve

Richard Fuller couldn't believe it when the Air Force sentry refused him entry through the gate that led to Vandenberg's Coast Road. Even though Lieutenant Colonel Lansford had put him on the security list, the guard had explained that the route southward was temporarily closed to remove silt deposited on it by the tidal wave. Frustrated by the fact that Lansford had been the one to personally invite him down to the Arguello storage facility in the first place, Fuller pulled into the holding lot to wait for the road to reopen.

Leaving the confines of his car, he stretched his limbs and looked out to the sea that crashed onto the rocks less than a quarter of a mile away. It continued to be an usually clear afternoon. Absent was the thick fog that had perpetually veiled the coastline for days on end. Absorbing the pleasing warmth of the sun as it crept down towards the western horizon, Richard remembered the day's traumatic sequence of events.

It had all started out early that morning, when he had learned what the warning sirens had been activated for. As it turned out, his frantic dash down to the beach, to make certain that Miriam and her crew were safe, had been accomplished with only minutes to spare. For no sooner had they climbed onto the canyon's summit when the wave had been first spotted.

The initial sign of its approach had been when the frothing surf-line visible below them suddenly was sucked westward. Within seconds, the powerful riptide had pulled the waters back, exposing almost a mile-wide band of sloping, wet sand. One of the young male students had first sighted the tsunami itself. Still far out to sea, the wave's spiraling curl had stretched the entire length of the horizon. This sight in itself had been breathtaking.

Soon Richard had been aware of a distant, gathering roar. Like the sound of an approaching freight train, the crashing surge of water had steadily increased in volume. By the time the full extent of the wave's size could be appreciated, its accompanying sound had been almost deafening.

For the rest of his life, the sights and sounds which he had breathlessly watched take form in the distance would be deeply ingrained in his consciousness. From that day onward, whenever he looked out to the sea, a single, awesome vision would be instinctively triggered.

Over three times as large as the massive surf that had pounded into Hawaii's north shore, the tsunami had seemed to continue to grow in size until the moment it exploded onto dry land. The very earth below them had rumbled as the seventy-five-foot wave struck the beach with the speed of a jet aircraft. Richard had been unable to do anything but cower.

The top of the canyon had provided them a safe, bird's-eye view of this momentous event. They had only become aware of the force and volume of water involved when the bubbling, crashing surf had instantly flooded the beach, inundated the surrounding sand dunes, and engulfed the very valley where they had been digging less than a half-hour before. All eyes had been focused on the swirling deluge as it bit into the canyon's previously dry, mud-baked walls. Less than a minute later, the waters had receded and it was all over.

Ever so gradually, that portion of the earth's surface had returned back to normal. A confused gull had cried out from high above, and a gust of ripe wind had blown in off the Pacific. Few words had been exchanged among the group of shocked onlookers, who had sat there looking at the flooded beach, vainly trying to grasp the enormity of the force they had just witnessed.

It had been decided to wait a bit longer to make certain that another wave wouldn't follow. When they eventually had returned, it had been by way of the railroad tracks. The going there had been slow and awkward, yet all agreed that the debris-laden beach was just too risky.

Of course, the group had been mainly concerned about how their camp had weathered the deluge. After an exhausting, tedious hike, they had anxiously peered down from the trestle and were afforded their first view of Ocean Beach Park. All had breathed a sigh of relief upon finding the parking lot flooded, yet with their trailers still parked in the familiar semicircle. Apparently the hill on which the tracks had been mounted on had blocked the main onslaught of water, and thus kept their valuables from being swept away.

Heedless of their personal belongings, the group had rushed down the hillside to see to the safety of the Chumash relics they had exhumed. Only when

285

they had been found safe had a collective shout of pure joy issued from the team's lips.

One instrument that had not been working was the telephone. Miriam had been in a hurry to notify the University that all was well with them. While the kids began the cleanup, Richard volunteered to take their instructor into town to make the call. Though the parking lot had been covered with several inches of seawater, his car started up and they had easily made it to Ocean Avenue. From there they turned eastward towards Lompoc.

It was from his condo that Miriam had initiated the call. While she was engrossed in a lively conversation, Richard jumped in the shower and then made a quick change of clothes. By the time he was out of the bedroom, Miriam had been off the phone, and well into her preparation of a quick lunch. The morning's excitement had done wonders for their appetites, and they hungrily gobbled down two tuna-fish-salad sandwiches apiece.

They had just finished eating when the call had arrived from Lansford's office. Speaking for the senior officer, Master Sergeant Sprawlings invited Richard to the Arguello storage facility, which had successfully weathered the wave's fury. Sprawlings had hinted that something extremely important waited for the NOSC researcher there. Richard's curiosity had been fully aroused, and he wasted no time locking up the condo and getting them back on the road westward.

He had dropped Miriam off back at Ocean Beach Park with a promise to drop by sometime the next day. Backing out of the still-flooded lot, he returned to the intersection of Ocean Avenue, and this time had turned to the right, away from Lompoc. A half mile later, he reached the closed security gate, where he sat presently.

Merely recreating this morning's activities caused Richard to shake his head in wonder. Who knew just what surprises the afternoon held? Like one who dangles a piece of chocolate in front of a child, the master sergeant had been toying with him. Though he wouldn't say what awaited Richard at Arguello, his mere tone of voice had indicated that it was something of major significance. Maybe they had found a portion of the Titan that indicated exactly what caused it to fail, or perhaps they had chanced upon the prized nose cone itself. Whatever it was, just knowing that it lay invitingly close, only a few miles from his present location, was most frustrating.

The squeal of car brakes sounded behind him, and Richard diverted his glance away from the blue Pacific. Turning to focus his glance on the guard gate, he saw two Air Force sedans in the process of stopping before the sentry. What caught Richard's attention was the fact that they had been coming from the south. This meant that the road there had to be clear. Jumping back into his car, he pulled out of the lot and approached the gate himself.

By the time he reached the sentry, the two sedans were well on their way northward. The uniformed guard met him with a salute and proceeded over to his open window.

"Sorry about the delay, Doctor, but I just got word that the road to Arguello is open now. Please drive carefully, and look out for any debris that has yet to be removed."

Nodding in response, Richard was full of anticipation as he hit the accelerator and pulled onto Coast Road. It didn't take him long to notice that this portion of thoroughfare had indeed been hard hit by the tsunami. Though the pavement was still intact, much of the road's shoulder was covered with sand and other debris. Upon rounding Point Arguello, he viewed a tractor crew in the process of removing a huge boulder that had been apparently tossed up onto the shoulder from the surf below. No stranger to the wave's awesome strength, Richard knew that they were very fortunate not to have lost the road itself.

Soon Slik 6 was passing on his left. Because it lay high on a surrounding hillside, the space shuttle's launch site was well out of the tsunami's reach. Wondering if the Air Force were still going on with its ill-conceived plan to send it skyward, he crossed the railroad tracks and set his eyes on the metallic roof of the external-tank storage facility, shimmering in the distance.

As he parked and exited his car, he noticed the protective, eight-foot-high sand wall that had been hastily bulldozed up to protect the building. Part of this temporary wall had been washed away, yet it was evident that the main force of the wave had been focused on the north-facing beaches. Otherwise, the wall would have been completely decimated. It was only because the facility was built on a beach that faced the south that it had survived.

A pair of armed sentries stood at the building's entrance, and Richard had to be cleared before being allowed inside. As was the case when he had last entered this massive structure, it proved to be completely empty except for a small knot of curious figures gathered at its center. His footsteps echoed off the concrete floor as he approached them. Only when he was approximately ten feet away did he recognize two of the seven individuals standing there.

The only non-uniformed figure in the bunch was David Downing, the young, bearded McDonnell-Douglas engineer, who was dressed in a white shirt, red tie, and gray slacks. Beside him, in the process of leading the discussion, was Ensign Louis Marvin, of the DSRV Marlin. Richard had flown back from Hawaii with the skinny, balding officer, and had a genuine fondness for his warm sense of humor. The other men present were blue-suited Air Force officers of a much more senior rank.

As inconspicuously as possible, the NOSC researcher made his way to this circle of figures and peered in between them to see what they surrounded. He did a double-take upon viewing the object that sat on the pallet before them.

The six-foot, six-inch piece of bullet-shaped cowling could only belong to a missile's nose cone. Formed of fire-scarred, white metal, it had the distinctive emblem of the U.S. Air Force imprinted on its base.

Not believing what he was seeing, Richard pushed his way through the circle of men. Seconds later, he was recognized.

"Dr. Fuller!" greeted the excited ensign. "We did it. We found the Titan's nose cone!"

Still totally speechless, Richard stared out at the piece of debris, while Marvin continued, "As I was just explaining, the amazing part of it all was that this discovery was totally by accident. If it weren't for that tidal wave almost pulling us down to our deaths, we would have never chanced upon it. Isn't that incredible?"

Barely able to nod in recognition, Richard proceeded to the nose cone's opposite side, while the ensign continued on with his blow-by-blow account of the fateful series of events that had led them deep into Arguello Canyon. As he knelt down to examine the nose cone's surface more closely, he was joined by the other civilian present.

"Your expression says it all, Doctor," whispered the bearded engineer. "The really strange part was that the Titan's payload was still snug inside the fairing when they brought it up. Although it's damaged way beyond repair, just knowing that the Russians can't get their hands on it is the best news of the day."

"Talk about the hand of God protecting our country," said Richard. "It's almost like some sort of miracle."

"Good things happen to good people," offered the engineer with a grin.

It was as Richard traced the portion of metal skirting that lay on the nose cone's lower edge that he spotted a strange aperture cut into the fairing's skin. A bit smaller than a fist, the hole was certainly not part of the rocket's original design.

Noticing Richard's line of sight, Downing spoke out carefully. "Interesting, isn't it? I noticed it also, yet our Air Force friends are still too excited with the mere fact that this nose cone is here in the first place to give this orifice much attention. I'm not certain what in the world caused it, yet whatever it was, it must have been moving at an incredible velocity to pierce this multi-layered sandwich of steel as it has."

Absorbing this observation, Richard suddenly shivered in awareness. His limbs trembled, and a cold sweat formed on his forehead, as his mind's eye raced back to the past.

The time was over twelve months ago. The place, San Diego's Duvalier Laboratories. He had been invited by the amiable Frenchman who owned the firm to witness a demonstration of an electromagnetic rail-gun. This novel weapon was a part of the nation's Strategic Defense Initiative. It operated by accelerating a projectile to ultra-high speeds, using electric and magnetic energy instead of chemical means. In return, the velocities monitored were rated at an astounding 46,000 miles per hour.

On the day in question, he had seen the launcher fire a half-pound plastic projectile, and had watched it easily penetrate a two-inch-thick steel plate. The fist-sized hole it had left was almost exactly like the one he currently stood before. Of an even stranger coincidence was the test that had immediately preceded that launching. A four-inch-thick steel plate had been fired at. Because of an improperly packed bullet, the projectile had disintegrated upon striking its target. Left in its wake had been a circular pattern of pellet damage that seemed to match that found on the first section of cowling pulled from the Pacific earlier. Could an electromagnetic rail-gun be responsible for the Titan's demise?

Remembering how Lansford had reacted when he had last brought up even the idea of sabotage, Richard struggled to keep his suspicions to himself. He knew he could voice them to only one person.

"Are you all right, Doctor?" questioned the engineer, who noticed Richard's trembling limbs and vacant stare.

Brought back from his deep inner thought, the NOSC researcher wiped his forehead and slowly stood. Louis Marvin was just describing the stone-paved road, and the strange monument it led to, when Richard excused himself. Escorting him to the building's exit was David Downing.

"You think that hole was caused by an outside

source, don't you, Doctor?" probed the alert engineer.

Halting at the doorway, Richard solemnly looked him in the eye. "What do you think, Mr. Downing?"

The engineer didn't hesitate to express himself. "I don't know, but I'll be damned if anyone's going to tell me that the puncture was caused by a piece of the Titan. Though it is vaguely possible that an explosion could propel part of the rocket through the steel skin, the dynamics are all wrong. That nose cone was just too far from the boosters for such a thing to have happened."

Richard grimly nodded in agreement. "You know what talk like that will get you around here. But in all good conscience, I'm not about to just sit around and let the same thing happen to that shuttle. I hope Secretary Fitzpatrick is more open-minded than the rest of the Brass around here."

"If you need the opinion of another expert, just give me call," offered the engineer. "You can reach me twenty-four hours a day by calling the local McDonnell office."

"I just might take you up on that," replied Richard, who offered his handshake.

Ducking outside, he passed the guards and made his way over to a narrow, rocky ledge that overlooked the sea beyond. His heart was still pounding in his chest as he surrendered his thoughts to the scene unfolding on the western horizon. There, the setting sun was in the process of just dipping beneath an advancing wall of thick, gray fog. Taking in the muted colors of this strange dusk, he scanned that portion of ocean that was still visible. The inky depths swelled with a threatening malevolence. From the same waters that the deadly tidal wave had been spawned in, another danger could very well be awaiting them. Yet, this time, it was exclusively man-made.

Knowing full well that a submarine could be easily adapted to carry a weapon such as a rail-gun, and ever conscious of the flurry of activity which was taking place at nearby Slik 6, he gathered the inner strength to pass on these suspicions to the one person who could do something about them. Now, he could only pray to God that this individual would listen.

Deep beneath the very seas that had so thoroughly captivated the NOSC researcher, the Soviet attack sub Volga plunged almost silently. Powered by a nuclear reactor, the 350-foot-long vessel was one of the quickest and most sophisticated in the Russian arsenal. It carried a complement of one hundred and twenty officers and seamen.

From the boat's attack center, Captain Mikhail Antonov found himself hunched over the periscope, in the process of scanning the surrounding seas with his one good eye. Behind him, taking in this procedure, were Grigori Yagoda, Dmitri Andreyev, and Konstantin Lomakin. Having just completed a light meal of beef stroganoff, rice, fresh black bread, and fruit compote, the three Spetsnaz operatives were anxious to get on with the difficult mission.

"Ah, excellent," observed the captain as he backed away from the scope. "It indeed appears that we have these waters all to ourselves."

A devilish gleam emanated from his eye, as he approached the commandos and continued, "The fog is thick and the dusk ever darkening. These ideal conditions shall get you to shore without being spotted. Are you ready, comrades?"

Accepting their nods, Antonov addressed his Officer of the Deck firmly. "Take us up, Senior Lieutenant. We shall show our sail only."

As the OOD conveyed these orders, the captain returned his attention to his guests. "Your country is proud of you, comrades. May the spirit of the Motherland protect you always. And don't forget, we'll be right here awaiting your signal when you're ready to go home."

While Konstantin and Dmitri were busy seeing to last-minute adjustments to the black-rubber wet-suits and waterproof equipment bags that they would carry, Grigori took Antonov aside.

"Thank you for your hospitality, Captain. Merely spending these couple of hours on the Volga have been like taking one last visit home."

Antonov proudly beamed. "You are as gracious as your father, Lieutenant Yagoda. Now, go with courage, and may you strike the enemy a crippling blow!"

A muted hiss of venting ballast was followed by the deep voice of the Officer of the Deck. "We're ready to disembark, Captain."

After personally hugging each of the commandos, Antonov watched them follow the warrant officer up the conning tower's hatch. Though he had only known them for a very brief period of time, he already felt emotionally attached to them. Their loyalty and bravado were a shining lesson to every member of his crew. This fearlessness was especially apparent in their leader.

Grigori Yagoda was the kind of son a warrior dreamed of having. Courageous and bold, yet innately sensitive as well, the young officer had accepted his new orders without blinking. Seemingly oblivious to the fact that he was being asked to penetrate a heavily guarded military complex, on the enemy's own shoreline, and then shoot down its most cherished space platform, Yagoda did not flinch. If anyone could achieve this impossible goal, it would be Yagoda and his brave team. Of this fact, the captain was certain. Instinctively checking the wall-mounted clock, he knew that they would all too soon be alone to meet their destinies.

Meanwhile, above deck, the air was fresh and noticeably cooler. To the sound of the water slapping against the Volga's streamlined sail, the commandos gathered before the rope ladder that the warrant officer had just thrown overboard.

The fog was thick and the visibility limited to but a few meters as Dmitri unfolded the life raft. Holding the heavy rubber craft over the side by its bow line, he triggered the compressed air charge that instantly inflated its rounded hull. Settling it down into the choppy waters, he handed the bow line to the warrant officer and cautiously climbed down into the raft's interior. Konstantin handed him the heavy, plastic duffel bags inside of which were stored their fatigues, supplies, and weapons.

Once this process was completed, Konstantin climbed down into the boat. Before Grigori followed him, he turned to accept the warrant officer's firm handshake.

"Good hunting!" offered the sailor proudly.

Waving in response, Grigori pivoted and began his way down the rope ladder. No sooner had he settled himself at the raft's stern than the warrant officer cast off the line and pulled in the ladder. By the time he disappeared from the sail's top, they had already pushed away from the conning tower and begun paddling.

Checking his wrist-mounted compass to make sure that they were headed eastward, Grigori looked up when a muted, bubbling roil sounded nearby. It was then that he noticed that the Volga's sail was no longer visible.

Totally alone now, they put their backs into their paddling. The thick shroud of fog veiled the enormity of the distance that they had to travel, yet the men established a vigorous rhythm. As they kept their conversation to a whispered minimum, all was silent except for the slap of sea water against their hull, and the lonely cry of a distant fog horn.

An hour passed, and still their rhythm did not falter. Satisfied with their progress, Grigori allowed them the briefest of breaks. It was during this period of blessed rest that they first heard the faraway sound of breaking surf.

"We're there already!" observed Konstantin victoriously.

Signaling the overly enthusiastic commando to keep his voice down, Grigori rechecked his compass. "We'll proceed another half a kilometer before leaving the raft. Come on, comrades, let's get it over with."

His teammates responded by picking up their paddles and continuing their full strokes. Beyond, the sound of the crashing surf continued to intensify, and soon Grigori gave the orders to halt. Without a further word spoken, they stowed the paddles and opened their sealed sea bags. From these waterproof sacks, each man removed a pair of goggles, a snorkel, and a set of fins. After resealing the bags, and mounting them on their backs, they donned this skin-diving equipment and slipped into the awaiting ocean.

Grigori's sea bag was the heaviest and most awkward of the group, yet he managed to get overboard with a minimum of noise. The water was chilly, and it took him some effort to remove his knife and slash the raft's hull. Once this was accomplished, he again checked his compass and beckoned his men to follow him.

Because of his load, he found the easiest stroke to manage was the breast stroke. Always a powerful swimmer, Grigori extended his arms in front of his head fully, while drawing his knees forward and outward. This was followed by a sweeping backward movement of both his arms and legs. By the time he had completed but a dozen such strokes, the low water temperature was hardly noticeable. Warmed by his pounding blood and insulated wet-suit, he found himself enjoying the swim. Ever conscious of his two teammates, who easily matched his pace, the commando emptied his tangled mind of any thoughts but those of his stroke. Time quickly passed, and the loud, pounding sound of the surf signaled that their goal was near.

Spitting his snorkel from his mouth, Grigori halted and began treading water. His teammates did likewise and gathered around him.

"We are just about there," managed Grigori. "Remember not to fight the riptide and keep a sharp lookout for those rocks."

"Yes, Mother," responded Konstantin facetiously.

Slapping a handful of water at Konstantin's mask, Dmitri shook his head at this attempt at humor. Grigori seemed to ignore it, as he cleared his snorkel and pointed toward the east.

As they resumed their stroke, each man recognized

that they were now contending with a strong offshore current. Most likely resulting from a return flow of waves, this force made their progress tedious. To counter it, each swimmer had to apply a strenuous effort.

Grigori was just beginning to tire when the first curl of surf broke over his head. Spitting the water from his snorkel, he countered the resulting pull of the riptide by continuing on in a lateral course. This change of direction was starting to pay off when he spotted a jagged shelf of rock protruding from the water immediately before him. Doing his best to signal its presence, he fought the tide that was now drawing him ever closer to this dangerous obstacle. Utilizing every last ounce of muscle, he pulled himself backward and just missed the razor-sharp ledge by less than an arm's length. Much to his relief, his alert teammates did likewise.

The tide continued its unyielding pull, and they soon found themselves on the opposite side of the rock shelf. Still masked by the fog, the surf there appeared to be a bit more even. Doing his best to scan the waters for hidden obstacles, Grigori decided that that spot looked as good as any other. Signaling that fact, he put his head down and initiated a smooth, powerful stroke forward.

Again a line of surf broke over his head, yet this time its crashing wake pulled him in the same direction in which he had been headed. Doing his best to nestle his body in this wave's curl, he felt a sudden surge of velocity as the surf hurled him forward in a burst of fluid speed. Seconds later, the wave smashed onto the beach and he was aware of a gravelly layer of coarse sand beneath him. With muscles straining and his chest heaving, he pulled himself out of the water and gratefully caught his breath.

Dmitri Andreyev followed close behind. Gagging on the sea water that he had swallowed during the maddening ride in, he did his best to muffle the coughing seizure that possessed him.

"Easy now, comrade," prompted Grigori, who crawled over to the commando's side to attend to him.

Slipping Dmitri's sea bag off his back, Grigori slapped him hard between the shoulder blades. As a result, Dmitri gagged and the coughing fit passed.

"Thank you, comrade," offered Dmitri weakly. "I hope Konstantin remembered to keep that big mouth of his shut."

Suddenly aware of their teammate's absence, Grigori slipped off his own equipment bag and turned to scan the shoreline. His gut tightened upon viewing nothing but fog, sand, and the ever-frothing white surf.

"He must be still out there!" cried Grigori, his tone filled with concern. "I'm going to go out and see if I can find him."

Without further hesitation, he pulled on his mask and plunged back into the surging foam. As it turned out, he didn't have to proceed far to find the missing squad member.

Hanging lifelessly amid the line of pounding surf, Konstantin's limp body was impaled on a mangled arm of rusted steel. With eyes still open, he seemed to be looking westward, to a homeland he would never return to again. As the fog wrapped its misty tentacles around his soaked corpse, Grigori struggled to contain his grief. They had gone through much together, and for his brave friend to die in such a needless way was a supreme travesty of justice. Knowing that the mission would have to go on regardless, Grigori pulled himself together. Certainly, Konstantin would have done likewise if their fates had been reversed.

Because the body had no identification on it, the corpse could be left where it was. He needed only to remove the weapons pack. Then, if Konstantin were subsequently discovered, the authorities would only have the unfortunate death of yet another unknown skin diver to contend with.

With some difficulty, Grigori managed to cut the straps of Konstantin's sea bag. Doing his best to remain free of the rusty snare that lay in the water, he shouldered the sack and took a last look at his dear comrade. The tears had already stopped flowing down his cheeks by the time he arrived back at the beachhead.

"Well, where is he, Grigori?" quizzed Dmitri as he helped the blond-haired commando from the water.

Slipping off his mask and fins, Grigori was solemn. "I'm afraid there must have been some sort of shipwreck out there. Our good friend Konstantin was impaled on the remaining debris. Hopefully, his death was quick."

Though he had been expecting as much, Dmitri let forth a wail of anguish. "He never did know how to stay away from trouble, that one. I can't imagine how the world will be without him."

"Well, get used to it quickly," retorted Grigori. "He knew the risks, just like each one of us who dons the black beret. Now, to insure that his death is not in vain, let's get on with our mission. We must find a secluded spot to change into our fatigues and bury our wet-suits. Then we must be off for the hills above Space Launch Complex 6."

Taking the extra sea bag that Grigori had been carrying, Dmitri regathered his composure. "You are right, comrade. There will be time for mourning later, after we have finished our task. Right now, tears mean not a thing. While you were gone, I found a hidden ledge of rock further up on the beach."

"Excellent," returned Grigori. "Lead the way, Comrade Andreyev. I knew I could count on you."

The beach was narrow, and surrounded by a wall of volcanic rock. At the base of this ledge was a cramped, cave-like formation. It was there that they began peeling off their wet-suits, replacing them with camouflaged Green Beret fatigues. After the skin-diving equipment was buried beneath a rocky niche, they shouldered their weapons. Grigori slung the encased Stinger package over his back and led the way upward.

The climb up the cliff was steep, yet there were plenty of jagged footholds available to allow them access to the summit. The ledge of rock they soon found themselves on was relatively smooth and flat. As they slowly proceeded inland, Grigori spotted a strange-looking object mounted on the ground before them. Appearing like a ghostly apparition in the swirling fog was a large, rusted anchor, lying on a concrete slab, with a thin, iron-link rail around it. Gathering in front of this apparent monument, the commandos passed a moment of hushed silence.

"I wonder if this anchor came from the same wreck that caused the death of our beloved comrade?" said Dmitri grimly.

"Perhaps it did," answered Grigori, who was suddenly startled when a strange sound came from somewhere close by.

Because the fog served to mask this noise's exact source, Grigori spun on his heels in an attempt to track it down. Instinctively crouching beside him,

Dmitri pointed to their left. There, two distorted, pinprick shafts of bright light illuminated the swirling mist, approximately one-quarter of a kilometer distant. It was most obvious that they emanated from a pair of flashlights, and that whoever carried them were headed straight for the commandos.

Taking his knife from its sheathe, Dmitri made a cutting motion over his throat. Signaling that this wasn't the type of response that he wanted, Grigori instead motioned toward the ledge they had just climbed up from. Disappointed, Dmitri followed his teammate back to the wall. Carefully edging down its sharp face, they lowered themselves just far enough so that only their foreheads still peaked over the jagged summit.

Thirty seconds passed until voices could finally be heard. Long before their mist-veiled figures became visible, the Spetsnaz operatives, who were fluent in English, could readily make out the rambling conversation.

"I still wish I had my surfboard down here when that wave hit this morning," boasted a high-pitched male voice. "That would have been the ultimate ride of a lifetime."

"It would have also been your last," returned his deep-throated companion. "Sometimes, Johnson, I don't think you're playing with a full deck."

With this, two uniformed sentries emerged onto the rock plateau. Positioning themselves beside the anchor monument, they rather halfheartedly shone their lights in the direction of the sea.

"This sure is a night for spooks," offered the surfer. "I can just visualize the ghosts of those destroyer boys who were lost here back in 1923."

"That disaster was a tragic one, all right," responded his companion. "But enough of that spook talk. This place gives me the chills without that nonsense. Now come on, we'd better get on with our rounds before the sergeant throws a shit-fit."

Without another word spoken, the sentries turned from the sea and disappeared eastwards. A full minute passed before Grigori gave the signal to climb back onto the plateau.

"Such is the fierce nature of our adversaries," spat Dmitri. "They babbled on like mere schoolboys."

Grigori's tone was a bit more cautious. "Don't let them fool you, comrade. The Americans might seem slow to anger, but pity the poor enemy that it is not prepared to counter their wrath once it is aroused. We must be ever alert now for both more sentries and electronic surveillance methods. The closer we get to that missile site, the thicker they'll be, so let's take advantage of this cloak of fog while we still have it. We shouldn't rest until we are well hidden in the hills to the east of the launch complex itself."

Dmitri stepped aside and beckoned with his hand. "I'm ready whenever you are, comrade. Merely lead on."

Doing just that, Grigori readjusted the load that lay slung over his back and began his way inland. After passing the anchor, they followed a narrow, earthen pathway over a desolate plain littered with razor-sharp thistle and spiky cactus. Continuing on the trail as it climbed up a steep ravine, they crossed a set of railroad tracks and were forced to dive to the ground for cover when a pair of bright headlights suddenly pierced the mist before them. Pressing their noses into the sandy, dry soil, they looked up in time to see a convoy of large trucks pass on a road that lay another half kilometer to the east. The powerful roar of their diesel engines rumbled through the night, and Grigori couldn't help but grin.

"I bet they're headed for the launch site," he whispered softly. "It has to be nearby."

"Either that, or we've been mistakenly dropped off on one of their so-called freeways," offered Dmitri with a nervous wink.

Only when he was certain that no other traffic was in the vicinity did Grigori dare stand. Leaving the path they had been following, he led Dmitri directly toward the nearest portion of pavement. Though their progress roused a startled long-eared jackrabbit, they managed to stay well clear of the sharp, low-laying brush and dreaded rattlesnakes that abounded there.

When they finally made it to the road, they found it to be a good-sized thoroughfare. Paved with black asphalt, it was wide enough to handle the largest of transports. Its flat surface looked awfully inviting, yet Grigori knew that it was fraught with too many unseen dangers. Proceeding by way of the surrounding hills would be much more practical.

Grigori needed a running start to get to the top of the hill that lay on the other side of the roadway. As his boots bit into the soft sand that comprised this summit, his glance strayed immediately before him, to the east. His eyes subsequently opened wide with wonder as they took in the scene on the distant horizon. For the fog had temporarily lifted. Visible another kilometer away was an immense, brightly lit complex of massive concrete-and-steel structures. Positioned at the center of this conglomeration of blockhouses and towers was the very vehicle he had been sent to destroy. Shimmering beneath the banks of spotlights, the spotlessly white shuttle sat perched on its trio of boosters. Looking deceptively close, it beckoned him forward like a father welcoming a long-lost son.

How very easy it seemed to merely set up their weapons right there and just blast away at it. Yet Grigori knew his Stinger's infra-red guided warhead would have a much easier target once the rocket's main engines ignited.

Since the security there seemed almost non-existent, for the first time he actually thought that the mad scheme might succeed after all. Ever aware that over-confidence could be their worst enemy, he swore that they would proceed with caution. They had come too far to fail by accident now. Konstantin Lomakin's tragic fate must not be their own.

Chapter Thirteen

Richard Fuller arrived at Slik 6's launch control center at 8:00 A.M. sharp. He had anticipated the ever-present early morning fog that made driving down to the coast a time-consuming proposition, so he had made certain to leave Lompoc extra early. As it turned out, he arrived just in time for his appointed meeting.

The launch complex was buzzing with activity as he passed through the dual security gates and drove by the payload-preparation area. Dozens of hard-hat-wearing, white-smocked technicians milled about the various assembly buildings located there. As he continued on toward the partially buried concrete-block structure housing the main control center, he had a brief view of the shuttle itself. Barely visible in the swirling fingers of fog, the shiny white orbiter was lit by a bank of powerful spotlights. Perched as it was on its boosters, the vehicle appeared ready to fly. A renewed sense of urgency prompted Richard's actions, for he knew that he had wasted enough valuable time already.

The previous night had been one of the most frustrating evenings of his life. After leaving the Arguello docksite, he had returned to his condo with hopes of immediately contacting Secretary of the Air Force Fitzpatrick. Subsequent calls to both the Pentagon and to the Secretary's current Vandenberg quarters had gotten him nowhere. Apparently in the process of entertaining a group of Congressmen, who were also visiting the base, Fitzpatrick had been impossible to reach no matter what the problem involved. Richard had been asked to leave his name, number, and a brief message. The Secretary's coldly efficient aide had then recommended that Richard contact Lieutenant Colonel Todd Lansford instead. Realizing that he had nowhere else to turn, the NOSC researcher had reluctantly done so.

It had been Master Sergeant Sprawlings who had set up this morning's early meeting at the control center. Though he couldn't help but get the feeling that they were merely patronizing him, Richard knew that it would be better than nothing. Still positive that the Titan had been taken down by an outside source, and fearing that such a fate awaited the shuttle, he renewed his determination. Certain of the validity of his suspicions, he pulled into the control center's parking lot.

At the block structure's entrance, he was met by a pair of heavily armed, grim-faced sentries. They checked his ID and found his name on their clipboard, but Richard was not allowed further entry. He was told that Lieutenant Colonel Lansford would have to be paged, and was forced to wait for him outside. While one of the guards proceeded inside to notify Lansford, Richard's face flushed with anger. Here he was a personal guest of the Air Force, and they didn't even trust him enough to allow him into their precious control room. Turning from the remaining sentry, he diverted his irate gaze to that portion of the facility that lay before him.

Fighting the impulse to jump back into his car and leave this place altogether, he scanned the grounds, and upon seeing the silhouette of the barely visible shuttle again, knew that he'd have to give it one more try. This was his first time inside the launch complex itself, and he couldn't help but be impressed. Contrasted against the green hillsides, the mammoth white, gray, and red structures made a most unnatural scene. It was evident that no expense had been spared in its construction.

The fog momentarily parted, and he took in the series of mountainous ridges that lay to the east of the facility. Richard wondered if that were where Miriam's original dig site had been located. More wide and desolate than he had imagined, the countryside there was vast and rugged. Surely it had changed little since the time of the Chumash.

Lowering his line of sight, he took in the pair of barbed-wire-topped, chain-link security fences that separated this wilderness from the facility itself. Sandwiched in between these steel barriers was a fifty-yard-wide clearing of common ground, where several rifle-toting sentries could be seen walking their rounds. Though they would probably be able to keep the perimeter free from a minor frontal assault, such a token security force would be totally ineffective in countering such threats as the one Richard feared they were facing. Determined as ever to present his case as logically as possible, he pivoted when a voice called out behind him.

"Good morning, Dr. Fuller. Sorry for the delay, but things are a bit hectic inside."

Lansford's overly cheery tone didn't disguise his inner preoccupation, and Richard held his tongue while the officer approached him. Noticing his guest's somberness, the Air Force officer added,

"Please forgive me for not being able to get you inside, but at the moment it's crowded enough in there. Do you mind if I'm able to stretch these old, cramped legs while we talk?"

Nodding that this was fine with him, Richard followed his host down a narrow footpath that lay immediately inside the security perimeter. As they passed the eight-foot-high, chain-link fence on their left, Lansford spoke out cautiously.

"I understand that you tried to contact Secretary Fitzpatrick last night. Is there anything that I could help you with? I'm afraid the Secretary has other concerns at the moment."

"Yeah, like wet-nursing a bunch of eager Congressmen in order to get bigger appropriations for next year's Air Force budget," shot back the angry NOSC researcher.

Fighting to restrain his own temper, Lansford countered, "That tone of voice really isn't called for, Doctor. All of us are under an unusual amount of pressure lately with today's rushed launch and all, and patience is something each of us could use more of. I'm sorry if it seems as if I've been ignoring you, but lately there just haven't been enough hours in the day."

"So you're going ahead with the launch today," observed Richard thoughtfully.

"That's the intention," returned Lansford. "But for the life of me, if we make it, I'll never know how we did it. We could have used weeks to get the Condor out of mothballs, not days. This whole effort is unprecedented. Once again, our men have done the impossible, and then some. Now, how can I help you, Dr. Fuller?"

With firm resolve, Richard spoke out. "I realize your great responsibilities, Colonel, and I'm sorry to be such a pest, but there's something that I just have to get off my chest."

"Then shoot," returned Lansford directly.

Clearing his throat, Richard continued, "Yesterday afternoon, per your invitation, I got down to the Arguello storage facility and had a look at that Titan nose cone. If you'll just hear me out, I think I have that irrefutable proof of sabotage that you demanded earlier."

"So you're still on this sabotage business," mumbled Lansford.

Ignoring this interruption, the NOSC researcher merely kept going. "Upon close examination of the nose cone's base, I noticed a fist-sized hole in its steel cowling. At first I assumed that it was just a byproduct of the massive explosion that brought the rocket down, yet upon further contemplation, I realized that I had seen such damage before. One year ago in San Diego, I witnessed a test firing of an electromagnetic rail-gun. At that time, a half-pound plastic projectile was shot at a steel plate of approximately the same thickness as the nose cone's skin. The results were too similar to be ignored.

"This coincidence led me to think about another test firing that failed because of an improperly packed bullet. In this instance also, it left behind a familiar pattern of damage that matched that found on the first piece of Titan cowling that we pulled up the other day.

"Backing up my theory is a McDonnell-Douglas engineer, who examined both pieces of debris and agrees that it is extremely unlikely that the Titan's nose cone was penetrated by its own shrapnel. If you'd like, I could contact him and you could speak with him personally."

"I don't think that will be necessary at the moment," returned Lansford, who cautiously added, "Have you shared your theory with anyone else?"

"Of course not," answered Richard. "Though I do think it's substantial enough to inform Secretary Fitzpatrick of."

Suddenly halting his forward movement, Lansford looked up into the face of his guest. With this abrupt glance, Richard also stopped walking. Standing on the dusty footpath, with the security fence beside them, the senior Air Force officer pointed out toward an object that lay immediately behind the NOSC researcher. Turning to see what his host had spotted, Richard was afforded an excellent view of the shuttle as it sat on its launch mount. Visible less than a quarter of a mile away, the white, delta-winged spacecraft appeared like some sort of prehistoric bird ready for flight. Tendrils of venting liquid hydrogen could be seen swirling from its boosters, and Richard realized that the fog was already rapidly dissipating.

"She's a beauty, isn't she?" reflected Lansford proudly. "She cost over a billion bucks, and if you ask me, she's worth every penny of it. In less than an hour five brave men are going to ride up that access tower and be loaded into the orbiter's command module. Then, at the stroke of noon, if all continues as scheduled, those boosters will trigger with a force of over six million pounds of combined thrust. Seconds later, our boys will be well on their way into the heavens."

Angling his line of sight downwards, so that it directly met that of his guest's, Lansford added, "I truly appreciate your concern about the Condor's safety, but do you really think that I would in any way jeopardize this project's safety? My God, Doc, this is my life's work that you're talking about! I've dedicated thousands of hours of time so that this day, and

311

many others, could come to pass. If I had the merest hint that something was amiss, I'd see to it at once.

"Now, as to your concern about sabotage, let me just remind you that the security around this complex is airtight. No one in their right mind would dare try to challenge us here. I'd just like to see someone try to smuggle a weapon the likes of an electromagnetic rail-gun into this valley. Even if such a newfangled gadget were indeed operational, it would need an extremely powerful energy source to activate it. And that's not even taking into consideration such a device's huge, bulky size. No, Doc, I'm afraid this one I'm just not going to buy."

Well aware of the reason for the professional soldier's natural recalcitrance, the civilian offered him a new idea. "What do you think about the possibility that the threat we're facing is not a ground-based one? Isn't it possible that a naval vessel could have been adapted to carry a weapon such as a rail-gun? Powered by a nuclear reactor, such a device could have deadly capabilities."

"Next you'll be telling me that it's loaded on the back of that Soviet sub that's rumored to be in these waters," returned Lansford lightly.

"Why not?" retorted Richard. "Such a vessel would serve as the ideal platform!"

The lieutenant colonel merely shook his head. "Easy does it, Doc. I hear you, but it's still not registering. I must admit that your idea could have some merit, and that it should be explored in the future, but as for right now, it just doesn't apply. There's no way that I can stop this launch on a mere hunch. You wouldn't believe the pressure that we've been fielding from Washington to get the Condor skyward. I'm not about to be the one who's going to call the President to cancel this launch because of a

312

slight possibility that something might go wrong. That's just not how it works at this stage of the game."

Taking this as his final word, Richard knew that he had failed. Not willing to waste any more effort in vain, he shrugged his shoulders and turned back toward the launch-control center.

Behind him, Lansford was most aware of his disappointed guest's sullen expression and rushed to catch up with him. Forced to increase the length of his steps to keep up with the NOSC researcher's full stride, Lansford spoke out between breaths.

"I'll tell you what, Doc, since you're so set on this thing, I'll go halfway with you. As soon as I get back to the control room, I'll ring Bill Rose, our security chief. We've got a good three and a half hours left until launch, so there's plenty of time to initiate a complete sweep of the area. We'll even send out the choppers to patrol the coastline, to make certain that there are no bogy submarines prowling in the waters there. What do you say to that?"

Taking these remarks as the conciliatory gestures they were meant to be, Richard didn't even bother responding. Increasing his pace, he decided that only one vessel could save the Condor now. Turning off the path to head directly toward the parking lot, he prayed that he would find the U.S.S. Razorback still moored at Port Arguello.

At 0900 Commander Philip Exeter was seated at the head of the wardroom table. Dressed in a clean pair of khakis, he had an icebag set on his right knee. Contentedly sipping on a cup of coffee, the senior officer studied a chart of the course that they would be undertaking once they left Arguello. Seated opposite him was his XO. Patrick Benton was reading a well-worn copy of the latest issue of *The Submarine Review* while chewing on the stem of his favorite pipe.

Both men hardly looked up when Lieutenant Scott Willingham entered the wardroom and approached the captain's side. "Sir, the boat is ready to get underway."

Still deep in his study of the chart, Exeter responded, "Very good, Lieutenant. What's the status of the Marlin?"

Willingham was quick to answer. "The DSRV is secured in its transfer skirt. Commander Pierce and his crew are presently topside, double-checking the mount in preparation for our embarkation."

"Good," returned the captain, who only now looked up into the alert eyes of the young lieutenant. "Please let the commander know that we'll be sitting on the surface until we reach our release point. They're more than welcome to join us for breakfast once we get under way."

"Aye, aye, sir," responded Willingham as he continued on toward the access trunk that was located on the other side of the officers' staterooms.

While the junior lieutenant began his way up the ladder that would take him topside, Patrick Benton put down the copy of the magazine he had been reading. After removing his pipe from his lips, he asked, "How far will we be taking the Marlin out this time?"

Exeter readjusted his weight and seemed to wince when this movement caused him to jerk his injured limb. "Ah, damn this knee anyway! I'm sorry, Pat. I guess I'm just not used to being handicapped yet. To answer your question, it's been decided to drop them along that portion of the debris field that lies closest

314

to shore. It seems now that they've got their nose cone, the powers that be want to take a look at what's left of the Titan's engines."

"I sure bet that tidal wave shifted that debris field some," reflected the XO. "I still can't get over how it seemed to lead the Marlin right down to that nose cone. I would have sure liked to see their faces when they chanced upon that temple, or whatever it was. Talk about the hand of fate. It was almost as if this whole thing was meant to happen this way."

"Don't get metaphysical with me, Pat," said Exeter, his face in a grin.

Before the XO could respond, the comm line rang out. Patrick Benton reached over and picked it up.

"XO here . . . Yeah, the captain's still in the wardroom. . . . Hold on, and I'll see what he has to say."

Holding his hand over the transmitter, he looked up. "Captain, it's Lieutenant Willingham. It seems there's some hotshot from NOSC topside. His name is Dr. Richard Fuller, and he says that it's urgent that he has a word with you before we put to sea."

Checking his watch, Exeter responded, "We've got a couple of minutes yet. Check his ID and then send him down."

After relaying this information, the XO hung up the receiver and sat back in the booth. "I wonder what this is all about."

"Commander Pierce mentioned something about flying over here from Hawaii with some scientist who's giving the Air Force a hand with the salvage operation. I'll bet you this is the guy."

Exeter took another sip of coffee, and was in the process of carefully readjusting his ice pack when a tall, tanned, blond-haired civilian rounded the corner and entered the wardroom.

"Dr. Fuller, I presume. Good morning, I'm Commander Philip Exeter, and this is my Executive Officer, Patrick Benton. Welcome aboard the Razorback. Please sit down. Can we get you a cup of coffee?"

Nodding that this would be most welcome, Richard exchanged handshakes with the officers and took a seat on the captain's right.

"You don't know how good it was to see this vessel still tied up here when I got down to the docks," remarked Richard, who accepted the mug of coffee that the galley mate soon served him. "I was afraid that you would have already gone to sea."

"As it turned out, you just caught us in time," replied the Captain. "I understand that you're with NOSC. We're stationed in San Diego ourselves. You wouldn't happen to know a Dr. Roselle over there, would you?"

"I sure do," returned Richard. "He's my boss."

Exeter smiled. "No kidding. We worked together several years ago on the ADCAP program. That man didn't miss a thing."

"He's still as sharp as ever," reflected Richard. "You really don't appreciate how brilliant he is until you work for him. He's a source of constant amazement."

"Well, you guys continue to do excellent work. I hope you know how much it's appreciated. Now, how can we help you this morning?"

Richard answered the Captain's question carefully. "Scuttlebutt has it that the Razorback has been on the trail of a suspected Soviet submarine in these waters lately. I have good reason to believe that not only was this same vessel directly responsible for the Titan's demise, but that it could very well threaten the space shuttle Condor as well."

Taking in this revelation, both officers appeared

astounded by what they were hearing. It was Exeter who broke the silence.

"That's a mouthful, Dr. Fuller. If this so-called bogy does indeed exist, how in the hell could it be responsible for knocking a missile out of the skies?"

Richard didn't hesitate. "It's carrying a nuclear-powered, electromagnetic rail-gun. Able to induce velocities of up to forty-six thousand miles per hour, such a weapon would only have to hit the Titan a single time to send it hurtling back to earth.

"Recently, I completed an examination of this same rocket's nose cone. Etched in its base was a hole that provides what I consider to be indisputable proof that such a weapon made the Titan fail. What concerns me now is the fear that the same fate awaits the Condor."

Though no words were spoken, the glance exchanged between the Razorback's two senior officers said it all. They were definitely receptive to his warning, and then some.

Playing devil's advocate, Patrick Benton asked, "If you're so certain of all this, then why hasn't the shuttle launch been postponed? I believe that the latest news dispatch showed the Condor still going up today at noon, as scheduled."

Richard could only shrug his shoulders. "That's the alarming part. Though I presented my concerns to the Air Force colonel in charge of operations here, the man wouldn't even pass them on. I even tried to inform Secretary of the Air Force Fitzpatrick, who's currently visiting Vandenberg, yet he was totally unreachable. I felt as if I was knocking my head against a brick wall. And then I remembered the Razorback. Even if they won't cancel the launch, at least you can be out there on the lookout for any unwelcome intruders."

317

Again checking his watch, the Captain responded, "That's an interesting theory, Dr. Fuller. We'll certainly keep it in mind when we begin our patrol, which should be in five more minutes. Though we'd love to have you along, I'm afraid we'll have to ask you to leave now."

Confident that he had gotten his point across, Richard rose. "Thanks for your time, gentlemen."

"And yours," countered Exeter, who removed the ice pack and struggled to stand himself.

Holding onto the wall while he got his balance, the Captain added, "Let's just hope to God that you're wrong, Doctor. But in the meantime, you can count on us to make certain that no harm comes to the Condor from the sea. Can you find your way back topside?"

Nodding that he could, Richard took a last look at the two men who now had the responsibility. Sighing in relief, he then turned to make his way out of the stern access trunk.

That left the wardroom empty except for the Captain and his XO. It was the XO who tested the waters.

"Well, Captain, what do you think about all that?"

Exeter released a sigh of his own. "That was sure one for the books. Electromagnetic rail-guns still sound like science-fiction, yet if he's working for Roselle, he's got to be a smart one. My first impression said he could have a screw lose, yet my gut tells me that Dr. Richard Fuller just might have stumbled onto something hot."

"I agree," returned the XO. "The sooner we get out there, the quicker we'll all know for certain."

"Then let's do it, Pat. Get that deck crew down here, and notify Willingham. I want us making steam just as originally planned, so get these kids moving!"

318

As the Razorback inched its way into the Pacific, Grigori Yagoda and Dmitri Andreyev sat nestled in a circle of rocks, a quarter of a kilometer away from Slik 6's northern security perimeter. Appearing to blend in with the surrounding terrain, the camouflaged commandos studied that portion of the launch complex visible before them.

Beyond the dual set of barbed-wired-topped fences was a large bunker filled with snaking pipes and various-sized tanks. Both operatives assumed this to be the gas-storage area. Separating this facility from the launch pad itself was a wide, barren plain, empty except for a series of access towers. This afforded them an excellent view of the shuttle vehicle as it sat perched beside the trio of boosters that were designed to guide it into the heavens.

The fog had long since lifted, and the sky was crystal blue, without a cloud visible. Already the warmth of the sun was noticeable. After wiping dry his soaked forehead, Dmitri Andreyev rechecked the magazine of his M16 rifle.

"I tell you, Grigori, this all looks too simple. You would have thought that the Americans would show a little more concern for the safety of their precious shuttle. This will be like shooting a fat chicken that's locked in its pen."

His blond-haired teammate looked up from the sixty-inch-long tubular weapon that he had been working on. "Don't underestimate the crafty Americans so readily, comrade. Though we've seen only a minimal show of security so far, they're out here all right. I'll guarantee you that they have video cameras and other electronic monitors covering every square centimeter of that perimeter. Just you try penetrating it."

"Who needs to penetrate it bodily?" returned Dmitri with a wink, as he gently patted the shiny black, bazooka-like instrument that Grigori had been assembling. "With this baby, that fence will be completely useless."

"Let's just hope that there are no major delays with the launch," reflected Grigori. "We've only got provisions for two more days at the most."

"If that occurs, we've only got to go into the nearest town for supplies. We've got plenty of U.S. dollars, and I understand that their supermarkets are most adequately stocked with any food that you might desire."

Grigori shook his head and fought to hold back his laughter. "I could just see us merely walking into one of their stores dressed like this, comrade. We don't exactly look inconspicuous."

"I don't know about that, Grigori. After all, this is a military town. Most probably, they'd never even take notice of us."

A familiar, muted chopping sound was heard in the distance, and both men instantly scanned the skies for its source. It was Dmitri who pointed out the dark green helicopter that was sweeping in over the rugged hills that lay to the east.

"It's a UH-1 Huey," he observed breathlessly. "And it seems to be headed straight for us!"

Without hesitation, Grigori carefully lowered the Stinger. "Help me with the camouflage netting, comrade!"

Both men reached out for the piece of brown and green netting that lay spread out behind them. It took them only seconds to grab each of its sides and pull it over their heads. Appearing almost indistinguishable from the surrounding terrain, the disguise was soon put to the test when the helicopter seemed to hover

320

directly above them.

The sound of the chopper's engines roared with a vengeance, and Dmitri had to speak right into his teammate's ear to be heard. "Perhaps their video cameras have spotted us, Grigori. Do you think that you should blast them from the skies with the Stinger, and then turn it on the shuttle before we're discovered?"

"That would be much too risky," returned Grigori calmly. "Without the hot plumes of the booster engines pointing the way, there's too great a chance that our missile would miss its mark. And besides, I doubt if we've been caught yet. Most likely, it's only a patrol."

This observation was confirmed when the sound of the helicopter's engines suddenly began to fade. A minute later, the distinctive clatter was completely absent. They poked their heads from under the net, and a quick scan of the skies verified this fact.

"You are right once again," commented Dmitri. "I guess I'm getting a little too over-anxious."

Grigori slyly grinned. "That's only natural, comrade. Like any good hunter, you smell the kill before your nose and instinctively crave for satisfaction. Yet, with this quarry, it's going to be patience that makes the hunt succeed. Calm down, my friend. Our time will soon be here."

Pulling the net completely off them, Grigori sat up and lifted the now-fully-assembled Stinger to his shoulder. Peering through its telescopic lense, he centered the cross-hairs on the target that had sent them to this desolate plain in the first place.

Beginning with the stubby nose of the gleaming white orbiter, Grigori slowly scanned its box-car-like fuselage, finally coming to a halt on the insignia painted on its delta-shaped wing. Without the need of additional magnification, he was able to easily make out the five-pointed-star emblem of the United States Air Force. Beneath this etching was printed the word "Condor". Well aware now of the precise identity of his prey, Grigori sat back to await the moment when the hunt would begin.

Chapter Fourteen

Five and a half miles from Point Arguello, the U.S.S. Razorback sailed on a westward course. In the process of detaching the DSRV Marlin from its back, the sub bit into the cool waters fifty feet beneath the Pacific's surface. Below in the vessel's sonar room, the two seamen currently responsible for monitoring the series of sensitive microphones mounted on its hull listened to the noise caused by the DSRV's parting.

"Brother, is that sucker ever creating a racket," commented Lefty Jackman disgustedly. "Every submarine in the Eastern Pacific is bound to hear us now."

"The Marlin will be on her own soon enough, pawdner," answered Seaman Second Class Seth Burke, who pulled off the headphones he had been wearing. "Then we'll be able to go about business as usual."

Following his co-worker's lead, Lefty also removed his headphones. While massaging his sore earlobes, he reflected on their state.

"That will sure be a welcomed relief, Tex. Maybe this time we'll be able to tag that Soviet sub once and for all. It's still eating on me that they were able to shake us like they did."

"If they're still around and we hear 'em, we'll get 'em all right," returned the gangly Texan. "At least this time, we don't have to go runnin' around with our active sonar pingin' up a storm."

Lefty reached for his coffee cup. "Amen, brother. I still can't believe the Skipper hasn't ordered us to activate it as yet. Maybe we're finally done with that boring salvage duty."

"I wonder if it could have something to do with that up-coming space shuttle shot," offered Burke, who went for his own coffee cup. "I heard some Air Force honchos back at Arguello sayin' that it could go up anytime now. It sure has been a while since the last shuttle, Challenger, went down."

"I'll say," answered Lefty solemnly. "That's one morning I'll never forget. Even now, I can see it as clear as day. I was sitting in my high school science class watching the launch preparations live on TV. All morning we were hearing about how great it was to finally have a real, live teacher in space. When the orbiter exploded right before our very eyes, my first reaction was that this couldn't be really happening. When the reality finally sunk in, I walked around in shock for an entire week afterwards."

After taking a long sip of coffee, the Texan voiced his own experience. "Well, join the crowd, pawdner. I was helpin' my dad string fencin' down in the south forty, when one of the hands arrived and told us that the shuttle had exploded. It's funny, but even out on the west plains of Texas, I was able to visualize just what that explodin' space ship must have looked like. Even my dad was choked up by the news, and that's one old coot who don't get riled by nothin'."

Shaking his head in response, Lefty momentarily

placed one of his cramped feet on the lip of the console. Just as he was in the middle of a wide yawn, Chief Petty Officer Lawrence Desiante barged into the narrow compartment. Catching the Senior Seaman as he pulled his foot quickly downward, the chief didn't waste any time in expressing his wrath.

"Oh, and what do we have here, a coffee party? I hate to be a nuisance, but would you mind telling me who's running the store while you jokers are sitting here with your feet up jawing?"

Guilt filled their faces as the two seamen set their coffee cups down. While the moustached chief squeezed his bulky figure forward, Lefty looked up sheepishly.

"I'm sorry, Chief, but we were only waiting for the Marlin to complete its detachment. There was so much racket going on out there that there wasn't much else that we could hear anyway."

"Oh, so you two decided to have a little coffee klatch," spat the still-fuming chief. "And here I was only minutes ago having the riot act read to me by the XO, that we should be especially on the ball these next couple of hours. You should have heard me bragging how you two were the best in the Navy, and that you'd never let us down. If the XO had walked in with me, I could have never shown my face in front of him again."

Sliding on his headphones, Lefty reached out to get back to work. "Don't worry, Chief. If those Russkies are still out there, you got the right guys to find them."

Softening a bit, Desiante responded, "That had better be the case, Jackman. I don't go about boasting about every wet-eared seaman who answers to me. Now, let's see what we've got out there!"

Reaching out for an auxilliary set of phones, the chief snapped on a headset himself. His breath was heavy as he sat down on the stool immediately behind the two sonar technicians. Rubbing his creased forehead, he struggled to clear his mind of everything but the series of sounds that was now being funnelled into his ears.

Responsible for the source and volume of this noise was Lefty Jackman. By turning a thick plastic dial, the senior seaman was able to determine which of the Razorback's hull-mounted hydrophones were to be isolated. A sweep of the waters to the west, the direction in which they were currently heading, picked up nothing but the loud, distinctive chattering of millions of shrimp. As he turned the dial to penetrate the waters to the south, they heard the playful, squealing voices of a pod of dolphins. Oblivious to the almost human-like moans and clicks that filled the seas there, Lefty rotated the scan to check their baffles. There, they had to be extra careful to listen over the steady drone of the Razorback's own engines.

It was while inching the dial forward with the most delicate of touches that Lefty isolated one of the stern hydrophones and picked up a faraway muted vibration. To the average listener, this sound would have been practically indistinguishable from the myriad of other noises audible. But to Lefty Jackman's sensitive ear, this resonance was as noticeable as an improperly tuned musical instrument. Turning the dial quickly backward to isolate the exact location of this sound, Lefty felt his pulse quicken. Only when he turned the volume gain to its maximum level did he turn to address his co-workers.

"Do you hear it? It's some sort of man-made

pump!"

The chief's brow narrowed as he vainly attempted to verify the seaman's observation. "I'm not so sure that I agree with you, Jackman. From this distance, it could be almost anything."

"Maybe it's the Marlin," offered Seth Burke.

"No way," countered Lefty. "She's smack in our baffles, and nearly half the distance closer. Besides, the Marlin's signature is nothing like this one. My first hunch is that it's coming from that Russkie nuke that thinks it can fool us by playing possum."

Though he still didn't agree, the chief looked up to determine the sound's heading and relative rough range. With the XO's spirited briefing still fresh in his mind, he knew this was an instance when it was much better to be safe than sorry. Since there was obviously no propeller whine audible, if it were another sub, it would have to be indeed hovering. Even this fairly silent process produced some sort of noise. This was particularly true of the nuclear-powered boats, with reactors that never stopped running. Deciding that there was the slightest of chances that this could indeed be the case, the Chief cautiously reached out to pick up the comm line. Watching the chief speak into the receiver, the two seamen looked on anxiously.

The Razorback's maneuvering room was located on the vessel's second deck, in the stern half of the boat, between the crew's mess hall and the engines themselves. Fondly known as Razorback Power and Light, the room controlled and monitored all aspects of the sub's power capabilities. Usually staffed by a complement of a half-dozen men, the compartment was home to dozens of voltage meters, pressure indicators, levers, switches, and valves. These instruments measured not only the state of the boat's three 1,500-horsepower diesel engines, but the condition of its pair of huge propulsion batteries and its trio of 940-kilowatt DC electric generators as well.

Because the Razorback was currently completely submerged, it was being propelled by battery power only. In this state, the vessel's diesel engines had to remain idle, because of the lack of an adequate supply of fresh air. Presently standing before the bank of meters that indicated the amount of charge left in these batteries was Exeter, Benton, and the boat's Engineering Officer, Lieutenant Ted Smith.

Over the nearby drone of the propulsion unit itself, the three officers were locked in conversation. They were only a few feet from the engine room but even so, the compartment was uncharacteristically hot. This temperature was high enough to cause wet rings of sweat to stain their uniforms. It was this abnormal environmental factor that was the subject of their present conversation.

"I still don't want you taking any chances, Lieutenant Smith," cautioned the Captain. "If that main condenser goes, this entire boat will be like a hot house in a matter of minutes."

"She'll hold, Captain," returned the Engineering Officer firmly. "There's no way that I'd needlessly jeopardize the safety of the Razorback if I knew differently."

"I realize that," said Exeter. "But meanwhile, you guys back here are taking the brunt of the discomfort."

"At least make certain that the men drink plenty of fluids, and some salt tablets wouldn't hurt either," interjected Benton.

Watching Exeter reach down and carefully rub his right knee, Lieutenant Smith replied, "Will do, Mr. Benton. It's going to take more than a little heat to melt this tough bunch. By the way, Captain, how's that injury of yours holding out?"

Shifting his weight onto his left leg, Exeter answered with a wink, "Don't forget that I'm an ex-engineering man myself, Lieutenant. No little bash on the knee is going to keep me down. I'll manage all right."

Punctuating these words was the harsh buzz of the comm line. An alert seaman answered the phone and called out, "Lieutenant Benton, it's Chief Desiante, sir."

Without wasting a second, the XO walked over and picked up the receiver. His eyes lit up with interest as he took in the report that the chief hastily conveyed.

Closely watching his expression change was Exeter. The Captain found his hopes rising when the XO flashed him a victorious thumbs-up. Seconds later, Benton was off the phone and back at his side.

"Sonar's got a contact, Captain. The bearing is one-two-five, at a rough range of thirty thousand yards. The chief still can't say for sure, but he feels we could have caught a nuke hovering there."

"Good work, Pat," shot back Exeter. "My instincts told me that something was out there. Now, if it's just that Victor."

Checking his watch, the Captain added, "Get into sonar and take a listen, Pat. I'm going to stop up in my stateroom for some aspirin, and then get over to the control room, where you can reach me. Let me know the second that you can get a positive on them.

"And, Lieutenant Smith, the next couple of hours could be critical. I'm counting on you to hold us together at least until noon."

"No sweat, sir," returned the confident Engineering Officer.

Following the lead of his XO, Exeter began his way toward the sealed, watertight doorway that led toward the boat's bow. Doing his best not to hobble, the Captain ducked through the hatch that Patrick Benton efficiently opened for him. Halting before the ladder that would take him up to his stateroom, Exeter took a brief moment to address his XO.

"If it's indeed the Soviets, Pat, you know what this might mean. Dr. Fuller's prophecy could unfold right before our very eyes."

"For some reason, I kind of hope that it does," countered the XO, who reached into his breast pocket to exhume his pipe. "It's our turn to show those guys that Uncle Sam doesn't take trespassers lightly."

"Especially those who shoot down his missiles," added Exeter, as he began the painful climb up toward his stateroom.

Watching his progress, Patrick Benton knew that any lesser man would have been laid up on his bunk hours ago, but not their Captain. Stubborn and pigheaded to the very end, Exeter would command the Razorback from his very deathbed if it were necessary. Praying that he would never have to see that day come to pass, the XO turned to continue on through the hatch that led into the crew's mess hall.

The smell of bacon and coffee met his nostrils as he entered the galley. Approximately a dozen sailors sat in the various booths that lined this rather spacious compartment. They were either deep into their breakfasts or watching the movie that was playing from the mounted video screen, and a hushed silence prevailed. Without taking the time to disturb them,

Benton continued on past the kitchen area and into an adjoining passageway. It was at the end of this narrow corridor that his goal lay.

The sonar compartment was dark and cramped. Stacks of electronic equipment lined its walls. Slowing his progress some to allow his eyes time to adjust to the dim light there, the XO entered the room cautiously. He soon picked out three figures seated in the compartment's far corner. It was towards the chief petty officer that he addressed himself.

"The Captain thought it would be best if I had a listen myself. Is it still out there, Chief?"

Turning to the unexpected visitor, Desiante responded, "It sure is, Mr. Benton. Have a seat while we get you a set of headphones."

Scooting off the stool he had been seated on, the chief reached forward and plugged another headset into the console. While he did so, both Lefty Jackman and Seth Burke became aware of their new guest. Sitting up straight in their chairs, the seamen looked on as the XO positioned himself immediately behind them. With his customary corncob pipe protruding from the corner of his mouth, Benton slipped on the auxilliary headphones. He then closed his eyes, to more fully concentrate on the obscure noise emanating from the southeast at a distance of some 30,000 yards.

For the first couple of seconds, Benton had trouble picking up anything unusual. Only as his pulse settled did he hear a muted surging sound, barely audible in the background.

The XO knew that if they were on one of the new 688-class attack subs, they would merely have to feed this sound into the computer. The signature would then be analyzed and its source identified. On board the Razorback, this task had to be accomplished the old-fashioned way. Emptying his mind of everything but the unknown surging, he wracked his brain in an effort to determine what was causing it. Though he still couldn't say for certain, the only thing that he could compare it to was the unwanted sound created by a reactor cavitation problem that he had experienced on one of his previous commands aboard a nuclear-powered Sturgeon-class attack sub.

Opening his eyes, he met the chief's inquisitive stare and responded accordingly. "There's something out there, all right. It sounds like an internal, closed-loop cavitation signature, emanating from a nuclear-powered submarine. Most likely, they're just sitting there hovering, thinking that we'll merely pass them by. But we'll show them otherwise, won't we, gentlemen?"

The XO was in the process of picking up the comm line when Lefty Jackman called out excitedly, "Sir, I'm picking up another unidentified contact! This one lies in the northeastern quadrant, at a heading of zero-eight-zero. Relative rough range is thirty-eight thousand yards. You know, it sounds like it could be another diesel-electric!"

As this new signature was channeled into their headphones, Patrick Benton momentarily delayed his call to the control room. There was no doubt in his mind that the new sound they were now hearing was indeed the familiar drone of a battery-powered submarine. Yet one fact immediately stood out in his mind. Since the only other two diesel-electric vessels in the U.S. Navy were in Japan, in the midst of ASW exercises, this meant that this contact had to be of foreign origin. He was most aware that any one of the two vessels they had just picked up could hold the threat that the NOSC researcher had warned them of earlier. Hastily checking his watch, he saw that in another hour the Condor was due to be launched from nearby Vandenberg. With this in mind, he activated the comm line, to present their dilemma to the Captain.

Six and a half miles due east of the Razorback's current position, Deputy Commander Bill Rose of Vandenberg's 4392nd Security Police Group sat in the co-pilot's seat of a UH-1 Huey helicopter. Presently hovering only a few hundred feet above the jagged hills that comprised Slik 6's eastern border, the chopper had its nose pointed westward. From this position, the launch complex itself was just barely visible to the left. His attention was instead riveted straight ahead, on the desolate plain that was situated to the immediate north of the launch pad's security perimeter. There, a quarter of a mile from the fence itself, lay a circle of large, angular boulders. It was toward this rocky mass that his stare was centered.

The roar of the Huey's engines sounded loudly overhead, and to compensate for it, Rose was forced to speak firmly into his chin-mounted radio transmitter. "That's affirmative, Colonel Lansford. The preliminary infra-red helicopter scan shows a pair of mammalian life forms hidden within the circle of rocks. We're almost certain that it's not coming from either a bear, cougar, or any other form of wildlife. It's got to be human. I hope you don't mind, but I've taken the liberty of deploying Strike Team Able."

"Of course I don't mind," responded the crackling voice of Lansford as it emanated from the helmet-mounted speakers. "It's urgent that you clear the

333

area as soon as possible. Use whatever force is needed to accomplish this task at once."

"Yes, sir," snapped Rose. "I'll notify you as soon as the sector is secured."

Switching the two-way radio's frequency, he dialed that of Captain Tim Geller, the strike team's leader. A momentary crackle of static was followed by a familiar bass voice.

"This is Able Team leader, go ahead."

Breathlessly, Rose addressed him. "Roger, Able Team leader, this is Commander One. You are cleared to initiate housecleaning. Use whatever elbow grease is necessary."

"I read you, Commander One. Will send in the mini-maids, over and out."

As the helicopter inched its way over the surrounding hilltops, Rose strained to see his men in action. Strike Team Able was his personal creation. Comprised of two dozen crack members of the 4392nd Security Police Group, the squad was created for incidents such as the one they currently faced. It appeared that this would be the first time in its two-year history that a call it was responding to was a real emergency and not a simulated one. Armed with M16's, M79 grenade launchers, a pair of M60 machine guns, and a 90-mm. M67 recoilless rifle, the group included the base's top marksmen. It was designed to repel an invading force in the unlikely event that such a group of terrorists were able to breach Vandenberg's security perimeter.

Not having any idea who they could be presently facing, Rose scanned the plain that lay before him. Because his men were dressed in camouflaged fatigues that blended into the surrounding terrain, he had to use a pair of binoculars to pick them out. They were currently deployed approximately 200 yards from the rock formation where the intruders had been spotted. Positioned in a semicircle, they covered the northern, western, and eastern perimeters. This left only the southern flank open. Rose leaned forward expectantly as a tall, lean figure stood and beckoned his men to continue their advance. Crouched low to the ground, they slowly began their way towards the circle's axis in unison.

"Attention intruders, you are currently trespassing on a United States military installation. Please immediately stand up with your hands clearly extended over your heads!"

As this amplified warning was repeated, Grigori Yagoda returned the startled expression that he saw on his teammate's face. This look of astonishment turned to near panic when Dmitri Andreyev poked his head up through the camouflaged netting that was spread out on top of them and took in the advancing line of troops that approached on three sides.

Ducking back down, his voice trembled. "There's a whole army of them out there, Grigori! Where in the world did they come from?"

"I told you not to underestimate the Americans," retorted his blond-haired co-worker coolly.

"That's easy to say now," returned Dmitri, who reached down to ready his weapons. "Perhaps we'll be able to fight our way past them."

Grigori beckoned his teammate to calm down. "Easy now, comrade. There is still another alternative for us to consider."

Placing his Uzi on the ground beneath him, Grigori put on his green beret. He then pushed aside the net and stood.

"Are you going to surrender?" quizzed Dmitri, who remained crouching and watched as Grigori opened his palms and raised his hands up over his head.

Ignoring this question, Grigori climbed up onto the rock ledge and faced the line of armed soldiers, who were now some fifty yards away. Upon spotting him, they immediately froze. A single tall, lean figure broke from their ranks and spoke through a battery-powered megaphone.

"Please have your accomplice join you also!"

Surprised that they knew that there were two of them present, Grigori beckoned Dmitri to join him. As he shakily did so, Grigori yelled out in perfect English, "Good morning, gentlemen! We're both assigned to the Army's 7th Infantry Division at Fort Ord. We've been sent down here on direct orders of the Secretary of the Defense, to attempt to penetrate your defenses."

The gangly American Air Force officer was quick with his response. "We know nothing about such an operation. Please remain standing still, with your hands overhead, while I send a team in to check your credentials."

He signalled to his right, and two brawny soldiers appeared. One of these individuals held a large German shepherd dog by a taut leash. Pulling out their handguns, they began walking quickly forward.

Dmitri watched their progress and felt his heart pounding in his chest. He knew very well that, although their accents and uniforms might temporarily fool the Americans, they had no proper credentials. His mouth was dry and breath heavy when he suddenly swooned back dizzily.

This sudden, unexpected movement caused the Americans to abruptly stop dead in their tracks. As they simultaneously crouched to raise their weapons, the German shepherd lunged forward and its leash slipped from its handler's grip. Angrily growling, the huge tan-and-black dog raced towards the nearby circle of rocks.

Disoriented by his loss of balance, and guided by the illogical grasp of fear-induced panic, Dmitri reached for the .45-caliber pistol that he had hidden beneath the belt at the small of his back. Raising it before him, he managed to hold it steady and shoot the dog smack in its head. No sooner had it tumbled to the ground than Dmitri turned the weapon on the dog's handler. Another shot rang out, and this time an American soldier fell, mortally wounded. Dmitri was already turning the pistol toward the startled American who stood at his fallen comrade's side when an iron-like grasp pulled him down behind the shelter of the rocks. A second later, the first bullets whined into the stone ledge.

"Have you gone insane?" cried Grigori as he scrambled for the weapons that they had left on the floor beneath them. "Why in hell did you do such a foolish thing? Not only did you almost commit suicide, but now you've just about doomed the success of our mission as well!"

Having snapped back to his senses, Dmitri timidly picked up a M16. "I'm sorry, comrade. I don't know what got into me."

The blast of an exploding grenade sent a shower of ricocheting stone down onto their heads, and both men ducked for cover. As the fragments settled, Grigori grabbed for his Uzi.

"You've left us no alternative, comrade. Now, we

337

must fight for our very lives."

Peeking up over the rim of protective rock, he sprayed the horizon with a hail of 9-mm. bullets. Ever conscious of the unalterable course of violent action that he had brought down on them, Dmitri grabbed the M16 and joined his teammate. He raised its sights in just enough time to center them on the chest of an advancing American. The soldier had just pulled the pin from a grenade and was about to lob it over his head when Dmitri's shot took him down. When the wounded man dropped the already primed grenade, it exploded in a showering torrent of razor-sharp shrapnel. As a result of this, two of his country-men fell to the ground beside him.

Dmitri concentrated on protecting their western and northern flanks, while Grigori took aim at the line of soldiers coming in from the south. Because they had a well-protected vantage point and plenty of ammunition, they were able to stop their attackers from closing in all together. Prone on their bellies, a good fifty yards away, the Americans could only hope that a lucky shot would hit its mark.

"Commander One, this is Able Team leader. I'm afraid the opposition is a bit stiffer than we had anticipated. Five of my men are down. Some air support would sure be appreciated."

Taking in this breathless request, which was delivered with a background accompaniment of staccato-like rifle blasts, Deputy Commander Bill Rose instantly replied, "We're coming in, Able Team. This won't take long."

Signaling the pilot with a raised right fist, Rose held on as the Huey gained altitude and shot over the hills they had been hiding behind. It didn't take him long to spot the circle of rocks from which an occasional puff of gunfire broke. Circling the battlefield, he determined the positions of their own men. He couldn't help but notice that several of these young soldiers were sprawled out on the sandy soil, their limbs blood-covered and not moving. His face tightened in anger, and he pointed towards the enemy's position.

"Let's get those bastards, Lieutenant!"

In response to this passionate directive, the pilot guided the Huey in to attack. On their first two sweeps, they saturated the rock ledge with 7.62-mm. bullets spat forth from their chin-mounted mini-gun. It was on the third pass that they began blasting into the stone itself, with their TOW fire-and-forget anti-tank missiles.

A resounding explosion followed the detonation of the first of these powerful missiles. This was accompanied by a thick cloud of dense white smoke. Well aware that they still carried another five TOW's in reserve, Rose anxiously licked his lips in anticipation of the next approach.

"My goodness, Grigori, what was that?"

Dmitri's shaken voice emanated from deep inside a crevice of rock, where the Spetsnaz operatives had crawled to escape the Huey's bullets. With his ears still buzzing from the deafening blast that only seconds ago had shaken them, he caught the look of solid confidence on his teammate's face.

"That, comrade, was most likely one of their TOW anti-tank missiles," whispered Grigori. "I doubt if we'll be able to take many more concussions like that one, without the entire ledge sliding down on top of us."

Slipping out of the crevice, Grigori reached for the Stinger that still lay inside its protective case. Rather meekly, Dmitri followed him out into the cramped clearing, which the rocks surrounded. He looked on as his teammate hastily took hold of the shiny black, tube-like weapon and efficiently made some last second adjustments.

"How do you plan to counter this anti-tank weapon, Grigori?"

"Reload your M16 and prepare to give me some covering fire, comrade. We still have a single chance. I'm going to take out that Huey, then turn the Stinger on the space shuttle. If the fates are still with us, my aim will be true, and we'll accomplish our glorious mission after all. Now, take courage, Dmitri Andreyev. Our finest hour has finally arrived!"

Inspired by these words, Dmitri took a last fond look at his teammate, then reached out to insert another cartridge case into his rifle. Seeing that Grigori was ready for action, he stood upright and, resting the barrel of the M16 on top of the rock ledge, began spraying the surrounding landscape with bullets.

Grigori wasted no time taking a position behind him. A quick scan of the horizon allowed him to catch sight of the helicopter as it prepared to sweep in from the north. No sooner had the first bullets begun blasting from its mini-gun than the Spetsnaz operative calmly sighted his quarry and pulled the launcher's trigger. Instantly, the weapon kicked backward and the air filled with an ear-splitting report. A resonant roar sounded as the Stinger's smooth-case fragmentary warhead shot out in a blinding burst of supersonic speed. Guided by the red-hot exhaust plume of the approaching chopper, the missile soared upwards and smacked into its target. A resounding blast followed and the sky filled with flaming debris.

Conscious that the helicopter would give them no more problems, Grigori reached down to begin the process of reloading the Stinger. The still-smoking barrel was scorching with heat, yet he shoved the new missile inside it anyway. In the process of pivoting to set its sights on the southern horizon, Grigori noticed that the chatter of the M16 had stopped behind him. Just as he looked over to see what was keeping Dmitri from firing, his friend's body brushed up against his back. One look at what was left of his blood-soaked face and Grigori knew his comrade had been killed almost instantly.

A new purpose inspired his actions as he turned and again shouldered the Stlnger. As he peered into its sights, a tear momentarily clouded his eye. Wiping it away, he centered the cross-hairs on the gleaming white, delta-winged space craft that sat invitingly on the other side of the security fence.

It was just as he pulled the trigger that a 90-mm. M67 recoilless rifle round struck him at the base of his skull. A milli-second later, Grigori Yagoda was nothing more than a few bloody scraps of skin and bone.

Oblivious to his death, the Stinger streaked from its launcher. Yet this time its aim was errant, and the warhead harmlessly exploded at the base of the security fence. All too soon this detonation faded, and the plain was silent again, except for the rush of the wind and the distant cry of the ever-pounding surf.

Captain Tim Geller was the first one to make it to the blood-spattered circle of rocks. Ever so cautiously,

341

he peered inside, and came to the instant conclusion that their unknown enemy no longer threatened them. Only then did he somberly reach for the two-way radio, to convey this fact to Launch Control.

Lieutenant Colonel Todd Lansford took the deaths of Bill Rose and the seven Able-Team members quite hard. Ignoring the distinguished, pin-striped individual seated beside him, he gazed up at the launch monitor, his stare vacant.

It all seemed so unnecessary. Why anyone in their right mind would send in two men to initiate a job that would take a full battalion was beyond him. He could only guess that they were terrorists of some sort. He wondered what Dr. Richard Fuller would have to say about all this. Then he snapped back from his reverie as his esteemed guest spoke up.

"I'm sorry about your men, Todd. They went to their deaths with all the valor and bravado befitting members of the United States Air Force. The entire country can be proud of them."

Secretary Fitzpatrick's words caused Lansford to sharpen the focus of his line of sight. He took in the shiny white orbiter perched at its launch mount. The digital clock that was superimposed in the bottom right-hand corner of the monitor screen showed that the launch was being held with thirty-one minutes and fifty seconds to go until lift-off. The senior officer stirred when the white-haired figure who sat beside him again spoke.

"Don't you think it's time to reinitiate the count-down, Todd?"

Massaging the pounding ache that possessed his forehead, Lansford sat forward. As if emerging from a horrible nightmare, he suddenly became conscious of his present location. Seated at the rear command console of Shuttle Mission Control, he absorbed the dozens of anxious technicians who were stationed before their own keyboards and monitors in front of him. A hushed sense of anticipation filled the air and Lansford realized that it would take only a single order from his lips to get the ball rolling once again.

With renewed composure, he turned to address the veteran Defense Department bureaucrat who sat to his right. "I'm sorry, Mr. Secretary. I thought you wanted to hold the Condor until it was determined if the intruders had any accomplices close by."

The Secretary shook his head. "I don't think that's necessary any longer, Todd. Your preliminary infrared scan showed that those two individuals were the only unauthorized figures on the entire southern quadrant of the base. I'd say that it's safe to presume that they were working by themselves. Thus, I see no reason to hold the Condor any longer."

Calmed by the Secretary's tone of voice, Lansford sighed. "You're right, Mr. Secretary. I'm sorry for hesitating. I'll restart the countdown at once."

While the lieutenant colonel picked up the intercom to convey this decision, Fitzpatrick watched him with a practiced, shrewd eye. At that moment, he could have sworn that there was something important that the senior officer was keeping from him. His years in Washington had taught him that he could trust no man absolutely. He could only hope that, whatever his host was holding inside, it wouldn't jeopardize the further safety of the delta-winged space craft that filled the monitor screen above him. A breath of relief passed his lips when he noticed that the digital clock had again started moving. This meant that in a little over a half-hour's time the Condor would be released into the heavens.

Fitzpatrick's eyes gleamed as he visualized the sophisticated reconnaissance platform secured in its cargo hold. For there lay the future security of the entire Free World. Confident that no further obstacles lay in their way, he sat back and watched the seconds left to lift-off continue to tick away.

Chapter Fifteen

Captain Philip Exeter stood in the Razorback's control room, his attention locked on the navigational chart that showed their current position. Beside him was huddled the sub's Navigator and Weapons Officer. They too studied the graph, on whose surface was drawn a triangular design. Laying at the apex of this polygon was a mark indicating the Razorback. From this position two straight lines were drawn of approximately equal length. The top one stretched to the northeast, and showed the location of the still-unidentified diesel-electric submarine. The opposing arm of the triangle extended to the southeast, and terminated at the spot where the supposed nuclear vessel currently hovered. Since spotting these two contacts, the Razorback had turned around. Headed back toward the east now, it was in the process of bisecting the triangle, putting the sub equally distant between both targets.

Ever conscious that noon was only a quarter of an hour away, Exeter shifted his weight impatiently. Making his indecision even more difficult was his aching right knee. Still feeling the pain, he wondered when the three aspirin he had just consumed would finally take effect.

The captain knew that from their current position they could easily take out both contacts. Yet, since either one had yet to make a hostile move, he found himself hesitant to do so. After all, they weren't in a declared state of war. All that he had to go on were the frantic ramblings of the NOSC researcher, whose theories could very well be so much hot air. Waiting anxiously for one of the vessels to make some sort of belligerent maneuver, he could do little more than have the Razorback primed for action. To insure their readiness, he would depend on the two junior officers who studied the chart at his side.

Clearing his dry throat, Exeter first addressed his Navigator. "Mr. McClure, I'm going to need you to pull those bathygraphs of these waters. Somewhere beneath us, the Marlin is probing the sea floor. If we are forced to attack, we've got to be certain that the DSRV doesn't stand in our way."

"Aye, aye, sir," responded the Navigator, who turned to rummage through his chart box.

This left Exeter facing his Weapons Officer. "Mr. Willingham, I'm relying on you to give me a constant update on those firing solutions. Since both contacts are under suspicion, you'll have double the work. I want all six torpedo tubes loaded with Mk-48's. Each is to be ready to fire at my command."

"What exactly are we waiting for, Captain?" asked the alert junior officer.

Exeter met the young man's inquisitive stare. "I'm not really sure, Lieutenant. All I know is that, if one of them is going to play its cards, it will be within the next fifteen minutes."

Checking his watch, the somewhat puzzled Weapons Officer nodded and began his way across the compartment to the boat's Mark 101-A fire-control console. It would be from this position that the final firing bearings would be determined and, if needed, the torpedoes subsequently fired.

Returning his attention to the chart, Exeter mentally traced the Razorback's new course eastward. By extending this route past the two unknown contacts, a journey of a little more than three more miles would take them right back to Point Arguello. Philip couldn't help but wonder what was presently taking place on the desolate plains a mile inland. Surely, the Condor was in the midst of its final countdown. If Dr. Richard Fuller's warning was to have some validity, the enemy would have to ascend soon. For not even an electromagnetic rail-gun could penetrate the ocean's icy depths. He rubbed his knee, and his weary eyes again went to the wall-mounted clock as the seconds continued to tick away to lift-off.

A deck beneath the control room, the Razorback's Executive Officer found his glance diverted once more to his watch. Barely visible in the dim light of the sonar compartment, he counted the minutes left until 1200 hours. Like the Captain, he too realized that if the enemy were to indeed make a hostile move, it would have to occur within the next couple of minutes.

Sitting in front of him, the two younger sonar technicians were hunched over their consoles. Both were wearing headphones that were connected to the series of microphones encased in the sub's hull. As a result of his recent briefing, they were each monitoring one of the two contacts that lay approximately a mile off their bow. Their first priority was to listen for any venting ballast that could indicate an ascent. Secondly, they were to be ever alert for the activation of any unusual deck machinery. If an electromagnetic rail-gun existed on one of those vessels, its bulky length would most likely be concealed somewhere on the sub's upper deck. Surely, they would hear it being activated. Only then would they know which target needed to be eliminated.

When he had relayed these final instructions, Seaman Lefty Jackman had asked for a description of just what they were so desperately listening for. Unwilling to reveal its exact nature, Benton had veiled his response. For, if the NOSC scientist's suspicions proved wrong, he preferred that Fuller's last-minute warning go no further than him and the Captain. Jackman had soon realized that he was not going to get a precise answer to his question and had merely shrugged his shoulders and immersed himself back in his work. The XO hoped that this was as far as the enlisted man's curiosity would go, yet such was not to be the case.

Unknown to the XO was the senior seaman's undying inquisitiveness. Not one to be thrown off the trail so easily, Lefty sat at his station with his thoughts spinning. As his subconscious mind took in the constant muted drone of the diesel-electric sub that slowly cruised the depths some 25,000 yards off their port bow, his conscious thoughts centered themselves on the strange briefing that the XO had just shared with them. The senior officer had instructed them to listen for something, yet he wouldn't even explain precisely what it might be. Lefty was no stranger to the fickle ways of Command, but this incident really took the cake.

Lefty could only assume that his co-worker, Seth Burke, was right, and that this whole thing revolved around the launch of the space shuttle. Perhaps the Soviets were trying to interfere in some way. That could be the reason why the Russian Victor was presently prowling these waters. He even supposed that the diesel-electric boat that they had just chanced upon could be working with the Victor. What he couldn't understand was that, if this was indeed what Command feared, why they didn't blow away both vessels and be done with it. These were their waters. Another foreign nation had absolutely no business there. How much better it was to be safe now than sorry later.

Looking forward to the day when America would quit being the nice guy and start playing hardball along with its hard-nosed adversary, Lefty reached up and readjusted the filter mechanism. After increasing the volume gain another full notch, he did his best to focus his total concentration on the contact's present sound signature. His heart jumped when the familiar drone of the unknown vessel's electric engines was abruptly overridden. In its place rose a noisy, liquid surge that was more characteristic of a nuclear reactor than an electric generator. Only after he double-checked his headphone connection, to make certain that he wasn't monitoring the contact that lay to their southeast, did he turn to inform the XO.

"Sir, you're going to have trouble believing this, but that diesel-electric that we've been following has just turned nuclear on us!"

"What?" quizzed the XO, who hastily clipped on the auxillary headphones to hear for himself.

Quick to pick out the hiss of a reactor's coolant loop, he looked puzzled. "Are you certain that you're tuned into the right vessel?"

Lefty's voice didn't falter. "I'm positive, sir. One second she was purring along on her batteries, and the next, this racket overtook her. Unless there's another nuke right on top of her, it's got to be coming from that same submarine."

It was with this observation that an idea dawned in Patrick Benton's consciousness. What if this reactor had been carried inside the diesel-electric's hull all this time? Only recently activated, it was to be utilized for a single purpose, to power a weapons system that demanded much more energy than its fossil-fueled generators could provide. This supposition was seemingly confirmed when a bubbling whirl of venting ballast emanated from this same vessel.

"She's ascending!" cried Lefty Jackman excitedly.

Without a second's hesitation, the XO reached out to grab the comm line.

Philip Exeter was standing at his usual command position at the center of the control room when the call arrived from Benton. Hastily checking the time, he knew that he had to make his final decision quickly. In another seven minutes, it would be too late.

"Mr. Willingham, give me a firing solution on the contact whose heading reads zero-three-zero," ordered the Captain firmly.

The Weapons Officer fed this request into the fire-control console, and was quick to respond. "Final solution entered and looks good, Captain."

"Prepare tubes one and three for firing!" countered Exeter, who again checked the time.

Before giving the order to release the torpedoes, he hurriedly went over his alternatives. Of the two targets before them, only the vessel off their port bow was ascending. The sudden activation of a nuclear reactor aboard this same boat surely meant that this sub needed a powerful boost of energy for something other than propulsion. Even though the NOSC scientist's prophetic warning seemed to be coming to fruition, it was not every day that a peacetime Naval officer gave the orders to willfully sink another vessel. What if this submarine had no hostile intentions, and was merely caught up in a web of coincidence? Or perhaps the sub laying off their starboard bow contained the real enemy. Were the two somehow working together?

Exeter knew he could go on second-guessing himself all day long and never be the wiser. Guided by his instincts alone, he summoned the courage to make the difficult decision that only he was responsible for. Ever conscious of the billion-dollar vehicle that would soon be blasting off into space, and gambling that Dr. Richard Fuller knew what he was talking about, Exeter turned to his right and ordered his Weapons Officer to fire both torpedo tubes.

Seconds later, the Razorback's hull trembled under the force created by two sizzling explosions of compressed air. To a loud, popping roar, the pair of Mk-48 torpedoes shot from their tubes and bit into the surrounding waters. As they plunged forward under their own power, each weapon found its course directed by the stream of information entering its guidance system from an ultra-thin wire that was being constantly played out from its tail. Still connected to the mother ship, the torpedoes headed for their targets with the Razorback's sensors guiding their ultimate destiny.

Taking in the strained silence that possessed the control room's complement, Exeter prepared himself to accept the consequences of his actions. Instinctively crossing his fingers at his side, he could but pray that he had made the right decision.

Nowhere was the sound of the advancing torpedoes

more audible than from the Razorback's sonar compartment. Perched before the console, Lefty Jackman clearly heard the dual, high-pitched whines of the pair of Mk-48's. It didn't take him much effort to determine which target they were intending to take out. Overjoyed that the Razorback was finally showing some teeth, he glanced to his left as Seth Burke unexpectedly called out, "That other sub, it's moving!"

Having completely forgotten about this other contact, Lefty hastily switched frequencies. As he tuned into the sector of water that his co-worker had been monitoring, he picked up a most familiar, distant, surging noise, the source of which was all too obvious.

"I knew it was that Victor!" cried the Senior Seaman. "Just listen how they're high-tailing it out of there! It's like they can't get into the open ocean quick enough. I wonder what's keeping the Skipper from taking them out too?"

The authoritative voice of the XO broke from behind him. "You've got to learn to trust your captain, Mr. Jackman. He know's what he's doing. Now, what's going on with our torpedoes?"

Reaching over to flick on the compartment's elevated external speakers, Chief Desiante channeled the sound of their attack for each of them to hear. In return, the room filled with the whir of the Mk-48's as they prepared to make their final run.

As the frequency of this whine increased, a dull, bubbling blast of venting air could be picked up in the background. This was followed by a loud, continuous, vibratory hum. It was Lefty Jackman who identified it.

"They just blew their emergency vents! That hum is the sound of their main engines. Those poor bastards are trying to run for it!"

Each of the men listened to the frantic sounds produced by the diesel-electric sub as it attempted to reverse its ascent and pour on the speed. Yet continuing to overpower this rising racket was the hornet-like whir of the ever-pursuing Mk-48's.

The XO's gut tightened when the lead torpedo initiated its final approach. As its signature seemed to merge with that of its quarry, he braced himself for the explosive blast that should follow any second. Yet only a sickening silence ensued.

"The first Mk-48 overshot its mark," observed Lefty, his tone clearly disappointed. "We've got to get them with this last one!"

Again the XO picked out the high-pitched whine of the remaining Mk-48 as it initiated its final approach. Drawing in a deep breath, he pulled his pipe from his mouth and nervously bent forward. An eternity seemed to pass, and then the room filled with a thunderous, resounding explosion.

"We got them!" exclaimed Lefty triumphantly.

"Ya hoo!" added Seth Burke.

Hesitant to join in on the celebration just yet, Benton took in the joyous grin on the face of Chief Desiante. Unable to answer it with a smile of his own, the XO wondered if their torpedo had taken down a boat full of innocent men. Doubtful that they'd ever know for certain, he looked down at his watch. Even in the dim light of the sonar compartment, he could see that it was 1200 hours exactly.

The stroke of noon found Richard Fuller emerging onto the plateau that formed the summit of the canyon located immediately south of Ocean Beach Park. There the NOSC researcher set his eyes on the back of Miriam Rodgers, who sat on the lip of the rock ledge, her gaze locked on the sea beyond. Without revealing his presence, Richard anxiously scanned the southern horizon.

The sky was a deep, clear blue, the fog having long ago lifted, and he was afforded an excellent view of mountainous Tranquillon Ridge and the hills that surrounded it. Checking his wristwatch, he wondered what was keeping the Condor from lifting off as scheduled. Since this vantage point would offer them an excellent view of the launch itself, it was most evident that there had been some sort of delay. Could it have been caused by something that the Razorback had chanced upon, while plunging beneath the seas off the coastline? Having no way to find out if this was indeed the case, Richard continued on to the summit's western edge.

"Good afternoon," he greeted. "I hope I'm not disturbing you."

Surprised by this voice, Miriam turned around and spotted her visitor only a few steps away. With that, a warm smile turned the corners of her mouth.

"Well, look what the wind blew in," she answered. "To what do I owe this honor?"

Halting at her side, Richard crouched down and kissed her on the lips. "To tell you the truth, I could think of no place I'd rather be than with you at the moment."

Catching a bit of weariness in his tone and expression, Miriam cautiously probed. "Is everything all right, Richard? You look beat."

Calmed by her concern, the NOSC researcher sighed. "I guessed I didn't sleep much last night. It's the same old frustrating story again, Richard Fuller against the Establishment. You know, things haven't changed that much since college after all."

354

After kissing Miriam once more on her lips, he sat down beside her and angled his glance westward. Taking in the view of the wide, sloping beach and the frothing surf beyond, he added, "Lord, is this a gorgeous day!"

Miriam followed the direction of his stare. "I'll say. Since we've been in Vandenberg, this morning has topped them all. I can't believe this visibility."

"It's as if that tidal wave washed away all the fog," reflected Richard, who noticed that Miriam had a notebook and pen on her lap. "I hope I'm not keeping you from your work. Joseph told me I'd find you up here."

Miriam set the notebook down on the ground beside her. "I was only making some entries in my journal. It was nothing earth-shattering. How are the kids doing down there, anyway?"

"The last I saw of them, they were digging away at the base of the canyon. That's a mighty spirited group you've got down there, Madame Professor. How do you keep them so motivated?"

Miriam grinned. "Actually, they do most of it themselves. That's one thing about the kids today. When they want something bad enough, they go after it with everything they've got. Not even the U.S. Air Force could keep them away from this dig."

Richard once again checked his watch. "Speaking of the devil, did you know that the space shuttle was due to be launched five minutes ago? I kind of thought you and I would have the best seat in town."

"As always, that's news for me," returned the archaeologist. "I didn't think we were supposed to be seeing a shuttle flight for at least another year."

"Neither did I," reflected Richard, who suddenly remembered a fact that he wanted to share with his lover. "By the way, there might be some sort of

355

archaeological find awaiting you on the sea floor several miles off the coast here. I recently heard that one of the vessels that is searching for the debris of that downed Titan chanced upon some kind of stone monument that appears to be man-made and of great age."

Genuinely interested in this revelation, Miriam abruptly turned towards him. "Exactly where was this formation spotted?"

Most aware that he had her curiosity aroused, Richard pointed out to sea. "That's the weird part. The vessel was at least fifteen miles off the coast, directly west of here, when they came upon it, at a depth of over two thousand feet below sea level."

"That's incredible," commented the archaeologist. "It sounds to me as if it could be some sort of submerged land mass that was possibly pulled down by an earthquake. You know, the Chumash had a legend that told of an island that was said to be located directly west of Point Arguello. Its name was Similaqsa, and it was known as the portal of the dead.

"If this formation is indeed of Chumash origin, we might have an amazing discovery on our hands. When's the soonest that you can introduce me to the men who made this initial find?"

Richard was just about to answer when his attention was diverted by a clearly audible, throaty roar that sounded in the distance. Immediately aware of what this signaled, he redirected his line of sight towards the south. There, against a crystal-clear backdrop of rolling green hills and deep blue sky, the shuttle was just visible, on its way towards the heavens.

"It's the Condor!" exclaimed the NOSC researcher, whose pulse quickened at the magnificent sight.

Close at his side, Miriam also viewed the ascending spaceship. She found herself thrilled as the roar of its boosters rose to an almost deafening pitch. The very ground beneath them seemed to vibrate in response.

Both figures were speechless as the tips of the boosters became visible. Belching fire and smoke, the mighty engines reverberated with a thrust of over 6 million pounds. As the rocket continued upward, the orbiter itself could be clearly seen. The white-skinned, delta-winged vehicle, which was about the size of a DC-9 jetliner, lay gripped onto the rust-colored main engine. Attached to each side of this central structure were the two detachable, solid-rocket boosters. Clear from the flames themselves, the black-nosed orbiter slowly began to rotate.

Watching as it began arcing up over the ocean, Richard restrained his innocent awe with a single realization. If his theory held true, this would be the most critical phase of the flight. Hastily, he scanned the surrounding seas, in a vain effort to locate any possible adversary. Yet, much to his relief, only the ever-surging waters were visible.

The Condor continued climbing, and soon was but a tiny speck high in the cloudless sky. Thankful that his supposition was apparently a foolish one after all, he reached out for the thin, inviting waist of the woman who sat at his side. Pulling her towards him affectionately, he felt her warmth and his tenseness instantly dissipated.

"It looks like they made it," said Miriam, who reciprocated with a hug of her own. Feeling his need, she was in the process of turning her lips up to meet his when a high-pitched, crackling male voice was suddenly heard.

"Miss Rodgers, you've got to come down at once!

Joseph has found some sort of sealed cavern dug into the base of the canyon!"

The spell was broken, and Miriam turned to identify the source of this news. Behind them, the tall, lanky figure of Mick Thompson was just emerging onto the plateau. Clearly out of breath, with his thin body soaked in sweat, the student had obviously run all the way up the trail that led there. Richard caught her puzzled glance and playfully winked in response. Both of them then stood, and began their way toward the path that would take them back down to the floor of the valley.

Chapter Sixteen

Five hundred and forty feet below the Pacific, the DSRV Marlin cautiously approached the remains of the submarine taken out by the Razorback's torpedo. Located five and half miles due west of Point Arguello, the Marlin was guided by its usual three-man complement.

Lieutenant Lance Blackmore sat in the co-pilot's position, his gaze locked on the DSRV's active sonar. Beside him sat Commander Will Pierce, whose hands tightly grasped the airplane-like steering column. Crouched behind the two officers, Ensign Louis Marvin scanned the controls, in a vigilant effort to make certain that all systems were operating properly.

The hollow ping of a sonar return resonated over the Marlin's P.A. system, and Blackmore reached over to determine the exact distance between the source of this return and their own bow. Familiar now with the DSRV's systems, the young lieutenant determined that a mere 400 yards of water separated them from the crippled submarine.

Because they had been nearby when this vessel was hit, they had been able to monitor the entire attack sequence. Blackmore would never forget the sounds of the approaching torpedoes. For a tense moment, he had even feared that the Mk-48's were being aimed at them. Yet they had streamed by the Marlin and, eventually, one of them had made contact.

And to think that he had thought DSRV duty was going to be dull! Since he had been deployed on the Marlin, the action had been almost non-stop. First there had been the rescue off the coast of Kauai. This had been followed by their surprise flight to Vandenberg, the arrival of the tidal wave, and then the recovery of the Titan's nose cone. And now to witness actual undersea combat! This was the Navy that Lance had always dreamed of serving.

He had found himself excited when Commander Pierce had relayed his decision to temporarily halt their present debris search. The grizzled veteran couldn't resist taking a closer look at the vessel that had incurred the Razorback's wrath.

Blackmore was finally beginning to have a genuine liking for the beard-stubbled veteran. He was unlike any man he had ever met before. Direct and to the point, Pierce held back no punches. If he didn't like you, he'd tell you right to your face. Yet if he saw even a hint of promise in your make-up, he'd be the first to give you a chance to prove what you were made of. This was how he had allowed Lance to come of age.

Only a few days had passed since Blackmore was standing on the deck of the tender Pelican, feeling sorry for himself. How much he had learned about life since then! He could place the blame for this newfound maturity squarely on the back of a single individual.

Though the commander certainly had his faults, when it came down to basics, there was no one Lance would rather have responsible for his life than Pierce.

His technical expertise couldn't be questioned. He knew the Marlin inside out. Utilizing it as a mere extension of his own self, he knew just how far he could push the vessel. Time after time he had shown what kind of stuff he was made of whenever duty called. Yet throughout it all he had remained a human being. This point had struck home the morning the tidal wave had almost swept them to their deaths. Plunging into the icy depths without any hydraulic control, Lance had thought that he would be the only one to show his fear. Yet when the lights had suddenly flashed on, even Pierce's face had been contorted with terror.

Not embarrassed by this show of emotion in the least, the commander had taught him that fear was only natural. What one had to be wary of was when panic veiled logical thought. That was when it could prove fatally dangerous.

From that moment on, Lance had felt accepted. Looking at the commander in a new light, he had accepted his duty draw wholeheartedly. Even Louis Marvin was beginning to rub off on him. The ensign, who always seemed to have a smile and joke to offer, was currently perched behind them. Competent and bold, he could be relied on when the going got rough.

Proud to be an integral part of such a team, Lance sat forward to get a better look at the sonar screen. As they continued their approach, the exact shape and position of the wreck was most evident. The sub rested upright, on a relatively level, sandy sea bed. Its hull appeared intact, though there was considerable damage apparent aft, the probable result of an explosion in its stern.

The hushed silence that had prevailed for the previous couple of minutes continued, as Pierce activated the Marlin's spotlights and guided the DSRV up over the disabled vessel's hull. Bending over to peer through the viewing scope, he took in the incapacitated sub's blunt bow. Two plane fins protruded from each side of the hull, with a single fin projecting from its upper deck.

Twenty feet or so behind these planes extended the vessel's sail. Unusually long and thin, the conning tower's surface was void of any identifiable marks that would hint at its nationality.

As the Marlin continued its slow sweep down the sub's hull, Lance spotted a strange-looking object sticking up from the deck behind the sail. Tubular-shaped and over eight feet long, it appeared to be made of some sort of steel piping. It extended into the sub itself, under the cover of a partially extended piece of protective cowling. Having no idea what its purpose was, he picked out the smashed bulkhead that lay behind it. A gaping, jagged hole lay in this portion of the pressure hull. Though the inner hull still appeared intact, thick globs of black oil constantly strained from its seams. The torpedo appeared to have struck the upper portion of the stern with an upward, glancing blow. If it had hit it with a direct angle, he doubted if the vessel would still be in one piece. Appreciatively taking in this damage, Blackmore looked up when a deep voice sounded on his left.

"I've got to admit that I've never seen a sub with this particular design before," observed Pierce. "The Soviets must have been hiding it from us. Though the engine room is surely in a shambles, I bet she can still support life. What do you say about attaching Marlin onto her bow escape trunk and us having a firsthand look inside?"

"Sounds good to me," returned Marvin. "If they're still kicking in there, Ivan will sure be glad to see us."

Blackmore knew that such an effort could be doubly dangerous. Beyond the threat of encountering a poisonous atmosphere inside was the manner in which they would be received if there were indeed survivors aboard. For what kind of reception could one expect from a crew that had just been torpedoed? Yet, with all this in mind, he couldn't help but find himself curious as to the nature of the crew. Would they encounter a group of iron-fisted Soviets or a boatload of crazed terrorists? Just knowing that the Marlin's crew could be the first to reveal their identities provided reason enough for the lieutenant to nod his head in consent.

"Good," replied Pierce, as he began turning the Marlin around to return to the sub's bow. "Ready the boarding equipment, Ensign. It's time you earned your keep around here anyway."

While Marvin ducked back inside the pressure capsule to initiate this task, Blackmore caught the boyish expression that lit the commander's face. Looking like a child who was about to break into a candy store, Pierce beamed in anticipation. This enthusiasm was contagious, for Blackmore felt his own nerves tingle when the Marlin dropped onto the submarine's upper deck. A loud, metallic clap followed as the DSRV rested firmly on its hull. Using the viewing port to complete a flurry of last-minute maneuvers, Pierce inched the Marlin forward. He looked up only when a voice cried out from behind.

"We've got it, Skipper! The way it looks now, the transfer skirt just fits."

An expression of relief filled the commander's face as he released his safety harness. Reaching up to grab the DSRV's underwater telephone, he dialed the frequency band that was reserved for international emergencies. His voice was firm as he spoke into the

363

transmitter.

"Disabled submarine, this is the DSRV Marlin calling. We are presently attached to your forward escape trunk. We mean you no harm. We are here only to assist in your rescue. Do you copy?"

A blast of raucous static was the only answer that he managed to pick up. Replacing the telephone, Pierce began pushing himself out of his command chair. Careful not to hit any of the controls, he managed to crawl into the tight hatchway that separated the two pressure spheres. Before disappearing altogether, he took a moment to address his concerned co-pilot.

"Don't look so glum, Lieutenant. You didn't think that I could merely sit here and miss all the action, did you? I'll be back soon enough. In the meantime, I'll be leaving the Marlin in your most capable hands."

With this, he turned and continued on back into the middle sphere. Blackmore watched as he took hold of the steel "bang-stick" that Marvin soon handed him. This spear-like object had an explosive charge on its tip. The Commander angled it down through the transfer skirt, and placed its tip up against the disabled sub's hull. Pierce wasted no time triggering it. With a sharp blast, the charge activated and the submarine's hatch was penetrated. It was Marvin who lowered the miniature testing device through the tiny hole that this blast had created. Using this instrument, he would determine if the vessel's atmosphere were dangerous or not.

"There's no radioactivity apparent, Skipper. What little air that remains is sour, but it should be breathable for a short amount of time."

"That's all I'm going to need," answered Pierce, who began climbing down into the transfer skirt.

Using the end of his flashlight, he rapped sharply on the visible portion of the hatch cover. Seconds later, the grating sound of twisting metal could be heard down below.

"It looks like someone's home after all," added the commander, as he took a last fond look at his crew before descending into the now-open hatchway.

"Give my regards to Ivan!" offered Marvin.

Shutting the transfer skirt behind Pierce, the ensign stood up and caught the serious glance of the Marlin's co-pilot. "I pity those poor Russkies if they try to pull any shenanigans with the Skipper. If they do, they're going to wish that they were sunk for good."

Absorbing this comment, Blackmore wondered if he would have the nerve to do what Pierce was attempting. Shifting around in his seat, he placed one of his hands around the emergency disengage lever, just in case it were suddenly needed.

It was pitch black as Will Pierce climbed down the steel ladder of the disabled sub's escape trunk. The air was cool and smelled vaguely like rotten eggs. Careful to take only the shallowest of breaths, he reached the final rung and dropped down onto the deck. Switching on his flashlight, he angled its beam upwards. A rack of torpedoes was visible to his right, and he knew that he was in the torpedo room. Only when he slowly pivoted did he illuminate the face and figure of the individual who had opened the hatch for him.

Tall and blond-haired, the muscular figure was dressed in black slacks and a matching turtleneck. His ageless, weather-worn face was dominated by a piercing blue stare. Little emotion showed on his face as he nodded in greeting. When he spoke, his accent was thick his very tone clearly admitting defeat.

"*Bonjour, Commandant.* Welcome aboard the attack submarine Ariadne."

In instant response, Will Pierce's face blushed with astonishment. For this was far from the type of reception he had planned on receiving.

"Captain, you're never going to believe the message that we just picked up from the Marlin."

The XO's words were delivered as he rounded the open door to Philip Exeter's stateroom. Seated at his desk, in the process of logging a detailed description of the attack they just completed, the Captain caught the excited glance of his guest and replied flatly, "Try me, Mr. Benton."

Fighting to compose himself, the XO took a deep breath before continuing. "Commander Pierce contacted us from the radio room of the same sub that we took out with our Mk-48. There're apparently twenty or so crew members still alive and kicking. I can't believe that he had the nerve to board them."

Indeed fascinated by this revelation, Exeter pushed away his log and turned to face his XO. "You don't say. That guy's not afraid of the devil himself. How have the Soviets treated him so far?"

Benton's eyes flashed. "This is the hot part, Skipper. They're not Russians, they're French!"

Hardly believing what he was hearing, Exeter did a double-take. "Say again, Pat?"

"You heard me, Skipper. That sub we took out was a French Agosta-class attack boat. And don't worry that we might have blown away a bunch of innocents, because there was a full-scale, operational, electromagnetic rail-gun mounted on its stern deck."

"Sweet Jesus," sighed Exeter, his mind reeling. "So it wasn't the Soviets all along. Wait until we inform Dr. Fuller."

"That guy deserves the Medal of Honor," returned the XO as he pulled his pipe from his shirt pocket and poked its stem between his lips. "And by the way, I made certain to tell Commander Pierce that the Condor made it into orbit without a hitch. That little bit of news really made his day."

"As it's made each of ours," added the Captain. "I imagine that the commander is going to want to initiate a transfer of survivors as soon as possible. We'd better get the Razorback ready for them. Prepare the crew's mess hall as a holding area. I guess it would be a good idea to put together a squad of armed security guards. Have Lieutenant Willingham lead them."

The XO nodded. "Aye, aye, Skipper. I'll get on it at once. Should I ready a transmission for COMSUB?"

"I'll take care of that, Pat. I'd love to be there to watch the admiral's face when he hears this one. I have a feeling that there's going to be some mighty curious Intelligence types waiting for us back at port. Now, you'd better get going on that security detail. Thanks again for all your help, Pat. With this bum knee and all, I couldn't handle the boat without you."

"I don't know about that," retorted the XO. "You're doing an awfully fine job as it is."

Flashing a warm grin, Benton turned and disappeared out the passageway. Still seated at his desk, Exeter reached forward to massage his knee. While he did so, his mind struggled to absorb the shocking information that had been just revealed to him.

No matter the nationality, he found himself satisfied that at least the right enemy had been eliminated. Again he thanked the Lord for Dr. Richard Fuller's warning. Without the NOSC researcher's guidance, there was a very good chance that the Condor would have never made it out of the earth's atmosphere.

Anxious to learn of the motive that had inspired the attempt to interrupt the flight in the first place, Philip turned back to his desk. A proper dispatch would have to be drafted and then relayed down to San Diego. As he went to pick up his pen, his eyes drifted to the picture of Carla and his girls, mounted on the wall before him. Wondering if he'd ever be able to share that morning's incredible events with them, he shook his head and returned his attention to the duty that awaited him.

Colonel Jean Moreau was no stranger to difficult days, yet this one that was just passing was one of the worse he had ever experienced. It had all started early in the morning, when he had been awakened from a sound sleep by a telephone call. His assistant, Jacques LeMond, had wasted no time in revealing that the Third Brigade had struck once again. This time a group of three young mothers had been found hacked to death outside the installation's central living quarters. Sticking up in the blood-soaked ground nearby had been a single machete with a red bandana tied to its hilt.

When the mutilated bodies were initially discovered, a wave of panic had spread among the other workers. Aware of just who this calling card belonged to, they had already begun to talk of abandoning their jobs for the very safety of their families. Fear could be dangerously contagious if it weren't stood up to, and Moreau had ordered his assistant to stem the hysteria at its very source. If need be, the Legion was to be called out. For, if the terrorists weren't stopped cold in their tracks, Moreau could soon have a massive insurrection on his hands.

No sooner had he arrived at this office than he had received word that the series of a half-dozen Japanese communications satellites that they had been contracted to put into space would be delivered from three to six months late. Such a delay could have serious consequences for their already threatened cash-flow position.

If that news weren't frustrating enough, he had spent the rest of the day with one eye on the clock and the other on his private telephone line. For hours on end, he had waited for the telephone call that still had yet to arrive.

A half hour before, he had left his office and driven straight home. There he had mixed himself a Pernod and soda and headed at once for the solace of his veranda. With his telephone beside him, he had stretched out on his favorite rattan lounger and watched the dusk engulf the thick jungle that lay only a few steps away, on the other side of the screened-in porch.

As always, the steaming humidity was all-oppressive, and not even the constantly whirling ceiling fan was able to draw down a decent cool draft of air. To the ever-increasing, hypnotic throb of the night creatures, he breathed in the very scent of the jungle. The smell of pure, green life itself met his nostrils, and he found himself longing for the dry, sweet fragrance of the meadow in which he had been born and raised.

Did such a world really still exist? Sometimes Moreau wondered. For seven long years, he had known little else but the confines of this malaria-ridden sweat-hole called French Guiana. Dedicating his every effort to the success of Ariadne, he had sacrificed the prime years of his life to see this dream come true. Yet no matter how long and tediously he had applied himself, there had always seemed to be one more insurmountable obstacle facing him. And now, to think that all this selfless toil depended upon such desperate measures as Operation Diablo.

Just thinking about this plan that he had been forced to implement soured his mood to an even greater degree. For, though he would have liked to purge its essence from his very mind, his conscience would not cooperate. Try as he could to justify their actions, he knew it all came down to one basic fact. It was one thing to take down an unmanned Titan 34-D missile, but to interfere with a manned space shuttle flight placed them in the same league as the misguided terrorists of the Third Brigade.

A decade ago, Moreau had sworn his allegiance both to the Commandant and the cause he served. During the years that followed, he had certainly had his share of unsavory tasks to fulfill, yet this was the first time that he seriously questioned his involvement. Did this mean that his days there were already numbered?

A rustling sound came from behind him, and Moreau realized that he was no longer alone. Seconds later, Theresa sauntered up before him an ice-filled glass in her hand.

"I thought that you would like another drink, *mi amore*," she greeted seductively.

Slowly replacing his empty glass, the pert teenager did her best to linger at his side as long as possible. Though her initial appearance had upset Moreau, he couldn't help but take in her tight, tanned body. Dressed in her briefest shorts, and a thin, stringed halter-top, the Brazilian beauty exuded a raw sensuality. His loins instinctively stiffened in response. For a brief second, he even considered throwing her to the ground and mounting her right there. Like an animal in heat, he'd lose his worries deep in her wet, primal abyss. Yet the ringing phone cut through the dusk like a shriek of terror, and in an instant any passionate intentions on his part dissipated.

Moreau's hand shot out for the receiver, and the moment he heard the familiar faraway hiss indicating a long-distance call in the background, he waved Theresa away. With his weary eyes locked on the jungle, he listened as a deep voice somberly greeted him.

The next couple of minutes moved with the ponderous pace of a nightmare. For the most part, the Commandant did all the talking. Moreau could but summon the fortitude to occasionally grunt in meager response.

For the first time in his recollection, the esteemed figure he respected most in life spoke with the tone of one who had been totally subjugated. The dismal news that he soon relayed was as grim as his intonation.

Operation Diablo had been a complete failure. Not only was the Ariadne presently lying disabled on the floor of the Pacific, but the Americans had boarded her as well. A handful of surviving sailors had been taken into U.S. custody. Over four dozen of their brave comrades hadn't been so fortunate. Their stiff corpses still lay within the sub's crushed hull.

As a direct result of this tragic turn of events, the Condor had been able to successfully attain its orbit. Already, its precious payload had been released. Whereas the Americans were now back in the space business, the Ariadne project was now finished.

Only minutes before, the President of the Republic

had ordered the Commandant to resign his position at once. Labeled a disgrace to his country, he even faced the possibility of criminal charges.

The Commandant's voice was quivering with emotion as he thanked Moreau for his years of service. He left him with a single sentence, the ominous overtones of which still rang in his ear even after his trembling hand had managed to hang up the receiver.

"Now do what you have to do, my son, for you deserve much more than the shame that your country is about to call down upon your once-honored name."

Stunned by this conversation, Moreau sat upright, his limbs twitching uncontrollably. Waves of sweat poured down his forehead, and he struggled for each successive breath.

So this was what it was like when a man's very life caved in around him. All of his efforts, all of his work, in vain!

A frail voice broke out from behind him, its tone emanating as if from a different dimension. "Are you all right, *mi amore?*"

A warm, tiny hand hesitantly stroked his shoulder, and Moreau found himself possessed by a fit of blind fury. Dizzily, he stood. Angling his clenched fist downward, he smacked it into Theresa's jaw. As she fell to the ground, he turned and stormed out the back door. He was well on his way over the strip of grass that lay between his house and the jungle when a confused, whimpering voice called out to him.

"*Mi amore*, what is the matter with you? Is it something that I did? Please come back. The jungle at night is no place for you to be. You could get killed out there!"

This fragile plea registered in his consciousness, yet Moreau plunged onward into the tree line. The dark, sticky, heavily scented boughs of the jungle reached for his limbs, and the cries of the night creatures throbbed with a million different voices. Yet all that Jean Moreau could think of was that, if he were lucky, his demise would be mercifully quick. And such was his fate, as the night fell over French Guiana.

Chapter Seventeen

Vandenberg's underground situation room was a large, cavernous structure buried three stories beneath the surface of the base's main administrative area. Built specifically for the Strategic Air Command, this control center was utilized to initiate and monitor the launches of Vandenberg's Minutemen, Titan II, and MX ICBM's. Although it was primarily designed as a test range, the base did have sixteen missile silos on its northern sector that maintained a latent Emergency War Order capability. It was for this seldom-used function that the room currently found itself being occupied.

Seated at one of the two dozen digital consoles that filled the room, Lieutenant Colonel Todd Lansford pondered the startling series of events that had sent him scurrying from the shuttle launch center to this one. It had all started soon after the Condor had attained its orbit. The mission had been proceeding perfectly, and they had been able to deploy the Keyhole platform right on schedule. After being successfully activated, the recon satellite had begun its first sweep over the central Soviet Union.

It was Kauai's Kokee satellite-tracking station that had relayed to them the shocking photos that were soon to bring the world to the very brink of war. Those digitally transferred snapshots were of the Soviet ICBM fields at Tyuratam. There, the SS-18 silos were clearly visible. Huddled around the lips of these underground structures were an odd assortment of vehicles and personnel. A detailed analysis of the film showed the workers to be in the midst of replacing the missiles' warheads. Intelligence was certain that this new warhead package was what was known as the Tartar system. It would allow each of the SS-18's to be armed with ten MIRV'd warheads, with enough yield and accuracy to knock out even the most hardened target. It was common knowledge that this package was not only a flagrant violation of the current nuclear weapons treaty, but also indicative of a possible imminent first strike.

In response to this revelation, the President of the United States had immediately activated the hot line to the Kremlin. The infuriated Chief Executive had soon reached Premier Viktor Alipov. Yet, much to the President's dismay, Alipov had flatly denied his accusations. This had left him with no alternative but to bring his country's own strategic forces to a state of DEFCON Two, only a step away from war itself.

With this directive, America's Triad had been activated. Beneath the seas, America's powerful force of strategic missile submarines had been sent to their action stations. On land, the country's B-52 and B-1B bombers had been dispersed from their vulnerable airfields and sent flying toward their fail-safe positions. And finally, from deep inside their launch-control silos, the countdowns had begun on the United States' own arsenal of Titan II, Minutemen, and MX ICBM's.

Lansford was well aware that a flight of Minutemen

III missiles sat in their silos only a few thousand yards from his current position. He visualized Vandenberg's very own contribution to the Triad, as the sleek group of sixteen missiles waited for the launch-release codes that would come from this very room.

The officers who would relay these launch signals sat before their consoles around him. As they went about their macabre business with a cool efficiency, Lansford wondered if they ever thought about the consequences that would follow a real launch. Surely they were well aware that their actions would most probably signal the end of the civilized world as they now knew it.

Though he was a veteran Air Force officer himself, Lansford had never actually thought this fateful day would ever come to pass. World War III had been like a grim specter on the horizon, always threatening, yet never a reality. But the continued existence of the doomsday weapons that made this conflict so unthinkable had made this day inevitable. Man was only fooling himself if he thought otherwise.

Lansford looked out on the hushed room that surrounded him, and wondered if this afternoon would be the moment when humankind's luck finally ran out. He was well aware of the fact that that morning's skirmish with those suspected Soviet commandos could have been the first military engagement of the war. If so, at least the Americans had emerged from that brief battle victorious.

Of course, confusing the matter was the submarine that the Razorback had sunk while prowling off the coastline. Was its crew really French as the preliminary reports indicated, and was an electromagnetic rail-gun indeed mounted on its stern? And if this were true, was the Condor its target? Perhaps those so-called Frenchmen were really Soviet agents in disguise!

However it would eventually turn out, there could be no denying Dr. Richard Fuller's prophetic warning. If he ever lived to see this day through, Lansford promised himself to convey to the NOSC researcher his sincere apologies. Too busy to take the time to seriously listen to Fuller's wise counsel, he was extremely fortunate that his inattention hadn't ended up in serious tragedy. He shuddered to think what would have happened if the Condor had been shot down. Without the Keyhole in place, the Soviets would have been free to finish the rearming of their SS-18's, and could have even launched them without America's awareness. Such a fate would have been the most tragic of all possible.

Stirring with this realization, Lansford looked to his immediate right as the red plastic telephone positioned on the desk there rang with a harsh buzz. Quick to pick it up was the steady hand of the Secretary of the Air Force, Walter Fitzpatrick. At his side during this entire crisis, Lansford had been impressed with the Secretary's cool, collected firmness. Never once had he outwardly shown any visible emotion. That was why Lansford was surprised when a broad grin filled Fitzpatrick's face as he listened to whoever was on the other end of the line. Anxious to know what this abrupt change meant, the lieutenant colonel sat forward, expectantly. When he finally did hang up the receiver, Fitzpatrick took several seconds to savor what he had heard before turning to share it with his host.

"That was the Secretary of Defense, Todd. Only minutes ago, Viktor Alipov called the President on the hot line. Genuinely upset that our strategic forces had been brought up to DEFCON Two, he conveyed the following. The rearming of Tyuratam's SS-18's had apparently taken place without either his approval or knowledge. Alipov pleaded that the incident had been the result of the treasonous actions of two of his most trusted aides. Arrested, and currently being held in custody for the crime of treason, are General Vadim Sobolev, Commander-in-Chief of the Strategic Rocket Forces, and Alipov's senior aide, Valentin Radchenko. Both men have pleaded guilty and are ready to admit their crime publicly.

"To substantiate his country's peaceful intentions, Alipov has already ordered the MIRV'd warhead packages to be removed. To corroborate this, the silos at Tyuratam will be opened for inspection during the next pass of our Keyhole.

"The President has apparently accepted this admission, and has ordered us to step down to DEFCON Three. It's over, Todd. We've dodged the bullet one more time."

Taking in this observation, Lansford looked from the Secretary's relieved face to the emblem mounted on the wall behind him. The insignia was that of the Strategic Air Command, and showed a mailed fist holding a lightning bolt and an olive branch in its grasp. Beneath this crest was printed, "Our Profession is Peace." Ever mindful of how true this motto was, Lieutenant Colonel Todd Lansford turned to join the joyous celebration that was taking place around him.

Seven and a half miles due south of the subterranean control room, Richard Fuller followed Miriam into the narrow entrance of the newly discovered cave.

Inside it was dark and musty, and it took them a good thirty seconds to adjust to this sudden decrease in light. As their night vision gradually came to them, they picked out the various artifacts that lay scattered against the cramped cavern's walls. Dozens of colorfully decorated, lap-sized stone bowls sat next to a variety of baskets of every shape and size imaginable. Interspersed between these objects were hundreds of sharply tapered stone arrowheads, spearpoints, bone-fishing hooks, and awls.

Continuing on into the cave's interior, they passed a set of full-sized, whale-bone chairs. Draped over them were several rabbit- and bird-skin capes. Because of their excellent preservation and authentic appearance, it was most obvious that this site had been completely sealed off from humanity for hundreds of years. Not knowing what they could find next, the two astonished figures gathered at the center of the cavern's polished stone floor.

There the NOSC researcher broke the solemn silence that had accompanied them since they had entered. "My Lord, Miriam, is this place for real?"

Bending down to carefully touch the hem of the rabbit-skin cape that lay beside her, the archaeologist spoke with quivering excitement. "If I'm dreaming, now's the time to wake me, Richard. It's as if we've entered a museum that's been closed for a millennium. This is the find of a lifetime!"

"Hey, you two, quit fooling around out there and come back and take a look at this. It's unbelievable!"

The muted voice was that of Joseph Solares, and emanated from deeper inside the cave's interior. Miriam looked to Richard, and both of them pivoted in an attempt to track the voice's source. Seeing nothing but darkness beyond, they linked hands and cautiously proceeded further into the cavern's cool depths.

The walls gradually narrowed, and soon they were unable to walk shoulder-to-shoulder. Forced to hunch over, Miriam led the way, with Richard close on her heels. As it turned out, they didn't have to travel in this way for very much longer, for the narrow rock corridor opened to a fairly good-sized chamber. Following Miriam in through the entrance to this room, Richard halted beside his newfound love, and took in the wondrous sight awaiting them there.

Illuminated by a thin band of direct sunlight that entered from a minuscule hole cut into the jagged rock roof was the bare-chested figure of Joseph Solares. Appearing much the way his ancestors must have looked centuries before, the dark-haired Indian knelt before the chamber's far wall. His complete attention was focused on a section of polished stone, on which an expertly crafted petroglyph was drawn. There, catching the full brunt of the ever-falling rays of sunlight, was etched a massive condor. It was caught in the process of soaring on a thermal. The bird's long hooked beak could be seen, growing almost straight out from its flat forehead. Its head seemed completely bald, except for a bright yellow plume that crowned the very top of its skull. The rest of its body was covered with black feathers, except for a narrow strip of white ones situated under the front of each elongated wing.

So expertly drawn was this etching that the condor's face seemed to be imbued with life itself. Appearing wise beyond its years, the shaggy-feathered bird seemed to be trying to express its innermost thoughts. Unbeknownst to the three mortals, who were swallowed by its gaze, was the fact that in each of their minds the exact same mental picture was being transferred. With lonely fortitude, this king of living beasts, representing the last of his species in the wild, told of his struggle to survive at all costs. For life was the most precious of essences known to this world, and to needlessly waste it was the greatest tragedy of all.

BLACK EAGLES
by John Lansing

They're the best jungle fighters the United States has to offer. No matter where Charlie is hiding, The Eagles will find him! They're the greatest unsung heroes of the dirtiest, most challenging war of all time!

#1: HANOI HELLGROUND	(1249, $2.95)
#2: MEKONG MASSACRE	(1294, $2.50)
#7: BEYOND THE DMZ	(1610, $2.50)
#8: BOOCOO DEATH	(1677, $2.50)
#9: BAD SCENE AT BONG SON	(1793, $2.50)
#10: CAMBODIA KILL-ZONE	(1953, $2.50)

Available wherever paperbacks are sold, or order direct from the Publisher. Send cover price plus 50¢ per copy for mailing and handling to Zebra Books, Dept. 2139, 475 Park Avenue South, New York, N.Y. 10016. Residents of New York, New Jersey and Pennsylvania must include sales tax. DO NOT SEND CASH.

ASHES
by William W. Johnstone

OUT OF THE ASHES   (1137, $3.50)
Ben Raines hadn't looked forward to the War, but he knew it was coming. After the balloons went up, Ben was one of the survivors, fighting his way across the country, searching for his family, and leading a band of new pioneers attempting to bring American OUT OF THE ASHES.

FIRE IN THE ASHES   (1310, $3.50)
It's 1999 and the world as we know it no longer exists. Ben Raines, leader of the Resistance, must regroup his rebels and prep them for bloody guerrilla war. But are they ready to face an even fiercer foe—the human mutants threatening to overpower the world!

ANARCHY IN THE ASHES   (1387, $3.50)
Out of the smoldering nuclear wreckage of World War III, Ben Raines has emerged as the strong leader the Resistance needs. When Sam Hartline, the mercenary, joins forces with an invading army of Russians, Ben and his people raise a bloody banner of defiance to defend earth's last bastion of freedom.

BLOOD IN THE ASHES   (1537, $3.50)
As Raines and his rugged band of followers search for land that has escaped radiation, the insidious group known as The Ninth Order rises up to destroy them. In a savage battle to the death, it is the fate of America itself that hangs in the balance!

ALONE IN THE ASHES   (1721, $3.50)
In this hellish new world there are human animals and Ben Raines—famed soldier and survival expert—soon becomes their hunted prey. He desperately tries to stay one step ahead of death, but no one can survive ALONE IN THE ASHES.

Available wherever paperbacks are sold, or order direct from the Publisher. Send cover price plus 50¢ per copy for mailing and handling to Zebra Books, Dept. 2139, 475 Park Avenue South, New York, N.Y. 10016. Residents of New York, New Jersey and Pennsylvania must include sales tax. DO NOT SEND CASH.